Also by Amy Rose Bennett

Curled Up with Earl

with

an

Amy Rose Bennett

sourcebooks
casablanca

Published by Sourcebooks Casablanca, an imprint of Sourcebooks
P.O. Box 4410, Naperville, Illinois 60567-4410
(630) 961-3900
sourcebooks.com

Printed and bound in the United States of America.
OPM 10 9 8 7 6 5 4 3 2 1

To Richard, my love, my everything.
As always, this book is dedicated to you.

Chapter One

Hampstead Heath, Summer 1858

AT THE AGE OF EIGHT-AND-TWENTY, MISS LUCY BERTRAM could easily, perhaps even quite confidently, define the sort of person she was: thoughtful, analytical, observant, practical, diligent, imaginative, kind.

Also, most unfortunately, quivering-like-a-barely-set-blancmange nervous around strangers—particularly members of the opposite sex who were prospective suitors. Indeed, the mere idea of entering a high-society gathering such as a ball or a soiree—even a dinner party—where countless sets of eyes were bound to settle upon her, was enough to make her feel positively faint with terror or cast up her accounts. Possibly both.

Although at this present moment, Lucy was completely alone in a deserted rural laneway—unless one counted her family's ancient pony, Juniper, as company—so she wasn't nervous *precisely*. However, she could certainly own to feeling more than a little anxious and a great deal flummoxed. And while her powers of observation still appeared to be intact, her practical streak had all but deserted her. Because she simply had no clue how to dislodge the mired back wheel of her gig from a muddy ditch. At all.

As if that wasn't bad enough, there was a summer storm grumbling on the horizon. The roiling bank of dark-as-a-bruise clouds that had been brewing over London since midday was drawing ever closer, and the ominous low rumbles of thunder were making poor Juniper stamp and snort and twitch.

Of course, when Lucy had set out from her home, Fleetwood Hall, less than an hour ago to run a few errands in the nearby hamlet of Heathwick Green, she *had* noticed clouds amassing above Hampstead Heath, along with an unmistakable heavy sultriness in the air. It was the sort of sticky humidity that promised a downpour. But she'd dismissed any nagging concerns because Heathwick Green was so close to home, and it wasn't as though she hadn't made this trip with Juniper a thousand times over. And while the lane was muddy from a heavy rain shower earlier in the day, for the most part it wasn't particularly boggy or hazardous.

However, what Lucy *hadn't* counted on was the enormous brown hare that had decided to dart from the prickly briar hedge, straight across Juniper's path. The hare's lightning speed and proximity had startled the usually unflappable pony and sent him off course toward the verge where the drainage was poor, and now they were well and truly stuck. No matter how much Lucy attempted to coax Juniper forward with gentle flicks of the reins and encouraging words, the gig hadn't budged more than an inch.

Fudge and fiddlesticks and fiddledeedee. Huffing out an exasperated sigh, Lucy resigned herself to the fact she was going to get dirty and probably drenched to the bone as she gathered up her wide crinoline skirts of faded blue muslin and climbed down from the gig. As her kid leather boots sank into a patch of sucking mud, she winced. To say that her maid, Dotty, would not be happy would be an understatement.

Lucy wasn't particularly happy either, not when she glanced under the gig and spotted the extent of the problem—or should she say the depth of it? The ditch was a veritable quagmire, and there was no doubt in her mind that Juniper wouldn't have the strength to pull the vehicle free. It was rather a shame that "brute strength" wasn't one of her own defining attributes, because then she might be able to give Juniper a helping hand with a bit of a heave-ho from the rear.

On the positive side, Fleetwood Hall wasn't that far away. If she unstrapped Juniper and led him home—there was no way Lucy could ride bareback in her present attire—they'd be there within twenty minutes, and they *might* escape the approaching tempest. But that would also mean she'd have to abandon the gig, and while she liked to think that no one would make off with it, someone might.

That eventuality would be nothing short of a disaster. Her father, Sir Oswald, could ill afford such a loss. They were already down to a skeleton staff at Fleetwood Hall, and as it was, Lucy was constantly battling to make ends meet with the limited household budget her father had allocated. The loss of the gig simply couldn't be borne. Not by her father, or herself. The little two-seater carriage meant that she could go wherever she liked, whenever she liked…even if that was just to Heathwick Green or to the village of Hampstead to run errands. Or, most importantly, to the train station so she could travel to London to meet with her friends and fellow Byronic Book Club members, Jane Delaney and Artemis Winters, the newly wedded Duchess of Dartmoor.

Or to search for her brother.

Monty… It had been over four months since her older brother had fought with Father and then disappeared into the night with a valise, and without a word since. Lucy missed him desperately and, because she was certain he didn't have any independent source of income, she was worried sick about how he'd been faring. And Father would not be drawn on the subject either—about whether he'd heard from Monty or what had led to their estrangement. But then, it wasn't unusual for her father to be uncommunicative, even grumpy of late. As soon as Lucy got back to Fleetwood, she would check the small bundle of mail she'd picked up from Heathwick Green's posting inn, the Wick and Whistle, to see if Monty had written to her. Just like she always did.

But first she had to get home.

Lucy impatiently pushed an errant lock of hair off her sticky cheek and glanced up and down Fleetwood Lane to see if anyone was headed her way—someone who might be able to render assistance. But the thoroughfare was deserted. Which wasn't all that surprising; no doubt other folk in the vicinity had already hurried home because of the impending storm.

As though the elements had heard her thoughts and wished to mock her for her hubris, the thunderclouds emitted a low warning growl and a sharp breeze caught at Lucy's bonnet and gown. Even the sun had now retreated.

There was nothing for it. She would have to free Juniper and take her chances that no one would steal the gig.

With another sigh, Lucy lifted up her skirts as best she could and gingerly picked her way through the treacherously slippery sludge to Juniper. The gray pony tossed his head and snorted as if to say *Now hurry up. I don't have all day* and Lucy laughed.

"I'll have you free in a jiffy, my dear old boy," she said as she tugged off her gloves, tossed them onto the worn leather seat of the gig, then began to unharness the pony from the traces. There were ever so many straps and buckles, but since her father had laid off Fleetwood Hall's coachman and their one and only groom several months ago, Lucy often helped the young stable boy, Freddy, with Juniper, so she knew what she was doing. Although, her father had recently mentioned that he might have found a new groom who not only possessed a solid recommendation but was willing to accept a reduced wage. Lucy was firmly of the opinion that he couldn't start soon enough.

She'd just started to loosen the pony's breast collar when there was an almighty clap of thunder and lightning flashed. A flock of jackdaws sheltering in a nearby oak tree shot into the air squawking and shrieking, Juniper whinnied and shied, and in the very next moment Lucy's feet went out from under her, and she fell backward, plopping unceremoniously onto her derriere with bone-jarring impact. Mud squelched between her fingers and oozed around her stocking-clad ankles and this time she couldn't stop herself from cursing aloud.

"Barnaby Rudge and buckets of fudge," she grumbled. Could this day get any worse?

It seemed it could, because a shadow that was darker than the encroaching storm fell across her. Looking up, Lucy couldn't suppress a startled gasp. A ruggedly handsome man was staring down at her, his towering, broad-shouldered frame silhouetted against the mass of roiling black clouds behind him. For one wild moment, she fancied that one of the ancient gods of the sky like Thor or Jupiter had descended from the heavens. If the stranger had been brandishing a thunderbolt or two instead of a carpetbag, she wouldn't have been the least bit surprised.

His cobalt-blue eyes were almost hidden by a tousled sweep of sable-brown hair. Save for the flicker of a dimple in one lean cheek and the twitch of amusement at one corner of his wide mouth, he'd be forbidding if not altogether intimidating. He seemed like the sort who could fell a man with one well-aimed punch. Or help to liberate a gig from a ditch.

He was certainly the type who could set someone like her to the blush. Especially when he doffed his wide-brimmed felt hat and drawled in a deeply rumbling Scots brogue, "Can I help you, lass? You look like you're in a wee bit o' trouble."

"I..." Lucy's whole face felt as though it was burning. Her mouth had gone dry, and her stomach was a mass of knots. "Yes. Yes, thank you," she managed at last with a feeble smile.

"You're no' hurt, are you?" he asked as he put down the sizable carpetbag and then extended one large, bare hand toward her. His knuckles were scarred and scraped, his palms callused—not the hands of a gentleman, by any means.

Gentleman or not, Lucy couldn't very well refuse his offer to help. And despite his looming bulk, at this particular juncture she couldn't see any reason *not* to trust him. His demeanor was pleasant enough.

Lucy wiped her mucky palm upon her skirts before she placed her hand in his. "My pride might be a little dented, but that's all," she muttered in answer to his question as she clambered to her feet. Although if truth be told, she was a little winded and her tailbone might be a tad bruised. Not that she'd admit any of that to the stranger. Instead, she murmured an embarrassed "Thank you."

Casting her gaze downward, she rubbed her hand upon her gown again and tried not to notice the snug fit of the stranger's buff breeches and top boots—the way the fabric and leather seemed to be molded to his muscular thighs and calves. She certainly couldn't bring herself to meet the man's eyes. Indeed, she couldn't bear to think what he thought of her at this present moment. If one looked up *mortified* in any dictionary, "Miss Lucinda Bertram" would be a fitting definition.

"It's no' a problem," he said, pulling a kerchief from the breast pocket of his dark green jacket. "Although I'd be lying if I didna admit I'm more than a wee bit curious about what happened here..."

Lucy gratefully accepted the pristine square of linen and cleaned her fingers. "An unexpected series of mishaps, I'm afraid," she began, then proceeded to describe in a great rush how the gig had become mired and what led to her fall. "If it hadn't been for that darned hare. The way that it shot out of nowhere without warning… Rather like a skittish March hare, I suppose. We get a lot of them on the heath… Only it isn't March, of course…" Oh dear, she was blathering on like *she* was utterly harebrained. She drew a deep breath in an attempt to halt her runaway tongue and to give herself a moment to order her tumbling thoughts. "At any rate, unless I can free the gig, I'll have to leave it here. It truly is stuck."

The Scot grunted as he took back the soiled kerchief and wiped his own hand. "Aye. I can see that." His chiseled lips tipped into a wry smile. "But no' for much longer."

Relief surged, but ingrained politeness made Lucy say, "If you're sure it's not too much trouble…"

"Of course it's no', lass. You dinna want to get caught in the storm, do you?" At that very moment, thunder boomed above them and the trees and briar hedge shivered and shook as a gust of icy wind tore past, chasing away any lingering sultriness in the air. It wouldn't be long before the downpour hit.

"Well, no…" Lucy conceded.

"Good." The stranger moved close to Juniper and began to reharness the pony with an efficiency that was impressive. "I'm glad we agree. If you wouldna mind hopping back in your seat…"

Lucy frowned. "You can't mean to free the gig while I'm sitting in it. I'll just add unnecessary weight."

He glanced over his shoulder, openly smirking. "A slip o' a lass like you? I dinna think so. Although…" He shucked off his jacket and tossed it, along with his hat, onto the gig's seat as though he were claiming a spot. "If you could persuade your pony to put a *wee* bit more effort in while I'm pushing from behind, it would be greatly appreciated."

A splinter of irritation pricked. "The wheel *is* quite bogged," said Lucy. "And Juniper isn't as young and sprightly as he used to be. Are you sure you can manage this? I'd be happy to hold onto Juniper's bridle and coax him forward while you push."

"And risk having you get trampled or run over if you lose your footing again?" The Scot began to unfasten his cuffs and roll up the sleeves of his cambric shirt, exposing corded forearms that were strangely transfixing. "No' a chance. Trust me, pushing the gig while you are in it willna be a problem," he said. "So you'd best stop your havering and hop in before I pick you up and *put* you in."

What? Lucy's mouth dropped open. *What a managing, overbearing rude-word-that-rhymes-with-farce.*

Of course, she was grateful for the stranger's intervention, but she wouldn't be ordered about or manhandled like a sack of potatoes…even if it *might* be quite true that she could very well slip again. However, before Lucy could formulate any sort of response—unlike her dear friend Artemis, witty retorts were not her forte—a raindrop, cold and heavy, plopped onto the tip of her nose. This was followed by a barrage of more icy raindrops; so rather than argue, Lucy swallowed her chagrin, hiked up her skirts, and scrambled into her seat.

As she took up the reins, the Scotsman rounded the back of the gig. At his signal, she urged Juniper forward with a few encouraging clicks of her tongue and a gentle snap of the reins. Within moments, the vehicle lurched forward and they were free of the mud. But not free of the rain.

It was now coming down in sheets and the wind had grown wilder, ripping at Lucy's bonnet with angry, icy fingers. If she didn't make haste, the gig would surely get washed away.

Thunder cracked and lightning briefly illuminated the air. And then the Scotsman, carpetbag in hand, leaped into the gig beside her.

"Weel, what are you waiting for, lass?" he demanded over the roar of the storm. "I dinna ken where you are headed, but I'd suggest you get us out of this infernal weather before we drown or get struck by a bolt from above."

Despite his high-handedness, Lucy couldn't really quibble with the man's logic—he *had* gone out of his way to help her, and she couldn't begrudge him a safe place to shelter—so she snapped the reins again and Juniper took off at a spanking clip. No doubt the pony wished to be home too.

Within the space of five minutes, they were turning the corner into the beech-lined lane leading to Fleetwood Hall. The Scotsman gave a low whistle as they passed between the estate's grand iron gates and followed the gravel-lined drive toward the three-story, whitewashed manor house. "You live here?" he asked as he raked a dripping curtain of dark hair away from his brow and his gaze wandered over the building's ivy-clad facade.

Even though she was soaked to the skin, filthy, and shivering, Lucy couldn't hide her own slightly smug smirk. "Yes," she said as she directed Juniper around the back of the house toward the stables. "I do. Welcome to Fleetwood Hall. I'm sure my father, Sir Oswald Bertram, would like to meet you…Mister…"

"William Armstrong," he said, and Lucy had to press her lips together to suppress a laugh.

"Mr. Armstrong… How apt," she said before she could stop herself.

William Armstrong slid her a sideways glance from beneath the dark sweep of his spiky, rain-wet lashes. "You wouldna be laughing at my name now, would you, Miss Bertram?" he asked, wry amusement lacing his tone. "It is Miss Bertram, I presume?"

"I... Yes. It is. Lucinda Bertram." Despite the cold air, Lucy felt her cheeks grow warm. It seemed she had indeed teased the braw Scotsman.

How entirely singular. It was not like her at all. Miss Lucy Bertram didn't tease or flirt with gentlemen, especially not handsome-as-Heathcliff strangers with rough hands, granite-hewn jaws, sharply cut cheekbones, and shoulders wide enough to fill a doorway. She usually turned bright red and stumbled over her words and retreated into her shell, much like a Galápagos tortoise. It was almost as though the raging storm had unleashed a reckless, more brazen streak inside her. One that she'd hitherto been unaware of.

How...novel.

They'd reached the stables and Lucy drew the gig to a halt in the yard beneath a slate-tiled portico. The cobblestones were awash and the rain still teemed down in buckets, but at least they were now out of the worst of the weather. The stable lad materialized from the shadows of the stalls and Lucy tossed the reins to him. "Make sure Juniper gets a nice rubdown, Freddy," she called down to the lanky youth, who'd already begun to release Juniper from the traces. "And an apple with his oats when he's cooled down. It's been a rather wild afternoon and he deserves a treat."

Freddy bobbed his head. "Yes, miss." He darted a curious glance at Mr. Armstrong but didn't say anything as the Scotsman leapt down from his seat and rounded the gig to Lucy's side.

Before she could finish gathering up her sodden skirts in preparation to alight, the Scot grasped her about the waist. "Here, let me give you a complete demonstration that I do indeed live up to my name, Miss Bertram. Just so you dinna have any doubt."

Oh... Doubt was the furthest thing from Lucy's mind as she was lifted down from the gig as though she weighed nothing at all. As her feet met the slick cobblestones, she found herself looking up into William Armstrong's harshly handsome face. Somehow, her hands had landed upon his rock-hard chest—a chest that was clad in nothing but soaking wet, practically transparent linen.

Even more disconcerting was the fact that she could feel the Scot's touch as it lingered about her waist. The pressure of his fingers and the warmth of his palms seemed to penetrate her muslin gown, boned corset, and shift, heating her flesh beneath. The scent of rain, leather, and shaving soap—pleasantly astringent with notes of musk and spice—teased her senses. And his deep-blue gaze, the way it held hers before dipping to her mouth... Every part of Lucy seemed to tighten yet soften at the same time. Goose bumps of awareness spread over her skin and her breath quickened as something hot and dark and thrilling unfurled inside her. Even the air around them seemed to crackle with expectation.

As Lucy's gaze brazenly lingered on the Scotsman's face, she was suddenly overwhelmed by the strangest sense that she'd met him before. That he was somehow familiar. But for the life of her, she couldn't quite place him.

Although perhaps she'd once met him in a dream. Or in a book...

When her nose *wasn't* buried in a scientific journal or she wasn't gardening or peering through a microscope at a sample, she was invariably reading a Gothic romance novel. Yes, her fertile imagination had simply cast William Armstrong as the "brooding hero" in the unfolding drama of "getting caught in a late-summer storm."

Thunder growled and lightning flickered and the strange spell enveloping Lucy was instantly broken. Mr. Armstrong seemed to wake up as well, as he dropped his hands and stepped back. "You should go inside, Miss Bertram," he said gruffly, nodding toward Fleetwood Hall. "Before you catch cold." His gaze had become shuttered. Remote. Decidedly unfriendly.

"Yes…" Lucy wiped the rain from her eyes, suddenly feeling chilled to the bone and oddly disappointed. But he was right. She should return to the house. She *was* cold and wet and grubby, and it wasn't as though she hadn't a thousand things to do. Her father's latest journal article for the Linnean Society on strychnine trees endemic to Ceylon wouldn't get written by itself.

Nevertheless, decorum decreed that she couldn't just leave Mr. Armstrong here in the stables. She summoned a smile that she hoped would pass for inviting rather than uncertain. "You must accompany me. I can at least offer you a cup of tea and a slice of cake to say thank you for your help. And I'm sure you'd like to dry off." Goodness, he *so* needed to dry off and don more clothing because the way the man's shirt clung to every hard plane and contour of his well-muscled upper body…it was most distracting. Lucy swallowed and, with an effort, dragged her attention back to the Scotsman's face. "I'm sure my father will want to thank you as well, Mr. Armstrong."

But the Scot shook his head. "No. That willna be necessary. At least no' for now. I'll stay here and help Freddy with Juniper and the gig."

Help Freddy? Lucy's astonishment must have shown on her face because Mr. Armstrong cocked an eyebrow before he executed a perfect bow. "Your father has recently hired me, Miss Bertram. I'm Fleetwood Hall's new groom and coachman. I'm to start today."

"Oh…I…" Lucy blinked. Why hadn't her father said anything about Mr. Armstrong's planned arrival? But then, this wouldn't be the first time he hadn't shared his plans with her. Time and again she'd been the last to know what was going on. At least they had a new groom. She was more than happy about that.

Mr. Armstrong must have mistaken her surprise for disbelief, as he said, "I have a letter from Fleetwood's steward, Mr. Gilchrist, confirming my appointment to the position in my coat. And my references are in my carpetbag. I can fetch them if you'd like."

"No…no, you don't need to do that, Mr. Armstrong. But I'll let my father and Mr. Gilchrist know that you are here. And welcome. Please, do pop into the house for that tea and cake. Or perhaps you'd like something more substantial? Mrs. Gilchrist—she's our cook—will be more than happy to put something together for you. Some soup or a sandwich? I know there's some leftover roast beef and Mrs. Gilchrist makes the most excellent mustard pickles. There might even be a pork pie in the larder. And a barrel of small beer. We get it from the Wick and Whistle Inn at Heathwick Green. I don't drink it myself— I'm partial to tea and on special occasions a sip of elderberry wine or sherry—but I know my father likes to have a glass or two after a hard ride…"

Oh, figgy jam and spotted dick. Lucy bit her lip to curb her babbling. The idea of seeing William Armstrong every single day was too much. She couldn't quite decide if her heart was tripping with nervous dread or excitement.

At any rate, Mr. Armstrong tilted his head in acknowledgment of her panicked outpouring. "All of that sounds verra satisfactory, Miss Bertram. As soon as I'm done here in the stables, I'll make myself presentable and put in an appearance." Then he turned his attention to Freddy and Juniper. Lucy was clearly dismissed.

Ha! To describe William Armstrong as high-handed would

be an understatement. Lucy retrieved her basket and shopping parcels from the storage box at the back of the gig, then rushed across the stable yard toward Fleetwood Hall's rear entrance that led to the kitchen. As she paused in the open doorway, unlacing her mud-encrusted boots, she glanced back toward the stables and had the oddest sensation that Mr. Armstrong was watching her with his dark-as-a-midnight-sky eyes.

Surely not, thought Lucy. It was more likely the case that he was laughing as he recalled the moment he came upon her. A baronet's daughter, wallowing in the mud.

Oh, how lowering. Of course, she suspected the groom would never mention the incident again, but that hardly signified. Whenever she saw him, whenever she needed the gig or decided to go riding and he accompanied her—Father would insist that he did—she would know he'd be thinking about it. Not only that, she'd also be forever thinking of the moment she'd foolishly imagined Mr. Armstrong might kiss her.

Lucy emitted a disgruntled sigh and firmly shut the door on the rain and her ridiculous fancies. She was the spinsterish daughter of a practically impoverished, somewhat eccentric baronet. She'd be more likely to achieve the impossible and gain entry to a university to study the botanical sciences and be accepted as a member of the male-dominated Linnean Society than wed any man, let alone someone like him.

The opinion of the mercurial Scots groom—*a servant,* she reminded herself, *that you met only half an hour ago*—shouldn't matter one iota. So why oh why was a tiny part of her tempted to ask Dotty to press her best pink silk gown and dress her hair in ringlets and dig out her rose-scented perfume like she was some silly young debutante out to impress a gentleman at a ball?

Oh, Lucy Bertram. You are such a goose, she lamented as she entered the deserted kitchen and deposited her things on the scrubbed oak table. *The fall on your derriere didn't just knock the stuffing out of you. It knocked out all of your common sense.*

Her mind refocused, she began to unpack her basket. She'd purchased a lovely washed-rind cheese and a wedge of crumbly yellow cheddar from the Heathwick Purveyor of Fine Foods and Tea Shoppe, and a jar of the lavender-scented honey her father liked on his morning crumpets. And then she pulled out the post and cursed. Somehow the rain had penetrated the gig's storage box and her wicker basket. Father would be miffed with her if anything important was damaged. She leafed through the small bundle, checking each slightly damp envelope. When she got to the last one, her heart all but stopped.

There *was* a letter addressed to her. And it was from Monty.

Chapter Two

DAMN, BLOODY DAMN. WHAT THE HELL IS WRONG WITH ME?

Will "Armstrong" shoved his dripping hair out of his eyes as he watched Miss Lucinda Bertram dash across the stable yard to the rear entrance of Fleetwood Hall. He hadn't even officially started his new post here, yet he'd almost lost his head and kissed the pretty-as-an-English-rose lass. *So, so stupid.*

Deliberately flirting with his employer's daughter was bad enough. Why he'd felt the need to put on a ridiculous masculine display of strength by lifting her out of the gig, he had no idea. He was behaving like some mindless buck strutting around showing off his antlers during rutting season.

With a grunt, Will turned his back on the far-too-appealing sight of Miss Bertram removing her dainty but muddy boots, exposing her slender, stocking-clad ankles, and focused on assisting the stable boy, Freddy, with unharnessing Juniper. "How old are you, lad?" he asked as they led Juniper into one of the freshly mucked-out empty stalls.

Freddy looked at him shyly from beneath a shaggy fringe of bright carrot-red hair. "Thirteen, sir."

"Och, just call me Will. I'm no' one to stand on ceremony."

Freddy bobbed his head and smiled. "Yes, sir... I mean, Will."

"Verra good." Will patted the stocky gray pony on the rump. "If you dinna mind, I'll leave you to tend to Juniper. I should make myself known to your master, Sir Oswald. I take it there's a place I can change into fresh clothes?"

Freddy pointed beyond the neighboring stalls, which housed a pair of matched chestnut carriage horses and another sleek black mount. Thoroughbreds, by the look of them. "Yes, just up the back, over there," said the lad. "Will the tack room do? Don't worry about Tom though. He's big but he doesn't mind strangers."

"Tom?"

Freddy grinned sheepishly. "Fleetwood's barn cat. He's a very good mouser."

"Perfect." Will nodded toward the gig. "When I return, I'll help you with the cleaning. It'll be a fair job."

Freddy's nose wrinkled. "It looks like it got stuck in a bog on the heath."

Will couldn't help but laugh. "No' quite, but close. I'll be as quick as I can."

As he retrieved his coat, hat, and carpetbag, he caught himself casting a glance toward the back of the manor house. Miss Bertram had disappeared. He gritted his teeth and, yet again, inwardly admonished himself for acting like a daft, lust-bitten beast. It probably didn't help that he'd already met the lass months before—albeit briefly—and had felt a spark of attraction even then. A spark that apparently hadn't dimmed in the slightest when he'd come upon her in the laneway this afternoon.

Despite her disheveled state, he'd recognized her immediately, but had pretended he didn't know a thing about her. He trusted that she hadn't recalled him. At least he didn't think so, considering the circumstances surrounding their first encounter in a crowded ballroom. He'd been in a different disguise that time, posing as a wealthy American industrialist—a Mr. Adam Whittaker—not a gruff, nose-to-the-grindstone Scots groom. The only person at that ball who'd known his true identity had been the host, Lord Castledown.

One thing was clear—he *needed* to crush this inconvenient attraction for his employer's daughter and keep his mind on the job at hand. And that job wasn't just to play the part of Fleetwood Hall's groom and coachman. No, his real role was to track down a murderer within the Linnean Society. Someone had poisoned the prominent, noble patron Viscount Litchfield and, via a series of letters, had directly threatened to do away with another half dozen of the society's preeminent council members unless Charles Darwin was expelled from the society by summer's end. The perpetrator's reason? The society supported Darwin and his controversial views on natural selection and evolutionary theory—ideas that were recently disseminated at a Linnean Society meeting on the first of July.

On the list of Scotland Yard's chief suspects, Sir Oswald was near the top. Not only was he a member of the Linnean Society and a botanical poisons expert—he'd written an entire book on the subject and cultivated an extensive poisons garden here at Fleetwood Hall—but he was also a man who was rumored to need money quite desperately. In addition, there were whispers in certain circles that he'd held a grudge against Lord Litchfield for reneging on a deal they'd struck earlier in the year. The viscount had supposedly agreed to fund an expedition to the Malay Peninsula that Sir Oswald was to head, but had then changed his mind, leaving the baronet high and dry and embittered.

The problem was there was no concrete evidence implicating Sir Oswald in the crimes of either the murder of the viscount or the poison-pen letters. Not one speck. Under recent questioning by Scotland Yard detectives, Sir Oswald had been unshakable in his claim that he was innocent of any wrongdoing. He insisted that he had no issue with Darwin's views or anyone else who put credence in them, and that there'd been no bad blood between him and Lord Litchfield despite the circulating rumors. But according to Scotland Yard's divisional surgeon who'd conducted the postmortem examination, Lord Litchfield had been poisoned with strychnine. While strychnine could be found in rat poison, the powder that Litchfield had ingested appeared to be far more potent and more readily soluble. Only someone with expert knowledge could have produced it.

For that reason, Will had been tasked with conducting a clandestine investigation: to monitor Sir Oswald's comings and goings, who he met with, his correspondence, the poisons he possessed, and if he *did* actually object to Charles Darwin and everything he stood for.

While it would have been easier for Will to gather intelligence if he'd taken up a position inside the Bertram household—perhaps as a footman, valet, or butler—word was Sir Oswald's stables were short-staffed. Hence the persona of Scots groom-cum-coachman "William Armstrong" had been created with a suitable reference from an acquaintance of the baronet's, Lord Castledown. Fortunately, scarcely anyone outside of a chosen few at the Home Office and Scotland Yard knew Will by the name he was born with, William Douglas Lockhart, or his courtesy title, the Earl of Kyle. Given Will's decade-long absence from both Edinburgh and London high society, barely anyone save for his reclusive grandfather, the Duke of Ayr—a man he despised beyond all measure—would recognize him or refer to him as Lord Kyle anymore.

Once Will had brushed the mud from his boots and had donned fresh breeches, a linen shirt, woolen waistcoat, black necktie, and only *slightly* crumpled sack coat, he raked his fingers through his still-damp hair and scowled at his slightly distorted reflection in the cracked mirror on the tack-room wall. He could do with a shave, but he didn't want to waste any more time. Besides, his shadowed jaw made him look rougher, less approachable, and that would make it easier for him to keep his focus on the investigation and away from far-too-pretty flaxen-haired distractions. Of course, he suspected Sir Oswald would want Will to accompany his daughter on rides and excursions as grooms customarily did, but if Miss Bertram viewed him as uncouth, she might decline his escort. Cultivating an unkempt appearance and overbearing, brooding facade would surely work in his favor.

"What do you think?" he asked the ginger barn cat, Tom, who blinked at him sleepily from a pile of saddle blankets stacked on a nearby shelf.

Tom closed his large green eyes and snuggled back into the blankets. The cat was clearly disinterested in Will's sartorial choices.

Keeping his glowering expression in place, Will emerged from the tack room and, with his references and letter of appointment in hand, sprinted across the stable yard, heading for the back entrance of Fleetwood Hall.

Let the investigation begin.

Lucy sat in the window seat of Fleetwood's study and scanned her brother's letter for what seemed like the hundredth time. If one could even call a few hastily scrawled lines a letter. Said lines told her nothing at all beyond the fact that Monty was all right. Of course, he'd also entreated her not to worry nor look for him, but how could Lucy not do *both* of those things?

He was gone, and she had no idea when she would see him again.

Or worse, *if* she would ever see him again.

She examined the water-stained envelope. There was no

return address, and the postmark on the Penny Black stamp was so smudged, it was virtually indecipherable. It *could* be a London postmark. But even with the aid of a magnifying glass, the numeral five was the only part discernible. It would be virtually impossible to work out which branch of the London District Post Office had stamped it.

With a sigh, Lucy dashed a frustrated tear from her cheek and tucked Monty's letter into the sleeve of her plaid poplin gown. She should get on with her father's work—*her* work, really—before anyone came upon her and noticed she was upset. Although Father didn't seem to notice all that much about her these days. Unless he was critiquing a journal article she'd written for him or she approached him about the household budget or the management of Fleetwood's extensive gardens. That reminded her—she had to consult Mr. Rolfe, the gardener, about trimming back the cherry laurels in the poisons garden. They were far too overgrown, and it was such an involved process. And then she should check on the new monkshood and hemlock seedlings in the hothouse—

The sound of her father's voice in the hall outside had her hastening to her rosewood escritoire on the other side of the room. But before she sat down, the door opened to reveal he wasn't alone.

Mr. Armstrong hovered on the threshold just behind her father's spare form. She'd been right... The groom's muscular shoulders *did* practically fill the doorway. She met the Scotsman's watchful eyes and promptly blushed. She couldn't help it. He surprised her by glancing away first. It was almost as though she'd been dismissed again. Or she wasn't worthy of his interest. His gaze traveled about the room as her father addressed her.

"Ah, Lucy. I knew I'd find you here," Sir Oswald began

without preamble. "I understand you've already met our new groom and coachman, Will Armstrong?"

"Yes," she said, keeping her gaze trained on her father. Even though a peculiar mixture of annoyance and self-consciousness and disappointment brewed inside her chest because the Scot was ostensibly ignoring her, she was determined to appear just as unruffled and unaffected. As cool as a cucumber in an ice-house in midwinter. "I have."

"Ah, very good." Sir Oswald crossed the room to his own desk, a grand mahogany affair, and took a seat. "I have some rather pressing correspondence to attend to and Mr. Gilchrist has gone out to inspect some flooding in the lower-lying pad-docks, so I'll leave it to you to show Will around. But don't dillydally. I want to see the slides of the Ceylonese *Strychnos nux-vomica* seeds you've prepared for me."

"They're beneath the microscope, waiting for you to examine. I've rendered preliminary sketches of the samples for your article too," she said.

Her father nodded. "Excellent. Oh, and before I forget, if you wish to resume your custom of taking a morning ride out on the heath, Will may accompany you. It will be nice for Titan, Nutmeg, and Mace to be exercised regularly again."

Lucy bowed her head. "Of course, Papa. It will be. Nice, that is. Once Mr. Armstrong has his bearings, I'll be back to finish the first draft of your article. I won't be long."

"Ah…" Her father raised a hand, halting her progress toward the door where Mr. Armstrong still waited. "Just one more thing before you go, Lucy. A friend of mine, a fellow member of the Linnean Society, Mr. Zachariah Thorne, has recently returned to London from his Yorkshire estate and will be joining us for dinner this evening. He's due to arrive at seven." He arched a grizzled brow and peered over his silver-rimmed spectacles at her. "I trust that Mrs. Gilchrist will be able to prepare something suitably impressive? Given Thorne's wealth and prestige—he's quite the entrepreneur—I'm sure he's used to the very best of everything. I'm expecting four courses at the very least."

"I…" Dismay welled in Lucy's chest. Trust her father to leave something like this to the last minute. If she'd known, she would have picked up additional supplies in the village. Nevertheless, she hid her clenched fists in the folds of her skirts and mustered a smile as she said, "I'll see what we can do."

"Oh, and I expect you to wear something pretty. Something that's not…" Sir Oswald waved a hand in her direction. "Well, not a dull plaid like that. If you recall, I did furnish you with a whole new wardrobe for the Season."

Lucy had to unclench her teeth to reply. "Yes. I recall." How could she not? Before that fateful night when Monty left, her father had been determined to sell her off to the highest eligible male bidder in the London marriage mart. Aside from the few occasions when she'd been able to catch up with her Byronic Book Club friends, Artemis and Jane, to talk about life and all things wonderfully bookish, she'd hated every other moment of her short-lived "Season."

And then another thought occurred to her. One that was entirely horrible and made her heart sink faster than a deflating hot-air balloon. Was her father trying to marry her off again? To this Zachariah Thorne? Why else would he ask her to wear "something pretty"? Most of the time he didn't give a flying fig about her attire.

Behind her, Mr. Armstrong cleared his throat and irritation scuttled in to replace Lucy's dread. Not only had the groom heard the entirety of that rather awkward exchange about her *dull plaid* gown, but he also had the audacity to give her a signal to hurry up?

Ugh. Hiking up her chin in an effort to hide her embarrassment, Lucy spun around and the groom stepped back into the hall so she could pass. "This way, if you please." If her tone sounded slightly shrewish, she didn't much care.

But the Scot didn't say a word and followed her in silence. Well, relative silence. Lucy couldn't help but notice the echo of his booted footsteps on the wooden floorboards as they made their way through the house. "I take it you haven't eaten yet, Mr. Armstrong?" she threw over her shoulder.

"Will," he said. "Almost everyone calls me Will. And to answer your question, no, I have no', Miss Bertram."

"Very well. Will it is. I'll take you to the kitchens so you can meet Mrs. Gilchrist."

The jovial cook greeted the Scots groom with a wide smile as soon as Lucy made the introductions. "My word. Aren't you a big handsome lad, then?" the woman crowed as she planted her flour-dusted hands on her broad hips. "Now don't you be flirting with the young housemaids or some of us older staff members might get jealous." And then she winked.

Lucy's eyebrows shot up. Good heavens, the woman was *married*.

Will, on the other hand, didn't seem perturbed in the slightest, given the smile tugging at the corner of his mouth. "I promise you I'll be on my verra best behavior at all times, Mrs. Gilchrist," he said. "And I'm sure there's more than enough to keep me busy in the stables."

"Yes," agreed Lucy stiffly. "I'm sure we'll hardly notice Mr. Arm… I mean 'Will' is here."

Mrs. Gilchrist released a throaty chuckle that made her ample bust wobble like a barely set flummery. "You might not, Miss Bertram. But I know I will." She winked at the groom again, then said, "Now, what can I be fixing you? A beef sandwich or a pork pie? We've small beer too. A large lad like you must work up a decent thirst and appetite."

"I dinna want to put you out," he said. "A pork pie and perhaps a mug of small beer?"

"I'll get them," offered Lucy, heading for the larder. "You keep working on that pastry, Mrs. Gilchrist. Father has just informed me that he has an important guest, a Mr. Thorne, coming for dinner. And he expects four courses." She returned to the table with the pork pie. "At a minimum."

"What?" Mrs. Gilchrist threw her hands in the air, sending up a cloud of flour that caught in Lucy's throat and made her cough. "There goes my plan for steak and kidney pie, then. That's far too plain for a fancy gentleman caller. And we've nothing at all for the fish course."

"Yes, it will be a challenge to come up with a suitable menu," said Lucy, placing the pie on a china plate and then passing it and a linen napkin to Will, who'd already taken a seat at the far end of the oak table where the air was flour-free. He nodded his thanks. "But I'm sure we'll work out something together." She filled a mug with small beer and handed this to Will too.

Mrs. Gilchrist wiped her forearm across her wrinkled brow and huffed out a heavy sigh. "Yes, I'm sure we will, miss. Right." She clapped her hands together. "I need to crack along."

"After I've shown Will to his quarters, I'll gather some sorrel. That would at least cover the soup course." Lucy glanced through the sash window to the kitchen garden and the stable yard beyond. The chickens had emerged from their henhouse and were now pecking at the ground, hunting for worms. "At least it's stopped raining. For the moment."

"Aye, it has." Will dabbed the corner of his wide mouth with the napkin, then rose to his feet. It appeared he'd consumed the pie and beer in just a few mouthfuls. "That was delicious, Mrs. Gilchrist."

The cook beamed. "There's plenty more where that came from, my lad. And just so you know, breakfast is at eight o'clock, luncheon at noon, and supper at nine. But do drop by anytime you're hungry. I wouldn't want you to go without."

The groom inclined his head. "Thank you, Mrs. Gilchrist. I'll keep that in mind." He caught Lucy's eye. "I'm ready whenever you are, Miss Bertram."

Lucy nodded and managed to reply without blushing. "Very good." Really, she had so much she needed to accomplish this afternoon that she didn't have time to worry about when the far-too-handsome groom might be popping into the kitchen at all hours of the day or night, or what he might or might not think of her. Or indeed if he thought about her at all beyond the fact she was his employer's daughter.

She led him back toward the stables and then past them, along a flagged path to the head groom's quarters—a small thatched, whitewashed cottage adjacent to Fleetwood's ancient apple orchard. "I trust you'll be comfortable here," she said as she unlatched the door and revealed the simple, barely furnished sitting room. "The bedchamber is just through there," she added, indicating another door that was slightly ajar. The end of a wrought-iron bed frame and a single mattress covered with a quilted counterpane in various shades of blue were just visible. "There's a water pump just around the side by the orchard. I don't think you'll fancy carting water all the way from the pump near the horses' trough. But if you require anything else at all—extra linen or blankets, or towels, or if you find the place a little dusty and would like it to be cleaned—do let Mrs. Gilchrist know. Or me, for that matter. We'll send one of the housemaids over."

Will's dark brows pulled together in a deep frown. "Ye dinna have a housekeeper? I dinna wish to trouble you unnecessarily."

"I… No…no, we don't, I'm afraid. Not at the moment." Lucy really didn't wish to discuss her family's slide into penury and the associated penny-pinching with a man she barely knew. And a servant, no less. Aside from the fact it just wasn't *done*, it was rather embarrassing to acknowledge that her father had squandered much of the Bertram fortune on self-indulgent expeditions abroad in his quest to discover every obscure poisonous plant beneath the sun. She forced a smile. "In any event, it will be nice to have a head groom and coachman again here at Fleetwood. I'm sure Freddy is over-the-moon happy."

Will gave a noncommittal grunt and his gaze traveled back to the stables. "I'd offer to help you with picking the sorrel to stop your skirts getting mucky again, but I also promised Freddy that I'd help him clean the gig."

"Oh… That's quite all right. It's only a workaday gown and the plaid pattern is dark enough that it should hide any stains. And I quite agree. Cleaning the gig is a priority. Father might ask you to pick up Mr. Thorne from the station at Hampstead, and it's far too much bother to ready the carriage for such a short trip."

The groom stepped outside. "Verra well." His mouth slid into a smile. "I'd best get on with it, then. I wouldna want to disappoint your father or Mr. Zachariah Thorne."

"Of course." Lucy shut the door. "I shall see you anon, I expect." While part of her would love to go riding in the morning—it had been months since she'd done so—she expected she would be far too tired, given everything that had already happened today and the myriad things she had left to do. Like Will, she'd "best get on with it" too.

Besides, the mere idea of riding with the new groom was enough to make her all hot and bothered. It was best not to think about that.

She started down the path, Will following. At the stables, just before she crossed the yard to the kitchen garden, he said softly, "It might only be a workaday gown you're wearing, Miss Bertram, but I like it. And it's no' dull at all. Plaid suits you."

Lucy paused and dared to glance back, and when the groom's eyes met hers, he added, "But perhaps my Scots blood makes me a wee bit biased." Before she could respond to his unexpected praise, he executed a swift bow, turned on his booted heel, and then disappeared into the deep shadows of the stables.

Oh… Fiddlesticks and candlesticks! Her cheeks burning with a flush of pleasure, Lucy picked up her skirts and hastened across the muddy yard. Why did Mr. Armstrong have to go and say something like *that*? She didn't think a man had paid a compliment about her appearance before. Indeed, compliments of any kind from anyone, even her father, were as scarce as hen's teeth of late.

Lucy sighed as she collected a basket from the storeroom where all the gardening tools were kept. Instead of dismissing the Scot from her mind as she'd been determined to do earlier on, she was certain her thoughts would continue to stray to him for the rest of the afternoon. And evening. How was she to focus on writing her father's article on Ceylonese *Strychnos nux-vomica* seeds now?

Fiddlesticks indeed.

Chapter Three

THE RAIN HELD OFF FOR THE REST OF THE AFTERNOON AND into the early evening when Will set out for Hampstead Station in the freshly cleaned gig. Which was fortunate, because as soon as he met Mr. Zachariah Thorne, Will was certain the man would have been most put out if his immaculately tailored jacket of black superfine with velvet lapels, satin-covered top hat, and gold-rimmed monocle had been besmirched by rain-drops. Although the man's black hair was so slick with Macassar oil, the droplets probably would have rolled off it like water off a duck's back.

Indeed, Will quickly formed the impression that Thorne was a bit of a pretentious prig despite the fact he spoke with a strong Yorkshire accent. Will also suspected Mr. Thorne, the "entrepreneur," definitely possessed "new money" rather than old—a fortune amassed from milling or mining or railways or something else "industrial." In Will's experience, that sort of man often tended to be the worst kind of toff. He was always out to prove something. That he was not only wealthier, but that he was more tenacious, ruthless, cannier, and that he had better taste and better opinions than anyone else despite his humble upbringings. That even though his speech and manners were coarser, he was just as well-to-do as any noble member of high society.

That he "belonged."

Will's theory that Zachariah Thorne was a bit of a prat was

confirmed in full when within moments of meeting him, the man took one look at the gig and his upper lip curled. "*That's* what Sir Oswald expects me to ride in this evening rather than his carriage?" he all but growled. "If I'd known, I would have arranged for my own carriage to ferry me here from Belgravia." He gave an exaggerated sigh, then made a show of fishing out his gold pocket watch and checking the time, then pushing it back into his paisley satin waistcoat. "Wait here."

With that, Thorne turned on his heel and marched straight over to the telegram office on the platform. A few minutes later, he returned and said in a voice that was as hard and cold as a Yorkshire hoarfrost, "Right. Take me to Fleetwood House, then." Climbing into the gig, he leaned back in his seat and flicked a speck of nonexistent lint off his sleeve. "Oh, and for your information, I won't be catching the train back, so this"—he waved his hand at Juniper and the gig—"won't be required later this evening. I've sent for my carriage."

"Verra good, sir," said Will, taking his seat. Despite his best efforts to keep to his side of the small conveyance, his knee accidentally bumped the Yorkshireman's when they hit a rut in the still-muddy laneway, earning him another lip curl. In hindsight, he probably should have asked permission to ready Sir Oswald's carriage. He certainly didn't envy Miss Bertram having to entertain the grumpy Northerner. While Will was determined to adopt a grumpy demeanor himself, to keep his mind on his mission and to keep the comely Miss Bertram at a distance, he suspected Thorne genuinely was a disagreeable sort of man. The sort who would find fault with the smallest of things. If there was a smudge on his wineglass or the sorrel soup wasn't served at precisely the right temperature, he'd be sure to let his hosts know.

A sliver of anger penetrated Will's chest at the thought. Sir Oswald didn't appear to value his clever, sweet-natured daughter or the amount of work she was lumbered with. Not only did the baronet expect her to be his research assistant—Will had never met a woman who actually knew what a microscopic slide was, let alone how to prepare one—but she had also taken on the entire role of housekeeper in the absence of one. Of course, Will was aware he'd arrived at Fleetwood Hall less than six hours ago, but he believed he'd already accurately ascertained the "lay of the land." As a covert inquiry agent, it was his job to make quick and accurate assessments of a situation and to read someone's character swiftly. To find out all of their quirks and vulnerable spots so he could manipulate a situation to his advantage in his quest to ferret out the truth.

He was supposed to be objective. Analytical. However, the idea that Sir Oswald might actually be planning to marry his daughter off to the block of Yorkshire granite sitting beside him filled Will with inexplicable ire. He must have unconsciously tightened his grip on the reins, as poor Juniper began to snort and toss his head in protest. *Sorry, old boy.* When they got back to the stables, he'd give Juniper a lump of sugar to apologize.

As they approached Heathwick Green, Will didn't think it would hurt to venture a remark. "I hear you are in the Linnean Society. Like Sir Oswald."

Thorne snorted. "I don't see how that's any of your business. I'd suggest you confine your interest to horses, mucking out Sir Oswald's stables, and other equally menial matters befitting someone of your station."

What an asinine ass. Will barely resisted the urge to roll his eyes. As it was, he only just managed to stop himself from deliberately steering the gig through a sizable puddle that would have splashed Thorne's evening attire. He didn't regret trying to coax information out of the Yorkshireman or mind Thorne's subsequent put-down. He was here to find out all he could about Sir

Oswald and any of his associates at the Linnean Society. A man had been murdered and others had been threatened with the same fate if Charles Darwin wasn't ejected from their ranks within a few weeks' time. The clock was ticking, and he had to get a result.

Thorne obviously had the funds Sir Oswald needed, so gleaning all he could about their relationship was a priority. It was a pity that Thorne wasn't a braggart. Although if the Yorkshireman tended to keep things close to his chest, maybe he had something to hide…

They'd passed through the village and its small cluster of shops and cottages, and a little farther on rose the spire of a church above a dark canopy of yew trees.

Thorne grunted. "Last time I was here, I didn't notice the local church. I take it that it's a Protestant establishment, not some papist abomination."

Papist abomination? Now that was an interesting choice of words. Was the man a religious zealot of some sort? Will slid the Yorkshireman a sideways glance and, sure enough, the man's face was a picture of derision. "I couldna say, sir," he said carefully. "I'm verra new to the area. Although I expect it's an Anglican church." Of course Will did know this for a fact. Before he'd headed to Fleetwood Hall, he'd conducted a quick inspection of the village shops, the inn, and St. Edmund's Church. But he was rather interested in provoking Thorne into revealing more about himself.

"Humph. One would hope so," said Thorne. "I would also expect that Sir Oswald demands that his staff attend church services regularly. *I* would never employ someone who refused to observe the Sabbath. Given you're a Scot, I take it you're a Presbyterian or a member of some other Episcopalian denomination?"

"Presbyterian," said Will. "At least my mother was." It was

interesting indeed that a discussion revolving around religion had seemed to loosen Thorne's tongue.

The man puffed out his chest. His sonorous voice was resonant with pride as he said, "Many years ago, I aspired to become a minister myself and to work in the colonies, doing God's work as a missionary. My father was a staunch Calvinist, and I came to learn from an early age that one must do what one must to save one's soul." His dark eyes settled on Will. "Even if one is predestined to end up in the fiery pit."

Ha! Will had to bite the inside of his cheek to stop himself from laughing out loud. If Zachariah Thorne only knew the myriad sins *he'd* committed over the years—in the name of Queen and country, of course, when he'd served as an officer in the British army and now as an agent for the Home Office—the man would be looking at him like he was a minion of the Prince of Darkness himself.

Sir Oswald must be desperate for money indeed if he'd begun to associate with a prickly-as-a-conker Calvinist. The Calvinistic concept of predestination—that whether a person went to heaven or hell was determined upon entering the world and there was little that one could do about it—had always seemed particularly harsh to Will. With such narrow, uncompromising views, he could well imagine that Thorne had fire and brimstone running through his veins rather than blood.

They lapsed into a strained silence—no doubt Thorne was already speculating that Will was destined to go to Hades because of his irregular church attendance—but thankfully, it wasn't long until they were turning into Fleetwood Hall's drive. As they drew to a halt in the graveled forecourt before the house, the front door was opened by a pair of liveried footmen and Sir Oswald emerged in the company of Miss Bertram.

Will's gaze snagged on the sight of her. There was no possible way he could ignore her.

Damn it.

She'd done as her father asked and had indeed donned a pretty gown. One might even say an extravagant, haute couture gown. A confection in petal-pink satin and fine lace, she looked like she'd floated in from Fleetwood's rose gardens that bordered the drive. Her flaxen hair had been arranged in becoming clusters of ringlets that framed her perfect oval of a face. The phrase *breathtakingly lovely* wouldn't even do Miss Bertram justice.

Telling himself he shouldn't gawk like a lovestruck mooncalf, Will tore his gaze away and busied himself with the reins. Good God. He'd already broken his vow to keep his distance when he'd paid her a compliment about her plaid gown earlier on. He needed to remember that he was a thirty-two-year-old man, not a boy. A hardened military officer who'd survived fighting in the Crimean War. A covert "inquiry agent" assigned to difficult missions both here and occasionally abroad. A man who never got emotionally entangled with anyone at all, let alone the daughter of a murder suspect. It would be unprofessional to do so. It could endanger his investigation by scrambling his judgment.

He definitely didn't need such a complication. Somehow he had to harden his resolve. Harness his runaway lust. Repair the cracks in the armor surrounding his heart.

Thorne jumped down from the gig and strode up the steps to the covered portico. Sir Oswald greeted his guest with a smile and a handshake. It was almost as if they were long-lost friends.

Miss Bertram executed a perfect curtsy as Thorne bowed over her ungloved hand. Even from where Will was sitting, he could see the frank appreciation in the Yorkshireman's heavy-lidded gaze as it slid over Miss Bertram's fine face and figure.

Bloody hell. It appeared that Sir Oswald might actually have real plans to marry off his daughter to the odious man. Somehow Will smothered another unexpected pulse of hot anger that swelled and throbbed inside his chest. It was not his place to interfere. Or feel anything at all.

But it *was* his duty to find out how well Sir Oswald and Thorne knew each other. And if either of them had been involved in Viscount Litchfield's death and the death threats received by Charles Darwin and other members of influence within the Linnean Society.

He suddenly wished he were in the shoes of one of the footmen who would no doubt be present at dinner.

Now there was a thought…

His gaze narrowed on the tallest fellow, sizing him up. At a pinch, his livery would do. Although Will would have to act swiftly to put his plan into action. With a flick of the reins, he roused Juniper and they headed off to the stables at a brisk trot. There was no time to lose.

―――――

Lucy somehow mustered a polite smile as Mr. Zachariah Thorne took her hand and she curtsied. While etiquette decreed that she shouldn't have to curtsy at all—she was the daughter of a baronet and Mr. Thorne was a commoner—her father had directed her to do so before they'd stepped out of the front door to greet him. "We need to impress him, Lucy. A pretty gown is only part of the equation. I expect you to play the part of perfect hostess. You know how flighty you get when you're nervous. I can't afford to offend this man."

"I'll try to, Papa," she'd said, even though her stomach

churned and her knees felt as though they were made of butter left out in the sun too long. Her father had categorically confirmed something that she'd already suspected: that *she* was the one who needed to impress Mr. Thorne. And meeting strangers of the opposite sex—especially "eligible" gentlemen who might have marriage on their minds—was never easy for her. Well, that was an understatement.

The whole scenario terrified her.

Now that she was face-to-face with the wealthy Mr. Thorne, Lucy was no less petrified. Especially when the man's dark-as-obsidian eyes traveled over her like she was an item at auction and he was estimating her value. She imagined the checklist running through his mind as he appraised her attributes.

Attractive enough? Yes.

Good teeth? Yes.

Biddable? Amiable? So far, so good.

Child-bearing potential? In the right age bracket. Hard to judge the size of her hips beneath that frightfully wide skirt.

If he was the sort of man who expected women to be seen and not heard, he would not be disappointed. Because Lucy was determined to keep her lips clamped together lest she start babbling nervously, which would only lead to awkwardness and embarrassment for her. And of course it would irk her father.

She rather hoped the man might be entirely bored with her company and that she would soon be disregarded. If she could have disappeared into the faded flocked wallpaper in the drawing room where they'd just repaired for a predinner sherry, she would have.

Clarke, one of the two footmen still employed at Fleetwood, entered the room bearing three brimming sherry glasses on a silver tray. Healey, the other footman, must be making sure everything was laid out perfectly in the dining room.

When Lucy reached for her glass and noticed the tray was slightly tarnished around the edges, she inwardly grimaced. She really should have made sure Fleetwood's butler, Redmond, had checked all of the silverware this afternoon, but she'd been so busy with other things. And then of course Redmond, because of the staff cuts, was also acting as his master's valet, so he was run ragged with far too many duties as well.

With a small sigh, Lucy seated herself with an appropriate degree of demureness upon a settee by the fire and tried to pay attention to what her father and Mr. Thorne were discussing. But it was a rather dull conversation about new railway lines and the price of wool bales and mills and shipping costs and some of Mr. Thorne's other business interests in the north. She learned he owned a fine town house in Lowndes Square in Belgravia, was a member of Boodle's and the exclusive Raleigh Club, and his preferred tailor was in Savile Row.

Although, every now and again, Lucy was aware of Mr. Thorne's regard drifting her way. He was stationed by one of the wide sash windows, facing the room and her. Indeed, she rather felt like a specimen in a jar. It was quite unnerving, to say the least, and she tried very hard not to squirm or fidget. If she revealed how disconcerted she was by look or by action, surely he'd notice.

Cool-headed. That's what she aimed to be. Just like her friends Artemis and Jane. She hadn't seen them in an age and missed them terribly. Artemis was still abroad on her extended honeymoon with her delicious duke, but Jane was still in London. Perhaps she could stop by Delaney's Antiquarian Bookshop tomorrow to see what her friend was up to. A Byronic Book Club meeting with just the two of them wouldn't be quite the same without Artemis, but it would give her something to look forward to. And Jane was always so sensible and gave excellent advice—

"Lucy."

At the sound of her father calling her name, Lucy jumped and nearly spilled her sherry all over her skirts.

"Are you woolgathering, my dear gel?" Without waiting for her to respond, he continued, "I was just telling Mr. Thorne that I think it's time we went in to dinner."

Lucy glanced at the mantel clock. Mrs. Gilchrist had been informed that the first course should be served at precisely eight o'clock, but it was only a quarter to the hour. "I..." She deposited her glass on a nearby table and rose to her feet. "I should probably check with the kitchen. You know how it is..."

Even though Mr. Thorne's expression was a study in neutrality, Lucy had the impression the man was slightly irritated. Her father, on the other hand, was the picture of disgruntlement. Nevertheless, he simply inclined his head in acquiescence rather than find fault. He clearly didn't want Mr. Thorne to witness any bickering. "Very well," he said. "I trust you won't be long."

"Of course," said Lucy, starting for the door where Clarke waited. "I'm sure bringing dinner forward won't be a problem." To the footman, she murmured on her way out, "Perhaps you could refill their sherry glasses."

But as she approached the kitchen, she stopped in the hallway outside, gaping. Because coming straight toward her was Will Armstrong, attired in a footman's uniform. The navy satin breeches, butter-yellow waistcoat, and white hose fit him well, though the navy-blue serge jacket appeared to be pulling tightly across the bulk of his biceps. "What... Why are you...?" She paused and inhaled a steadying breath. "Why are you wearing livery? Where did you get it? Is it Healey's? Is he all right?"

Will adjusted his cravat. "Aye, it's Healey's. I'm afraid he's taken ill," he said. "Nothing serious, I believe, but he's retired to his quarters to rest. Rather than bother you while you were entertaining your guest, Mrs. Gilchrist asked if I could fill in. And because Mr. Thorne doesna wish to catch the train back to London later this evening, your butler, Mr. Redmond, agreed. Mr. Thorne has already sent for his carriage and everything in the stables has been taken care of…" He paused, his gaze lingering on her face, making her blush. "I hope I havena overstepped. I got the impression your father wishes to impress his guest."

"Oh… I… Yes. He does. And I suppose that would be all right," she murmured. "You filling in. Thank you, Will, for helping out."

Ugh. But it wasn't all right. Now Lucy would have to endure a dinner of four courses with Mr. Thorne watching her while she tried not to gawk like a besotted ninny at Will Armstrong. Would this frustrating, testing, horrid day ever end?

Chapter Four

"Miss Bertram, this roast chicken is very good," said Mr. Thorne. "My compliments to your cook."

Oh, hurrah, huzzah, and hallelujah! Lucy summoned a smile. "I'll be sure to let her know." *Unlike all of the other petty complaints you've made.* Like the sorrel soup was a tad bitter (it wasn't) and the mushrooms in the vol-au-vents, which Lucy had foraged from the nearby woods several days ago, might be poisonous. (They weren't—Lucy knew her mushrooms.) Or that the claret was too dry and the Chablis was too sharp. (She couldn't really give an informed opinion on the wine because she drank it so infrequently.) Oh, and how disappointing there wasn't a fish course. According to Mr. Thorne, there was nothing quite so wonderful as a well-cooked piece of fish, like monkfish or plaice or turbot, smothered in hollandaise, to really satisfy one's appetite.

The ungrateful man was lucky she didn't upend the sauceboat on his head.

Smothering a genuine smile at the thought of how he would splutter and fume as Mrs. Gilchrist's excellent bread sauce dripped into his eyes and neatly trimmed muttonchops, Lucy sliced into her portion of breast. Taking a dainty bite, she chewed carefully, noting the chicken *was* actually very good. When she looked up from her plate, her attention wandered across the vast expanse of white linen covering the dining table to the shadows at the edge of the room, and her gaze connected with Will Armstrong's. His lips twitched with something like wry amusement, and then he winked at her as though they were sharing a private joke. That he'd somehow intuited what she'd been thinking.

Surely not.

Disconcerted, Lucy felt her cheeks heat with a self-conscious blush, and she hastily looked away and tried to focus on what her father and Mr. Thorne were talking about.

"Richard Owen? The man's delusional," said Mr. Thorne with a sneer. "Anyone who seriously believes that *Dinosauria* species once existed must be mad."

Richard Owen might be many things, but Lucy didn't think he was mad. She'd heard him speak on more than one occasion at public lectures, and it was said that he also tutored the Queen's children in natural history. Only seven years ago, the Royal Society had awarded him a Copley Medal. She simply couldn't let such a comment go unchallenged.

Drawing a steadying breath, she said, "I, for one, think the sculptures of *Iguanodon*, *Megalosaurus*, and *Hylaeosaurus* that he commissioned for the Crystal Place Exhibition are most fascinating. I've viewed them many times, and they never fail to fill me with awe. And there is quite a bit of evidence to support Owen's theories that dinosaurs once walked the earth."

"A handful of bones and fossils?" Thorne snorted. "Owen's only saving grace, in my eyes, is that I've heard that he disagrees with Darwin and his ridiculous theories about the transmutation of species and the so-called process of 'natural selection.' It is heretical to believe that humans aren't unique. We are *not* related to other animals. One species does not simply transform into another. That goes against the laws of both God and nature and everything I believe in. Species are an unchanging part of an intelligently designed hierarchy. A *divine* hierarchy."

Hmmm. Ignoring her father's warning look—his grizzled brows had descended into the realms of "ferocious scowl"—Lucy ventured, "I take it, Mr. Thorne, that you've read Darwin's recent contribution to the *Zoological Journal of the Linnean Society* which just came out? 'On the Tendency of Species to Form Varieties; and on the Perpetuation of Varieties and Species by Natural Means of Selection'?"

Thorne grunted. "Of course. In fact, I was present at the reading of his cowritten paper at the Linnean Society meeting last month. What a load of dangerous rot. The Church should have something to say about it. And the society, for that matter. In fact, I believe that Darwin should be expelled for bringing the society's name into disrepute."

"I'm sure he hasn't done that," said Lucy. "And it's not as though the theory of transmutation of species hasn't been around for some years now. It's rumored that even our Queen and Prince Albert have read *Vestiges of the Natural History of Creation* by Robert Chambers."

A muscle flickered in Thorne's cheek. "More rot," he ground out as he dissected the drumstick from the thigh on his plate with great vigor.

"I'll concede there are flaws within the author's arguments," continued Lucy. "But it's interesting reading, all the same." For some reason she couldn't quite explain, she didn't have any qualms about needling a stick-in-the-mud like Thorne. In fact, it was rather fun.

Her father clearly thought otherwise, as he all but glared at her across the table. "You've read that book? We don't own it."

Goodness. Lucy had never before seen him quite so agitated by something she'd said. He was usually pleased when she contributed something to a conversation that was more than panicked gibberish. She put down her fork and knife and dabbed at the corner of her mouth with her napkin. "I borrowed a copy from Delaney's."

"Delaney's?"

Now Lucy was frowning. Why was her father being so obtuse? "I'm sure you know it. It's a bookstore in Piccadilly, not far from Burlington House and the Linnean Society's headquarters. I meet my friends there for our Byronic Book Club meetings to discuss Gothic literature."

Oh, no! Why had she mentioned *that* particular detail? The wine must have loosened her tongue. She glanced at Will, whose dark-blue eyes seemed to be glinting with some emotion she rather thought might be barely suppressed mirth.

"Humph." Her father tapped his empty wineglass and Will immediately stepped forward to refill it with Chablis. "You said that you borrowed a copy. It's not a circulating library as well, is it?"

"No," said Lucy. "But Jane, my friend... Well, her grandfather owns the shop. And he was quite happy to lend it to me. I'm sure I could obtain a copy of *Vestiges* for our library here if you—"

Her father cleared his throat rather pointedly. "No, I don't think so. And that's quite enough talk about Byronic Book Clubs and transmutation and natural selection."

Thorne emitted a derisive chortle. "Yes, next thing your daughter will be trying to convince us that galvanism can reanimate the dead. Actually, I did wonder if I spied a rather large lightning rod on the roof as I arrived. You don't have any clumsily stitched-together corpses in a secret laboratory in your attic, do you, Miss Bertram? Or any vampiric bats roosting in the rafters?"

Lucy pressed her lips together as embarrassment and frustrated anger coalesced into a wave of heat that engulfed her entire face. How dare Mr. Thorne openly mock her! She knew for a fact that her father didn't really think any of those things. He'd been quite interested in Darwin's paper and subsequent article and had accompanied her to the Crystal Palace at Sydenham to view the *Dinosauria* statues on more than one occasion. He'd never dismissed her or her love for Gothic novels before tonight. That he hadn't defended her and now appeared to take Mr. Thorne's side instead spoke volumes.

Talk turned to Thorne's interest in investing in phosphate-based fertilizers and how they could help his coffee plantations in Ceylon yield more crops, and Lucy's attention quickly drifted away. If her father was quite adamant that she must accept a suit from Zachariah Thorne, she was in deep, deep trouble. She couldn't possibly consider marrying such a man. He might be handsome in an objective sense—all black hair and hooded eyes and sharply cut features. And he was certainly wealthy enough to please her father. But his ideals, his interests, his narrow views, and his pernickety personality were irritating in the extreme.

The question was how could she persuade her father that Mr. Thorne was the wrong man for her? That he would make her miserable? In fact that being married at all would make her miserable?

She took a sip of her wine, but it tasted sour and didn't sit well in the pit of her stomach.

She needed an ally. Someone who would support her in her decision to defy her father. A certain someone that her father *might* actually listen to.

Now, more than ever, she needed to find her brother.

———————————

Byronic Book Club?

Well, well, well, wasn't the lovely Miss Lucy Bertram full of surprises?

Will had already fathomed that his employer's daughter was intelligent. She'd certainly given Zachariah Thorne a run for his money. Will had had to ruthlessly tamp down the urge to laugh out loud or call "touché" several times during the dinner service when her subtle verbal jabs had bested the prat. But he'd had no idea that this seemingly demure young woman who blushed at the drop of a feather also harbored such a singular taste in literature. To learn that she enjoyed dark, passionate stories featuring brooding, troubled protagonists, and perhaps even supernatural elements, was intriguing indeed.

He suddenly burned to know if Thorne was actually the sort of man who would capture her interest. Of course, it was clear that she didn't agree with Thorne's views about many things, but he was also physically attractive in an austere way. He certainly grunted and sneered and growled enough to be characterized as "brooding."

Will also sensed that Miss Bertram was chagrined. And so she should be, given that Thorne had cruelly ridiculed her for her literary tastes. Indeed, he'd had to tamp down the urge to grab the man by the scruff of his neck and bang his head into the table until he apologized for being so rude. When the conversation had turned to the manufacture of fertilizers and Thorne's agricultural interests in the colonies, Miss Bertram had become withdrawn, perhaps even downcast, and an unfamiliar pang— something like concern—had squeezed Will's chest. So much for his resolve to remain unaffected and objective.

At least Thorne and Sir Oswald had both revealed a good deal more about their beliefs. It was certainly evident that Thorne resented the fact the Linnean Society supported Charles Darwin. The industrialist definitely had an issue with the naturalist's recently unveiled theory on natural selection.

At this rate, Will suspected that his clandestine investigation would yield results sooner rather than later. As he helped Clarke to clear the plates and platters of food before dessert was brought in, he patted himself on the back for trusting his gut and weaseling his way into the dining room. Of course, he did feel a trifle guilty that he'd had to dispose of Healey for the evening. He'd slipped a fairly strong dose of laudanum into the man's small beer just before dinner began and it had taken effect almost instantly, making the footman dizzy and drowsy. Will had helped him to his bed, and by the time he'd changed into the young man's livery, Healey was snoring away. Hopefully, the footman would be none the wiser when he woke in the morning and would simply feel well-rested.

Will, on the other hand, doubted he'd get much sleep tonight. As soon as the dinner party was over, Thorne had been farewelled, and Sir Oswald and Miss Bertram had retired to their rooms, he'd help Clarke lock up the house. And then, when everyone was sound asleep, he'd search Sir Oswald's study for further evidence of the baronet's involvement in the plot to get rid of Darwin and murder any Linnean Society member who openly supported the naturalist.

Locating any correspondence that Sir Oswald had exchanged with Thorne would be a good place to start.

Chapter Five

LUCY COULDN'T SLEEP. HER THOUGHTS WERE RUNNING amok down all sorts of twisted pathways as she lay in the muted darkness of her room, staring at the shadowy canopy of her four-poster bed.

The same useless litany of unanswered questions tumbled through her head, over and over again. Where on earth was Monty and how could she find him? How could she convince her father that she could never marry someone like Zachariah Thorne? How deep were the family's financial straits, and how much longer could they continue to penny-pinch unless she agreed to wed Thorne or someone like him? To make ends meet, would Father soon sell off parcels of the estate's unentailed land? Or some of Fleetwood Hall's artwork and furnishings or even their carriage and horses? Her father kept everything related to the family's worsening finances very close to his chest so she really didn't have any idea how bad things were. But she was beginning to suspect they were very bad indeed. Although he *had* just appointed Will.

Ugh. Will Armstrong with his deep-blue eyes and fallen-angel's mouth, rough hands, and a physique that made her so hot and bothered and restless, she could hardly think straight. Why oh why couldn't she stop fantasizing about this perplexing, mercurial man in all kinds of completely inappropriate ways?

Like what would it be like to kiss him? And more…

How frustrating it was to be a spinster sometimes. And a

baronet's daughter too—a woman who was *always* supposed to be on her best behavior. Who would be looked down upon if she dared to step outside the strict boundaries society had set in place for her. Yet here she was, harboring impure thoughts about a man—a stranger—who was in her family's employ.

She knew she needed to stop torturing herself like this. But she couldn't seem to help herself.

Eight-and-twenty and never been kissed. How sad and lonely and uneventful her life seemed sometimes.

Lucy was suddenly envious of her friend Artemis and the life she now led. She was still away on a Grand Tour of the Continent with her charming yet broodingly handsome husband, the Duke of Dartmoor. What she, Lucy, wouldn't give to explore the world, handsome husband or not. To go on expeditions like her father had done—and would continue to do so if he could secure the funding he needed. To make outstanding botanical discoveries and document them in articles and books and to be recognized for her contributions to the field of botany in her own right…

She sighed again. *If wishes were horses…* She hadn't even managed to finish the first draft of the article on Ceylonese strychnine for Father like she'd promised.

She thumped her pillow and rolled over to stare at the dying fire.

Outside, rain was falling, pattering like the drum of impatient fingers against the windowpane, while the branches of the oak tree outside her room scratched intermittently at the glass. Thunder rumbled in the distance, and flashes of lightning illuminated the edges of her curtains and penetrated the room. The very air around her seemed to pulse and crackle, setting her on edge.

With an exasperated sigh, Lucy threw off her covers and sat up. The mantel clock softly chimed the half hour—eleven thirty. It wasn't *that* late, and she had no reason to rise early in the morning. Perhaps she'd sleep better if she could get rid of one of the vexing issues on her very long list.

She stuffed her feet into slippers and threw a soft cashmere wrapper over her thin night rail. There was enough spark left in the glowing coals in the grate to light a taper and then a candle, and with a brass candlestick in hand, she quit her room and descended as silently as she could to the lower floors. However, she paused in the main hall, suddenly undecided about which direction to take. The rain was heavier now, hurling itself against the Hall in angry fits and starts, and a draft eddied about her, making the flame of her candle gutter.

She shivered and pulled her wrapper tight about her shoulders. Of course, she could set to work on her father's paper straightaway—it lay waiting in the study on her escritoire's blotter—but a nice, soothing cup of chamomile tea would certainly be welcome to ward off the chill night air.

Mind made up, Lucy headed for the kitchen.

Mrs. Gilchrist had banked the fire in the cast-iron range, just as she always did, so Lucy fed the coals some kindling and coaxed the flames to life once more. When the fire was dancing merrily, she put the kettle on the hob, then assembled a china teapot, a tea strainer, and the chamomile tea caddy on the oak table. As she retrieved a cup and saucer from the dresser, a metallic noise, the rattle of a latch, made her start, and in the next instant the back door leading to the garden swung open. Tom, the barn cat, dashed in along with a blast of frigid air and rain. And then came Will.

Lucy gasped and the Scot's eyes widened momentarily before his dark brows plunged into a frown.

He managed to find his voice before she did. Pushing the door shut, he leaned against it and said, "I'm verra sorry to startle you, Miss Bertram. I had no idea you would be up so late."

"I…" Lucy swallowed and the cup only clattered slightly in its saucer as she placed it on the table beside the teapot. "That's all right. I don't usually haunt the kitchen at this hour. I couldn't sleep."

Will nodded, then wiped a hand through his sodden hair, pushing it away from his face. Even though the kitchen was only bathed in the uncertain light emanating from the stove and her lone candle, Lucy noticed a faint scar on his forehead. It descended from his hairline, traveling jaggedly downward until it bisected his left eyebrow.

Goodness. Before she could dwell on what sort of injury he'd sustained to leave such a scar, Will's hair fell back into place. "I couldn't sleep either," he said. "You ken, new bed. New place. And then there's the storm…" A corner of his mouth quirked with a small smile. "I did wonder if a drink of warm milk might help. But I wouldna have barged in if I'd known you were up and about. Mrs. Gilchrist mentioned I could stop by any time…"

"Yes…yes, she did. And of course I don't mind." Lucy pulled the tea caddy toward herself. "I'm making chamomile tea. I'd be happy to pour you a cup too. Or I could put some milk on the hob to warm…"

"Och, I dinna wish to be a bother, Miss Bertram."

She smiled. "It won't be. At all. I'm sure Tom would like some milk too. Wouldn't you, my poor wet puss?"

But the cat didn't respond. He was ensconced on the hearthrug, the warmest spot in the room, legs shamelessly splayed, busily licking the fur on his belly.

Will didn't say anything else either. While Lucy went about heating the milk and finishing the preparation of her tea, he waited by the door, broodingly silent. Watching.

All at once she recalled she was barely wearing a thing. Just a thin nightgown and her wrapper. Her hair was loose, hanging down her back, and she was certain it was a tangled mess from all of her tossing and turning. She self-consciously tucked a wayward strand behind her ear as she stirred the milk in the saucepan to stop it catching on the bottom.

Will, most disconcertingly, was also in a state of dishabille. He was coatless and attired simply in buckskin breeches, boots, and a loose cambric shirt that the rain had dampened again. The shirt's fabric was plastered to the muscles of his shoulders, chest, and bulky upper arms, and the open neck revealed a tantalizing glimpse of bare skin. Dark stubble shaded his lean jaw. He looked thoroughly disreputable. Maybe even a little dangerous, like a ruggedly handsome brigand or pirate.

A Scottish incarnation of Heathcliff who'd just come in from the moors.

But surely he wasn't *dangerous*. Her father and Mr. Gilchrist had vetted his references. Sometimes she did let her imagination run away with her.

Although if anyone entered the kitchen right now, explaining the situation away might prove to be a tad difficult. It might be fine for her to go riding with Will as an escort, but lingering here with him when they were both quite scandalously attired and quite alone was not the "done thing." While she trusted that no one would come upon them at this particular moment, she'd best get on with making her tea so she could retire to the study to finish that darned article…just in case.

"Here we go, Mr. Armstrong," she said as she at last poured his milk into a mug and placed it on the table. Handing it to him seemed like far too dangerous a prospect. If their bare fingers brushed, she'd blush or stammer or say something foolish. Using his Christian name also seemed far too intimate a thing to do, so Mr. Armstrong he would be for now.

The Scot approached, took the mug with a murmured

thanks, then sipped it slowly as he watched her give Tom his saucer of milk. The silence extended as she finished preparing her tea. She should have invited Will to sit down, so he wasn't still hovering by the door, but she supposed he was being a gentleman and waiting until she left the room before he did so.

At last her tea tray was ready, but as she picked it up, preparing to take her leave, he stepped forward. He was so close she could smell his masculine scent, which was enough to make her go quite weak at the knees. Indeed, the tea things had begun to rattle when he said in a low, rumbling voice that seemed to vibrate through her and made her toes curl in her slippers, "Can I carry that for you, Miss Bertram? I'd be verra happy to."

"Oh… No. Thank you." Lucy licked her lips. A nervous gesture that he no doubt noticed, as his gaze dropped to her mouth. To her alarm, her nipples straightaway pebbled to tight points beneath her nightgown. Thank heavens her wrapper covered her unbound breasts and her body's response to his nearness. "I'm just going to the study," she murmured breathlessly. "I have some work I need to do. For my father. I'll…I'll leave you in peace to enjoy your milk. Good night, Mr. Armstrong." Indeed, how she made it out of the kitchen without dropping the tray, tripping over her own feet, or stumbling over the hall rug as she all but scurried away was a complete mystery.

It was only when Lucy reached the study and was installed at her desk sipping her tea that she wondered how Will had been able to enter the kitchen at all. Clarke and Healey usually locked up the house at night before everyone retired. Unless Mr. Gilchrist had furnished him with his own key… Or he'd borrowed one after locking up with Clarke.

In any event, she supposed it didn't really matter. Her imagination was simply running off in fanciful directions again.

Christ and all His saints.

Will cursed beneath his breath as the door closed behind Miss Bertram. How bloody unlucky could he be to bump into her in the kitchen when it was almost midnight? She was certainly conscientious, if nothing else. In his opinion, she worked much too hard for her ungrateful father.

He pulled out a chair, sat down at the table, then rubbed his face with both hands. So much for conducting a covert murder investigation. If Miss Bertram made a habit of staying up half the night, she was going to make his life difficult. Indeed, he'd been in danger of giving himself away when he'd first burst into the kitchen. Well, at least until he'd made up some feeble excuse about wanting to drink warm milk.

Actually, he hated warm milk. Give him a dram of whisky or a tankard of ale any day.

Although Tom seemed to be enjoying his saucerful.

Will pushed his own mug away and blew out an exasperated sigh. He couldn't afford to stay up all night waiting for Miss Bertram to retire again. He'd probably fall asleep at the table before she disappeared upstairs. His eyes were already gritty with exhaustion, and for the second time today he was cold and wet.

Although dashing through the rain in the dead of night was *almost* worth it, considering the glorious sight he'd stumbled across. Miss Lucy Bertram wearing nothing but her night attire with her pale golden hair cascading about her shoulders was not something he'd forget in a hurry.

Or ever, for that matter.

He yawned and scrubbed a hand down his face again. He might be exhausted, but how the hell was he to get to sleep after witnessing *that*? It felt as though he'd just encountered Mab or the Queen of Elfland and had been bewitched by her beauty. Entranced, unable to help himself, he'd approached her, offering to carry her tea tray. To serve her in whatever way he could. When he caught her floral feminine scent, he'd almost come undone. Nearly swept her into his arms and plundered her sweet, lush petal-pink mouth.

And now…now he was agitated. Restless.

Hungry, but not for food.

Worst of all, his objectivity was shot to pieces.

Tom, quite unexpectedly, twined himself around Will's boots and the legs of his chair, then went and sat at the door, meowing to be let out. Will rose. Clearly, it was his cue to leave too. He was sure that when he returned to his quarters and climbed beneath the quilt, all he'd be able to think about now were wet pussies and pink lapping tongues.

Worst of all, it seemed the image of Miss Bertram in her linen nightgown had already become burned into his brain. Good God, when she'd stood in front of the range fire, it had been like the most exquisite of tortures he'd ever had to endure. Of course, he'd tried very hard not to notice the way the light shone through the thin-as-gossamer fabric, highlighting the dip of her slender waist and the flare of her hips and the curve of her luscious, peach-shaped derriere. And when she'd turned toward him with the saucepan of warm milk in hand, he swore he'd glimpsed a shadowy triangular-shaped thatch at the juncture of her thighs.

His errant cock had twitched in his breeches, and he'd thanked heaven that his shirt was hanging loose, covering his groin.

If his dash through the rain didn't dampen his ardor, Will knew he was going to have to scratch his itch before he could fall asleep. And it was best he did so. He couldn't allow his sexual frustration to distract him and cloud his judgment. It wasn't Miss Bertram's fault, of course. It was all his. It had been such a long time since he'd had sexual relations with a woman—over a year, in fact—so no wonder he was as randy as an alley cat.

Or a barn cat.

Tom had disappeared into the night, so Will shut the door behind him, pulled up his collar, and then made a run for it. He'd best conduct his search of Sir Oswald's study another night. Hopefully tomorrow. And this time he'd do it closer to dawn so he wouldn't run the risk of bumping into any scantily clad females who addled his thinking.

Of course, he'd have to return the key he'd pocketed earlier when he'd been helping Clarke lock up, but that shouldn't be a problem. He was a dab hand at discreetly breaking into properties.

He wouldn't be put off again. He couldn't *afford* to be put off again.

He had a killer to catch.

Chapter Six

IF WISHES WERE HORSES, BEGGARS WOULD RIDE... OR AT THE very least, the "beggar"—Lucy, in this instance—would be sitting beside Will Armstrong in the driver's seat of the carriage, enjoying the fresh air and the view, not trapped here in the stuffy cabin with a disgruntled baronet. Especially now that it had stopped raining.

Since Will's arrival a week ago, it seemed like a deluge of biblical proportions had descended upon Heathwick Green and London. As a result, Lucy had been confined to Fleetwood Hall, unable to go riding or walking or anywhere at all. So she'd worked on her father's deuced journal article, but he'd been restless and hard to please and kept nitpicking away at things that didn't need "fixing." Something was on his mind besides rare varieties of Ceylonese strychnine. She was certain of it.

Lucy swallowed a sigh so her father wouldn't hear. Attempting to explain to him, for the third time, the precise meaning of the second passage of the conclusion she'd finally finished penning at three o'clock in the morning was giving her an eye twitch. But then again, her twitchy eyelid could simply be attributed to fatigue.

It would be far easier, of course, if the Linnean Society would let her through the front doors into its sanctified headquarters at Burlington House so *she* could also converse with her father's colleague—a gentleman who was a well-regarded botanist on staff at the British Museum with connections at

Kew Gardens. But alas, that was not allowed. Which was most unfortunate because at the present moment, the minute chemical differences in the alkaloid structure of the toxin found in *Strychnos cinnamomifolia* versus the more common *Strychnos nux-vomica* seemed to be confounding her father.

Sir Oswald leaned back against the leather squabs and rubbed the bridge of his nose as though his spectacles pinched. "Ugh. I think I grasp enough to convince Bennett that this"—he waved the article in the air before casting it onto the seat beside him—"should be included in the society's next edition of the *Botanical Journal*. Rest assured, I'll master the details before I present this at any meetings or public lectures."

"I know you will," said Lucy. Then she frowned. "Do you have a megrim, Papa? You should have said something before we set out. I could have made you some willow bark tea."

Her father grimaced. "Don't feel too sorry for me. I imbibed far too much poor-quality port after dinner last night, so I'm afraid my sore head is self-inflicted. It will fade."

Lucy tried to hide her worry with a smile. "I hope so." Her father was drinking more alcohol than usual, but it wasn't her place to pass judgment or remark upon it. She picked up her article, which she'd titled "The Genus *Strychnos* in Ceylon: Endemic and Rare Varieties of Note"—now her *father's* article, she reminded herself—and carefully reordered the discarded pages before sliding them into a leather folio for safekeeping.

She might not be a member of the Linnean Society, but she was a member in her own right of the Botanical Society of London and had been for several years. It was one of the few scientific societies that actually admitted female members. However, while Lucy had once regularly attended their fortnightly meetings to listen to lectures—though she was too terrified to ever present her own work—it had been well-nigh impossible during this past year with everything she had on her plate. And in the next twelve months, she didn't quite know how she would be able to scrape together the annual subscription fee.

Sadly, the past papers she had authored for the Botanical Society's journal were largely if not altogether disregarded by her father and other "serious" botanists. It seemed she and other like-minded females would always be looked down upon, as though their work was of less value and scientific merit than that of their male counterparts. Men who were members of more lauded, male-dominated scientific societies and possessed academic degrees from esteemed universities like Cambridge and Oxford.

Or had enough money to buy themselves a scientific society fellowship…

Men like Zachariah Thorne.

Lucy gave a resigned sigh and looked out the carriage window at the passing traffic and pedestrians. They were almost in Piccadilly, and it wouldn't be long until she was walking through the door of Delaney's Antiquarian Bookshop. Hopefully, Jane would be in today. Seeing her friend would make her feel better. And Jane was certain to have some advice on how she could deal with Mr. Thorne.

She also had Monty's letter in her reticule. She wanted a second opinion on the postmark, and Jane, who helped her grandfather appraise and restore books and had a good eye for detail, might be able to decipher the other smudged number on the stamp.

As the carriage at last drew to a halt outside of Burlington House, her father leaned forward and patted her arm. "Thank you again, my dear, for getting this article done. I shall see you in an hour?" He winked. "I might even be able to afford to take you to the tearoom in Fortnum & Mason's after my meeting."

"I'd love that," she replied with a heartfelt smile. Her father had been so oddly behaved of late—cross and demanding and critical one moment, then kind and magnanimous the next— that she really didn't know what to make of his moods.

But then, he wasn't the only temperamental man in her world at present. A certain Scots groom, who alternated between states of grumpy and charming like a fluctuating electric current, constantly flummoxed her as well. As Healey handed her down from the carriage, she couldn't resist sliding a glance up to the coachman's seat. It was as if Will Armstrong had some strange magnetic effect on her. His pull was almost impossible for her to resist.

As their eyes connected, he doffed his hat but didn't smile. *So he's still wearing his "grumpy" persona*, thought Lucy as she tilted her head away. Indeed, he'd been in that sort of mood before they'd even left Fleetwood Hall. The heavy rains had apparently damaged some of the track along the Hampstead line, so Will had been asked to prepare the carriage. With only Freddy to help him, no doubt it had been a huge undertaking; the carriage had been gathering dust and cobwebs in its lonely corner of the stables since Lucy's short-lived Season ended so abruptly.

But after Will had finished with it, the conveyance was spick-and-span both inside and out. All the brass fittings had been polished, the black wood exterior gleamed, and the interior had been aired and swept. Even the velvet cushions on the seats had been plumped, and the carriage horses were so well groomed, their chestnut coats gleamed.

The bell over the front door of Delaney's tinkled as Lucy entered. Jane's grandfather, Joseph Delaney, was manning the counter and put aside a stack of books to greet her. "Miss Bertram, how lovely to see you, my dear." The deep lines around his eyes crinkled even more with his wide smile. "It's been an age. I expect you're wanting to see Jane?"

"Yes, I am. Is she in?" Lucy winced. "I'm afraid I didn't message ahead."

"As luck would have it, yes, she is. She's helping to repaper and rebind a few books because I'm a bit behind. Why don't I show you to the back, and then you can chat with Jane while she finishes up?"

"That sounds perfect."

Jane's grandfather ushered Lucy into a small, cluttered workroom. As soon as Jane caught sight of Lucy, she put aside the book she was working on and enveloped her friend in a warm hug.

"Oh, Lucy. I was just thinking about you, and here you are."

Lucy laughed. "I always suspected you had preternatural senses, Jane."

Jane released her and bade her take a stool at the long wooden worktable. The scarred oak surface was cluttered with piles of books, spools of binding yarn and cord, stacks of paper and fine vellum in various colors, and baskets of tools for cutting and binding and embossing. The smell of glue, leather, and old books permeated the air.

"Please excuse the mess," Jane said with a grimace as she pushed a loose strand of her glossy brown hair behind one ear. As usual, the rest of her thick locks were constrained in a tight, no-nonsense bun so that the long scar that arced across her left cheek was clearly visible. "I shouldn't be too long with this." She indicated the open book on the bench in front of her. "I'm just waiting for the glue to dry on these marbled endpapers. And then we'll go upstairs for tea and a chat. How does that sound?"

Lucy arranged her lilac-hued skirts around her as she sat opposite Jane. "Wonderful."

They chatted for a little while about inconsequential matters while Jane waved a vellum fan over the inside cover of the book. Like Lucy, Jane had been burning the candle at both ends lately. The gray light filtering in through a large high window highlighted the shadows of fatigue beneath her friend's lovely green eyes.

Jane's widowed mother had recently remarried, and Jane had been recruited to act as a "sometimes" chaperone for her new younger stepsister. "Honestly, I'm considering moving into my grandfather's rooms upstairs," said Jane with a sigh. "He has a spare bedroom, and he could certainly do with an extra pair of hands about the shop. And it would save me having to traipse back and forth between here and Kensington where Mother now lives. Piccadilly is much closer to Fleet Street so I won't have to travel as far to hand in my various literary review articles for the papers."

"That sounds eminently sensible," remarked Lucy. "And then you won't be at your mother's and stepsister's beck and call quite so much. Perhaps when Artemis returns from her Grand Tour, you can take up a teaching position at her new academic ladies' college. I recall she did offer you a position if you wanted one."

"It's something I'll definitely consider," said Jane, lightly running her fingertips over the marbled endpapers. "Now, enough about me." Obviously satisfied the glue was now sufficiently dry, she put aside her fan and focused her full attention on Lucy. "I want to hear all about what sort of mischief you've been getting up to."

Lucy winced. "Not mischief so much. Several hideously embarrassing incidents spring to mind though." And then she proceeded to tell Jane about her gig-in-the-mud accident (without disclosing anything but the scantest of details about the new ruggedly handsome groom her father had appointed, lest she blush and give away the fact she was developing a very inconvenient tendre for the man). She also lamented the fact that her father was pressuring her to consider the disagreeable Mr. Thorne as a prospective suitor. And last of all, she mentioned Monty's letter and her need to find him.

"I rather hoped that you might be able to help me decipher the postmark so I can work out where Monty posted it from," she said, pulling the envelope from her reticule and pushing it across the table to Jane. "I've examined the second number through a magnifying glass, but I can't quite make it out. It could be a three or a five…"

"Hmmm." Jane picked up the envelope and took it closer to the window. "It might be…" Returning to the desk, she opened up a drawer and withdrew a large magnifying glass with a brass rim and handle. After a moment she said, "I think it might be a five. So the number of the receiving house this was posted at is—"

"Fifty-five," finished Lucy. "I have no idea where that is, but I'm sure we can find out at any London District Post Office."

Jane grinned. "The nearest one is but a five-minute walk away in Regent Street."

She put away the magnifying glass, removed the pinafore protecting her gown, and grabbed a bonnet and a green wool jacket off a hook on the back of the workroom door. "Come on. Let's go."

They emerged onto Piccadilly and Lucy glanced back toward Burlington House where Will and Healey still waited with the carriage. If Will noticed her departure, it was impossible to tell, but for some strange reason she imagined she could feel the groom's eyes on her as she and Jane crossed the road and then set out in the direction of Regent Street.

Within the space of ten minutes, Lucy had learned that the receiving house that stamped all letters with the number fifty-five was in the High Street of St Giles.

"St Giles," murmured Lucy as they exited the post office and began to wander back toward Piccadilly. Her stomach felt like it was weighted with lead. It was one of the worst parts of London, home to the notorious "Rookery" where crime was rampant and the poorest of the poor lived cheek to jowl in over-crowded lodgings.

She couldn't even begin to imagine her bright, handsome, jocular brother in such a place.

"Just because Monty posted his letter there doesn't mean he resides there too," reasoned Jane. "Covent Garden and all the theaters are close by. Perhaps he was in the area to see a play. Or picked something up at the markets."

"Perhaps..." Lucy didn't know why she had such a bad feeling—a sense of foreboding—hovering over her, but she did. She had to find Monty. She just *had* to. What if he was in trouble? Destitute? Her heart cramped with fear, and her mind began to tumble with so many terrible possibilities that her head spun.

Jane stopped in the middle of the street. "Lucy, please promise me that you won't go off searching the streets of St Giles on your own. It's far too dangerous. And Monty might not even *be* there."

Lucy met her friend's gaze and forced a reassuring smile. "I promise that I won't," she said, even though that was a complete lie. How could she *not* look for her brother?

Jane seemed satisfied with her answer though. She gave a nod. "Good." She slid her arm through Lucy's, and as they began to walk again, she added, "Now, let's return to my grand-father's store and I'll have our maid-of-all-work prepare us a tea tray. And then I'll show you some of our newest Gothic litera-ture titles. I have one I think you'll love—"

It was Lucy who stopped abruptly this time and Jane asked, "What is it? You've gone awfully pale."

"I…" Lucy's heart was tripping as she pointed across the street to a carriage that had pulled up near the corner of Jermyn Street, less than a hundred yards away. "My brother's former valet is over there. In footman's livery. I'm certain it's him. He might know something about Monty. About what happened that night. Hughes! Mr. Hughes!" She waved madly and before Jane could stop her, she was picking up her skirts and stepping off the cobbled pavement into the street, waiting for a break in the traffic so she could cross.

Lucy was breathless by the time she reached the man's side. He'd been helping his master alight from the carriage and was now in the process of putting up the steps when she drew to an abrupt halt. "Mr. Hughes," she managed between panted breaths, her gloved hand at her throat. "I'm…I'm so sorry to bother you like this—"

Hughes's middle-aged master, who hadn't traveled that far, swung around and glared at her. "Now see here, young lady," he snapped, black brows bristling with indignation. "Why are you accosting my staff in the street and creating a spectacle?"

"My apologies, sir." Lucy bobbed a swift curtsy. "That was not my intention. I…" She felt herself blushing as the import of what she was doing hit her. Breaking so many rules of etiquette *did* border on scandalous. But she wouldn't be put off. "Mr. Hughes here was once in my father's employ. I just wanted to ask him…ask him a quick question."

"And your father's name?"

Lucy opened her mouth, then shut it. It really wasn't any of this man's business who her father was. Hughes might very well tell his obviously high-in-the-instep master later on, but she wouldn't divulge such a detail herself in case it got back to her father. And she couldn't have that. "I'm not in the habit of giving out my family name to strangers, sir."

"And I'm not in the habit of letting strange, hoydenish young women verbally harangue my footmen in the street. Have you no shame, gel?"

Lucy straightened her spine. "I am no hoyden, *sir*. If you must know, my father is…is a baronet. And I'm not haranguing anyone. As I said, I merely wish to ask Hughes a question. That's all."

The gentleman crossed his arms. "Well, ask away. I haven't got all day."

Lucy chanced a glance at Hughes, who'd been standing steadfastly at attention this whole time with his gaze fixed on some distant point. Although there was a wash of ruddy color across his high cheekbones, so he was clearly a little disconcerted.

"I…ah… It's a private matter," Lucy said.

The gentleman snorted. "Private matter?" His gaze slid over her in the most insulting fashion, assessing her, and all at once Lucy's whole countenance was ablaze with anger and humiliation. Good Lord. Could this man seriously be thinking that she and Hughes…? That she would ever dally with a…with a footman?

But you have already thought of dallying with Mr. Armstrong, haven't you, Lucy?

Lucy pushed away the bothersome thought and drew a fortifying breath. Lifted her chin. "You, sir, are no gentleman," she gritted out. Tilting her head in Hughes's direction, she added, "I apologize for creating such a fuss, Mr. Hughes. I wish you well." And then she turned on her heel and marched stiffly away to join Jane, who still waited patiently on the other side of the street.

As soon as Lucy reached Jane's side, her friend grasped her arm. "Are you all right?" she asked gently. "Maybe I should have followed? I couldn't quite see what was going on. There was a carriage in the way, and with all the passing traffic..." Her frown deepened. "*Was* it your brother's valet? You seem rattled."

Lucy sighed. She *was* shaken but was determined to put on a brave face to cover how embarrassed she was by the whole awkward and humiliating scene. And disappointed. "It was. But he couldn't tell me—"

"Miss Bertram?"

Lucy turned to discover Hughes was standing but a few feet away. "I apologize for my master's behavior," he said. "Lord Branston can be a bit of a disagreeable prig sometimes."

Lucy summoned a smile. "I really do hope I haven't made any trouble for you. I–I just wanted to ask you a question or two about the night my brother left. We had a quick conversation the next morning about what my brother had taken with him— the things you noticed were missing from his belongings—but then I had to pack and then we were gone, and my father had let you go. I had no idea he would do that." She winced. "I hope he gave you a good reference, at the very least."

Hughes inclined his head. "He did. And I'm happy to answer any questions." He shrugged a wide shoulder. "But I'm afraid I don't know much beyond what I've already shared with you."

Lucy nodded. "I suppose I wondered if the night before, when my father and brother were arguing, whether you over-heard anything. The reason for the disagreement. You see, my brother hasn't returned home since that night, and I really have no idea where he's gone. If I had more information to go on, any sort of clue, perhaps I could find him."

Hughes frowned, then scratched his jaw as he glanced away. He looked uncomfortable.

"I won't judge you or think ill of you if you *did* eavesdrop a little," said Lucy. "As awful as it sounds, I'm quite desperate for any tidbit or crumb. Anything at all."

The footman nodded. "I was in your brother's dressing room that night, organizing his night attire, when he entered his sitting room... Sir Oswald followed and..." Hughes shuffled his feet. "Your brother shut the connecting door between the bedchamber and sitting room, so I didn't hear a lot, mind you. Mainly raised voices, but most of the words were indistinct. An angry rumbling more or less."

"I understand. But you said 'most' of the words. Did any *particular* words stand out?"

Hughes winced. "I can't say for sure, but I might have heard a name? Roger perhaps? Not only that—" He broke off and his cheeks grew red as though he was embarrassed. "There was something else, and of course, it might be neither here nor there, but..."

"Please go on," Lucy prompted gently.

Hughes nodded. "Very well. When your brother first came home, not long after you and Sir Oswald got back from the theater, I did wonder if there was someone else with him. In the drawing room downstairs? The house was very quiet, and I thought I heard laughter and another voice. An unfamiliar gentleman's. I don't know if *his* name was Roger, and of course, it wasn't my place to pry. As I said, I'm certainly not one to listen at keyholes." The footman shrugged. "I'm sorry I can't offer you more, Miss Bertram."

Lucy frowned, casting her mind back to that night. She hadn't heard any voices coming from downstairs, but then her bedchamber had been situated toward the back of the town house while the drawing room was near the front door. And the name Hughes might have heard...*Roger*... It meant nothing to her. She had no idea if Monty or her father knew a Roger.

But she couldn't very well ask Father. He was certain to

remain tight-lipped, just like he always did. And really, what did it matter if Monty was conversing with someone in the drawing room late at night? Unlike young, unmarried women, bachelors could do almost whatever they liked whenever they liked with whomever they liked.

Lucy offered Hughes a smile, hoping it hid her disappointment that she hadn't learned anything useful after all. "Thank you so very much for taking the time to talk to me," she said. "I hope Lord Branston doesn't give you any trouble."

The young man bowed, and after he'd bid her farewell, Lucy and Jane started walking toward Piccadilly again.

Once they reached the corner of Sackville Street, Lucy cast her gaze over the imposing facade of Burlington House up ahead, with its enormous arched entrance and endless rows of colonnaded windows, and wondered if her father was still busy. What a pity she couldn't simply march inside and demand answers from him. How much easier things would be.

But they weren't. They were messy and complicated and too frustrating for words.

Although now she had *one* significant clue, which was more than she had yesterday.

On a sigh, she turned to her friend. "Thanks to you, Jane, I now know where Monty might be. And before you say anything else, I promise you, hand on my heart, I won't venture into the streets of St Giles on my own."

Jane nodded. "Good. At the very least, take someone like Hughes with you. Even a pair of footmen, for that matter. Now, let's get that tea. I'm parched."

"Actually, I have a much better idea," said Lucy with a grin. "It will be my way of saying thank-you for all your help."

Chapter Seven

"*Guten Nachmittag*, Miss Bertram! How very lovely it is to see you again. It has been far too long since you graced our establishment with your delightful presence!"

Lucy tried not to blush at the effusive greeting of Herr von Schmidt, the flamboyant maître d'hôtel of Fortnum & Mason's much-vaunted tearooms, but it was a lost cause when her father's eyebrows shot up into the vicinity of his receding hairline. It probably didn't help that Herr von Schmidt was rather garishly attired in a jacquard satin coat in hues of magenta and fuchsia, which also clashed with his fiercely curled, butterscotch-yellow mustaches and neatly trimmed muttonchops. Compared with the subdued blacks and grays and blues of the other sedately attired gentlemen in the room, he really was a sight to behold. A bright peacock amongst a flock of plain pigeons.

"Why, thank you. You are too kind," she offered. "And I agree, it has been a while."

"And who have we here with you today?" the German gentleman asked, beringed fingers waving in the direction of her father and Jane.

Lucy made the required introductions and then Herr von Schmidt snapped his fingers. "Wilmot." A liveried waiter in black and white stepped forward and bowed. "Show Sir Oswald, Miss Bertram, and Miss Delaney to our best table. Over near the window. The one with the pink roses." He winked at Lucy and then leaned close and murmured, "And may I recommend the crab and watercress sandwiches and the cherry frangipane tartlet?" He pinched his fingers together and kissed them. "As they French would say, they are both *très magnifique!*"

"Goodness, he's quite the character, isn't he?" remarked Jane as Wilmot led them past other seated guests to an elegant table by a wide window that looked out onto Piccadilly. "I had no idea you were on such good terms with Fortnum & Mason's head waiter."

"Neither did I, Lucy," said her father. "It makes me wonder how often you've been coming here on your own without telling me. Obviously quite a lot."

"Well, I have to wait somewhere while you are conducting lectures or researching or consulting with colleagues, Papa," said Lucy quietly as she settled upon her seat. "There's only so long one can wander about browsing the shelves of Hatchards and Delaney's. And I usually only have a cup of tea and a biscuit or two. Maybe a sandwich. And I haven't always come on my own. M—" She broke off as she was about to say that Monty had sometimes accompanied her to the tearooms as well. But she didn't want to create discord by bringing up the subject of her brother so she told a white lie. "My friend Artemis would sometimes come too when she was in Town. Before she wed her duke."

"Humph." Her father claimed a seat with his back to the window while Jane sat directly across from Lucy. "I suppose I do lay claim to far too much of your time, my gel. But once you're happily wed and start your own family"—he reached out across the table and patted her hand—"you won't have to bother about anything botanical ever again."

"Oh… Oh, I don't mind helping you at all, Papa. You know how much I love the study of botany."

"But still…" Her father paused as he accepted a menu du jour from Wilmot and began perusing the page. "Actually, I was rather hoping Mr. Thorne might join us for afternoon tea." He peered over his spectacles at Lucy. "I bumped into him at the Linnean Society and extended an invitation. He just had to attend to a bit of banking first." Leaning closer, he added in a low voice, perhaps so Jane wouldn't hear, "Might I suggest you and Miss Delaney refrain from talking about Gothic literature? It's clear it's not his cup of tea."

Lucy's stomach pitched. *Buckets of fudge.* It seemed her father was determined to play matchmaker. She suddenly wondered if this spur-of-the-moment encounter had been engineered by her father and Thorne.

Ack. Why Thorne wanted to have anything to do with her she couldn't say. They appeared to have nothing in common, and if anything she felt as though the man looked down on her. He'd certainly made fun of her literary preferences.

Jane sent her a sympathetic smile across the table. At least Lucy could rely on her friend to give an honest opinion about the man when she met him.

The tea and a range of sandwiches and delicate petit fours arrived on a tiered cake plate only moments before Mr. Thorne made his entrance. As soon as she spied him, Lucy felt as though a dark storm cloud had entered the room, chasing away the cheerfulness of the occasion. Indeed, attired all in black save for a pristine white shirt, he all but resembled a thundercloud.

Herr von Schmidt himself ferried Thorne over. "Ah, look who has arrived to make your wonderful party even more merry," he declared in effusive tones, even though Thorne was glowering at the maître d'hôtel as though he found his bright presence a visual abomination. "I shall just ask Wilmot to fetch another teacup and place setting. Wil—"

Thorne held up a hand. "No tea. Coffee. Black, if you please," he said.

Herr von Schmidt bowed. "Of course, sir. At once."

As soon as the maître d'hôtel moved away, Lucy introduced Jane. Thorne studied her through his gold monocle for a moment, then smirked. "Ah, one of your fellow Byronic Book Club members, if I'm not mistaken." He then added with a bluntness that had Lucy gaping, "What happened to your cheek, Miss Delaney?"

Before Lucy could mouth "I'm sorry" to her friend across the table, Jane had pasted on a smile. "I was injured in a dog-cart accident, Mr. Thorne. Which leads me to ask… What happened to your manners?"

Thorne's black brows snapped into a frown, Sir Oswald spluttered and choked on his mouthful of tea, and Lucy pressed her napkin to her mouth to stifle a horrified laugh. *Touché, Jane,* she thought. Thorne deserved every bit of that perfectly aimed barb.

Nevertheless, Thorne quickly rallied. "My apologies for my bluntness, Miss Delaney. I'm a Yorkshireman. My father was a plain-speaking man of the cloth and I grew up in a mining town, so I do not always observe the proprieties. I tend to speak my mind."

Jane inclined her head, then picked up her tea and took a measured sip. The expression in her eyes clearly indicated she hadn't forgiven Thorne, but she didn't offer any further comment.

As Lucy was casting around for something to say to break the awkward silence, the unrepentant Yorkshireman's mouth twisted with a disdainful smile. "For instance," he continued as though nothing at all was wrong, "what in God's good name are we to make of the maître d'hôtel here? I thought dandies were as dead as the dodo. You'd think an establishment with the prestige of Fortnum & Mason would have better taste."

Horrified, Lucy's gaze darted to her father to see if he would defend the maître d'hôtel, but he didn't. Indeed, she was quite amazed to see his cheeks were now stained with a ruddy blush. "The garishness of Herr von Schmidt's attire does rather hurt one's eyes," he muttered into his tea.

Thorne selected a crab and cress sandwich for his plate. "I'd go farther than that, my good friend. The fellow's mere presence pollutes the place. I've a mind to have a word with the management about him."

Outrage at last loosened Lucy's tongue. "I happen to like Herr von Schmidt. Very much," she said quite clearly and smoothly even though her insides were roiling with fury. "And I don't think it's at all fair for you to impugn the man's character just because you don't like his manner of dress or the way he speaks."

Thorne's smile was mocking. "I assure you, it's a good deal more than his appalling apparel and effete manner that offends me, my dear." He traded a strangely pointed look with her father, who still wore an expression of extreme discomfort, before adding, "There's no doubt in my mind that *all* of Herr von Schmidt's tastes run to the unnatural. Not that you would know, Miss Bertram. But that's not your fault, of course."

"What on earth do you mean by that?" Lucy rejoined. "Are you intimating I understand less about the world and the way it works because I'm a woman?"

Thorne quirked a brow. "That's exactly what I mean. Frankly, I'd be shocked if you *did* know what I was talking about."

Lucy's father cleared his throat rather loudly. "Thorne, I've been meaning to ask for your opinion on the latest news coming out of India. Nasty business all round, hey what?"

"I'm rather relieved most of my coffee plantations are in Ceylon," Thorne replied, stirring a lump of sugar into his own cup of the steaming black liquid. "But yes, as you say, the rebellion is a nasty business."

Lucy exchanged a speaking look with her friend. Of course her father and Mr. Thorne would choose another topic of conversation that ladies shouldn't voice an opinion on. Lucy was personally horrified about what she'd read in the newspapers about the Sepoy Rebellion and all of the terrible atrocities that had been committed. It made her question why the British were in India in the first place; in her opinion, the East India Company had a lot to answer for. But of course what would she know? She was only a woman.

Talk eventually turned to more neutral topics and then Mr. Thorne surprised her by politely asking Jane about her grandfather's bookstore. "Miss Bertram indicated that Delaney's is an antiquarian bookshop. Am I correct in surmising your grandfather conducts appraisals and restorations of older books?"

Jane's manner was cool as she replied. "Yes, he does. And so do I."

"I see." Thorne nodded. "I might stop by at some point. I recently acquired a Bible at auction. A King James copy from the seventeenth century, highly ornamented, and printed by Robert Barker. Some of the gilt-edged pages and woodcut illustrations are a little worse for wear, so I'd like the opinion of someone experienced like your grandfather to advise me on what might be done to preserve or even restore them."

Jane's smile didn't quite meet her eyes. "Of course. I shall let him know you might drop by. I'm sure he'd be most interested to take a look. We're in Sackville Street, just across the way."

Thorne nodded, then removed a gold watch from the inner breast pocket of his coat. "I'm afraid I have another pressing appointment, Sir Oswald, ladies, so I must dash." He rose, bowed to Jane, then said to Lucy, "It's been most pleasant to dine with you again, Miss Bertram. I trust I might call upon you sometime?"

Lucy's mouth dropped open. Surely he didn't mean *any* of that. Nothing about this encounter or their last could be classed as "pleasant." And how dare he ask her in front of her father and Jane, when he knew she would feel pressured to acquiesce?

Her father leaned close and nudged her ankle beneath the table. "He has my permission, Lucy," he hissed. "Just say yes, gel."

Lucy hiked up her chin. "Thank you for the offer, Mr. Thorne. I shall consider it," she lied. There was nothing to consider. As far as she was concerned, the man could go jump in the English Channel and keep swimming.

Mr. Thorne must have sensed she was prevaricating because his mouth flattened and his black eyes glittered. He clearly wasn't accustomed to being naysaid by a woman.

Nevertheless, he bowed. "Of course." His disconcerting gaze moved to Sir Oswald, and he tilted his head. "We shall talk again soon, I expect." And then he turned on his well-shod heel and quit the tearoom.

"Lucy…" Her father was glaring at her. "I cannot believe you would be so rude as to—"

"And I cannot believe that you are seriously trying to foist me onto that horrible man," retorted Lucy. "This is not the Middle Ages and I'm not chattel." She tossed her napkin onto the table and stood. "I'll walk with Jane back to Delaney's and then I shall meet you at the carriage."

"I don't blame you at all for wanting nothing to do with Zachariah Thorne," said Jane when they emerged onto Piccadilly. "Aside from all of the appalling things he says, there's something about that man that doesn't sit well with me."

"Me either," said Lucy with a shudder. The cold, hard look in Thorne's eyes unsettled her. When she hadn't immediately accepted his offer to call on her, she imagined he was thinking of ways he might punish her for her temerity. "I think you can now see why I need to find Monty. I know in my heart of hearts that he would not want to see me wed to such a vile man."

Lucy farewelled Jane at the corner of Sackville Street, then returned to the carriage where Healey and Mr. Armstrong still waited.

The groom glanced down at her, and when his mouth tipped into a crooked smile for a fleeting second, her heart all but tripped over itself.

Fiddlesticks and flapdragons. How could it be that the only man who made her feel giddy with excitement was *this* one? A man she should barely regard at all.

Healey helped her into the carriage. While she waited for her father, her mind fell to contemplating how and when she could arrange a foray into St Giles.

Jane was right. She couldn't go on her own. But she didn't think she could ask Healey or Clarke either. The footmen had been in her father's employ for several years now, but while she trusted them, she also suspected they might not be game enough to do something behind their master's back. So many servants had been let go over the past year and no doubt they'd worry about incurring her father's displeasure if he discovered what they'd been up to. Mr. Gilchrist, Fleetwood's steward, was unswervingly loyal to her father, and Mr. Rolfe, the gardener, was far too old. Freddy was far too young and slight, and none of Fleetwood's female staff—the housemaids or Mrs. Gilchrist or Dotty—would be suitable either.

Which left only one person to ask. A sometimes high-handed man who Lucy suspected didn't always play by the rules. A man who was tall and strong and could liberate a stuck gig without breaking a sweat.

But how could she, Miss Lucy Bertram, persuade

someone like Will Armstrong to risk his position and go along with her plan?

And perhaps more important, could she trust him?

She needed to get to know him a little better, but she didn't have much time.

Chapter Eight

NOTHING. HIS LATE-NIGHT SEARCH OF SIR OSWALD'S LIBRARY and his study had yielded bloody nothing. Not one shred of concrete evidence linking the baronet to Lord Litchfield's murder or the sinister threats made to Charles Darwin and other prominent Linnean Society members.

Bloody hell.

Will flopped down into the chair behind the baronet's desk and huffed out a disgruntled sigh. He'd been at Fleetwood Hall an entire week, and tonight had been his first real opportunity to mount a proper search inside the house without fear of discovery. Between Miss Bertram and Sir Oswald burning the candle at both ends almost every night to get the baronet's paper written, and the darn barn cat Tom—one night when Will had sneaked in through the kitchen, the cat had also bolted in and had created a ruckus by knocking over the woodpile—he'd gotten nowhere. During the endless rainy days, he'd spent a good deal of his time getting to know Fleetwood's staff—servants were often a treasure trove of gossip—and he'd begun to fetch the mail from the Wick and Whistle so he could go through Sir Oswald's correspondence, but again, he hadn't found out anything he didn't already know.

He cast his gaze around the barely lit, shadow-filled room until it settled on Miss Bertram's neat rosewood escritoire. In the flickering flame of the one candle he'd dared to light, he imagined her sitting there, her lips pressed together in concentration and a slight line between her fine brows, working hard on some bit of research that her father would undoubtedly claim credit for.

He'd already contemplated and then dismissed the idea that Miss Bertram could be a suspect in this investigation. Yes, she did know a lot about botanical poisons. Perhaps even more than her father. But he couldn't fathom what her motive would be. Besides, Lord Litchfield had been murdered at the Raleigh Club—an exclusive, male-dominated "sanctum" for explorers or any man with ties to the British colonies. She might have the means, but she certainly didn't have the opportunity.

Will sighed and scrubbed a hand down his face. It was almost two o'clock in the morning, and his eyes were so gritty with fatigue that it felt as though he'd rubbed a fistful of cuttlefish powder from Sir Oswald's pounce pot into his eyes.

He should probably go to bed. He really had searched every nook and cranny he could think of, and he'd come to the conclusion that either Sir Oswald was innocent, or the proof that Will needed just wasn't here.

What did strike him as odd was the fact he hadn't come across a single bill or anything else pertaining to financial matters. For a man reported to be in deep debt, there must be some sort of records somewhere in the house. Perhaps in the steward's office or Sir Oswald's suite, away from his astute daughter's eyes?

But Will wouldn't search farther afield tonight. He didn't want to risk being discovered. Better to target Sir Oswald's rooms and the steward's office another night.

It would help if Sir Oswald could spend a night or two in London itself. Surely he did so on the odd occasion. Will didn't fancy searching the baronet's rooms from top to bottom while Sir Oswald was in residence. Although as a last resort he could slip him some laudanum. But he'd probably have to drug Redmond, the baronet's butler-cum-valet too. And he'd rather not resort to such underhanded tactics unless he absolutely had to. The more risks he took, the greater the chance he would be discovered.

He yawned and snuffed out the candle after licking his fingertips. He needed to get to bed and snatch a few hours' sleep. In the morning—well, when the sun rose—he was obliged to accompany Miss Bertram on a ride, weather permitting.

She'd asked him to do so after they'd arrived back at Fleetwood Hall, and Will had been surprised and intrigued, but also disgruntled. This far-too-captivating young woman had him tied up in all sorts of knots. Ensnared in some strange fairy net that he couldn't seem to escape from. He was enchanted and confused and frustrated as hell.

Today, when he'd sat in the coachman's seat and had watched her sauntering down Piccadilly in her pretty gown of light purple, he'd been transported straight back to Ayrshire. To Kyleburn Castle, the home of his youth. To the rolling fields of purple heather that he loved with such a fierce, bittersweet burning, it brought tears to his eyes. That beautiful countryside was about the only thing that he *did* miss.

Everything else about that place he would happily raze to the ground if he could.

Pulling a long, slow breath into his lungs, he closed his eyes and made himself unclench his fists. He cracked his neck and willed his taut shoulder muscles to relax so his arms would hang loose and limp.

Calm, he told himself. *Calm. You're here in Heathwick Green. Not at Kyleburn.*

You're no longer twelve years old.

You're no longer powerless and afraid and heartbroken.

By the time he got back to the groom's cottage, Will's

breathing had returned to normal. His heart no longer galloped as if he were a hunted beast and his chest no longer ached.

But he knew as soon as he fell asleep he'd be haunted by memories he could never keep buried, no matter how hard he tried.

———

When Lucy arrived at the stables early the next morning, she found that Will had already saddled one of the carriage horses for her to ride. He'd readied Titan, her father's temperamental Thoroughbred horse, for himself.

The air was cool and clear, and her breath misted as she waved her riding cane in the air and called a greeting to the groom. "It looks like it will be a lovely day," she said as she drew close and offered her mount, Nutmeg, a lump of sugar.

"Aye," said Will. "I hope you have a treat for Titan here too, or he's bound to get a wee bit jealous." He rubbed the black gelding's nose, and the horse shook his head and snuffled as though in complete agreement.

Lucy laughed and reached into the pocket of her sky-blue velvet riding habit for another sugar lump. "Well, we can't have that." And then she looked up through her eyelashes at Will, quite deliberately flirting. At least she *hoped* what she was doing would pass as flirting. She'd never done such a thing before, and she prayed she didn't look like a complete and utter ninny. "Are you sure you wouldn't like a lump too? I wouldn't want you to feel left out."

"What? You wouldna be suggesting that I'm no' sweet enough already, would you, Miss Bertram?" replied Will, his expression the epitome of solemnity. "By all accounts, I'm the embodiment of sugar and spice and all that's nice."

Lucy laughed. "Ha! Really? The man who told me to stop my havering when we first met?"

"Och, I do apologize for that, Miss Bertram. But you canna argue that we weren't in a wee bit of danger from the storm."

"Yes, well…" Lucy rubbed Nutmeg's nose. "At least there's no chance of that this morning." Indeed, as the mist wreathing the stable yard and Fleetwood's grounds began to burn off, it was clear it was going to be a beautiful summer's day. "I'm ready to head out if you are."

"I am." The groom led Nutmeg out to the yard and Lucy's pulse began to caper about. Will would help her into the saddle, which meant in moments his large hands would be on her. At her booted foot. On her ankles… Her cheeks grew hot just thinking about it. Indeed, if she had a fan, she'd use it.

She'd taken extra care with her appearance this morning. In fact, she'd risen early, before the sun had even peeked through her bedroom window. Dotty had been visibly grumpy about the unusually early start. Nevertheless, she dressed Lucy's hair in a low but ridiculously elaborate bun at her nape and secured a smart black topper that sported a swooping peacock's feather on top of her head at a suitably jaunty angle.

As Lucy had regarded her reflection in her dressing table mirror, she'd thought she looked fetching enough. As to whether she could entice Will into helping her… Deploying her feminine wiles to influence a member of the opposite sex was uncharted territory for her.

She really had no idea what she was doing. At all.

As she'd tossed and turned in bed last night, she'd already determined several possible outcomes to her venture. Will might laugh at her because her efforts were so feeble and awkward.

He might not notice she was flirting at all.

He *might* notice that she was attempting to flirt but ignore her because he was genuinely uninterested. (Oh, how mortifying that would be.)

But even on the very first day that she'd met Will, there'd been some sort of spark between them. When Will had lifted her down from the gig, Lucy was certain he'd been thinking about kissing her. And then he'd given her an unsolicited compliment about her plaid gown, and later on, during that awkward dinner with Thorne, he'd winked at her. Surely these were signs that he wasn't *entirely* indifferent to her. So he might be *slightly* interested, but perhaps he wouldn't want to risk his position by acknowledging the indecorous behavior of his employer's daughter.

The worst-case scenario would be that her efforts, and ultimately her scandalous proposition when she offered it, would be rejected outright. And she couldn't have that. If Will wouldn't help her to find Monty...

No, she just couldn't even entertain that particular train of thought for a second.

Her plan *had* to work.

Mustering her courage, Lucy looped the train of her habit over her arm, making sure to expose as much of her ankles and stockings as possible, then with her riding cane in her other gloved hand, she sauntered—she hoped the way she was swaying her hips counted as sauntering—across the hay-strewn cobblestones to where Will waited patiently with Nutmeg.

Had she detected a flicker of his gaze down to her ankles while he was checking on the girth strap and the stirrups? Oh Lord, she hoped so. She was certain her ankles were as comely as the next woman's and he *was* a man after all. According to her worldly friend Artemis, most men liked to look at women. They couldn't help themselves.

Although Lucy was beginning to think *she* liked to look at men.

Well, one particular man with dark-blue eyes and a tendency to forgo a razor far too often.

As she tightly gripped the saddle, Will squatted down, offering his strong, interlaced fingers for her to place her booted foot on. Lucy was momentarily transfixed by the sight of his breeches pulling tight over his thick, muscular thighs.

Oh, my... Had he noticed the direction of her stare? He *was* looking up at her through his long, black lashes with a look that bordered on wicked amusement as he said, "I'll give you a boost up on the count of three. Ready, lass? One, two..."

On "three," Lucy pushed off and sprang upward, and within seconds she was seated upon the saddle. She swiftly hooked her right leg around the fixed head of the sidesaddle and adjusted her grip on her riding cane so she could take up the reins.

Will straightened and placed a steadying hand on Nutmeg's neck. "May I check that your foot is securely in the stirrup, Miss Bertram?" he asked, all traces of impudence gone.

"Oh, of course," replied Lucy and she "helpfully" hoisted up the hem of her habit so that a good deal more than her left foot and stocking-clad ankle were exposed. Indeed, practically everything below the cuff of her knee-length riding breeches was on full display.

She chanced a glance at Will and noticed that his Adam's apple bobbed above his simple neckcloth before he gently slid her foot more securely into the stirrup and tested the strap. A bobbing Adam's apple *must* be some sort of sign that he was affected by what he saw.

He cleared his throat again. "I take it that both of your legs are secure and comfortable in the saddle, Miss Bertram?"

His voice was low and a little rough, and Lucy couldn't resist a tiny smile of triumph. "Yes, they are. Though if you like, you can check..." She began to inch her skirt a fraction higher so Will would be able to see that her left thigh was positioned securely beneath the leaping head, but he stayed her hand.

"No. That's quite all right. I'll take you at your word." He stepped back and bowed. "I take it you're all set, then?"

Lucy tilted her head. "I am."

"Verra good." Will returned to the stables to fetch Titan, and once he was in the yard, he swung up into the saddle with such athletic grace, Lucy's breath caught.

"You'll have to show me where you like to ride," he said as he drew alongside her.

"Out on the heath and then back through the woods on Fleetwood's grounds." Lucy nudged Nutmeg forward with a gentle tap of her cane and a flick of the reins, then glanced over her shoulder at Will. "I'll lead the way. I hope you can keep up!"

He grinned, his teeth flashing white against the dark stubble on his jaw. "Challenge accepted, Miss Bertram."

What the devil had gotten into Miss Bertram?

As they cantered across Hampstead Heath, Will couldn't fathom, at all, why the baronet's daughter had suddenly turned into a coquettish minx. Instead of sporting maidenly blushes, she was suddenly all fluttering eyelashes and sly feminine smiles that were sweeter and far more tempting than the sugar lumps she kept in her pocket.

And then, of course, she wouldn't keep her bloody hem down.

When she'd first appeared in the stables and gathered up her skirts to pick her way across the yard—he'd assumed that she'd done so to keep the fine blue velvet off the ground—he'd been hard pressed not to ogle her neat ankles and lower legs.

But then when she'd flipped up the bottom of her riding habit, brazenly exposing all of her shapely calf, he'd begun to suspect something was afoot. As to what, he hadn't a clue.

From what he'd seen of her this week, she was more a timid-as-a-church-mouse sort of woman, not a bold-as-brass seductress.

Regardless of Miss Bertram's motivation for blatantly flashing her shapely legs at him, Will had reminded himself to remain utterly detached and professional. To not stare or, worse, run his palm along the slender curve of her calf, tracing the shape of her until he got to her knee.

He was *not* that man. An opportunistic cad.

Now, as he followed her across the expanse of long grass on the heath, Will couldn't tear his gaze away. He told himself he was simply doing his job, making sure she was safe as he acted as her escort. But in truth, it was the sight of Miss Bertram's slender yet curvaceous figure moving in perfect unison with her mount that had him so enthralled. The rise and fall of her delicious derriere in particular was nothing but riveting.

She rode beautifully, flying over the open ground, clearing obstacles with ease. Indeed, she could be Epona, the Celtic goddess of horses, brought to life. And the bright smiles that she occasionally threw over her shoulder at him were like a siren's call, leading him on to God knew what sort of disaster.

Because if he acted on his impulse to sweep her into his arms and kiss her until she was breathless and disheveled, disaster of some sort would inevitably follow.

Somehow, some way, he'd rein in his desire, no matter what Miss Lucinda Bertram threw at him to tempt him. He had a mission. And the sooner it was over and done with, the better.

Miss Bertram eventually led them into the oak and beech woods bordering Fleetwood's grounds. Once the trees enveloped them, they slowed the pace of their mounts to a desultory walk along a well-trodden path.

The hushed shade was cool, but not unpleasantly so. A light

breeze ruffled the canopy overhead and the melodious warble of a bird greeted them.

They hadn't gone far when Miss Bertram uttered a soft exclamation. "Oh, look. There's a lovely troop of blusher mushrooms. Mrs. Gilchrist will have my head on a platter if I don't collect some." She halted Nutmeg on the path and cast a come-hither look at Will from beneath her eyelashes. "Would you mind helping me to dismount?"

"Of course not." Will slid down from Titan and tethered Sir Oswald's gelding to a nearby oak branch. Even though the horse seemed a little more subdued after a good hard canter across the heath, Will didn't want to risk having such a spirited and no doubt expensive animal bolt off if startled.

When he reached Miss Bertram's side, she'd already unhooked her legs from the sidesaddle. Drawing a steadying breath, he slid his gloved hands around her narrow waist, and when she grasped his shoulders, he lifted her gently down. There really was nothing much to the lass, yet somehow she seemed to knock the air from his lungs and all sense from his brain as she pressed herself against him and looked up into his face.

For several long moments, Will was frozen to the spot, completely mesmerized, his legs crushing into Miss Bertram's skirts. Her scent—something like roses and warm musky female—enthralled him. Although she was trapped between his own body and Nutmeg's, she didn't seem to mind. Her lavender-blue gaze was locked on his mouth, and when her perfect teeth pressed gently into the soft, pink flesh of her lower lip, he nearly groaned aloud.

Christ preserve me. Will swallowed and dropped his hands as though he'd been scorched, then stepped back. Wiped a hand down his face and looked anywhere but at her.

Not that it helped. His body was tense, all of his senses

on full alert like a beast about to pounce on prey it was set on devouring. Although, given that Miss Bertram was smiling like a cat who'd just been presented with a whole pitcher of cream, perhaps *he* was the hunted one.

One thing was clear: the lass was playing with fire. And one of them—if not both—was bound to catch alight if she continued with this game.

Good Lord. Her plan might actually be working. She *could* flirt.

Who would ever have thought she had it in her?

Her pulse racing faster than a horse galloping across the heath, Lucy watched Will retreat to a respectful distance. But she wasn't disappointed. She knew he'd been thinking about kissing her. She sensed he'd been watching her like a hawk ever since she brazenly lifted her skirt and flashed her leg at him.

Even now, as she turned back to Nutmeg's saddle to unstrap the small tin vasculum she used for collecting botanical samples, she felt Will's gaze on her. Oh, what a heady sensation, to feel him watching her, knowing he wanted her too.

Indeed, Lucy swore she felt a little giddy as she crossed the short expanse of grass to the base of an ancient oak where the mushrooms were clustered around the moss-covered roots. Kneeling down, she unscrewed the end of the vasculum.

"How do you know the mushrooms are safe to eat?" Will approached and then propped a wide shoulder against the oak's trunk.

Lucy carefully picked one and held it out to him. "There are a few ways to tell. But you *do* have to know what you're looking for," she said as Will took it and examined it. "These are definitely blusher mushrooms or *Amanita rubescens*, not its deadly cousin *Amanita pantherina*, or panther's cap. First of all, the blusher has a lighter-hued cap and the little scales on top are grayish in color. The *Amanita pantherina* tends to be a darker brown and has whiter scales. And see the little skirt hanging beneath the gills?"

Will turned the mushroom upside down and nodded. "I do."

"It has tiny striations on it, whereas the skirt on a panther's cap is smooth. The stems are also different at the bottom. And lastly…" Lucy picked another mushroom and delicately snapped a piece off the cap. "If you split the mushroom open, the white flesh 'blushes' or turns red when exposed to air. The panther's cap doesn't."

Will smiled and held the mushroom back out to her to add to her foraged pile. "Thank you for the explanation. I'm impressed by your expertise."

Lucy blushed and dipped her head to focus on carefully sliding the mushrooms into her tin. "Why, thank you, Mr. Armstrong. But I don't think my knowledge of British fungi varieties is all that singular. Now, if you asked me to talk about all the different varieties of the *Strychnos* plant native to Ceylon and India, or indeed all the different species of *Aconitum*—that's wolfsbane—or *Digitalis*—that's foxglove. Or *Atropa belladonna*—deadly nightshade—or hemlock, or cherry laurel which contains deadly hydrocyanic acid… Well, I am able to wax lyrical about them all for hours and hours."

Will's brows had drawn into a frown. "I must ask, how *do* you know so much about botanical poisons, Miss Bertram? It would seem most young ladies I've come across during my years as a groom tend to only care about ribbons and lace and the steps of the latest polka."

Lucy grimaced as she screwed the vasculum's cap back in place. "I'm my father's research assistant. In fact, I penned the first draft of his book, *A Discourse on Botanical Poisons in Great*

Britain, Both Common and Rare." She couldn't help but smile proudly then. "Its publication earned him a fellowship in the Linnean Society."

"But not you?"

Lucy couldn't suppress her sigh. "No. I'm afraid not. Although I have submitted the occasional paper to the Botanical Society of London, and they were all well received when they were published in the society's journal." She shrugged. "It's the best one can hope for when one is a mere female scientist."

Will smiled. "I'm verra glad to hear it. Talent and skill such as yours should definitely be recognized."

Lucy's cheeks heated, but she held the Scot's gaze. "I—I must say you are not quite the usual stable hand, Mr. Armstrong." She narrowed her eyes. "Have you always been a groom?"

Will straightened and tugged on the sleeve of his coat. "No, not always. But I've been around horses most of my life."

"I see… And what did you do before you became a groom? If you don't mind my asking, of course."

He gave her a lopsided smile. "No, I dinna mind." He stepped forward and took the vasculum from her, then crossed over to Nutmeg to secure the tin to the saddle. "I was a soldier in Her Majesty's army for some years," he said when he turned back to face her.

Oh… Lucy frowned. That probably accounted for the jagged scar she'd spied on Will's forehead when he'd come to the kitchen in search of warm milk. *And* his impressive physique.

It also occurred to Lucy that having served in the military, Will would know how to handle himself in an altercation. Not that Lucy was looking to place herself in a physically dangerous situation when she ventured into St Giles's Rookery, but one never knew who one might encounter in a dark alley. Now, more than ever, she was convinced that Will Armstrong was the right man for the job she had in mind.

Lucy brushed the dirt and leaves off the knees of her riding habit and wandered closer. "And do you have family?"

Oh, buckets of fudge! What if Will had a sweetheart or a wife? She'd never even considered the possibility. But her worry was short-lived as Will readily answered, "No one I'm particularly close to. My parents both passed away some time ago—my mother when I was twelve, just before I went—" He broke off, paused. "I was an only child," he said eventually. "I still have my grandfather but…" He shrugged. "We don't see eye to eye on a number of things. As I said, I'm not close to anyone. And I like it that way. It makes things…easier."

Oh, how terribly sad. Will sounded so…so alone. Lucy's heart cramped with sympathy. At least she had her father and her dear childhood friends, Jane and Artemis. And soon she'd have Monty back. But she *did* understand what it was like to lose a parent.

"I'm so sorry to hear that, Will," she said softly. "I lost my own mother when I was thirteen. She was in childbirth. Something went wrong and both she and the babe—a little boy—died." She forced a smile. "I–I do have an older brother. Monty. Although he doesn't live here at Fleetwood anymore… Not since April…" She paused. Bit her lip. "He's… We were always close as children—well, until he went to Eton, and of course I became the annoying little sister who kept getting in the way whenever he was home for holidays and wanted to spend time with one of his special chums. But that's neither here nor there, and I don't want to bore you with all the trials and tribulations of my youth. I suppose my point is I know what's it's like to be alone."

Will was studying her face, his expression grave. Now was the time she should present him with her proposition, but she found that her tongue had become tangled and her belly was a bundle of knots too. The coquette in her had fled and only tongue-tied Lucy remained.

The silence stretched. Extended with a tension that bordered on excruciating. Lucy had no idea what Will was thinking so she blurted out the first thing that sprang into her mind. "Would you help me in the garden? I mean, not today because you've only been here a week and you're probably still sorting things out in the stables and establishing a routine. But every now and again. When there's something that needs doing that I can't manage or Mr. Rolfe, our head gardener, can't quite tackle on his own."

Oh dear, where had all *that* come from? Did it seem like she was manufacturing reasons to spend more time with the handsome groom? But now that Lucy had made the suggestion, really it *was* rather a good idea.

One of Will's dark eyebrows lifted. "Of course. Although I dinna ken much about gardening, Miss Bertram."

Lucy pleated her hands together in front of her waist to stop herself from fidgeting. "Oh, that's quite all right," she continued in a rush. "You see, the problem is our Mr. Rolfe… Well, I'm afraid he's not as young as he used to be, so he's not quite up to doing everything that needs to be done about the grounds. For instance, the overgrown cherry laurels in the poisons garden desperately need trimming after all this rain. There is a man who usually comes up from the village to help out with the larger jobs—an undergardener, if you will—but he was recently injured…"

Oh no. Her tongue had come undone and now she was rambling, but she couldn't seem to help herself. She drew another breath and the words kept tumbling out. "I know you're already doing so much that's outside of your purview—you're the groom, coachman, even a footman on occasion—and I won't lie… Cutting back the laurel hedge does come with some risk because *Prunus laurocerasus* produces cyanide. Well, all laurels with the exception of the bay laurel do, but that's really by-the-by. In any event, what I mean to say is I would be most appreciative if you *would* lend a hand when Mr. Rolfe is ready. There's protective equipment we can use, and I really can't manage it on my own and—"

Will held up a hand. "Miss Bertram. It's quite all right. I would be verra happy to assist you. And dinna worry so much about my constitution. I'm a braw Scotsman and over the years I've survived a battle or two. I'm sure I can survive spending a few hours in a poisons garden."

"Oh… Thank you. Well…" Lucy summoned a grateful smile. "I suppose we should get back to Fleetwood, then."

Will tilted his head. "Aye."

This time Lucy behaved herself as the groom checked if her foot was securely in the stirrup. Even though she hadn't yet asked him to be her bodyguard, she'd learned several useful things. She *could* flirt a little. Will Armstrong hadn't laughed at her fledgling attempts. In fact, she was certain she'd detected a distinct glimmer of masculine interest in his eyes on more than one occasion. And given his past profession, she was certain she could rely on him in a difficult situation. But there was only one way to find out. Sooner rather than later she'd have to summon her courage again and plainly state her proposal.

She had to.

Chapter Nine

ALMOST A WEEK LATER, WHEN LUCY ENTERED THE MORNING room after her ride, it was to discover her father devouring a plate of eggs and kidneys and buttery toast while perusing the newspapers.

Since he'd submitted his article to the Linnean Society, he'd been in far better spirits. She, on the other hand, wasn't, although she did try to hide her despondency as she took a seat at the breakfast table. Yet another morning had gone by and she *still* hadn't drummed up the nerve to do what needed to be done: ask Will to help her find Monty. No doubt it wouldn't be long before Mr. Thorne came calling, so she really couldn't afford to dither much longer. If only she could rein in her self-doubt and nervousness as well as she reined in her horse.

Her father looked up from the *Times* as Clarke laid a napkin over her lap. "I hear that you took Nutmeg out again this morning and that Will exercised Titan. I'd say our new groom is working out quite well, isn't he? He seems quite capable."

Lucy focused on the stream of piping-hot tea that Healey poured into her cup. "Yes. I agree," she said, then busied herself with adding milk. "Quite capable." She was absolutely certain that Will would be adept at whatever he turned his hand to. *Good heavens, his strong capable hands.*

On my ankle. My calf. At my waist...

Lucy swallowed a mouthful of scalding tea. Hopefully her

father wouldn't notice that her cheeks were now as red as the strawberry jam in the crystal bowl in the middle of the table.

She'd been half-heartedly attempting to flirt with Will on and off—flipping up the skirts of her riding habit whenever she mounted her horse and casting him the occasional coquettish glance or smile—but it seemed it was all for naught. He remained steadfastly unmoved, the model of a perfectly appropriate groom. It was beyond frustrating and disheartening and her confidence was flagging by the day. Perhaps the expression "Practice makes perfect" didn't apply to flirting.

Her father pushed his plate away and dabbed the corner of his mouth with his napkin. "Oh, before I forget, you can let Mrs. Gilchrist know that I won't need dinner tonight. I have pressing business to attend to in Town. I'll be leaving before noon and won't be back until tomorrow."

"Oh… Are you staying at the Raleigh Club? Or Claridge's?" Her father had done so on various occasions in the past, but the Mayfair hotel, Claridge's, one of London's finest, was hideously expensive.

"No, at Zachariah Thorne's town house in Belgravia," he replied carefully. "I haven't mentioned it before, but we've been working on a joint project for a while now. He needs someone to advise him on establishing tea plantations in Ceylon. In fact, the reason I was able to employ our new groom was because Thorne recently recompensed me for my time." He frowned. "Now, don't look so po-faced, Lucy. I know you are not all that keen on Mr. Thorne. But I would ask that you give the man a chance. This project is… Well, it's something that I—that *we*, as a family— can't afford to turn down. In fact, I'm hoping that when I see Thorne today, I will also be able to tell him that you will accept his suit. I've given you ample time to get used to the idea."

Oh, fiddlesticks. Lucy's fingers crushed her own napkin. "I'm sorry, Papa. But that's the entire problem. We *don't* suit. I'm not right for him. As you know, I'm quite set in my bluestocking ways. I'm not biddable wife material. At all. From what I've seen so far, Mr. Thorne seems very exacting, and we have quite different beliefs and interests. I'm open-minded and, well, he isn't. If we wed, I would be miserable. You can't want that for me, Papa." Drawing a shallow breath, she added softly, "I'm sure Monty wouldn't want that for me either."

Her father's expression changed. Grew haunted. Was that a fleeting look of regret in his eyes? A tightening of his knuckles as he gripped the newspaper?

But then he seemed to gather himself together and he fixed her with a stern look. "Well, your brother isn't here, is he?" he said stiffly. "But if he was, I'm sure neither of you would want to live in a shell of a house with no servants and no horses and nothing to eat except for what you can forage from the woods. You need to be sensible, Lucy. At least until this venture with Thorne sorts itself out." His narrow shoulders rose and fell with a heavy sigh. "Look, I'm not saying you have to marry him just yet. But perhaps you could humor him a little? Go for a ride around Hyde Park with him a few times? Let him treat you to an ice at Gunter's Tea Shop? Go for a stroll about the British Museum or look at the latest Royal Academy art display at Burlington House? I–I would appreciate it."

Lucy regarded him for a moment as a cold, sick feeling settled in the pit of her stomach. She pushed away her tea. "How bad *are* things, Papa?" she murmured.

He swallowed, and the smile he gave her was so forced that Lucy thought it resembled a rictus of pain. "Let me worry about that, my gel. We'll pull through. I promise you. Just…I need you to at least *try* to do as I've asked."

Then he placed the newspaper on the table, pushed up from his chair, and quit the room, leaving Lucy with the certain feeling that something was very wrong in her father's world. Something that he was too afraid to tell her about and that Mr. Thorne was at the center of it.

―――――――

After Will returned from dropping her father at the Hampstead train station, Lucy sent word to the stables that it was time to help Mr. Rolfe trim the cherry laurels. It wouldn't be long before Mr. Thorne came calling, so she *had* to enact her plan. Thank the Lord her father would be absent tonight, which meant she could venture into St Giles at long last to find Monty. Come rain, hail, or shine, today was the day she'd present her proposition to Will. Dillydallying was not an option.

If only she didn't look quite so peculiar...

"You must promise not to laugh at me," Lucy called out as the groom passed through the wrought-iron gate into the walled poisons garden. She might be wearing a wide-brimmed cavalier-style hat to protect her complexion from the sun, but her face was already burning from preemptive embarrassment.

"Why would I laugh?" A puzzled frown creased Will's brow as his gaze traveled over her. Well, the top half of her body, because most of her lower half was concealed by a thick cluster of foxgloves that she was in the process of deadheading.

"Because..." Lucy winced. "I'm wearing my usual gardening attire, and it's a little unconventional. But on a hot summer's day like today, it's rather beneficial."

Will quirked a brow. "Unconventional? In what way?"

She sighed. "I'm wearing cotton bloomers à la Mrs. Amelia Bloomer, and my skirts only reach my knees... Some might think it scandalous, but it makes it easier for me to move around and do what I need to do in the garden. And before you *do* laugh and claim I look like Little Bo-Peep," she continued sternly, "just remember I'm wielding very sharp pruning shears, not a shepherdess's crook." With that, she stepped out from behind the flower bed. As she'd anticipated, Will snorted, then bit the inside of his cheek.

Lucy narrowed her gaze. "See, I *knew* you'd laugh."

He shook his head, barely suppressed hilarity dancing in his eyes. "I assure you I'm no', Miss Bertram," he said. "I wouldna dare."

Lucy placed a fisted hand on her hip and shot him a mock glare. "Lying does *not* become you, Mr. Armstrong."

"Verra well. I'll admit I'm a wee bit amused. It's no' every day that a man encounters a woman wearing"—he gestured at her attire—"whatever that is. You're right though. You do look a lot like Little Bo-Peep."

"Humph. Just wait until I get you to don a pair of cinder goggles," she said. "I'm not the only one who will be dressed up in outlandish clothing."

Will cocked a brow. "Cinder googles?"

"Yes, cinder goggles. Or train goggles. They're enclosed spectacles that protect your eyes from toxins. You'll be wearing them, as well as thick leather gardening gloves. When cut, the cherry laurel releases hydrocyanic acid, a vapor which smells a little like bitter almonds. You'll be safe enough in the open air though."

"Good God," said Will as he followed her toward the small shed where the gardening equipment was stored. "And I thought you were jesting about the risks involved in trimming a hedge."

"Oh, there's risk," she said as she pushed through the shed door. "You must assume that everything in this garden can kill you. And you must resist touching your face as much as possible. The tiniest bit of toxin entering your eyes or nose or mouth, or even via a tiny scratch on your person, could be the end of you."

"I'll take your word for that, Miss Bertram. Just as I'll place myself in your verra capable hands."

Was Will Armstrong deliberately flirting with *her* now? *Hallelujah!* But why did he have to mention *hands* of all things? Now all she could think about were *his* long, strong fingers and his thick wrists and muscular forearms... How it would feel to be wrapped up in his arms. Lucy was suddenly grateful for the dim light in the gardening shed. To hide how flustered she was, she occupied herself with providing Will with the equipment he needed to keep himself safe. Once he was kitted out and armed with his own pair of pruning shears, Lucy led him down a gravel path lined with beds of wolfsbane, deadly nightshade, and hemlock to the back wall, where Mr. Rolfe was already hard at work pruning the laurel hedge.

When the gray-haired gardener spied Will, his deeply lined face cracked with a wide smile. "Miss Bertram told me you were coming. With a strapping chap like you to help out, I've no doubt we'll be done in a few hours."

"I'll do my verra best, sir," replied Will.

"Excellent. If you wouldn't mind climbing up the ladder to trim the tops of the bushes, it would be greatly appreciated." Mr. Rolfe winced. "I'm afraid my balance isn't what it used to be."

Lucy smiled, but dipped her head as tears stung her eyes. She'd known Mr. Rolfe forever. To think that her father might have to let him and all of Fleetwood's other loyal staff members go hurt her heart. Fleetwood itself was safe from any creditors; the estate was entailed to the baronetcy and had been for several centuries. But if they were running out of money, it was true that anything of value within the stables and the house could be sold off to make ends meet.

The weight of responsibility suddenly sat so heavily on Lucy's shoulders that she felt like she might sink into the ground itself.

And then a wave of anger hit her. Engulfed her entirely, making her hands shake, and she had to turn away from Will and Mr. Rolfe. How dare her father put everyone in this untenable situation? How dare he make her feel obliged to wed a man she couldn't abide? The blame for this monumental financial mess they were in could be laid squarely at Sir Oswald Bertram's feet. If he hadn't spent so much money on countless scientific expeditions abroad, chasing fame and accolades for his achievements... Which a good deal of the time were *her* achievements, because she was the one who had penned his damn papers and his much-lauded book on poisons.

Barnaby Rudge and fudging buckets of fudge and foxing foxgloves and some other rude word that started with "f" that she'd once heard one of the footmen say.

She needed to calm down. "I'm... I'll leave you gentlemen to it, shall I?" she called over her shoulder as she began to retrace her steps. "I need to finish deadheading some of the spent flowers."

And she needed to stop beating about the bush with Will and move beyond "making eyes" at him. It was Freddy's afternoon off—he always went to visit his family in Hampstead—so as soon as Will returned to the stables, she'd go lay all of her cards on the table. She had nothing left to lose.

And if he said "yes"...well, tonight she'd be searching for Monty.

———

Will frowned as he watched Miss Bertram disappear down the garden path. Something was wrong. Very wrong. He could sense it like a hound scenting blood. It had been evident in the uncertain timbre of her voice when she'd suddenly announced that she was off to tend to another part of the garden. The rigid line of her slender shoulders as she'd walked away. Even the tilt of her head proclaimed something was amiss.

And it wasn't just now that she'd been acting strangely.

His mind returned to their previous encounters in the stables. On their very first ride, Miss Bertram had been uncharacteristically flirtatious…brazenly so. He'd been bemused, and God help him, he'd actually thought about kissing her on more than one occasion. Which was *not* an option. Subsequently, he'd been on his best behavior, and at the risk of hurting her feelings, he'd ignored her attempts to bedazzle him with her charming smiles and eyelash flutters and flipped-up skirts.

Although he'd been all ears when she'd shared snippets about her family. He was especially keen to find out more about her older brother and the nature of the rift between him and Sir Oswald. Miss Bertram quite clearly missed Monty, and Will sensed that she wanted to talk more about him. Beneath her coy yet coquettish veneer, it was obvious that she was troubled. If Will could find out more about the situation, he would. It might have nothing to do with the case, but he couldn't rule that out unless he knew the facts.

He wiped the sweat from his brow with his forearm, then adjusted his position on the ladder before he began to trim a new section of the potentially deadly hedge. Mr. Rolfe had begun to whistle quietly to himself, and Will was grateful he wasn't expected to engage in any idle chitchat. Of course, he could try to filch any number of details about the Bertrams from the gardener, but he sensed Rolfe had been with the family for many years and would be unswervingly loyal to them.

No, he'd probably find out more from Miss Bertram. She

was more likely to spill something useful in the way of intelligence without him needing to probe much at all.

Even though Will had known Miss Bertram for less than a fortnight, he already felt like he could read her fairly well... although he still hadn't worked out what the devil had been going on with her lately. When he'd helped her down from her horse this morning, the way she'd pressed herself against him... the way she'd focused on his mouth, he knew right down to his very bones that she'd been thinking about kissing him. It hadn't been the first time she'd done that either.

What on earth would make a baronet's daughter—an endearingly skittish but fiercely intelligent young woman—risk her entire reputation for the sake of a few snatched kisses with a servant? While it was a mystery to Will, he had to keep his eye on the prize. Later on tonight, he'd search Sir Oswald's rooms. With the baronet away, he wouldn't pass up this opportunity to do what needed to be done.

Chapter Ten

LUCY FLUTTERED HER EYELASHES, ATTEMPTED TO POUT SUG-gestively, then poked out her tongue at herself in the dressing table mirror.

Gah! To think a small part of her had entertained the idea that she was beginning to master the art of flirting. But her reflection told her otherwise. To her mind, the Lucy staring back at her looked like a complete and utter ninny whenever she tried to be something she wasn't—a seductive siren. She'd be lucky if Will didn't fall down with laughter when she offered her kisses as coin for his services as a bodyguard.

Lucy's gaze strayed to her lacquered jewelry box, and she flipped it open. Perhaps she should just offer him some expensive trinket instead. Her fingers sifted through the treasures within—a pair of pearl earrings, a garnet brooch, a peridot-studded bracelet. The problem was every single item had belonged to her mother and they all held great sentimental value for Lucy. It would break her heart to give anything away.

With a sigh, she closed the lid again. No, she'd just have to hope that Will found her pretty enough to kiss. She'd changed out of her "Little Bo-Peep" attire—which even she would admit was not the most glamorous garb—and was now more conventionally dressed in a light summer gown of pale-yellow silk. It showed off her dècolletage rather nicely, and the lace that cascaded from the ends of her sleeves added a nice feminine touch.

She didn't need to add color to her cheeks by pinching

them. Both the heat of the day and the thought of laying out her proposition to Will meant that her face was already flushed. She bared her teeth and leaned closer to the mirror. Nothing was stuck there, but perhaps she should chew on a comfit to make sure her breath was fresh. Oh, and she should add a few more dabs of lily-of-the-valley scent to her wrists and behind her ears. Perhaps even in the valley between her breasts. And maybe she should get Dotty to rearrange her hair and... She scowled at herself.

She was procrastinating. Again. She knew Mr. Rolfe and Will had finished trimming the cherry-laurel hedge. She'd heard the gardener's familiar tuneless whistle float through her open window as he'd wandered past five minutes ago, probably on the way to the kitchen to grab a tankard of small beer or a glass of lemonade to quench his thirst.

Which meant Will might be in the kitchen too. It wouldn't be out of place for her to check. She had to see Mrs. Gilchrist about dinner this evening anyway, and if Will wasn't there, she could take him something to drink. It would be a convenient excuse to visit him at the stables or at his quarters. A token of her "thanks" for going above and beyond his duties as groom and coachman.

Mind made up, Lucy applied more scent, then smoothed a few wayward strands of hair away from her flushed cheeks. She was ready... Well, as ready as she'd ever be.

However, when she entered the kitchen, it was to discover Will wasn't there.

When Mrs. Gilchrist mentioned there was a bottle of ginger beer in the pantry that the groom might like, Lucy claimed it. With a muttered thanks, she hastened away to hide her blush. If the canny cook had noticed that her mistress wasn't indifferent to the handsome Scot's charms, she didn't seem particularly bothered by it, thank goodness. Because if word got back to Sir Oswald that his daughter and the groom had started a dalliance—Lucy shivered—she doubted Will would be working at Fleetwood for much longer.

But then, she was well and truly putting the cart before the horse. She still had to get Will to agree to her proposal.

Upon reaching the stables, Lucy quickly ascertained the entire place was deserted apart from a few chickens scratching about. In the cool shadows, all could she see were empty stalls. The horses had to be out in the paddock behind the orchard, enjoying the beautiful day.

Will must be at his quarters, which, in a way, suited her purposes exactly. Heart pounding, still clutching the ginger beer in her damp palms, Lucy followed the flagged, lavender-bush-lined path around the side of the stables, heading toward the orchard and Will's cottage.

How on earth was she going to start this conversation that needed to be had? Perhaps she should have rehearsed something beforehand so her wits wouldn't completely fail her as they often did in challenging situations. Challenging for someone like *her*, at least.

"Mr. Armstrong," she said beneath her breath. *No, too formal.*

"Will, I have a proposal for you." *No, that sounds like I'm asking him to marry me.*

"Mr. Armstrong. Will…I need to speak with you about—" *Oh…* Lucy stumbled to a complete halt and almost dropped the ginger beer.

Will Armstrong was indeed at his cottage. In fact, he was outside, at the water pump, vigorously working the handle up and down to fill an iron pail…and he was barefoot and completely naked from the waist up.

Oh. My. Lord.

Lucy's mouth dropped open. The man was stunning. Breathtakingly beautiful. Sheer muscular perfection. When God created man, there was no doubt that He must have had someone like William Armstrong in mind.

The groom's back was to her so he hadn't noticed she was rooted to the spot, ogling the taut, sleek muscles of his lean upper body and the mesmerizing way they bunched and shifted as he pumped away. And then of course how could she ignore the man's narrow waist and hips and the firm mounds of his buttocks encased in tight buckskin leather? And below the breeches were his bare, muscular calves with their light dusting of dark hair, and then his long, shapely feet.

Liquid longing beat in Lucy's blood, and she swallowed past a throat tight with both panic and a strange burning hunger. She should make a sound. Clear her voice. Announce her presence. Turn around and run away. A sensible young lady, a *virtuous* young lady, would do that. But she didn't. And then before she *could* actually gather her wits together enough to do anything other than *stare*, Will bent down, picked up the brimming pail, and poured it over his head.

Water sluiced over him, drenching his entire body, and when he put the bucket down, he shook his head like a wet dog. Raked one hand through his dripping hair.

And then, horror upon horrors, he looked back over his left shoulder.

Straight at her.

Their gazes locked. Held for a heartbeat. And then Lucy whimpered.

"Miss Bertram?" Will's brows had plunged into a deep frown, but he didn't make any move to cover his nakedness. Indeed, he didn't seem embarrassed or perturbed in the slightest. When he turned to face her, hands on his hips, he asked, "Are you all right, lass?"

Oh, why did he do that? Turn around? And no, she wasn't all right or even in her right mind. She was both mortified and stricken by a wave of desire so strong she felt giddy, as if she must be drunk or drugged. If she tried to take a step forward, she was certain she would fall over because her knees would give out.

Somehow, though, Lucy tore her enraptured attention away from Will's lean, ridged torso and the water-beaded mounds of his pectoral muscles and met his dark blue gaze. "I–I brought you some ginger beer," she managed in a voice that was tellingly husky. "To say thank you for…for helping Mr. Rolfe. You didn't have to and… It's very hot. The afternoon, that is. The ginger beer is nice and cold." *Unlike my face, which is flaming like a Guy Fawkes bonfire.*

Will's mouth twitched. "Thank you, Miss Bertram. That's verra thoughtful of you."

"Oh, it's no trouble." Lucy managed to make her feet work and crossed the short expanse of lawn to where Will stood beneath the dappled shade of an overgrown apple tree. As he took the bottle, their fingers brushed and Lucy's breath hitched. Most of Will's face was in shadow, but she couldn't mistake the keen gleam in his eyes. Was it amusement at her befuddled embarrassment or something like masculine interest? No one—no *man*—had ever looked at her like that before, so she couldn't be certain.

He uncorked the bottle with his teeth, then tipped his head back and drank, his throat working with each deep, strong, pulling swallow. Good heavens, even the man's neck musculature was impressive.

When he'd had his fill, he lowered the bottle and wiped a hand across his mouth. "Thank you again, lass. I needed that," he said, his voice low.

She nodded. That was the cue "Sensible-Miss-Bertram" should take to leave. But "Desperate-Miss-Bertram" couldn't afford *not* to press ahead. Come what may.

"Mr. Armstrong. Will…" she began, then stopped.

Oh, flapping flapdragons. She really, *really* should have rehearsed what she needed to say. It would have come in handy, given Will was all wet and half-naked and entirely distracting, and of course her brain was still not working properly at all. She inhaled a fortifying breath. "I–I didn't just seek you out to bring you some ginger beer. I–I wanted to speak with you…privately…about a delicate matter. Actually, 'delicate' is probably the wrong word… It's more of a dangerous matter."

"Dangerous?" Will's frown was back as he crossed his arms over his chest. "I dinna like the sound of that, Miss Bertram. Are you sure you are all right?"

"I'm…" She sighed. "No. In all honesty, I'm not. And I'm not explaining any of this very well. Last week, you may recall I mentioned my brother, Monty. And that he no longer lived with us."

Will tilted his head. "Yes. I remember."

"Well, he and my father had a falling-out earlier this year—at the beginning of the Season—and Monty has ostensibly been missing ever since. Not missing, exactly. I mean, I believe he left of his own volition after he and Father had a dreadful row one night. He hasn't communicated a word to either one of us—me or Father—until just recently. The day you arrived, in fact."

Will placed the almost-empty bottle of ginger beer in the pail, then straightened. "Go on."

"I received a letter from Monty but it didn't say much at all beyond the fact that he is fine and I shouldn't worry about him. There was no mention of what had caused the estrangement between him and Father, nor did he say where he now resides. But I have been so, so worried about him for so long because

I know he doesn't have a lot of money…" She drew another deep breath. "In any event, I'm sure you've noticed that my father isn't particularly flush with funds at the moment. We used to have a lot more servants here at Fleetwood, but over the last year in particular we've had to cut back on expenses and, well…" This was the difficult part. "A logical way to save the family from certain penury is for me to wed someone wealthy."

"Thorne," said Will flatly. A muscle twitched in his lean jaw. "Your father wants you to marry Zachariah Thorne."

"Yes…" Lucy grimaced. "And I really don't want to. But you see, I'm certain Monty would take my side. He and I used to be quite close, and I just know he would be able to make Father see reason. But in order for him to do that—"

"You need to find him."

Lucy exhaled a shaky breath of relief. "Yes. And that's where you come in."

Will's frown was back. He rubbed his stubbled jaw. "I willna lie, Miss Bertram, it sounds like an almost impossible feat. I take it there was no return address on the envelope?"

"No. But…I do know where Monty posted it from. The postmark was smudged but a friend of mine helped me to decipher it. And we believe it was sent from the High Street in St Giles."

Will released a low whistle. "St Giles," he repeated. "That's no' a verra nice area of London, lass."

"I know. And of course Monty might *not* be living in St Giles. But the lodgings there would be cheap, and if he's running out of money…" She shrugged. "It's a possibility. I have to take a chance and at least try to find him. I can't sit by and do nothing at all with the knowledge I now have. Because if I *don't* find him…" Even though the afternoon was still warm, Lucy shivered.

Will's expression was grave, the light in his eyes as turbulent as a storm-tossed sea as he said, "So, just to be clear, you want me to accompany you into the St Giles Rookery. To go behind your father's back."

She swallowed. "Yes... I know it's a huge risk you'd be taking. And not just in a physical sense because you'd be escorting me through such a dangerous part of London. You'd be risking your position here too, because if my father finds out, he will *not* be happy."

"Aye. I'm thinking you'd be right on that score, lass."

Desperation suddenly gripped Lucy's chest. *What if Will said no?* "I hope you understand that I really have no other choice," she continued. "I must find Monty...or I'll be forced to wed Thorne."

The Scot studied her face. "I'll agree, you're in a verra difficult situation. But you're asking me to place myself in a difficult one too."

"I know. And it's horribly unfair for me to do so...but you are the only person I could think of to ask for help." Even though her heart was racing, Lucy moved a step closer. Dared to place her hand on Will's bare, corded forearm and raise her gaze to his face. Now was the moment to issue her scandalous, outrageous proposal. There was no turning back.

"I cannot offer you money for taking such a risk as I have little on hand. But...I did wonder..." She drew a bracing breath and lifted her chin. "I'd rather hoped that you might accept payment in the form of kisses... A kiss for every time we venture into the Rookery. I know it's not much, but when we are together, I feel something. A spark of electricity, a magnetic attraction that I simply cannot ignore. And I think you feel it too. Tell me I'm wrong, and I'll withdraw my proposition and walk away. I'll never speak of this again."

Beneath the palm of her hand, the muscles in Will's forearm went rigid. But his cobalt-blue eyes gleamed as his gaze honed in on her mouth. "You're not wrong, lass," he said huskily, "but this isn't right. You shouldn't have to trade kisses for my protection."

"Ordinarily I would agree. But my father wants to trade *all* of me so he can replenish the family coffers. And I loathe Zachariah Thorne. You've met him. He's simply awful. But you, Will Armstrong, I…" She firmed her voice even though her insides trembled. "I want you. Ever since we first met, I've imagined what it would be like to be in your arms, to feel your lips upon mine. I'm twenty-eight years old. A shy and ofttimes awkward spinster with singular scientific interests, and I've…I've never been kissed. Not once. In fact, I never thought I *would* ever want to be kissed. But then I met you and…and I do want this. Very much. Even though it's risky and wrong and—"

Will gently captured her chin between his thumb and forefinger. "Wheesht. That's enough," he murmured. "I'll kiss you, lass. You dinna need to beg. But I willna consider it, nor accept it, as a form of payment. Kisses should be given freely, so I'll kiss you because I want to and because you want it too. And I'll protect you from harm when you venture into St Giles because I want to do that as well. Are we clear?"

Lucy couldn't quite believe what she was hearing. Giddy relief washed through her. And desire. So much breath-stealing desire that her head was spinning and her heart was racing. Will had not only agreed to help her find her brother, but also admitted that he *wanted* to kiss her too. She could see it in the burning heat of his gaze. Feel it in the gentle hold of his fingers. "Yes, Will," she murmured. "We're clear."

One corner of his wide mouth kicked into a smile. "Good."

"So…" Lucy swallowed to moisten her mouth. "Are we… Are you…?"

"Going to kiss you?" The fire in Will's eyes intensified. "Do you want me to? Here? Now? Anyone might see us…"

Somehow Lucy summoned enough breath to speak. "No, they won't. We're hidden enough here behind your cottage." Good heavens, if Will *didn't* kiss her, she'd expire from want.

Will leaned closer still. "Then close your eyes, my sweet, bonny lass," he whispered, his breath brushing against her lips, and when she did, his mouth slanted across hers and Lucy melted.

She wasn't sure what she'd expected, but the reality of Will's kiss was everything she'd dreamed of, yet somehow nothing like it at all.

Nothing had prepared her for the blatant carnality of it. The raw intimacy of it… The feel of his firm yet supple lips pressing against hers. The rasp of his stubble. The delicious, sinuous glide of his mouth, encouraging her to move too. The warmth of his breath and the heat and hardness of his powerful body as one of his arms encircled her waist and drew her close against him. It was overwhelming and thought-robbing yet she'd never felt so alive, so galvanized. So *real*.

And then there was the wholly wicked yet wonderful feel of his tongue tracing the seam of her lips, coaxing her to open. When she did, he slid inside, caressing and tasting, teasing and exploring, and she thought she might die from the sheer decadent pleasure of it. Heaven had a taste, and it was something like ginger beer and sweet forbidden fruit and another mysterious ingredient that could only be classified as "Will."

And somehow, through it all, the scientific, analytical part of Lucy's brain registered and catalogued all of these wondrous sensations—indeed, every little thing Will did—within the space of heartbeats and shared breaths. Sighs and whisper-soft moans. When they at last drew apart, both of them breathless and smiling, Lucy knew she would remember these heady moments in every exquisite detail forever.

"There now," he said, gently brushing a strand of hair away from her cheek. "You've now been kissed. I hope you enjoyed it as much as I did."

Lucy swallowed. Licked her lips. "I did." *You'll never know how much.* "Do you think we might do it again sometime?"

He smiled. "You only need to ask, lass. I'm completely at your disposal."

Oh… Lucy smiled back. Then she realized her hands were still splayed against the hard wall of Will's naked damp chest, and she blushed and promptly removed them. "Well," she said. "Perhaps we might kiss again later this evening… Actually…" She drew a deep breath. "Now that you've kindly agreed to help me find Monty, I wondered if you would also be happy to accompany me to St Giles tonight. Because my father is away, it would be the perfect opportunity to go."

A flicker of a frown chased across Will's face but then it was gone. "Of course. What time do you want to leave?"

"I thought we could catch the nine o'clock train into Town. We can stable Juniper and the cart at the Wick and Whistle—we have an arrangement with the ostler—and it's not far to walk from there to the station."

"Verra well." Will's gaze traveled over her gown. "As pretty as yer yellow frock is, Miss Bertram, might I suggest you wear something a little duller and plainer with comfortable shoes? And perhaps dispense with a crinoline cage altogether? You dinna want to stand out, and if we have to run, it will be easier if you're wearing something a little more practical. A scented kerchief wouldn't go astray either. The St Giles Rookery is more than a wee bit…unsavory. If you take my meaning."

Lucy nodded. "I will do all of that. I trust your judgment.

Before we go, I'll also show you a photograph of Monty so you know who to look out for. It's rather small, but it's recent and a good likeness. He's fair, like me, and almost as tall as you."

"Tha' would be most helpful."

"I'll meet you at the stables at eight o'clock, then?" Before Will could respond, Lucy stood on her tiptoes and kissed his cheek. "Thank you. For everything," she murmured, and then she turned around and left her handsome bodyguard beneath the shade of the apple tree.

———

Christ on a cross.

Bloody hell.

Will ran a hand down his face. What the devil had he just gotten himself into?

Or more to the point, what had he just done?

Agreeing to Miss Bertram's plan was bad enough, but succumbing to temptation and kissing her like that... And then agreeing to kiss her anytime she liked...

He must have gone completely and utterly stark raving mad.

Indeed, when he'd first tasted her sweetness, reveled in her delightfully unschooled but enthusiastic responses to everything he'd done, he'd felt off-kilter. As though the world had suddenly tilted on its axis and he was sliding, falling headlong into some abyss he had no hope of escaping from.

Miss Lucy Bertram might look like an English rose and taste like ambrosia, but she was so very dangerous, and in more ways than one.

The sensible thing to do, of course, would be to keep the lass at arm's length. For one thing, he was potentially putting the entire murder investigation at risk by delaying what needed to be done. With Sir Oswald away, Will had been handed the perfect opportunity to go through everything in the baronet's rooms with a fine-tooth comb, without fear of discovery. However, now that he was acting as Lucy's bodyguard, he'd have to leave his search until later. Which meant he wouldn't be getting much sleep tonight. Again. And when one was sleep-deprived and distracted, one tended to make mistakes.

On the other hand, if sacrificing sleep was the price he had to pay for keeping Lucy safe, Will would do it. He couldn't leave her to fend for herself. He just couldn't.

She was… He sighed as he faced an uncomfortable truth. She mattered. And that was the most frightening realization of all.

There was no doubt in his mind that this business with Thorne and Lucy *was* compromising his judgment. Destroying his objectivity and distracting him far more than was wise. Indeed, the idea of Lucy marrying the likes of Zachariah Thorne, of that man touching her. Kissing her… Will clenched his fists. He felt like punching a hole through a wall. Smashing his fists against something again and again until they were bloody and bruised. Until this bloodred anger coursing through him subsided.

And those volatile thoughts, this savage feeling of blind anger, and the overwhelming urge to protect Lucy, they all shook him to his core. He'd never felt this way before about any woman. Good God, he'd only known Miss Bertram for a fortnight, and now he was acting like he was her bloody knight in shining armor.

Will sighed and retrieved the pail and returned to the cottage. He needed to dry off and cool down. To try and repair his shredded sangfroid.

He would do what he could to help Lucy—God, he was even calling her by her first name in his head now—but when all was said and done, he had a duty, first and foremost, to the Crown. There was a ruthless killer on the loose, and he had to do his utmost to gather evidence as swiftly as possible so that a successful arrest and prosecution could be made.

And it wasn't only Sir Oswald that Will had in his sights. Thorne's narrow religious views and obvious intolerance of Charles Darwin's controversial evolutionary theory marked him as a suspect too. Perhaps the prime suspect. As soon as Will could safely get word to his contacts at Scotland Yard about his suspicions, he would. He was reluctant to send a telegram from Hampstead Station because he didn't know where the loyalty of the telegraph office staff lay. They were supposed to be impartial and observe confidentiality, but they might also bear some sort of allegiance to the baronet. Or they might just be gossips.

In any case, even if Will composed a coded message, the address he sent it to wouldn't go unnoticed. Telegrams sent to Scotland Yard or the Home Office or the upper-class residence of one of his contacts in the peerage by a mere "groom" would be certain to raise an eyebrow or two.

While he could always post a letter, a meeting in person was best. But he couldn't just waltz off anytime he liked into Town to visit Scotland Yard or indeed anywhere else until it was his afternoon off. And that wouldn't be for another few days. Unless he discovered something of import… If that happened, he'd seek out Detective Lawrence straightaway.

Christ, Will hoped to God he did find something that was bloody useful before someone else died.

Chapter Eleven

LUCY WAS GRATEFUL THAT WILL HAD ADVISED HER TO WEAR comfortable shoes. Because by the time they'd walked from the Wick and Whistle Inn to Hampstead Station, and then the mile from Euston Station to St Giles, and then traipsed the length and breadth of the High Street, and then down nearby Shaftesbury Avenue, she was starting to develop a blister or two, along with a sense of mounting trepidation.

When Will had described the St Giles Rookery as "no' a verra nice part of London," that had clearly been an understatement. Lucy had imagined what it would be like, but the reality was vastly different. In fact, she felt like she'd stumbled into one of Hieronymus Bosch's hellish paintings. Either that, or one of the Dutch painter's nightmarish scenes had come to life.

Thank God for Will. As soon as they'd left the relatively well-lit High Street, he'd slid a hand around her waist, drawing her close as though they were a courting couple. She felt a little safer. It was almost as if she mattered to him. And that was rather lovely.

What wasn't at all lovely was the behavior of some of the men and women they passed—the brash costermongers and pestering peddlers and brazen "ladies of the night" soliciting a different sort of customer. Even though Lucy had followed Will's advice and was practically covered from head to toe— she wore a plain black straw bonnet, a dull-as-ditchwater walking gown of Prussian blue, and an old charcoal-gray, hooded cloak—she still somehow managed to attract unsolicited leers and whistles and jeers and insults from any number of unsavory characters. She was glad she'd concealed a small sheathed scalpel in her cloak's pocket. If, God forbid, she and her glowering bodyguard were separated for some unforeseen reason, at least she had *something* she could use to defend herself.

Indeed, the deeper she and Will journeyed into St Giles, scanning the faces in the crowded, rowdy streets for any sign of Monty, the more terrifying the area became. And the more wretched and malodorous. Lucy was also thankful for her lavender-scented kerchief as they passed piles of refuse and open sewers and narrowly dodged slops being hurled from windows into the street below.

The openings to dark, narrow alleyways gave glimpses into squalid, overcrowded, barely lit courts where patched and threadbare garments and linen hung from washing lines like limp, ragged flags. Barefoot, wraithlike children darted in and out of the shadows with scrawny dogs at their heels, while hollow-eyed women balanced crying babes on their hips. More coarse, harsh words than she'd ever heard in her life echoed in Lucy's ears.

And then there were the bodies, sprawled in lanes and doorways. Whether those poor souls were just drunk, or unwell, or worse, Lucy couldn't be sure, and it made her heart cramp with anguish. Could Monty really be here in a place like this? Surely he would return to Fleetwood Hall before he fell so low... The problem was she didn't know.

When they reached the busy Seven Dials junction, Will paused a few yards away from a public house that was packed to the gunwales with boisterous, drunken patrons. The sallow light from a nearby gas lamp briefly illuminated one half of the Scot's stern countenance before he bent low to speak in her ear.

"I dinna mean to sound like a doubting Thomas, Miss Bertram, but it feels like we're on a bit of a wild-goose chase. Your brother could be anywhere in this warren. Or no' here at all."

Lucy swallowed hard to clear the sudden lump clogging her throat. As the reality of the impossible task she'd set for herself hit her, so did a wave of despair. Searching for Monty was like looking for a needle in a haystack when one was blindfolded and had one's hands tied behind one's back.

But she would *not* be defeated. She would not give up. "I know it's difficult, but what other choice do I have? The postmark on his letter is the only clue I have to go on."

"I probably should have asked you sooner, but perhaps you could tell me the sorts of things your brother likes to do," said Will. "Is he fond of a drink? And please forgive my indelicacy, but is he the sort of man who might seek the affections of a…" His voice trailed away and he nodded discreetly in the direction of a woman sitting on the front steps of the pub. Her lips and cheeks were anointed with smudged rouge, and aside from a pair of torn stockings, she clearly wore no undergarments beneath her hiked-up skirts of garish green.

"A prostitute?" asked Lucy. "It's all right to say the word in front of me. I might never have been kissed before today, but that doesn't mean I'm completely naive about such things."

"My apologies," he said. "It's no' a subject one usually discusses with genteelly bred young ladies."

Lucy smiled. "Perhaps I should warn you now that I have a very practical streak. And because of my scientific background, a thorough understanding of the natural world and the base needs that drive species to reproduce." She drew closer to Will and murmured in his ear, "It might surprise you to learn that I even know how sexual intercourse works and that it's very different from how flowers propagate. I know there's a little more to it than the simple exchange of pollen from anther to stigma. Although fertilization follows, so perhaps it's not all that dissimilar."

Will cleared his throat. "I see."

When Lucy drew back, she was amused to see that Will might be blushing rather than her. There was a stain of color marking the planes of his high cheekbones.

She continued. "As to your other question about whether Monty likes a tipple or two… Yes, he does, but never to excess. He wasn't a slave to the 'demon drink' or even an 'opium eater.' As far as I know, anyway. But then, do brothers ever share what they are truly like with their sisters?"

Will's mouth twitched with a wry smile. "No, I wouldna imagine tha' they do."

"Monty also enjoys the theater," Lucy added. "At least he used to. And, like most gentlemen, enjoys the odd card game. But I'm certain he's never had a problem with gambling to excess either."

"Hmmm." Will looked thoughtful. "It's almost worth visiting a gaming hell or two. The problem is a club like tha' is one place I willna take you."

"But—"

"No buts, Miss Bertram. It's dangerous enough out here in the street. I willna take you into that sort of den of iniquity, especially on this side of Town."

Lucy sighed. "Perhaps we should walk past some of the theaters in Covent Garden. It won't be long until some of the plays and musicales end and theatergoers begin to emerge. I've assumed Monty has run out of money, but maybe he hasn't. It's all just guesswork on my part. In any case, we still have another hour before the last train back to Hampstead leaves Euston Station. If we have to, I can pay for a hackney."

She lowered her voice. "I brought my coin purse. It's in a hidden pocket—"

"You did what?" Will's voice was a low ferocious growl. "Good God, woman. Are you daft? Whatever you do, dinna reach into your pocket, let alone take it out. No' around here. There's cutthroats and pickpockets every-bloody-where."

"I'm sure it's all right," returned Lucy. "As I was trying to tell you, it's well hidden."

"Tha's no' the point—"

All at once there was a violent shout and then a whoop from the direction of the public house. Will grabbed Lucy by the shoulders and thrust her behind him, and then she saw what all of the commotion was about. A brawl had broken out between two men. They were locked together, awkwardly grappling each other, stumbling and grunting while a small crowd had begun to gather around them. Men and women cheered and laughed and called out obscenities and encouragement. Some even laid bets on who would win.

Lucy's stomach knotted with tension, and she slid her hand into her pocket. Her fingers curled around the scalpel's handle, and she wondered if she should slide the blade out of its leather sheath. The mood in the crowd was unnervingly gleeful, as though everyone's bloodlust had been aroused. It felt as if anything might happen at any second.

"We're leaving," Will gritted out. He grasped her gloved hand, but in the next moment, Lucy felt someone else roughly yanking on her other arm, trying to dislodge her hand from her cloak's pocket.

"Give it 'ere, you snobby bitch. I know you got somefink in there." Lucy whirled around to see who was attempting to rob her, and Will rounded on her would-be pickpocket. It was a lanky youth about Freddy's age, with a pinched face and hard eyes. But as soon as he took in Will's size, the way the Scot loomed and the ferocious expression on his face, the youth's eyes widened and he released Lucy at once. He lifted his hands, palms up, in a placatory gesture. "No 'arm meant, guv," he said and then bolted away through the crowd, faster than a rat ducking down a sewer.

"What the devil were you thinking, Lucy?" Will's voice was flat and hard with anger as he tugged her away from the violent brawl and bloodthirsty crowd.

Even though Lucy registered that Will had just used her first name, an intimacy that for some inexplicable reason made her want to do a little jig of pleasure, indignation also spiked. "What do you mean?" she demanded. "I didn't do anything wrong."

Will snorted. "Your hand was in your pocket and you have a coin purse in there."

Ugh. Lucy stopped abruptly, forcing Will to stop too. "That's not what I was reaching for, you great Scottish clodpole. If you must know"—she dropped her voice—"I have a weapon in my pocket. A nasty little scalpel. I was simply gripping it to make myself feel less…less vulnerable."

Will closed his eyes for a moment and ran a hand down his face. "Och, I'm sorry, lass. I shouldna have jumped to conclusions."

"Thank you," Lucy replied stiffly. "My purse is actually secreted beneath my skirts, and you have to know where the slit in the seam is to find it. I'm not completely 'daft,' as you put it."

"No, no, you're not. Again I apologize. But…" His gaze met hers, grave and uncompromising. "In the future, you must promise me that you will do exactly as I say. No questions asked. All right?"

Lucy nodded. "All right. And next time I won't bring a coin purse. Shall we be on our way?"

"Aye." Will slid his arm beneath her cloak so it encircled her waist. "I'm also verra sorry you feel so unsafe. But I promise I will protect you."

"I know you will. And it's not your fault I feel like this," she said. "I'm the one who asked you to bring me here. And I should also thank you for chasing off that cutpurse. I was very impressed by what a growl and a scowl can accomplish."

"It was nothing at all." A pause. Lucy sensed Will's gaze on her face. "He didna hurt you, did he?"

She winced. "Not really. I might have a bruise or two, but I'm sure it's nothing."

Will nodded. "Good." And then he fell silent as they hurried along the filthy, dark streets, all the way to Covent Garden.

Chapter Twelve

NOTHING.

Will's search—this time of Sir Oswald's private sitting room, bedchamber, and dressing room—had yielded bloody nothing.

Again.

Not one iota of anything useful that he could possibly present to Scotland Yard to justify further questioning of the baronet, let alone the issuing of an arrest warrant for Lord Litchfield's murder.

Bloody, blazing hell.

Will folded up the letter he'd been perusing by the light of a single candle and pushed it back into the pile in Sir Oswald's writing desk. While he *had* discovered that the baronet and Litchfield had corresponded on several occasions in the past, that in and of itself didn't add anything new to the investigation. There'd been talk of an expedition to the Malay Peninsula, but when it had fallen through, the baronet appeared to take it on the chin.

From what Will could tell, Sir Oswald did not seem to have an obvious issue with Charles Darwin or his controversial cowritten paper on natural selection either. Or the fact that Darwin was currently writing a book that would expand on his evolutionary theory.

Indeed, on the whole, Sir Oswald and Darwin appeared to have an amicable professional relationship, nothing more. There was no definitive proof that Sir Oswald had committed any crime.

In any event, Darwin was currently out of Town, so there appeared to be no immediate threat to the man's life despite the "poison-pen letter" he'd been sent. Although that didn't mean that the murderer wouldn't act again, and soon. Five other members of the Linnean Society had been sent threatening letters—all along the lines of "expel Darwin and publicly condemn his paper, or else face the consequences at the end of summer"—and they were all presently in London, so any one of them could be the next target. In a murder investigation, especially a case like this, there was no doubt that time was of the essence.

With a disgruntled sigh, Will pushed himself up from the chair behind the baronet's writing desk. Candle in hand, he made a circuit of the barely lit sitting room one more time to make sure nothing was obviously out of place.

It appeared this was the second wild-goose chase Will had been on today. The journey into St Giles to locate Monty Bertram had ultimately proved fruitless. At this point, Will had never been so frustrated by lack of progress in any direction in all of his life.

And so goddamned tired. The carriage clock on the mantelpiece told him it was almost four in the morning, and he needed to try to snatch a few hours' sleep before his duties called. Lucy—sweet Jesus, he couldn't stop calling her that in his head now—wouldn't be asking him to go riding with her at least.

By the time they'd gotten back to Fleetwood and Will had stabled Juniper, it had been half past one in the morning. And then he'd been obliged to wait a bit longer until he was certain Lucy and her lady's maid had settled for the night. He couldn't risk waking anyone in the part of the house where the bedchambers lay.

The only other place Will could think to search here at

Fleetwood was the steward's office, but he wouldn't do so tonight. The closer it got to dawn, the greater the chance there was of being discovered doing something he shouldn't by one of the servants. Of course, Sir Oswald might also have papers stored somewhere within the Linnean Society's headquarters itself. But that sort of search would have to be conducted by someone who wasn't "a rough Scots groom."

Will quietly quit the room. As he'd already determined, he would present his findings—or lack thereof—to his contact at Scotland Yard, Detective Lawrence, as soon as he could. He'd definitely mention his suspicions about Zachariah Thorne. Now *that* was a line of inquiry that should be followed up. Will would be interested to know if Thorne was also a member of the Raleigh Club. It would be easy enough for Detective Lawrence to find out.

Fleetwood Hall was as quiet as the grave as he descended the servants' stairs to the ground floor. He'd entered the house via the kitchen's back door, having picked the lock in less than a minute, and he intended to exit the same way. Despite his size, he could be light-footed when he needed to be. While he'd honed his reconnaissance skills in the military, he'd had years of sneaking around before that—at Eton to avoid detection by both bullies and overzealous dormitory prefects, and before that at Kyleburn Castle to avoid the biggest bully of all, his father.

But he didn't want to think of the man who'd made his life hell for so many years. The cur didn't deserve a single moment of Will's attention. So, just as he always did, he crumpled up the memory and stuffed it in the locked box in his mind labeled "Kyleburn."

Will was halfway out the door when he heard a snick of a latch behind him.

"Will?"

Damn. He turned to discover Lucy in the doorway on the other side of the room, dressed only in her white-as-snow nightgown and a light silk shawl. The flame of the lit candle she was holding flickered in the draft coming through the open kitchen door, casting dancing patterns of light and shadow over her face and unbound hair.

"What are you doing down here?" she asked, her expression curious rather than suspicious. Her gaze roamed over him, no doubt noting he was dressed simply in breeches, boots, and a loose shirt. As though he'd just thrown something on in a hurry.

Will threw her a sheepish grin, hoping it might charm her a little. "I couldna sleep again," he said, "so I thought another drink of warm milk might help. I have a lot on my mind." At least that last part wasn't a lie.

"Oh…" She closed the door behind her and crossed to the oak table. "It seems to be catching. I couldn't sleep either and came in search of tea." She glanced about the kitchen—the range was dark and cold—then frowned. "You didn't have your milk after all?"

"No…" Will shut the door and leaned against it. "In the end, it seemed like it would be too much bother to get the fire going."

"I don't mind making it for you," she said. "It will only take a few minutes."

Will inwardly groaned. Good Lord, he really did hate warm milk, but if the lass was offering and it helped to cover up the fact he'd been skulking about Fleetwood Hall in the wee small hours for another reason…

Smothering a resigned sigh, he nodded. "Thank you. If you need firewood or kindling, I'd be happy to fetch some."

"No, that won't be necessary," said Lucy, already moving

about the kitchen, efficiently assembling everything she needed. "I can see there's enough in the log basket by the stove. You sit down. I'm sure you're exhausted after the day and night you've had. It's the least I can do."

Will pulled out a chair and sat. "I willna lie, I am more than a wee bit tired," he said, rubbing the back of his neck. Although as he watched Lucy bending down to thrust a match into the range to light the small bundle of kindling inside, there was one part of him that stirred to life with eagerness.

Feeling guilty for ogling her shapely derriere, Will forced himself to look away, and instead studied the back of his clenched fists as they rested on the table. Then again, he wasn't the only one guilty of ogling. The lass had certainly been looking her fill when she'd caught him having a makeshift bath by the water pump beside his cottage.

At least he knew the lusting wasn't one-sided. Far from it.

The memory of Lucy's sweetly enthusiastic kiss, her first kiss, entered his mind. The taste of her and the little moans she'd made when he'd boldly slid his tongue inside her... His unruly cock stirred again.

Part of him was honored that he was the first man to have kissed Miss Lucy Bertram. He hoped it was everything the lass had been hoping for. Twenty-eight years was a long time to wait for something as simple as a kiss. Knowing that she'd offered her kisses to him as coin—the price she'd be willing to pay for his services as a bodyguard—both humbled and dismayed him.

It was unconscionable that Sir Oswald had driven her to such desperate lengths.

Even though he'd offered on impulse to kiss Lucy anytime that she liked, in that moment he had been sincere. Of course, for a thousand reasons, he really shouldn't. But Christ

Almighty, he wasn't a saint. And she was...she was a temptation he couldn't seem to resist.

When she'd told him tonight that she knew all about sexual congress, he'd been thrown and intrigued. And, he couldn't deny it, wildly aroused. Lucy was shy and anxious in many respects, but her matter-of-fact boldness when talking about the act was also damned appealing. He *shouldn't* assume that she was trying to let him know that she'd be interested in more than kisses...but try as he might, he couldn't stop himself from wondering if that *had* been her agenda all along.

The base male in him *really* wanted to find out.

A better, more civilized gentleman would not think about it at all. For one thing, Will would not be staying at Fleetwood for much longer. Once his search for evidence was over, he had no other reason to remain here. And it would also be grossly unfair to take advantage of Lucy's budding sensuality to assuage his own lust when in reality he couldn't offer her more than a few snatched moments of pleasure.

But damn it. Will's jaw tightened. Neither could he stand the idea that Sir Oswald would sell her off to Thorne. Someone like Thorne would destroy her...and Will realized he couldn't bear such a thing.

But what could he possibly do? He lived life in the shadows, pretending to be someone he wasn't, using false names and digging up people's dirty, shameful, and sometimes evil secrets, while Lucy was sweet and good and kind and amusing and intelligent and faultlessly honest... And so goddamn gorgeous he couldn't even think straight whenever she was around.

Especially when she kept bending over like that to check the fire she'd started. And oh, sweet Jesus...now she'd draped her shawl over the end of the chair, and through the thin fabric of her nightgown he could clearly see the outline of her perfectly round breasts. Breasts that reminded him of pomegranates or apples or any other sweetly fleshed globes he'd like to feast on.

He wiped a hand down his face and adjusted his position in the wooden chair to better accommodate his half-aroused cock in his suddenly far-too-tight buckskin breeches. God help him, his mouth was already watering, thinking about all the things they could do...if she would let him.

She'd begun to hum something he vaguely recognized as she stirred his milk and then took the kettle off the hob. "It's almost ready," she called softly over her shoulder. Her pale golden hair was loose and tousled, as though she'd been tossing and turning for hours, and Will itched to bury his hands in the thick cascading mass. To sift the silken locks through his fingers and—

"Here you are." Lucy turned and bought him a mug brimming with steaming milk. "I heated it slowly so it wouldn't catch and burn."

"Thank you, lass. You didna have to."

She smiled, her lavender-blue eyes gleaming softly in the candlelight. "But I wanted to," she said, then turned back to the stove to finish preparing her cup of tea.

She wanted to... What a strange, strange notion. Aside from his dearly departed mother, Will couldn't think of any woman who'd ever wanted to do anything for him out of kindness or caring. In his world, the women he usually consorted with did things that resembled affection. They whispered words to stroke his masculine pride, to arouse him, but none of it was honest or real. It was *convenient*, nothing more.

But this... Will's heart suddenly contracted in the most peculiar way. His chest was far too tight, and his throat ached. Even his skin felt all wrong. Like he no longer belonged in it. And devil take him, the bittersweet emotion suddenly surging through his veins, stealing his breath, cracking the granite encasing his heart was…too much. He didn't know what to do with this. Whatever *this* was… With any of it.

To hide how unsettled he was, he picked up his mug and took a mouthful of the milk. And then he had to swallow a violent curse as the liquid scalded his tongue. *Jesus Christ and all his saints.* He loathed warm milk, and burning-hot milk was even worse. But he'd drink it anyway because Lucy had made it for him and he didn't wish to offend her.

Lucy set a teapot and cup and saucer on the table, then took the seat at his elbow.

"How's the milk?" she asked as she poured out her chamomile tea.

"Verra good," he lied and offered her a reassuring smile. "I'll be sleeping like a wee bairn before too long."

She returned his smile over the rim of her cup. "I'm glad."

They drank in companionable silence for a while, and then Lucy put down her teacup on the saucer. Her gaze was troubled as it met his. "Will…we didn't really talk about this on the way home tonight, but I did wonder when you'd next be available to escort me around St Giles. The clock is ticking, so to speak…"

Guilt sliced deep into Will's gut. His days here were numbered, but nevertheless he felt an obligation to help Lucy as much as he could. He didn't know where the feeling stemmed from—he'd never be the hero she needed—but he couldn't ignore it. "I suppose it all depends on when *you* can manage to get away from here, lass," he said. "As yer father's groom and coachman, I'm obliged to accompany you whenever you venture out and about, so I'm assuming that would include Town. So it seems it's verra much up to you."

She fiddled with the handle of her cup. "Yes, of course, you're right," she said. "I'm clearly not thinking things through properly because I'm so tired and, I suppose, a bit anxious.

Actually, a lot anxious." A sigh escaped her. "As a last resort, I could appeal to one of my friends for help. The one I have in mind, she's rather elevated, but unfortunately, she and her new husband are abroad at present." She laughed, but there was no mirth in the sound. "I could always pawn some of my mother's jewelry so I could afford an English Channel crossing." Another sigh. "The only problem is I'm not exactly sure where my friend is at present. The last I heard she was in Switzerland, but she might have moved on to Italy by now. Her last letter came about a month ago."

Will frowned. "Surely it willna come to that."

Lucy shrugged a slender shoulder. "Unless I find Monty soon, I'm afraid it might. I will *not* marry Zachariah Thorne. If I have to flee England to avoid doing so, I will."

Will pushed his mug of milk away. "Lucy..." He halted at the realization he'd just breached the servant-mistress relationship so very badly. What a complete, imbecilic dunderhead he was.

Lucy had noticed, of course. "You used my first name," she murmured.

"My sincerest apologies, lass. I mean, Miss Bertram. I really shouldn't have used it. It's an unforgivable mistake on my part and—"

She reached out and covered his hand with hers. Her fingers were slender and pale and cool, but still somehow Will felt like he'd been scalded. "I don't mind. In fact, I think I rather like it," she said, her voice low and soft. Like a caress to his soul. "Say it again."

"I..." Will's gaze met her eyes, so large and luminous and as hauntingly beautiful as a mist-wreathed heather moor back home. "Lucy... I—"

He didn't know who moved first, but in the next instant, they were both on their feet and in each other's arms. This kiss was desperate and passionate and clumsy, yet achingly sweet at the same time. Lucy's hands were in his hair, urging him down, pulling him closer as her lips moved frantically beneath his. And her tongue—her tart, slick little tongue—was in his mouth, tangling with his. And his hands...his hands were everywhere. In her tumbling tresses, cupping her face, his thumbs dragging on her lower lip so she'd open wider.

When she yielded to his demand and he delved deep into her mouth, one of his arms lashed her hard against him. And God help him, when she felt his cockstand—she certainly couldn't miss it, he was harder than an iron bar—she ground her hips against his as if seeking satisfaction.

Lust surged hot and hard, and Will lifted Lucy onto the table. Her nightgown hiked up around her knees as her slender legs spread wide to accommodate his body.

"Will," she moaned as he pulled back briefly.

"Do you want to stop?" he managed between panted breaths. "I willna do anything tha' you dinna want me to do."

"No," she whispered huskily. "No, not at all. Just say my name again. I love the way it sounds on your lips."

"Lucy." Will lowered his head and suckled on her ear. Grazed his lips across her flushed cheek until they hovered over her mouth. "My bonny, sweeter-than-honey Lucy."

"Oh, Will." Lucy's kiss was hot and insistent, and Will was swept up in the fervor of it. There was no doubt she was a quick study. And eager and daring. When her hands slid beneath the hem of his cambric shirt and her fingers splayed over his bare torso, he groaned. If she kept this up, he'd be coming in his breeches before too long.

He pushed aside the thick curtain of her hair and dragged his mouth down her fragrant neck, inhaling her floral, feminine scent until he reached the hollow of her throat. He laved it with his tongue, then pressed his lips to the place where her pulse fluttered like delicate butterfly wings in flight. His hand found one of her breasts, and when he squeezed it gently, she moaned and pressed herself into his palm. Her nipple was a tight, hard bud and he ached to kiss and suckle it.

"Lucy… Kisses are not enough, are they, lass?"

"No…no, they're not," she whispered urgently. "I want your mouth on me."

"Here?" He thumbed her nipple through the fabric of her nightgown, and her breath quickened. Her fingers dug into his ribs.

"Yes. Please, yes."

With trembling fingers, Will released the buttons fastening her nightgown's bodice, then dragged the garment down her shoulder until one of her lovely breasts was fully exposed to his gaze. He'd been right. It was plump and perfectly round. Her skin was as satiny smooth as cream and her puckered nipple was as softly pink as a rose petal.

His mouth watering with acute need, he gently pinched that taut peak, then lowered his head and flicked it with his tongue, eliciting another sweet moan. Lucy's fingers speared into his hair. "More," she whispered, and Will couldn't refuse her. He swirled the tip of his tongue around her tight flesh, then captured that delicate bud between his lips, sucking gently, reveling in Lucy's response. How she writhed and trembled and whimpered and openly gave voice to her pleasure.

What a revelation she was. What a delight. Wickedly wonderful thoughts filled Will's head. Beat in his blood. He wanted to strip this woman bare. Introduce her to every carnal pleasure he knew of. God, if they were anywhere else but here in a kitchen—

A noise outside in the corridor made Lucy stiffen, and Will swore and stepped away from her.

"Quick, hide in the pantry," Lucy urged, frantically pulling her nightgown back into place. Will was already halfway there. As he pulled the door shut, he heard another familiar voice.

Mrs. Gilchrist. *Damn.*

"Miss Lucy, what are you doing up so early?"

A light, nervous laugh. "Oh, I couldn't sleep," Lucy replied. "I made warm milk *and* chamomile tea because I couldn't decide which one I wanted more."

"You poor thing. Can I get you something else? Are you hungry?"

"No, no. Well…I… Actually…I wouldn't mind a boiled egg. But when I was in the pantry just before, I noticed the egg basket was empty."

"Are you sure? I thought there were at least half a dozen. Let me check—"

"No, I'm sure there aren't. I can go outside to the henhouse—"

"In your night things? I won't hear of it. I'll fetch the basket and be back in a—"

"Oh, please don't trouble yourself with collecting a whole basketful now. It's far too dark. Just one will do."

A pause. "All right. If you're sure…"

"I am. I'll put the water on to boil while you're gone. There's already some in the kettle."

"Very well, miss."

The back kitchen door opened and closed, and then the handle of the pantry door turned. It was Lucy. "Quick, duck out into the corridor and then exit via the front door. I'll lock up before I return to bed."

Will slid into the kitchen. "Thank you," he murmured, then brushed a swift kiss across Lucy's flushed cheek. He wanted to say more. How sorry he was that he'd completely lost control and nearly brought disaster down on her head; how impressed he was by her ability to think on her feet; and lastly how utterly divine she was. But now wasn't the time or place.

Although, would there ever be a right time or place to tell Lucy anything beyond an apology for crossing a line he should never have crossed?

The sobering thought stayed with Will all the way back to his cottage. Lingered in his mind like a bothersome burr as he collapsed into his bed. Scratched at his conscience until at last his eyelids grew heavy, just as the sun was beginning to steal into his room.

Strange how the soft golden light reminded him of Lucy's flaxen locks, and it was only then that he was able to slip beneath the blanket of sleep...

Chapter Thirteen

THE SUN WAS HIGH IN A CLEAR BLUE SKY AND LUCY WAS busily deadheading the spent roses in the garden bed at the front of Fleetwood Hall when she heard the crunch of horse's hooves on gravel. Looking up, she watched Will ride into the courtyard on Mace, her father's second carriage horse. He flashed her such a roguish grin that her heart did a crazy little skip in her chest.

It had been two whole days since their fruitless foray into the St Giles Rookery and their unforgettable kitchen encounter. Two whole days of secret smiles and a few stolen kisses at odd moments. But there'd been no more middle-of-the-night encounters. Which was for the best, Lucy told herself firmly for the hundredth time. Even when her body longed for Will as she lay sleepless and wanting in her bed. Even when she longed for his company and the way he made her laugh and forget about her worries.

She shouldn't long for him in any way, shape, or form. Because nothing could come of this. It was a dalliance. A little bit of fun. Nothing more.

Will drew close and patted the fine chestnut gelding's glossy neck. "Thank you again for letting me take Mace into Heathwick Green," he said. "And for giving me the afternoon off. You didna have to. Especially after I overslept the other morning."

He didn't have to say "after our late-night tryst." The heated look in his gaze as it swept over her said it all. An unbidden image of her nightgown hitched up around her knees and Will between her thighs while he sucked on her bared breast popped into her head. Her cheeks burned and she imagined that they were probably as red as the roses she'd just been pruning.

Ugh. She clearly wasn't as worldly as she wanted to be.

"Think nothing of it. It's my pleasure," Lucy said as she dipped her head and adjusted her cinder goggles to hide how hot and bothered she'd become. "To be perfectly frank, I think you've been working far too hard and you deserve some time to yourself. And besides, Mace needs the exercise."

Will tipped his broad-brimmed hat at her. "You're sure it's all right for me to stable him at the Wick and Whistle?" His brow furrowed. "As I mentioned before, I willna be back until early evening."

"Yes, of course it is," said Lucy. Apparently Will needed to go into Town to attend to a few personal matters and intended to catch the train. "As far as I know, Father has no plans to take the carriage out today. I'm certain it won't be a problem."

Will nodded. "If you're sure…"

Lucy smiled. "I am. I hope you get everything done that you need to."

A shadow passed across Will's handsome face, but then it was gone, so perhaps it had been a trick of the light. "I expect so," he said, then tilted his head. "I shall see you in a few hours."

As he cantered away on Mace, Lucy briefly wondered what attending to "a few personal matters" entailed. Was it related to his family or was it was just something as prosaic as visiting a bank or making a purchase or seeing friends? She couldn't imagine a man like Will *wouldn't* have friends. Male or female… Of course, it really was none of her business.

She sighed and began cutting roses and placing them carefully in a basket to use in floral arrangements about the house.

She wasn't sure what the coming days would bring, but now, more than ever, she was determined to find Monty. And if she didn't, she *would* leave England altogether and seek refuge with Artemis rather than submit to her father's plan to marry her off to Mr. Thorne.

Sometime in the near future, she would venture into Town herself and conduct research into pawn shops. Mr. Delaney, Jane's grandfather, might know of some reputable ones. Given her current circumstances, it was best to be prepared for any eventuality. Although part of her also quailed at the idea of having to journey to the Continent all by herself. Her elderly cousin, Mabel Babbington, who resided in Shropshire, wouldn't be up to the journey. She could always ask Jane, but she would probably be reluctant to leave her grandfather who seemed to rely on her support in his bookstore more and more these days.

A male companion would be even more desirable, and part of her did wonder if Will might be persuaded to join her on the journey. She would pay him a proper wage out of the money she received from selling her mother's jewelry.

But when she found Artemis...*if* she found Artemis, then what?

Would Artemis's husband, the Duke of Dartmoor, help Will to secure another position, since Lucy wouldn't be able to employ the groom on an ongoing basis?

One thing was certain, there was no future for her and Will, no matter how much her heart did a little dance every time she saw him. In her romantic fantasies, baronets' daughters might be able to wed handsome, chivalrous grooms, but not in real life.

Besides, she didn't want to marry anyone, she reminded herself. She valued her freedom. And from what Will had told her, he didn't wish to wed either.

If she was at all sensible, she would end this highly improper "affair" before her heart really did become involved and she got hurt. That was the real danger, not falling pregnant and becoming an unwed mother. Thanks to Artemis, who'd once loaned her a quite practical book called *Every Woman's Book; Or, What is Love?*, and her own knowledge of biology, Lucy knew that there were several ways to prevent conception. Well, as long as the man one was involved with cared enough to prevent such an eventuality too. And Lucy had an inkling that Will might. If she was willing to continue their liaison.

She'd just moved on to the rose garden on the other side of the drive to cut a few more pink and apricot blooms when she heard the crunch of gravel again. Had Will forgotten something?

When Lucy turned and looked toward Fleetwood's gates, it wasn't Will at all. It was a smart black cabriolet and the gentleman mastering the reins was none other than Zachariah Thorne.

Barnaby Rudge and buckets of fudge. Why hadn't Father warned her that the Yorkshireman would be paying a visit today?

Lucy's stomach pitched as Thorne reined in his sleek bay gelding and the cabriolet drew to a stop beside her. Not because of what she was wearing—the more unappealing she looked the better, as far as she was concerned. No, it was simply because it was Thorne.

The Yorkshireman's hard, dark gaze slid over her, assessing her appearance, and his lip curled ever so slightly. "Miss Bertram, at the risk of sounding rude, I feel compelled to ask: What on earth are you wearing?"

Lucy refused to be shamed. She tipped her cinder glasses down and gave Thorne a speaking look. "Goggles and bloomers. I always wear them when I'm gardening, especially in Fleetwood's poisons garden. It protects me from anything noxious. Well"—she raised a brow—"usually."

Oh, did she really just say that? Mr. Thorne's thick black

brows arrowed into a frown, but before he summoned a response, Fleetwood's front door opened and her father appeared. "Thorne, welcome," he called. "I got your telegram." And then his uneasy gaze darted to Lucy as he descended the steps.

"Mr. Thorne will be joining us for lunch today," he said as he drew closer.

"And afterward, Miss Bertram, I propose to take you for a jaunt around Hyde Park," added the Yorkshireman.

Gah! Why was Thorne so persistent when his attentions were clearly not welcome? Unable to hide her chagrin at being ambushed like this, Lucy lifted her chin a notch as she addressed her father. "Why didn't you warn me about all of this earlier, Papa?"

Her father's cheeks reddened. "Now, now, Lucy," he said in a low voice, "I would be most grateful if you didn't make a fuss. It's only lunch and a brief excursion. And if you could change into attire that's more suited to the occasion, I would appreciate that too."

"Humph." Lucy picked up her basket of roses. "I suppose you'll also want me to check with Mrs. Gilchrist on how the lunch preparations are coming along."

"Yes…if you wouldn't mind. And perhaps you could also tell her that I won't require dinner tonight. There's a function at the Raleigh Club that I'd forgotten about. After Thorne returns from Hyde Park, I'll go back to Town with him. We're both attending."

Even though the idea of spending a few hours in Thorne's company rankled, Lucy decided she would comply to mollify her father. If he was busy in Town all night, she'd have yet another opportunity to look for Monty. So she bowed her head and murmured a suitably contrite "Yes, Papa" and prayed the afternoon wasn't going to be as hideous as she anticipated it would be.

———

Although he hadn't dispensed with his simple groom's attire, Will *did* discard his Scots accent when he met with his contact at Scotland Yard, Detective John Lawrence. Slipping into a refined, upper-class English accent—the one his grandfather used and the one he'd been forced to adopt at Eton to avoid being bullied—was something Will was able to do without any thought at all. "I hate to say it, Lawrence," he said as he removed his hat, then settled back into a cracked leather bench seat at the back of the Cockspur Tavern, "but since my arrival at Fleetwood Hall, I haven't been able to find any concrete evidence that incriminates Sir Oswald."

The detective frowned at Will over the rim of his tankard. Well, Will thought it was a frown. Lawrence habitually wore a grim expression and the Cockspur *was* rather dark and dingy. But it wasn't far from Whitehall, where the offices of Scotland Yard were located, so it was a convenient spot to meet.

"Well, that's a bit of a blow," Lawrence said, putting down his ale. "Nothing at all?"

"I'm afraid that anything I've gleaned is purely circumstantial." And then Will outlined what had led him to his conclusion. "However, I do have another firm suspect in my sights," he added. "An acquaintance of Sir Oswald by the name of Zachariah Thorne. He's a wealthy entrepreneur and a fellow member of the Linnean Society."

Lawrence drummed his fingers on the sticky, scarred table between them. "So are lots of men. You'll have to give me more than that."

"Of course. Thorne is somewhat of a religious zealot. A

fire-and-brimstone Calvinist. And he's staunchly opposed to Charles Darwin's theory of evolution by natural selection. Apparently he was very upset by the fact that Darwin's scientific paper on the subject was presented at the Linnean Society's meeting on the first of July, and that it recently appeared in the society's zoological journal. Thorne is also a member of Boodle's, which of course is probably neither here nor there, but it would be interesting to find out if he's also a member of the Raleigh Club. He owns coffee plantations in Ceylon, so he'd be eligible to join."

"Now you've piqued my interest." Lawrence's gaze narrowed. "I take it you've met this Thorne, then? At Fleetwood Hall?"

"Yes," said Will. "Unfortunately, that means it will be difficult for me to conduct any further investigation in and around the Linnean Society and the Raleigh Club. Both Sir Oswald and Thorne know me as William Armstrong, Scots groom."

"True," said Lawrence. "However, I wouldn't rule Sir Oswald out *just* yet. We both know that the perpetrator, whoever he is, must have procured the poison that killed Litchfield from someone with specialist knowledge. Not everyone knows how to turn regular powdered strychnine into such a potent, readily soluble form. But now that you have identified this Thorne as someone with an apparent motive, I want you to see what else you can dig up about him and his connection with Sir Oswald. Is it a friendship or is it a business relationship or something else entirely?"

Will's mouth twisted. "I know one thing. Sir Oswald seems determined to marry his daughter, Miss Lucy Bertram, off to Thorne. From what I understand, the baronet's financial situation is growing more dire by the day, but if his daughter and Thorne wed, he expects some kind of windfall. Miss Bertram detests Thorne and wants nothing to do with him, but Sir Oswald insists that she must accept the man's suit."

"Hmmm." Lawrence rubbed his chin. "My apologies for sounding blunt, but is that all this Zachariah Thorne gains? A wife? Why would he take on Sir Oswald's debts? We both know the marriage mart is full of young women with substantial dowries. So why Miss Bertram? Is Thorne in love with her?"

"Miss Bertram is extraordinarily pretty and intelligent, I'll give you that. But they only met two and a half weeks ago, so I shouldn't think so."

"Well, that's a line of inquiry that definitely needs further following up. If Thorne *isn't* besotted, what else does he get out of this apparent arrangement he has with the baronet? There must be something behind it. I'll definitely get one of my men to see if Thorne is a member of the Raleigh Club and if he was present on the night Litchfield was killed." The detective paused to take another sip of his ale, then added, "I should also let you know that there's been another development in the case in the last twenty-four hours."

The grim tone of Lawrence's voice, the man's dark expression, made Will's blood run cold. "What do you mean?"

"Our perpetrator has been busy sending threatening letters to Charles Darwin again."

Will frowned. "It's not well known where Darwin is staying though, is it?"

"No. Hardly anyone knows he's on the Isle of Wight. So that's interesting in and of itself. But that's not the only detail that's significant. On this occasion, the envelope didn't just contain a sheet of paper. There was also a substantial amount of an unidentified light-brown powder inside. Darwin thought it was simply pounce at first. But since handling the letter, a rash has broken out on his hands and arms, and he's been having bouts of vomiting. His physician isn't sure what ails him—apparently Darwin has suffered bouts of ill health on and off for some time, so his illness might not be related to the powder at all. Our man on the Isle of Wight will continue to monitor Darwin's condition and send word if, God forbid, he takes a turn for the worse. And of course, the powder will be analyzed to see if it contains strychnine or any other toxic substance. I'm expecting a sample to arrive later this afternoon."

"So you think someone definitely attempted to poison him?" Lawrence grimaced. "It would seem so. Time will tell."

Will nodded. "What did the letter say? Where did it originate?"

"It appears to have been sent from a post office just off Piccadilly, not far from the Linnean Society headquarters, two days ago. And it essentially repeated the same sentiments of the original missive: Quit the Linnean Society and cease spreading your heretical 'theories' about natural selection and evolution, or you'll meet the same fate as that evildoer Litchfield."

"Evildoer Litchfield?" Will frowned. "That language didn't appear in the previous letter Darwin received, did it? Or any of the other letters sent out?"

"No," said Lawrence. "But it makes me curious about Thorne. If he is a staunch Calvinist as you say, he might have very strong views on who he considers 'saved' or 'damned.' Who is good or evil."

"Agreed. But that also begs the question, what did Lord Litchfield do that could be classed as 'evil'? And how well did Thorne know Litchfield, if at all?" Will pondered the froth on top of his own ale for a moment. "Was Litchfield a Catholic perhaps? I've heard Thorne speak disparagingly of 'papists' before."

"No. As far as I know, the viscount was a member of the Church of England."

Will blew out a sigh. "I'm sincerely sorry I haven't unearthed anything else. And I do worry that I won't find what you need at Fleetwood Hall. I've still got the steward's office to search of course, but"—Will shrugged—"after that, I'm not sure what else I can do."

John Lawrence cast Will a sly look. "It sounds like you've gained the confidence of the baronet's 'extraordinarily pretty daughter' though, so continuing to cultivate that relationship might be worthwhile. At least for the moment. If nothing else, perhaps Miss Bertram will continue to shed further light on her father's situation and his odd acquaintanceship with Thorne."

"I'll do my best," said Will.

They briefly discussed a more efficient method for Will to get a message to Lawrence. The detective provided him with an address in Covent Garden he could safely send a telegram to without arousing the suspicion of the staff at the Hampstead telegraph office. And then they bid each other farewell.

When Will stepped outside the Cockspur onto the street, he rubbed a hand though his hair before donning his hat. As much as he wanted to return to Fleetwood Hall to see Lucy— and he really *didn't* want to think about why he wanted to see her again so soon after only a few hours away from her—he had one more thing he needed to attend to in Town.

The hansom cab he hired took only fifteen minutes to drop him at Kyleburn House in Belgravia. It seemed like forever since Will had walked through the sleek black door of his town house. In actual fact, it had only been two and a half weeks ago.

His butler, Hillier, greeted him in the vestibule. "My lord. Welcome home."

Will smiled as he handed his hat and plain sack coat to one of his footmen. "Thank you, Hillier," he said. "I won't be here for long. I just dropped by to check my correspondence."

The middle-aged butler bowed. "Very good, my lord. It's waiting for you on your desk in the library." He cocked a brow, "I assume you would like a pot of coffee sent up?"

"I would. And a few sandwiches too."

Hillier beamed. "I'm sure Cook will be delighted. She misses you, you know. I'll arrange it all at once."

Will scaled the wide, polished oak stairs to his library and sank into the comfortable leather chair behind the large walnut desk. His correspondence sat neatly in a pile in the middle of the dark-green leather blotter. With a sigh, he picked up a handful of missives and began to sort them. Bills, a few letters from his man of business. Another from his steward at Kyleburn... And then there was an envelope embossed with the Duke of Ayr's coat of arms.

Damn. What the blazing hell did his grandfather want? It had been over three years since Will had heard anything from him. He briefly contemplated burning the letter. But there wasn't a fire in the grate or any lit candles at hand at three o'clock on a fine summer's afternoon.

With a curse, he sliced open the gummed flap with the blade of his letter opener—oddly, there was no wax seal on the back—then pulled out the single sheet of fine paper...and his heart lurched, almost stumbling to a complete halt.

The letter wasn't from the duke, but his personal secretary.

My Lord,

I hope this missive finds you in good health. However, I'm afraid to report that the same cannot be said for His Grace. Unfortunately, your grandfather recently suffered an attack of apoplexy. Subsequently, he has requested that I write to you on his behalf to inform you of this turn of events as presently he cannot do so himself.

His Grace's physician has reported that while your grandfather's condition is likely to improve somewhat over the coming weeks—he has some facial and upper limb weakness on the right side of his body, but his other faculties seem sound—he may still suffer another attack which may have an outcome that is far worse. Such is often the case with apoplexy.

His Grace is resting comfortably and he wishes to invite you to Braeburn Castle, as he has a great desire to see you. He awaits your reply.

Yours faithfully,

S. Cathcart

Secretary to His Grace, the Duke of Ayr

Will put down the letter, pushed out of his chair, then crossed the room to pour himself a double dram of whisky. His thoughts careened about in his head, while his gut was a mass of complicated knots.

His grandfather, the man he'd despised for so long—the man he'd once told that the dukedom could go to Hades—could have died. And he still wasn't completely out of the woods yet. Which meant…Will had some soul-searching to do.

Should he abandon the Linnean Society murder case to rush to Ayrshire to visit the sickbed of a man he'd long ago decided deserved his back and nothing more? A man and a family name he'd reviled so much that he'd joined Her Majesty's army, not caring that if he perished on the battlefield the dukedom would die with him?

But if his grandfather did die, what then?

Will downed the whisky with barely a grimace and poured another before he returned to his desk.

Could he really turn his back on the dukedom and all of the

responsibilities that came with it? Like managing the Duke of Ayr's vast estates. His ducal responsibilities in Parliament. How could he continue to exist in the shadows, pretending to be someone he wasn't, for the rest of his life?

And how could he abandon Lucy? How could he leave her to deal with a beast like Thorne all on her own? A wave of fury rolled through him whenever he thought of that cur being *anywhere* in her vicinity. If he couldn't find the lass's brother in the next few days, he'd definitely help her to leave England so she could join her "well-elevated" friend on the Continent.

Will sighed as he pulled out a fresh sheet of paper bearing the Earl of Kyle's seal. One thing was clear: in a short space of time, the lass had managed to effortlessly twine herself around him, tangling him up in some sort of strange, delicate web that he wasn't sure he wanted to escape from. And that was a worry. In fact, he should be terrified.

Picking up a pen, he dipped the nib in the inkwell.

Even though he wasn't certain what the future might hold for him and Lucy, at least there was no longer a doubt in his mind about how he should respond to Mr. Cathcart's letter.

Chapter Fourteen

THE AFTERNOON *WAS* ALL KINDS OF HIDEOUS.

It hadn't taken Lucy long to regret her decision to appease her father. Sitting beside Zachariah Thorne for the half-hour journey into London, combined with nearly an hour-long drive around Hyde Park, was excruciating in the extreme.

Of course, Lucy knew their excursion was going to be off to a bad start as soon as she appeared in Fleetwood's drive in a plain gray carriage gown and black bonnet; it was attire more appropriate for someone in half mourning than going on a "jaunt" with a suitor on a fine late-summer's day.

After earning a lip curl from Thorne earlier on when he'd come upon her in the rose garden in bloomers and goggles, she certainly wasn't going to make an effort to "look pretty" as she'd done when he'd first come to dinner. Her carriage gown hadn't provoked another sneer, but the man's gaze was decidedly cool as he handed her into the cabriolet.

The cooler the better, as far as Lucy was concerned.

A chill atmosphere persisted, as they barely said anything to each other throughout the journey. And indeed, whenever Thorne did venture an innocuous comment or question about the weather or the traffic or the scenery in the Park, Lucy gave the briefest of replies. When Thorne eventually drove them through the Wellington Arch at Hyde Park Corner, Lucy did have cause to make a remark when he turned off toward Piccadilly.

"Where are we going?" she asked. "This isn't the way back to Hampstead."

"I know," he said in that harsh voice of his that reminded Lucy of unpleasant things like the grinding of metal or nails on a chalkboard. "I thought I'd spoil you by taking you to Gunter's, and Berkeley Square isn't all that far. I hear their ices are very good."

Lucy cast him a disbelieving look. *Spoil me? Ugh. Please don't prolong this whole awkward experience to impress me.* But she curbed her retort and instead said, "You've never been to Gunter's before? It's the most famous tea shop in London."

Thorne shrugged a shoulder. "I don't particularly enjoy sweet things," he said. "But I thought you might like some ice cream or sorbet. It is a warm day and you are wearing... Well..." Another shrug. "It looks like your gown is rather stuffy and I thought you might be hot."

"You don't like my attire?" she said flatly. Of course, her long-sleeved gown of gray cotton piqué was a bit prim and "stuffy," but why should she dress up in fine silk and muslin and lace and pretty beribboned hats for a man she could barely stand? Now if the man beside her was Will Armstrong...

Thorne directed his horse to turn into Berkeley Street before he spoke again. "I did hope that you'd make some sort of effort, considering the trouble I've taken this afternoon to woo you."

Lucy's mouth dropped open. This time, she couldn't contain her irritation. "Trouble you've taken?" she repeated. "Pray, sir, you do not need to trouble yourself on my account. Ever again. And if this is your idea of 'wooing,' I would prefer not to be subjected to it."

A muscle pulsed in Thorne's jaw, but he kept his eyes ahead on the traffic. "Your father told me you were amenable to my attentions."

"My father is wrong."

"Then why did you agree to spend time with me, Miss Bertram?"

"Believe me when I say I have no idea why." Of course she *did* know the reason why, but she couldn't very well say.

The Yorkshireman drew the cabriolet to a halt beneath one of the enormous plane trees beside the park in the middle of Berkeley Square. "You should at least give me an opportunity to prove myself to be a worthy suitor," he said stiffly.

Lucy had clearly pressed on a nerve, but at this point she didn't much care. Drawing in a bracing breath, she turned to face the man. It was about time she dispelled his illusions and put him out of his misguided misery. "Mr. Thorne," she began, "I'm sorry, but I have no idea why you have taken an interest in me. We have nothing in common. Our views and opinions on many fundamental matters do not align. And besides all of that, I do not wish to marry. It seems my father has led you to believe otherwise."

His jaw took on a mulish set. "It is unnatural for a young woman like you *not* to want to do so."

"Unnatural?" Lucy couldn't keep the note of incredulity out of her voice. "Next you'll be telling me that it is unnatural that some women want to study at university and have a professional career. Or write scientific papers or read Gothic novels. Or that they do not want to have babies."

His gaze was hard. "It is."

"Well, it seems we are at an impasse, Mr. Thorne. Because I believe the complete opposite to you. We do not suit now, nor will we ever."

"You're wrong. I firmly believe that I could help you to change. To see the error of your ways. To understand the Lord's grand design. If you were my wife, I could save you—"

"You want to marry me to *save* me? You think I'm a wicked

sinner and damned? Well, thank you so very much for impugning my character, and indeed my very soul."

Thorne shifted in his seat. It was the first time Lucy had seen him look uncomfortable. But his next words confirmed that he agreed with everything she'd just said. "No one is perfect and we are all tainted to some degree, Miss Bertram. Some more than others. However"—he faced her, and as he reached for her gloved hand, his dark eyes gleamed with a fervor which seemed almost lust-ridden—"I do believe it would be a shame for someone as pretty as you to end up in the fiery pit for all eternity. It is my duty as a Christian to rein in your sinful pride—"

Lucy snatched her hand away. "Oh, please. Spare me from your duty." A waiter from Gunter's appeared and she cast him a smile she hoped was friendly. "Sir, if you wouldn't mind helping me down…"

"What?" snapped Thorne. "You're leaving?"

"You expect me to stay after insulting me so roundly? And for taking liberties without asking permission?" Thorne had only clasped her hand momentarily, but there'd been something about the proprietorial way he'd done so that had unsettled Lucy greatly. The slightly taken-aback waiter offered a hand which she took and then alighted onto the cobbled ground.

"Mark my words, I'll be speaking to your father about your conduct, Miss Bertram," gritted out Thorne.

"Go ahead," said Lucy, shaking out her skirts. "Because I will certainly be speaking to him about yours too."

"I've been nothing but a perfect gentleman. And you seem to have completely missed the fact that I just declared you to be pretty."

"Oh, yes, but how perfectly gentlemanly it is of you to inform me that I'm also a damned soul in your eyes. Good day, Mr. Thorne. I'd rather walk my wicked self all the way back to Heathwick Green than spend another moment with you." And with that, Lucy turned on her booted heel and marched away across the square in the direction of Bruton Street. It wasn't so very far to Euston Station. She'd catch a train back to Hampstead, and if Mace wasn't still stabled at the Wick and Whistle, she'd walk home to Fleetwood Hall.

Maybe somewhere along the way she'd cool down.

———

The pavement in front of Euston Station was a swarming hive of activity when Will leapt down from a hansom cab. Nevertheless, he spotted Miss Lucy Bertram in the crowd almost immediately. She might be wearing a duller-than-dull gray gown, but her pale-gold hair and rosy-cheeked countenance caught his eye.

"Miss Bertram," he called out, waving a hand, and when she stopped and turned and their eyes met, her frown disappeared and a delightful smile broke across her lovely face.

"Will," she said when he reached her side. "We are well met indeed. I take it you've concluded your business in Town for the day?"

"I have." His gaze wandered over her face, drinking her in. And then he admonished himself for acting like a besotted schoolboy. He needed to be more circumspect, for both their sakes. Before things got out of hand.

When Lucy didn't say anything else, he ventured, "If you dinna mind me asking, why are you here? And all alone? I would have gladly come with you if you'd needed an escort."

"Oh…" She glanced away and a small line appeared between her finely drawn brows before her gaze returned to his face. "I was obliged to accompany Mr. Thorne into Town. He dropped by Fleetwood in his cabriolet, and then…" She sighed. "It seemed far easier to accept Thorne's invitation to go on an excursion about Hyde Park than to refuse and create a big fuss." Her pretty mouth curved into a smile that didn't quite meet her eyes. "What a mistake that turned out to be."

Now it was Will's turn to frown. "He isna driving you back to Fleetwood Hall?"

"We…we had a difference of opinion. A disagreement. I decided that I would prefer to make my own way home."

Hot anger flared and Will had to force himself to adopt a mild tone. "He didna hurt you, did he, lass?"

"Oh, no…nothing like that. Well, he did insult my character." Her smile became genuine as she added, "But I returned the favor, so I think we were even at the end."

"I'm verra glad to hear it."

"Well…" Lucy glanced toward the entrance to the station. "I suppose we could catch the train back to Hampstead together. Or…" She clasped her gloved fingers together in front of her chest in an entreating gesture. "I don't want to put any pressure on you, Will, because I did give you the whole day off… But we could venture into St Giles and take a look about the High Street for Monty. At this time, many of the shops will still be open and nightfall is hours and hours away. I'm sure it won't be as dangerous as last time… Not only that"—she gestured at her attire— "but I'm wearing a carriage gown sans crinoline. And look…" She pointed her toe out from beneath her skirts. "I've got boring half-boots on so if we need to make a run for it, it won't be a problem." She dropped her voice. "I'm afraid I do have my coin purse with me, but it's secreted in my pocket which I promise not to put my hand into. In fact, I'll have no need to because I didn't bring a scalpel with me either. All right?"

"Hmmm." Will scratched his jaw. "That's all well and good but… I dinna want to be a wet blanket, lass, but won't your father notice your absence? He might be worried about you when you dinna return from your outing with Thorne."

Lucy frowned. "You're right. Although I could dash off a telegram to let him know I'm fine and that I'm catching the train home. That should appease him. Honestly though..." Another sigh. "I don't think he'll care all that much because tonight he's returning to Town for a function at the Raleigh Club with Mr. Thorne. If he doesn't stay at the club itself, he'll probably spend the night at Thorne's Belgravia town house again."

Will's blood quickened. "The Raleigh Club? As in Sir Walter Raleigh?"

"The very same," said Lucy. "It's an exclusive gentlemen's club for men who have ties to the colonies or are fond of exploring or traveling abroad in general. My father and Mr. Thorne are both members."

"Ah. I see," said Will. What a bloody shame it was that he couldn't dash over to Scotland Yard right this minute to let Lawrence know. But he might be able to send a telegram... Lucy would notice, but he could always just claim he'd forgotten something on his to-do list. That might work.

He suddenly wished that he could take her into his confidence, but that was impossible given the nature of his work. Her father and her would-be suitor were prime suspects in an ongoing murder investigation. Unless and until he withdrew himself from the case, a lie it would have to be, no matter that it weighed heavily on his conscience. "Verra well, lass," he said. "Let's visit that telegram office. And then we'll go looking for your brother."

Chapter Fifteen

LUCY WASN'T SURE IF IT WAS BETTER OR WORSE VISITING ST Giles when there was still sufficient daylight.

In some ways, she felt safer because there were certainly more people about and they weren't hiding in the shadows: costermongers with their barrows and carts of oranges and onions and potatoes, herring and eel and pickled cockles, trotters and dripping, and loaves of bread; hawkers and peddlers of anything one could imagine—broken candles and buttons and rusted pots and pans, threadbare secondhand clothes and even birds in cages; newspaper boys and matchstick girls; street sweepers and weary-eyed vagabonds.

And then there were haggard men in their worn-out coats, huddled together in tight knots, or watching passersby from doorways and the dark mouths of alleys. The prostitutes who called out to Will and other women lugging buckets of water or emptying out slops or haggling with street vendors. And everywhere there were clusters of children, with their grubby faces and far-too-ragged clothes, sitting on steps and in the gutters or darting past. One blink and they were gone.

However, because darkness hadn't yet descended, it also meant that Lucy could be seen. Even though her clothes were plain, they weren't careworn or filthy, and despite the fact that Will was by her side, she quickly became a target for every single hawker selling something on the High Street and any nearby thoroughfares.

But the incessant noise and bustle and constant harassment

weren't the worst things. No, the most awful thing was the overpowering stench. The heat of the day had intensified anything that was malodorous, to the point Lucy could barely stand to take a breath. How anyone endured living here in this overcrowded, forsaken part of London she had no idea. It made her heart weep to think that some people lived in such dire circumstances their entire lives.

It made her lament the fact that her family's slide into genteel poverty would be unfortunate, but in no way could it compare to *this*. And it made her ashamed that she'd been living in such blissful ignorance for so long.

"Will, I'm such a fool," she said after her stoically patient bodyguard had chased off yet another peddler hassling her to buy his wares—this time chipped china and tarnished, mismatched silverware that had probably been pilfered. "This wasn't a good idea. We should leave."

Will's expression was grave but kind. "Aye, I think you may be right, lass." He nodded at the dark clouds amassing above the jagged rooflines and the nearby spire of St Giles-in-the-Fields Church. In the distance, thunder grumbled. "Besides, it looks like a storm is brewing."

Lucy sighed. Disappointment dragged at her and she had to swallow back a sudden rush of hot tears. "I can't even imagine Monty in this place—" She broke off.

There was a man. Tall with blond hair and wide shoulders in a plaid cap and dark sack coat, pushing his way through the crowd. Walking rapidly away from them with long-legged strides toward Shaftesbury Avenue.

She clutched Will's arm. "It's him. It's Monty," she breathed. "I'm sure it's him."

"Where?"

She pointed. "Up there. We must hurry."

Picking up her skirts, she started forward, but her progress was hampered by the thick, constantly moving throng of bodies and the maze of carts and barrows and random crates and barrels and baskets. Will somehow kept pace with her as she ducked and weaved, twisted and turned, stopped and started and sidestepped until she had no idea where she was and had completely lost sight of the man she thought might have been her brother.

When she at last stumbled to a halt, Will at her heels, they seemed to be in a narrow, shadow-filled laneway that was unnaturally quiet compared to the High Street. The buildings surrounding them were a hodgepodge of architectural styles, and any windows Lucy spied were cracked or broken and the holes stuffed with sacking or rags. A one-eyed cat sniffed at a nearby pile of rotting refuse.

Lucy leaned back against a rough brick wall to catch her breath, which came in ragged puffs. Perspiration trickled down her spine and she tried not to gag as she sucked in the fetid, humid air. Will, on the other hand, seemed barely out of breath at all. Curse him.

"We're not far from Seven Dials and Neale's Yard," said Will, his voice grim. He gently clasped her arm. "I dinna want to alarm you, but I do no' like the feel of this place. We should head back toward the High Street before—"

"Well, 'ello, 'ello, 'ello. Who do we 'ave 'ere? A pretty little ladybird an 'er 'andsome fancy man per'aps. Trespassin' on *my* turf."

Oh no... "Flapping flapdragons," Lucy whispered and her heart all but stopped. Standing but a few feet behind Will was a lean, sallow-faced man with long, limp hair hanging in matted strands about his shoulders. In his hand was a dull-bladed knife which he tossed in the air and caught again like he was merely playing with a ball. And just behind him was a smirk-ing, hard-eyed woman in a stained red sateen gown. The hem was ragged and the lace around the far-too-low neckline was tattered and torn. Her lower lids were smudged with something black like kohl or candle soot, and her pale-red hair was a tangled bird's nest.

Will turned around ever so slowly, reminding Lucy of a predator sizing up its prey before it pounced. Though his reply to the other man—a pimp, perhaps—was mild enough. "I'm afraid you've misread the situation," he said, his voice a low rumble. "We dinna want any trouble. We took a wrong turn, that's all. In fact, we're on our way back to the High Street."

"Oh, really? And why should I believe you?"

When Will didn't immediately answer, the pimp moved a step closer and somehow Will seemed to grow bigger. He stood taller and, beneath his coat, his broad shoulders were a rigid line. His change in stance must have put off the pimp as the man's dark eyes momentarily flared wide. But then his gaze grew hard. Watchful.

Calculating.

And still he tossed the knife almost lazily.

Oh God. Lucy swallowed. Her chest was so tight her breath felt like it was trapped in her lungs. Her legs were trembling so much she could hardly hold up her weight. If that man lunged at Will with that knife. Or threw it… She suddenly wished she'd thought to bring some sort of weapon with her. Not that her little scalpel could compete with such a large knife, which was really more of a dagger. But it would be better than nothing, surely.

The prostitute giggled, startling her. "Ain't you a fine strap-ping sort," she crooned, as her gaze wandered over Will. "I bet you're well hung—"

"Shut it, Polly," the man snapped. He waved the knife toward

Will, and Lucy couldn't contain a gasp. "Clear out yer pockets. Both of you. And I might let you go on your way unhurt."

But Will shook his head. "Let the lass leave. And then I'll do as you ask."

The pimp snorted. "I'm not bleedin' fick in the 'ead now, am I? Anyone can tell she's no' from around 'ere. Too 'igh in the instep, she is, wiv 'er far-too-pretty 'air and face and 'er fancy-Nancy clothes. I bet she's got coin somewhere on 'er. Oi, Polly." He waved the knife toward Lucy. "Go search 'er."

The prostitute started forward but Will held up a hand and she halted immediately. "Polly, I wouldna go near her if I were you." Over his shoulder, he called, "Lass. Run."

Lucy didn't have to be told twice. Her heart in her mouth, her pulse already bolting clean away, she picked up her skirts and took off. If she could make it back to Shaftesbury Avenue, or anywhere at all where there were others, she might be able to summon help—

And then there was a quicksilver flash and something darted under her skirts and between her feet—the blasted alley cat—and then she pitched forward, landing on the filthy cobblestones on her hands and knees.

Even though white-hot pain lanced up her arms and through her kneecaps, and terror gripped her insides, Lucy forced herself to move, to drag herself to her feet. And when she dared to look back to see how Will fared, or if anyone was in pursuit, it was to discover that the pimp was lying in the middle of the street, clutching his jaw and groaning, while Polly knelt over him, calling his name and crying. And the pimp's knife was in Will's hand. And he was all right.

Oh, thank God. Lucy emitted a sob and as she clutched at the bricks behind her, Will turned…and then he was rushing toward her with ground-eating strides. Thunder cracked, lightning flashed, and all at once the heavens opened and it began to pour as Will reached her side.

"Lass, I told you to—"

"I did," she returned, her voice no more than a fractured whisper, her face wet with tears and raindrops. "I did run... I'm sorry. I tripped and fell."

A muscle pulsed in Will's jaw. His hair was plastered to his forehead, and in the gloom, his blue eyes were as dark as midnight. "Are you hurt?"

"Just scraped and bruised knees."

He nodded. Once. "Good." And then he grasped the back of her head, pulled her in, and kissed her. It was hard and fierce and quick, and when he released her, he tossed the knife into the gutter, threaded his fingers through hers, and they hastened back toward the High Street, neither of them looking back.

———

In the end, they didn't catch the train from Euston Station back to Hampstead. Instead, Lucy offered to pay for a hackney cab to take them all the way back to Fleetwood Hall. She had enough in her coin purse to cover the fare, and considering her knees stung and ached and they were both soaked to the skin by the time Will hailed down a driver who was happy to make the journey, it seemed like a good use of what little money she had.

So much had happened in the Rookery that Lucy's mind was spinning as the hackney began to plow its way through London's teeming streets.

"Do you really think that was Monty?" asked Will. In the dark confines of the hackney, his blue eyes gleamed as they met Lucy's.

"I'm certain it was. I'd recognize him anywhere." She frowned.

"I desperately want to go back and continue our search, but after what just happened, it's clear to me it's far too dangerous."

"Aye," agreed Will. "I willna take you again. I hope you understand. If anything happened to you—" He broke off, and from the way his jaw clenched, Lucy knew he was recalling those fraught moments in the alleyway. "Your father would kill me, for one thing. And I wouldna blame him."

Lucy touched Will's arm. "What happened isn't your fault. It's mine. I made you take me even though I stood out like a sore thumb, and then I foolishly ran off. So I do understand." She sighed heavily, then added, "If only I had a network of spies in St Giles. Or at least the means to hire an inquiry agent. Why, a lookout who could keep watch would do too. But I have no idea how to go about arranging anything like that."

Will's expression changed. Grew thoughtful. "You're a canny lass," he said. "And dinna let anyone tell you otherwise."

He settled back against the seat and gathered Lucy close. She closed her eyes and for a few minutes allowed herself to bask in Will's praise and the simple joy of being held. How lovely it felt to be snuggled against his big strong warm body with her cheek against his chest. How comforting it was to listen to the steady thud of his heart. But then a vision of the smirking, knife-wielding pimp intruded into her mind and she couldn't stay there in Will's arms a second longer.

She withdrew from his embrace and sat up straight.

"What is it, lass?" he asked, his brows arrowing into a frown. His gaze was filled with concern as he studied her.

Outside, heavy rain beat against the hackney's windows—an erratic tattoo that matched the uneven rhythm of her own heart. "You could have been killed too..." she murmured. Her voice cracked and tears pricked. "I–I'm sorry. I should have said so before."

Will briefly pressed a finger to her lips. "Wheesht, lass. Dinna feel guilty and dinna cry on my account. Apart from a few bruised knuckles, I'm fine."

She nodded and brushed a tear from her cheek. "I know, but what if that man *had* hurt you? I'd never be able to forgive myself."

A smile tugged at one corner of Will's mouth. "Och, lass. I ken how to defend myself. He wasna a real threat. He was all bluff and bluster more than anything else."

Will said this with such quiet, firm confidence that Lucy believed him. And it made her wonder what sort of training Will had received in the army that gave him the ability to not only disarm a man but fell him in a matter of seconds. And with barely a discernible reaction.

He was...formidable. And brave and so very protective. His first thought had been about her. He'd told her to run while he'd faced a man with a knife.

"You saved me from harm," she whispered.

"Well, no' entirely... You did manage to trip over."

A bubble of laughter that was more like a hiccup escaped her. "That wasn't my fault this time. It was that darned cat."

He cocked a brow and smirked. "Just like it was the fault of that darned hare?"

"Exactly."

His smile softened. "I havena asked you how *you* are now. An experience like that—just the threat of being robbed or attacked—can be quite a shock. It can shake you up inside. And there's no shame in admitting it. Or crying about it. Just dinna cry for me. I'm as tough as old boots."

Lucy smiled. "You are tough, I'll give you that. But you do *not* resemble old boots."

He tilted his head. "Thank you. But tell me, how are your

knees? Are they sore? And what about your hands? It sounds like it was a hard fall."

"I do feel a little knocked about," Lucy admitted.

"Well, let's see then."

Lucy gingerly removed her gloves first. The soft, buttery leather was scuffed, but underneath, the heels of her palms were only a little bruised rather than scraped.

Will gently picked up one of her hands and turned it over to study it. Then he bent his head and tenderly kissed her wrist and her palm, sending a delicious shiver down Lucy's spine.

"And what about your knees?" he murmured.

"My knees?" she squeaked.

"Yes. Your knees. You know, they're halfway between your ankles and the tops of your thighs? The bits in the middle that bend so you can walk and sit down."

Lucy narrowed her gaze. "Ha, ha, Mr. Armstrong. How droll."

He gave her a quizzical look. "You wouldna be shy now, would you, Miss Bertram? I do recall that you're quite happy to flip up your skirts whenever we go riding."

Lucy blushed. Of course, he hadn't mentioned that he'd probably glimpsed her knees when she'd been sitting bare-bottomed on the kitchen table with her nightgown rucked up about her spread legs. "Yes, I know," she managed. "But on *those* occasions I was attempting to flirt with you. But now…"

"Now, what?" His gaze held hers, and for one breathless moment, Lucy thought she saw some sort of emotion like tenderness or hope flicker in the deep-blue depths of his eyes.

She swallowed and decided to avoid the subject of why this suddenly felt different. Like there wasn't only lust between them. That it might be something more. Because "more" was impossible.

Instead, she gave voice to the first excuse that came to mind. "Now my skirts and petticoats and drawers are probably covered in all manner of muck and filth."

"All the more reason to check for scrapes. Your wounds will need tending to so infection doesna set in."

Will was right, of course. "Very well," said Lucy. She drew in a breath and then gathered up her soiled skirts and petticoats until her knees were exposed. The fine white linen of her drawers was grubby and torn in several places, but no blood had seeped through.

"I dinna think you have any grazes," said Will, "but I should take a look, just to make sure." He raised a brow. "May I?"

Lucy's response was tellingly breathless. "Yes."

Will slid to his knees on the floor of the hackney and then with great care loosened the ribbons securing the bottom of her drawers before gently rolling each leg up. And then he unfastened her ribbon garters and rolled her stockings down. "They're only bruised," he said gravely, "no scrapes," and then Lucy's heart quickened as she wondered if he might bend his head and bestow a kiss upon each knee.

The thought of it made her pulse race and her lower belly flutter madly with anticipation. But then Will swallowed audibly and inhaled a deep breath, and then he proceeded to put her stockings and drawers to rights. Everywhere his fingers brushed Lucy's flesh pebbled and tingled. And by the time her skirts were in place and he was joining her on the seat again, she was caught somewhere between thwarted desire and disappointment and budding delight.

Will might not have kissed her bruised knees "better," but she knew he'd been thinking about it.

She *knew*. And the idea of it thrilled her rather than horrified her.

Perhaps Mr. Thorne was right after all.

She *was* wicked. And it was a fact she wasn't sorry about. Not one little bit.

Chapter Sixteen

WHEN THE HACKNEY ROLLED INTO FLEETWOOD'S DRIVE, Lucy didn't much care if anyone thought it was odd that she'd returned home all soaking wet with the groom as her only companion.

As it was, no one actually noticed. The hackney departed, Will respectfully bid her adieu before disappearing around the back of the house, and Lucy was only greeted at the front door by Redmond, who, like every good butler, didn't even so much as bat an eyelid upon seeing her sodden, disheveled state.

When she'd inquired if her father was still at home, Redmond informed her that he'd quit Fleetwood half an hour ago with Thorne, but that he'd received her telegram and had left a note for her in her room.

Oh, dear...

After Lucy had dealt with Dotty's fussing and had sent her off to arrange a warm bath, she picked up the single sheet of paper on her dressing table, broke the seal, and read...

> *Lucy,*
>
> *I read your telegram and, of course, Thorne told me his version of events when he arrived here without you. To say that I am not pleased would be an understatement. This "I will not get married" nonsense must stop. So much is at stake.*

I will talk with you on the morrow when I return home.

Father

Lucy sank onto the dressing table seat and sighed heavily. That was a talk she was *not* looking forward to, but it needed to be had. Of course, she knew what was at stake, but this nonsense with trying to marry her off to Mr. Thorne *had* to stop.

And if it didn't... She shivered. There was something about the way Thorne had looked at her this afternoon when he'd declared she was "pretty"—a heated gleam in his eyes that made her wonder if he might stop playing the gentleman at some point and try to force her into marriage another way... By compromising her.

What a terrible, terrible thought. A reality Lucy could barely stand to contemplate. But if she were sensible, she should.

Finding Monty had proved to be well-nigh impossible, so that meant there was only one other thing that she could feasibly do to save herself. She must leave London. She must seek sanctuary with Artemis, sooner rather than later.

Lucy pulled her jewelry box toward her and opened it. She didn't want to sell anything inside, but she had no other choice. Before her father returned home and they had their "talk," she would venture into London tomorrow morning and speak to Jane or her grandfather about finding a reputable pawn shop. And perhaps Jane might have a better idea where Artemis was at present. That would certainly be helpful.

Actually... Lucy frowned. She could always visit Dartmoor House, the Duke of Dartmoor's residence in Belgravia. Someone on the duke's staff like his personal secretary might know of his whereabouts, and Artemis's, on the Continent. And if they weren't happy to disclose the duke's and duchess's location to her, she could also try calling on the duke's sister, Horatia, Lady Northam. Lucy had met her at Artemis's and the duke's wedding in late May. She didn't know why she hadn't thought of making an inquiry there sooner.

She glanced at her haphazard reflection in the mirror and almost managed a smile. All was not lost just yet. Now, if only she could stop thinking about a certain Scots groom who had turned her into a besotted fool practically overnight. Because why else would her heart ache so much at the thought of having to say goodbye?

She removed her wet bonnet and tossed it onto a nearby chair, wishing she could discard her feelings just as easily. Having a little fun with a man like Will, living in the moment, was all well and good until one's heart started to become involved. And after this afternoon, she truly feared that might be happening. Not just hers, but his too.

Leaving William Armstrong behind might be one of the hardest things she'd ever have to do.

Unless he came with her…

She looked herself in the eye in the mirror. *But then what, Lucy Bertram? Then what?*

That was a question she could not answer. Or, more to the point, didn't want to answer. Perhaps for now, she'd just have to leave it be.

———

Yet again Will couldn't sleep, even though he was bloody exhausted.

He grunted, threw off the sheets and quilt of his narrow bed and scrubbed his hands up and down his face. He sure as hell wasn't going to go searching for warm milk.

His mind was abuzz with far too many thoughts.

He *really* should go and search the steward's office to look for further evidence linking Sir Oswald to the case. And maybe he'd find out more about the baronet's dealings with Thorne. Detective Lawrence was right. The Yorkshireman would gain a pretty wife, but nothing else of value from this union. So why not wed a pretty young woman from a wealthy family instead of saddling oneself with a father-in-law with mounting debts?

There must be something else going on between Thorne and Sir Oswald that no one knew about. And maybe that was the key to unlocking this case. But first Will had to find proof.

He also wanted to find Monty for Lucy's sake. He couldn't bear to see her so desperate with worry.

Indeed, he couldn't stop berating himself that *he* hadn't thought to hire an inquiry agent. He had the means—both the contacts and the funds—to do so, and he would employ one with knowledge of St Giles and Covent Garden as soon as he could. But letting Lucy know all of this was not an option at this point. He couldn't disclose who he really was and what he was doing at Fleetwood. At least not yet.

With a yawn, Will rose, pulled on a pair of cotton drawers, then struck a match to light a candle and then a lamp in the small adjoining sitting room. The carriage clock on the mantelpiece told him it was just after eleven. Outside, a soft rain was falling, pattering on the cottage's thatched roof and against the mullion windowpanes. In an hour or two, he could safely steal inside the hall and do what needed to be done. Everyone would be asleep and Sir Oswald was away again.

And then what?

Whether or not he managed to unearth any relevant evidence or additional clues, it was clear Will's time at Fleetwood Hall was coming to an end. His grandfather might suffer another stroke, and next time it could be fatal. Pretending to be Will Armstrong or Adam Whittaker or Billy Lockwood or anyone else other than himself, William Lockhart, the sixth Duke of Ayr, would then be impossible.

But that was a problem for another day. He'd written to his grandfather's steward to say he'd visit Braeburn Castle as soon as he was able to.

His grandfather might be disgruntled at the news, but it was the best he could do for now. The arrogant, ruthless, belligerent man—a man who was very much like Will's deceased father—was lucky he would visit at all.

To avoid thinking about his family or their fraught past, Will threw on a shirt, picked up a book, then settled back into the worn but comfortable armchair by the dark fireplace. He'd purloined a copy of *A Discourse on Botanical Poisons in Great Britain, Both Common and Rare*—the book Lucy had penned but her father had put his name to—from Fleetwood's library, but tonight, his tired eyes wouldn't focus properly on the words and his mind kept wandering.

Detective Lawrence had suggested that he continue to cultivate his relationship with Lucy, but it seemed unfair and underhanded and part of Will feared that he was venturing into water that was far too deep and dangerous. The fact he felt so guilty for lying to Lucy about who he was, along with the fact that he cared so much about her safety and what the future held in store for her, was telling indeed.

If truth be told, the simple fact that he couldn't get her out of his head also spoke volumes.

Good God, to think that this afternoon he'd almost succumbed to the urge to have his wicked way with her in the hackney. When she'd lifted her skirts and he'd exposed her pale slender legs so he could check her knees for injury, he'd experienced a rush of lust so strong, it had stolen the very breath from his lungs. Indeed, it had taken every ounce of discipline in him to resist the impulse to run his fingertips over the smooth, silken flesh of her calves. To feather soft kisses on the tender flesh inside of her knees and thighs just so he could hear *her* breath catch. To learn all of the ways she would like to be pleasured, if she'd let him...

But she deserved better than that. Her first time making love shouldn't be in the back of a grubby old hackney with a man who couldn't give her what she wanted and needed. Who couldn't be honest with her about who he really was and what he'd been up to all this time.

Aside from that, she'd be shaken to the core by an attempted robbery and threatened assault. It wouldn't be right to take advantage of her vulnerable emotional state, just so he could slake his rampant lust.

Aye, Will's bloodlust had been up after he'd downed that greedy, filthy pimp with one punch. So much so, he hadn't been able to crush the need to kiss Lucy in that squalid laneway. The sight of her quivering and in tears as she leaned against a dirty brick wall had nearly cleaved his heart in two. And it was his safety she'd been worried about. Her tears in the hackney had been for *him*.

Her heartfelt words echoed through his mind: *But what if that man had hurt you...? I'd never be able to forgive myself.*

Jesus Christ. He really didn't know what to do with the idea that this young woman might be starting to care for him. No one but his poor mother had ever loved him. And that had been such a long time ago when he'd only been a boy.

What he wouldn't do for a drink right now. Perhaps he'd help himself to a nip of brandy from Sir Oswald's stash in the drawing room when he snuck inside. Maybe that would put out the fire in his veins and blunt his own inconvenient emotions.

A light tapping at the door had him frowning.

What the devil...? He cast Lucy's book aside and padded barefooted across the rug. Perhaps there was something wrong with one of the horses and Freddy, who slept in a small cot in the tack room, had come to fetch him. All the animals had appeared to be fine when he'd stabled them for the night. Even Mace, who he'd picked up from the Wick and Whistle a few hours ago.

But it wasn't the stable lad knocking at his door at this late hour after all.

It was Lucy.

"Lass..." Will's gaze swept over her. She was only attired in a white cotton nightgown, a silk wrapper, and thin slippers. Her blond hair was unbound, and in the ambient light from the lamp, raindrops glittered in the pale golden strands that tumbled about her shoulders. He drew a breath, concern warring with a good dose of desire. "Is everything all right?"

"May I come in?" she asked.

"Of course." Will stepped aside, and then cursed silently as she brushed past and he caught her delicate floral scent. He should be wearing more than thin drawers and a cambric shirt. Then again, the baronet's daughter should be wearing far more than what she presently had on too.

None of this was appropriate. Not in the slightest.

But since when had that mattered? Will knew deep down in his heart that his distance and objectivity had been blown to pieces almost from the very start.

He shut the door and made sure the curtains were properly drawn. He was not expecting anyone else to be out and about in the rain at this late hour, but it was better to be safe than sorry.

When he turned around, it was to discover that Lucy was hovering near the darkened fireplace, looking as uncertain as he felt.

"Why don't you take a seat"—he gestured at the single armchair—"and I'll light a fire. It's cool outside."

But she was shaking her head. "No... That won't be necessary. It's just that..." She met his gaze. In the soft glow of the lamp, her eyes had turned a mysterious shade of misty blue and she was nibbling at her lower lip. Her fingers clutched her wrapper so tightly her knuckles had turned white, yet her cheeks were awash with a soft pink blush.

Will drew closer slowly as though he were approaching a skittish horse that was liable to bolt at any moment. "Lucy, what is it?" he asked gently. "You can tell me anything. I hope you know that."

She nodded, then offered him a small, nervous smile. "I know. I trust you, more than I can say. Which is part of the reason I'm here. Oh, no..." She frowned. "I just know I'm going to blather."

"I like it when you do."

She blinked. "You do? Truly?"

"Aye, I find it verra charming." It wasn't a lie.

"Oh... Well then..." She inhaled a little breath as though steeling herself to begin. "You see, Will, ever since that incident in St Giles this afternoon, I can't stop thinking about it. And how awful it was when that detestable man threatened you. I felt so helpless and imbecilic, and of course I'm responsible for placing you in harm's way. And indeed, for dragging you into a mess that isn't yours." She paused and drew another breath. "I know we've already been over this, and no doubt you'll tell me again that it's all right. That it doesn't matter. But to me it does. I feel so wretched, I–I can't sleep. And the house seems so big and echoing and empty...and all I can think of is you..." Her voice trailed off but her gaze still held his. "And I wondered..."

Will's heart was in his mouth as he prompted her, "Wondered what, lass?"

She swallowed, then the tip of her pink tongue darted out to moisten her lower lip. "I wondered if I might be able to spend the night here with you," she murmured huskily. "In your bed. In your arms. Just so I might be able to fall asleep. When I'm with you, I feel safe."

Devil take him. Will scrubbed a hand through his hair. Safe with him? Good God, if Lucy could see the wildly inappropriate thoughts running through his head right now, or if she knew that his blood had begun pounding and his cock was already hardening at the thought of her warm, luscious curves pressed up tightly against him, she wouldn't feel safe at all. Of course he wouldn't touch her. Wouldn't do anything she didn't want.

But…he knew she desired him too, and if they started to kiss and they both got swept up in the moment and carried away…

No, he wouldn't let it get that far. He would do the right thing. Be a perfect gentleman, even if his ballocks turned blue. Even if it killed him.

Of course, he *could* also just say no and refuse her request outright. Turn her away and send her back to her own bed alone. That would be the best course of action to take for both of them.

But the way she looked…all big lavender-blue eyes and flushed cheeks and breathless anticipation and *Christ*…he was *not* a saint.

No, he couldn't deny her. So he drew a deep breath and said, "Verra well, lass. But be warned. I may snore."

———

Lucy released the breath she'd been holding. He'd said yes?

She couldn't quite believe it. "Thank…thank you," she

murmured. "And honestly, I'm sure I won't mind it at all if you snore. As long as you don't mind my cold toes."

His mouth twitched. "I dinna think your cold toes will bother me for long." His smile grew wider. "I'll soon warm them up."

Oh, good Lord. Lucy's belly performed an odd little flip-flop. Of course, that's what she wanted, to feel warm and safe, but to hear him say something like that as he watched her with a keen gleam in his dark-blue eyes…when like her he wasn't wearing much at all…was all kinds of thrilling. Indeed, the flutters of excitement gathering between her thighs were not conducive to sleep. Far from it. To think that in a few moments she'd be pressed up against that hard, muscular body. That Will's legs and feet might entwine with hers. That he might drape an arm over her. Pull her close…

Could he hear the crashing of her heart? See that her chest was rising and falling with her quickened breathing?

To break the taut silence, she murmured, "Well…I suppose we should… I mean, I'm ready to…" Her gaze strayed to his bed. The light of a candle on the bedside table revealed that the covers were rumpled, and guilt immediately pinched. "I hope I didn't wake you."

"No, you didn't. I couldna sleep either," he said. "Why don't I hop in bed first so my back is to the wall, and then you can join me?"

She nodded. "All right."

He put out the lamp, and then ever the gentleman, he let her pass through the door into his bedroom first. While she was discarding her wrapper and slippers, he slid into the bed. Lying on his side with his head propped on his elbow, he looked—Lucy swallowed—too delicious for words.

When she lay down, her back to his front, he drew the covers over both of them. Then he licked his fingertips, reached over her, and snuffed out the candle before settling back into his narrow spot. His arm slid around her waist and his body heat cocooned her in warmth, and while Lucy's first instinct was to snuggle back against him, she didn't. She just lay very still, drinking in the heady sensation of being held by a man she'd come to care about far too much.

And in ways that were far from proper or wise.

Trying to ignore the desire curling through her, she closed her eyes and attempted to focus on her breathing instead. But Will's musky masculine scent and the hard press of his hips and thighs against hers, the way the hairs of his lower legs tickled her calves, the way his breath drifted across her temple, all of these things made falling asleep impossible. Her body was acutely aware of the slightest movement either of them made. Beneath the light cotton of her nightgown, her nipples were hard, aching points.

It hadn't been a lie when she'd told him that he made her feel safe. That all she could think about when she'd been on her own was lying in his arms, just like this.

Though she'd clearly been lying to herself, and to him, when she'd declared she'd just wanted to fall asleep.

"Will…" she whispered into the soft, velvet stillness.

"Hmmm…"

She sensed that it wasn't a sleepy *hmmm*. That he was listening expectantly, that like her, he was actually waiting for something to happen.

She rolled over and faced him. In the darkness, she couldn't see much at all, but a chink in the curtains let in the tiniest bit of light so that she could make out his temple and the line of his cheek. A wide shoulder.

"I haven't been completely honest with you," she began. "I didn't just come here to sleep. I came here because I can't stop thinking about you and me. The things we could do together. You may think me wicked and wanton"—she pressed a hand to his chest, and she swore she could feel his heart thud against her palm—"but I can't seem to help myself. I–I want you."

The silence extended for the space of a heartbeat. Then another. And just when Lucy began to despair that she'd made a terrible mistake and had shocked Will to the core, he murmured huskily, "I like wicked and wanton. And I don't just want you, lass. I burn for you."

And then before Lucy could even think of what to say, or draw another breath, his hand was in her hair, gripping the back of her head, and his hot mouth was on hers, devouring and plundering as though staking a claim. As though this kiss declared, "You're mine."

Oh, she so wanted to be his and his alone, even if it was only for one snatched night of wicked pleasure. Lucy yielded to his every demand, kissing Will back with a fervor that matched his. When his tongue entered her, stroking deeply, she opened wider and tasted him too. She slipped a hand beneath his shirt and clasped his lean torso, earning her a deep groan that only increased her own desire.

One of Will's legs slid over her hips, dragging her body closer, and she couldn't help but gasp with delight when she felt the insistent, unmistakable jut of his aroused manhood against the soft plane of her belly.

He *did* want her.

When he pulled away, his forehead resting against hers, he murmured raggedly, "Perhaps we should slow down…stop…"

But Lucy clutched at his shirt. "Slowing down is the last thing I want to do. I'm a twenty-eight-year-old woman. I know what I need. I know what the risks are. I know there are measures we can take to prevent any unintended consequences. I may be a virgin but I'm not naive, and I've told you before, I know how things work. And if the worst should happen..." Her voice caught. "If the worst should happen and if something unforeseen occurs... If for some reason I'm forced to marry Thorne against my wishes—"

Will's grip on her nape tightened. "That willna happen, Lucy. I swear to you it won't."

She drew a shaky breath. "No one can predict the future. But if the unthinkable *does* happen, at least I will have spent a night with a man I do desire. When you kiss me and hold me... Will, I burn for you too. Please show me pleasure. I need the memory of this—of us together—to store away in..." Her voice trailed away before the far-too-telling words on the tip of her tongue slipped out: *in my heart.*

"Och, Lucy..." Will cupped her face and kissed her so gently, with such sweet lingering tenderness that a lump formed in Lucy's throat. And when he drew back and whispered, "I'll do my best to make this special for you," Lucy's heart swelled with bittersweet joy.

Will was going to make love to her.

"Take off your shirt," she whispered, and he did. And then he was kissing her deeply, possessively, while one of his hands roamed over her body, exploring her dips and curves through the fabric of her nightgown. Each kiss was long and slow and drugging, and very soon Lucy's body was aflame. All her nerve endings were singing and her blood was pulsing with a desire so strong she could barely contain it.

Her own hands skimmed over Will's taut, muscular back, his shoulders, the bulk of his upper arms. Her fingertips pinched his furled nipples, earning her a hiss and a nip on her lower lip. His breathing was rough as he muttered, "Wench," but she could hear the laughter behind it. She imagined he smiled.

When Will at last slid the buttons fastening her nightgown undone and parted the fabric, exposing her breasts, she wasn't ashamed, only aroused. He coaxed her onto her back, and while he feasted on her neck with hot, sucking kisses, his clever fingers teased and pinched and taunted her hard-as-pearl nipples.

But soon it wasn't enough. And Will knew that too. His hot mouth slid to one of her bared breasts, and as he licked and suckled, she speared her fingers into his thick silken locks and gripped his head. The sensations he so effortlessly aroused... The delicious shivers, the gooseflesh, the searing bolts of pleasure that seemed to arrow straight through her, heating her blood and intensifying the throbbing in her sex... It was the most exquisite form of torture imaginable. And when one of his hands slipped beneath the hem of her rucked-up nightgown and settled on her lower belly, just above the curls hiding her mound, she moaned in frustration.

"Yes, touch me there," she urged, parting her thighs. She knew she was wet and slick, and while once she would have been mortified and, indeed, too shy to be begging and panting like a wanton, with Will it felt so right.

And so, so good. Especially when one of his wicked fingers found her drenched crease and slid between her folds, spreading moisture up to the pulsing, swollen bud of her clitoris. And then he began to tease the very center of her, with not just one but two fingertips. They moved in tight, tiny circles, rubbing and pressing and flicking and working her into a wild frenzy. Oh...it was almost too much.

She undulated her hips, grinding herself against his hand, mindlessly chasing pleasure, and when he pressed his mouth to her ear and whispered hoarsely, "Come for me, sweet Lucy. Let go," she did immediately, tumbling over the edge into bliss, gasping and crying his name.

"Oh…that was lovely. Actually, more than lovely…" she whispered between panted breaths. "It was marvelous… And so much better than when I—" She broke off as she realized what she'd just admitted.

Will withdrew his hand and nuzzled her neck. Tugged on her earlobe with his teeth. "When you what, Lucy? Touch yourself?"

"Yes…" Lucy felt her cheeks grow warm, which was ridiculous considering her nightgown was up around her hips and her breasts were bared and her body still hummed with deep satisfaction, courtesy of Will's thoroughly wicked ministrations.

"Next time you do so, my sweet, bonny lass," Will continued, his warm breath caressing her ear, "I want you to think of me and this night. And I promise you that I will do the same when I make myself come by my own hand. When I stroke my cock."

Lucy turned and pressed her hot cheek against the hard plane of his chest. His lewd, filthy words should appall her. But they didn't. Not at all.

"I would be honored if you did," she whispered. "And I *will* think of you… Only…" Some wicked imp inside her—a brazen part of her she'd hitherto been unaware of—made her tiptoe her fingertips down his chest to his taut belly and then lower, until she reached an intriguingly thin trail of hair that began just below his belly button. "I'm dying to know… Have you thought of me before? When you stroke yourself?"

A beat of silence. "Aye." His voice was rough and low. "I have."

"And may I ask, what am I doing when you think of me…?" Her fingers discovered that the trail of hair disappeared below the waistband of his cotton drawers. "What wicked things are *we* doing? What happens?"

A deep groan rumbled out of Will and he caught her questing hand. "If you go any lower, you'll find out."

"Do you want me to? Go lower?"

"God help me... Aye, I do." He released her, and Lucy slid her hand beneath his drawers and gently wrapped her fingers around the hot, steel-hard length of his erect manhood. His *cock*.

He was so impressively big and thick, and she swore she could feel his flesh pulse and swell even more when she squeezed gently and slid her closed fist up his rigid shaft to the surprisingly silken head. When she rubbed her thumb over the very end, she felt a tiny amount of moisture and Will gave another guttural groan. "Sweet Jesus, lass. At this rate I'll be spilling before you know it."

Lucy smiled and her heart thrilled at the idea that she'd so affected Will. The shy Lucy of old had disappeared and a seductress had taken her place. "Tell me what to do," she whispered. "Tell me how you like it. How to please you." She squeezed him again. "I want to know. Everything."

"I canna. If I tell you every wicked, carnal thought running through my head involving you right now, you'd be shocked."

Her own lust was building, growing, making her bold, and she swiped her thumb over him a second time. "Then just tell me *one* thing," she murmured thickly, "and I will do it."

He gripped her wrist. "Straddle me. I want to feel the wet folds of your sweet, hot cunny sliding along the length of my cock. I willna take your maidenhead though, lass, because tonight I dinna wish to cause you pain. As you ride me, I will take my pleasure and you will take yours. I want to make you come again too."

Oh... How could she say no to such a wonderfully wicked proposition? While her bruised knees were still sore, the mattress was soft, and indeed when she did rise up and settle herself over Will's groin, her knees were the last thing on her mind. All she could feel was how wet she was, and how hard and hot and thick his cock, and when she began to slide back and forth at Will's urging, she'd never felt so free and abandoned and powerful.

She bent low, taking her weight on her hands, and Will gripped her head and pulled her down for a fiery kiss. And when he released her, his hands found her breasts, cupping and fondling and squeezing her flesh as she continued to ride him, her pace growing faster and wilder.

"I'm almost there, Lucy," he rasped. "Come with me, lass." He slid a hand between their bodies and found her clitoris. And when he pinched it and sucked one taut nipple into the hot cavern of his mouth, she gasped and reached her peak at once, and Will followed. His seed erupted in thick spurts, coating his belly and hers and the mound of her sex.

It was sticky and messy and wonderful, and Lucy's body hummed with joy and deep satisfaction. "I made you come," she whispered, then leaned down and kissed Will. Her tangled hair fell around them and Lucy wished that she could see her lover's face.

But when he spoke, his voice was like soft, dark velvet and she knew he was smiling and satisfied too. "Aye, you did indeed," he murmured. His fingers threaded through her hair, gently pushed it away from her flushed cheek. "Let's get cleaned up. And then we should get some sleep."

Will slid from beneath the covers, and after he lit a candle he fetched a towel and some water and then gently wiped Lucy down and then himself. Returning to the bed, he gathered her into his arms, kissed her temple, and within minutes Lucy drifted into a deeply contented slumber.

Chapter Seventeen

WHEN LUCY AWOKE, IT WAS TO DISCOVER THAT SHE WAS AS warm as could be and that her legs were entwined with Will's. Sometime in the night, she'd snuggled up against him and now her head rested on his wide chest. Her mouth curved with a smile. She decided it was the most comfortable pillow in the world.

A sliver of pale morning light penetrated a chink in the curtains above Will's bed; it illuminated a narrow section of his handsome face—his tousled dark-brown hair, a high cheekbone, a slice of stubbled jaw, and a corner of his beautifully sculpted mouth. When his face was in repose, the stern expression he often wore disappeared. In fact, apart from his night beard, Will *almost* looked angelically boyish.

Although, last night put paid to the idea that he was either of those things. Lucy bit her lip as she recalled everything they'd done together in this bed. All the wicked things they'd said. Will was more like a fallen angel, and she'd quite happily followed him into sin.

But then, she was the one who'd come knocking on his door and had entreated him to share his bed with her. He really wasn't to blame.

A cock crowed in the distance and Lucy's toes curled. *Cock.* What a wonderful word for such a wonderful part of a man. If she had her way, she'd lie in this bed with Will for the rest of the day, learning all the ways he liked to be pleasured and what else he could do with his marvelous cock to please her.

And then she sighed. She couldn't afford to be a slugabed. Very soon she'd have to get up and steal back into the house and her own bedroom before anyone noticed her absence.

She yawned and stretched a little, and Will stirred.

"Lucy..." His voice, all low and husky with sleep, was music to her ears. "Good morning, lass."

She sat up a little and smiled down at him. "Good morning to you too. How did you sleep?"

"Like a log." Then he frowned. "What time is it?"

"I'm not sure, but judging by the light, I suspect it's still quite early. Before six o'clock?"

"Hmmm." Will pinched the bridge of his nose, then pushed himself farther up the pillows so that his face was now in the shadows.

There was something about the way he was looking at her—a solemn light in his gaze—that made Lucy feel uneasy. A frisson of apprehension slid down her spine. She swallowed. "Is anything wrong?"

His answering smile wasn't reflected in his eyes. Reaching out, he gently tucked a strand of hair behind her ear. "Yes...and also no," he said gravely. "We need to talk."

Lucy attempted to make her voice light. "Well, that sounds ominous."

When Will didn't reassure her that what he was about to say wasn't actually "ominous," Lucy's belly began to churn in earnest. "What is it?" She tried to smile. "You're not going to tell me that there's a Mrs. Armstrong somewhere, are you?"

Will shook his head. "No. Nothing like that. I'm definitely not married. Nor have I ever been wed. However, before I go any further, I want to make it clear to you that last night was wonderful and I enjoyed every minute of it. I'm honored indeed that you trusted me to show you pleasure. But..." He paused. "I do need to tell you something. About me." Another pause as Will inhaled a breath. His unflinching, unfathomable gaze met hers. "I havena been completely honest with you about who I really am. My first name *is* William. But my last name isna really Armstrong. It's Lockhart. And I'm no' a groom."

Lucy frowned as confusion filled her head. "Do you mean that you're still a soldier?"

"No... But I did serve in Her Majesty's military for seven years before I resigned my commission." Will's gaze grew more intense. His expression was so serious, Lucy's chest tightened as though she were about to receive a blow. "I need to take you into my confidence, Lucy. Can I trust you to keep a secret?"

Lucy's mouth was as dry as a desert in midsummer. She had no idea what Will was about to disclose, but she had the terrible feeling it was not going to be something she wanted to hear. Nevertheless, she managed to murmur, "Yes...yes, you can."

He nodded. "Verra well. I resigned my commission to become a spy for the Crown, and for the last three years I've worked for both the Foreign Office and the Home Office. Whoever needs me. And there's someone you know who can verify that all this is true if you ask him. I wouldna mind at all if you did."

"Who?"

"Lord Castledown. He works for the Home Office. You attended a ball—the first of the Season—at Castledown House in April."

"I remember."

"I was there that night, at Lord Castledown's behest. And you and I actually met—albeit briefly."

"We did?" Lucy's bewilderment deepened. Along with the unpleasant sense that she'd been tricked and played for a fool. "I don't recall you at all."

Will's gaze was steady. "I was using another name and my

appearance was slightly different. I was introduced to you as Adam Whittaker, an industrialist from New York."

Lucy gasped. "That was you? The man with the spectacles and the enormous mutton chops?"

Will winced and scratched his stubbled chin. "Aye. I will readily admit that I was glad to shave those off. I dyed my hair too, so it was a wee bit lighter and had reddish streaks. And I wore a padded waistcoat."

"I... We barely spoke that evening and anything I said to you was probably gibberish. I was so nervous..." said Lucy. "Although I do remember your eyes seemed a little familiar when we first met. I mean, when we met again. When you helped me down from the gig."

Will nodded. "I wasna sure if you would associate me with Adam Whittaker."

"No. I didn't. Not really. Were you..." She was so taken aback that she had to draw a breath before she could continue. "Were you spying on me at Lord Castledown's ball? On my father? He introduced us, if I recall."

"No, I wasna spying on either of you that night. I was involved with gaining intelligence for another unrelated case."

Unrelated case? Trepidation flickered through Lucy. A biting spark that had the potential to turn into something that scorched and burned and hurt. "Why are you here at Fleetwood Hall then, William?" she whispered. "Are...are you working on another case now?"

"Before I tell you what's going on, there's something else you should know."

This time when Lucy spoke, she couldn't contain her exasperation. "William Armstrong... No, Whittaker... I mean Lockhart. Whatever your name is. What else could there possibly be?"

Will scrubbed a hand through his hair, and for the first time, a shadow of apprehension flickered across his face. "Open the top drawer of the bedside table," he instructed. "You'll find a small silver box. Take it out and look inside."

Her heartbeat pounding in her ears, Lucy did as Will had asked. Upon opening the box, she discovered a ring inside—a very masculine signet ring of silver—nestled in a bed of deep-blue velvet. The actual signet itself was a heraldic coat of arms depicting three silver boars' heads on an azure shield. Below them was a chain-bound heart. "Is this a clan ring?" Lucy murmured. And then she met Will's gaze. "Is this yours?"

"Aye, it's mine… But it's no' just a clan ring. You see, not only am I a spy, but I'm also an earl. The Earl of Kyle, to be exact, and that's my official seal. My grandfather is the Duke of Ayr."

Lucy shook her head as pure, undiluted shock washed over her. "You mean to tell me that I'm curled up in bed with an earl who's also a spy for the Crown? Is this really true? Or are you mad? Or am I? I truly don't know what to believe."

"I know it's a lot to take in," Will said. "And you have every right to doubt me. And to be angry with me for deceiving you—especially after last night—but I had to."

"But why? Why all the subterfuge and duplicity? Why are you here, William Lockhart, Lord Kyle?" The sick feeling returned to the pit of Lucy's stomach and she grabbed a pillow and hugged it to her chest. "You didn't answer my earlier question, but I will ask you once again… Are you here to spy on me and my father? What on earth have we done? I don't understand any of this."

"I'm not here to spy on *you*, lass." Will hesitated, but only for a moment. His expression was so grave, Lucy shivered. "You told me before that I could trust you to keep a secret. Now you must promise me that you will not disclose a single word of what I'm about to tell you. To anyone. Do I have your word?"

"I–I don't know, Will. Or should I call you 'my lord'? I'm so confused."

"Lucy. Look at me," Will commanded, his voice low and deep yet somehow gentle. "We've only known each other for a short time—and I know I've misled you and lied to you about so many things, at every turn—but what does your gut tell you? What do your instincts tell you? Even after everything I've just told you, do you trust me?"

Lucy searched Will's gaze for long moments. Looked deeply into his eyes. She couldn't detect any hint of guile, nor any glimmer of uneasiness. It wasn't just her gut or her instincts that told her she *could* trust Will. God help her. It was her heart.

"Yes, I believe you, Will," she said. "Only the Lord in heaven knows why, but I do. And I won't say anything to anyone, I promise. Just please tell me. What is going on?"

———

Will released the breath he'd been holding as relief flooded through him. Thank God she trusted him and he trusted her too. He lifted her hand and kissed it. "Thank you. Now, to answer all of your questions… I currently work for Scotland Yard as a detective in disguise, so to speak. And I've been tasked to investigate the murder of Viscount Litchfield who was a member of the Linnean Society."

Lucy frowned. "Lord Litchfield? I never met him, but I do recall there was a big to-do about his death in the newspapers. About a month or so ago?"

"That's correct. No' a lot of detail about the case has been released to the public because there's an ongoing investigation in progress. But Scotland Yard believes Lord Litchfield was poisoned with an atypically potent form of strychnine. As soon as he ingested it, he died within minutes."

Lucy gasped in apparent horror. "Oh my God… You think my father is responsible?"

"I ken it's hard for you to hear, but he *was* originally at the top of Scotland Yard's list of suspects. Litchfield was poisoned at the Raleigh Club. Not only was your father there that night, but he also appears to possess a strong motive. Rumors have been circulating that Litchfield and your father were not on good terms after the viscount withdrew financial support for a proposed expedition to Malaysia. Your father was actually formally questioned by Scotland Yard detectives directly after the murder."

Lucy's face was ashen. "I honestly had no idea. He…he never said anything about being at the Raleigh Club that night or about being questioned. I knew Father was disappointed with Lord Litchfield when the expedition was canceled at the start of the year, but he appeared to have overcome his pique. At least I thought so. And just because my father *does* know a lot about strychnine and all of its different botanical varieties, that doesn't prove anything. Why, any apothecary or physician worth their salt could probably turn rat poison into something more potent."

"All good points," conceded Will. "And we have considered all of those possibilities too. But there's no one else with those sorts of qualifications who's both a member of the Raleigh Club *and* the Linnean Society."

"But what makes you think Lord Litchfield's death has anything to do with the Linnean Society in the first place?"

"Because in the days leading up to his death, the viscount received a threatening letter, and so did several other prominent members of the society's council…as well as Charles Darwin. It seems the killer took exception to Darwin's paper on evolutionary theory that was presented at Burlington House on the first of July. And unless Darwin is expelled from the society, there could be more deaths. In fact, Darwin recently received another threat. The envelope also contained an unidentified powder that caused him to break out in a rash almost immediately, and he's since been ill."

"As far as I know, my father's not opposed to Darwin or his theories." Lucy shook her head. "I just can't believe he would orchestrate anything like this. It sounds both diabolical and mad."

"I agree," said Will. "Since I've been here, I haven't discovered anything that directly implicates your father in Litchfield's murder or the sinister plot to expel Darwin from the society. Or worse, kill him. I don't think your father is involved. At least not directly."

Lucy cast him a narrow look. "That's why you've been sneaking about the house late at night, isn't it? You've been searching for evidence."

Will winced. "Yes, I was. But in a way, those searches have helped to eliminate your father as the chief suspect. At least in my mind. I certainly dinna want the wrong man to be arrested for these despicable crimes. In fact, since I arrived at Fleetwood House, I do have another suspect in my sights. One with a far clearer motive. A man who is also a member of the Linnean Society and the Raleigh Club and appears to hold Charles Darwin and his theories in contempt."

"Zachariah Thorne," breathed Lucy.

Will inclined his head. "Yes. In fact, the most recent letter threatening Darwin accused him of being an 'evildoer' like Lord Litchfield. Upon meeting Thorne, I was struck by how his view of the world is verra black and white. It seems like the sort of language he would use."

"'Evildoer.' That certainly sounds like something Thorne would say," said Lucy grimly. "Yesterday, he all but accused *me* of being a wicked sinner, but he thinks that if we wed, he can save me. I've never been so insulted in all my life."

Will gritted his teeth as a bolt of fierce anger shot through him. "He said that to you?"

"Not in those exact words, but more or less, yes."

"Lucy, I do believe you have good cause to be worried about Thorne. Last night you mentioned that you feared you might be forced to marry him."

"Yes. I just have this feeling that if I continue to refuse his overtures, he may do something that makes it impossible for me to say no to a marriage proposal. The truth is I don't feel safe with him. And because of that…" She looked Will straight in the eye. "I've decided that I cannot stay here, or indeed in England at all for the foreseeable future."

Will nodded. "I understand. And to hear you say that fills me with even more concern. If Thorne is behind Lord Litchfield's murder and everything else, it means he is a verra dangerous man. It also makes me wonder why your father is so beholden to him and why Thorne is prepared to take on your family's financial debt in exchange for your hand in marriage. Yet you canna abide the man, and Thorne, if you'll excuse my bluntness, he doesna seem enamored of you either."

Lucy sighed, the sound infinitely sad. "I really don't understand what is going on."

Will reached out and touched her arm, wishing he could offer comfort. "If you stayed in London, I was hoping you might be able to help with the investigation."

Lucy's eyebrows shot up. "Me?"

"Yes," said Will. "You. Maybe with a little prompting, your father might confide in you about why this match is so important to him."

But Lucy shook her head. "I doubt it. He's far too stubborn and proud. Whenever I've tried to talk about anything of import in the past—even about Monty and what caused their rift—he refuses. Aside from that, I really do think I need to remove myself from Fleetwood Hall and its environs. At least for now."

"Hopefully that won't be for too long." Will drew a breath. "About your brother. Your suggestion yesterday—to employ an inquiry agent—was inspired. And I will do exactly that later today. It will be someone who can keep watch in St Giles and Covent Garden around the clock. I'll just need to borrow that photograph of Monty that you showed me."

"You would do that?" Lucy breathed, hope dawning in her blue-gray eyes.

"Of course."

She kissed his stubbled cheek. "Thank you. Thank you so much."

Will barely resisted the fierce urge to turn his head and claim her delicious mouth. "You realize that if we catch Thorne, your problem is solved."

"True…" Lucy bit her lip, then sighed. "But how long will that take? And what if you can't find the evidence you need?"

Will conceded she was right. And as long as Lucy stayed here at Fleetwood without her brother to defend her, she could be in danger. He couldn't dismiss her fears. And then another idea occurred to him—something so obvious he could kick himself for being such a daft dunderhead. "I think I have another solution. One that will make the problem that is Mr. Zachariah Thorne go away."

Keen interest glimmered in Lucy's gaze. "I'm listening. What do you suggest?"

"What if you had an alternative suitor? One who's equally wealthy but far more powerful than an industrialist from Yorkshire?" Will cocked an eyebrow. "The Earl of Kyle, for instance."

Instead of smiling as Will had hoped, Lucy frowned at him.

"But how will that work? My father already knows you as Will Armstrong, Scots groom. How will you be able to explain your presence here working in his household, given your title? And then of course he might not even believe you're an earl. Either way, he has no reason to trust you. He's not likely to agree to your proposal to court me."

"I'm certain that I can mount an argument that will persuade him. And I can do it without revealing the real reason I've been working here. In any event, my days as a spy conducting clandestine investigations are numbered anyway." Will explained the situation with his grandfather and that according to the duke's physician, he might have another stroke that could take his life. "So you see, I need to reenter society as William Lockhart, Lord Kyle, sooner rather than later."

Sadness filled Lucy's gaze. "I'm so sorry to hear about your grandfather, Will. I know you are estranged, but still it must be difficult for you. As to whether you can convince my father to believe you, and to accept you as my new suitor, I have no idea if you will succeed. You can but try."

Will took her hand. "And in the meantime, we must keep you safe. My gut also tells me Thorne is unpredictable and not to be trusted around you. Do you have someone else in London that you can stay with until your elevated friend returns? I think you've mentioned a Miss Jane Delaney. Is that right?"

Lucy smiled. "Yes, I could probably stay with Jane. She divides her time between her mother's house in Kensington and her grandfather's apartment above his bookstore in Piccadilly."

"Excellent," said Will. "We should get ready for the day and then go into London as soon as possible. I need to visit Scotland Yard so I can discuss my changed situation with my contact there. And perhaps you can talk with Miss Delaney as soon as we get to Town. Actually, before we depart Fleetwood

Hall, I wondered if it would be possible to search one last place here—the steward's office. I know Mr. Gilchrist sometimes goes out and about to tour the estate and to visit the villagers. Do you know what his movements are this morning?"

"I don't," said Lucy, "but I'm sure I can send him off on an errand to keep him out of the way. He won't think it odd. He's quite amenable."

"Thank you. I meant to conduct the search last night"—Will smiled—"but then something else came up."

A rose-pink blush washed across Lucy's cheeks. "You could have said no to me."

"No. I couldna have." And he meant it. The fact that he'd do just about anything for Lucy Bertram didn't terrify him anymore either.

Lucy put down the pillow she'd been clutching against herself, and as she slid from the bed, Will added, "You might want to do up a few of those buttons, lass. You dinna want to shock anyone on your way back to the house."

Lucy looked down to where her neckline gaped open, and she squealed and clutched the fabric to her chest. "How long has my nightgown been like this?" she asked breathlessly.

Will shrugged. "The whole time we've been talking. But I thought you knew. I promise I didna look." Well, that was a lie. He'd tried very hard *not* to look but the curve of Lucy's pert, round breasts and the shadows of her pretty pink nipples beneath the thin cotton *were* very distracting.

"No, I didn't know," said Lucy as she began to fumble with the buttons. "I forgot so many were undone."

"Och, it's not like I havena seen your bosom before," said Will with a smile. "And a verra lovely bosom it is too. It seems such a shame to cover it—"

Lucy launched a pillow at him and Will ducked but not

enough. It caught him on the jaw and his grin widened. "Although I might be risking another drubbing with a pillow, I'd suggest you do all of those buttons right up to your chin now, lass, or I'll be dragging you back into this bed and you willna be leaving for at least another hour."

"Humph." Lucy affected a frown but the ends of her lovely mouth kept lifting into a smile. "If I didn't have to get back to the house, I wouldn't mind spending half the day in bed with you. And I want to let you know that last night was all kinds of wonderful for me too and I don't have a single regret. But…"

Will frowned. "Oh dear. Buts are never good."

"I just think I should make it clear that if Father does give his consent to our courtship, it won't be a real courtship that will end in an engagement and marriage. Because I do not wish to wed. I–I have plans that involve travel and research and writing a book on botanical medicines, and even though all of that seems impossible at the moment because of my family's financial situation, I just don't see how I can marry anyone without giving all of that up. As an earl, no doubt you'll want a conventional wife who wants to have your babies. I know you'll need an heir one day, especially when you are a duke. But I'm not sure that *I* want all of that." She winced. "I might be a little bit eccentric. My views *are* rather singular for a woman my age."

Will held her gaze. "I do understand and would never want to stand in the way of your dreams. It might reassure you to know that the reason I joined Her Majesty's army in the first instance was to defy my grandfather. The continuation of the family line was not a priority for me then. And now…to be honest I dinna know how I feel. Duty might call, but on the other hand…" He shrugged. "Suffice it to say, marriage is not on my mind either at present. It will be a courtship of convenience."

Lucy nodded. "Good. So we are both like-minded in that respect."

"Aye, we are. You dinna need to worry."

Just before Lucy hastened out the door of his cottage into the sunlit mist enveloping the grounds, Will pulled her in for a kiss. "I shall see you soon, my sweet Lucy," he murmured. "And hopefully, by the end of the day the Earl of Kyle will be officially courting you, at least in a public sense. I promise you that trusting me willna be a mistake."

Now all he had to do was convince Sir Oswald.

Chapter Eighteen

"YES, I'LL TAKE BOTH OF THE BLUE EVENING GOWNS, Dotty—the azure trimmed with silver and the one in Sèvres blue. And a few day gowns too," said Lucy to her lady's maid. "That should be enough along with suitably matching accessories. I trust your choices."

Dotty's mouth turned down at the corners, but she didn't say anything as she went about retrieving everything Lucy had requested from the dressing room and then filling a traveling trunk and valise. If she had noticed that her mistress had been missing from her bed half the night, and that her slippers were slightly damp and grass-stained, she hadn't remarked upon it. But Lucy did wonder if Dotty suspected something had happened given the fact she was wearing a perpetual frown this morning.

Ignoring her maid's moodiness, Lucy turned back to rummage through her jewelry box, deciding what she would be prepared to sell if she had to—perhaps the pearl and amethyst brooch and the earrings that matched. She needed to be mercenary. Sentimentality would not save her. Only money, should she need to quit England at a moment's notice.

Of course, given everything Will had done for her already— the way he'd helped her at every turn and shown her nothing but care and consideration and respect—Lucy had no reason not to trust him or take him at his word. She knew in her heart that he'd do his utmost to protect her. But still, something might go wrong. Even though Will was the Earl of Kyle, her father might very well reject his offer to court her.

One thing Lucy wouldn't do, though, was play the hapless maiden. She would *not* allow Zachariah Thorne to force her into marriage. Especially now that she'd learned the man might very well be a murderer.

Her father's note still lay on her dressing table like a silent rebuke, and Lucy unfolded it.

The words that worried her the most jumped out at her: *This "I will not get married" nonsense* must *stop*.

Well, if leaving was the safest option, that's what she would do.

At a knock on her bedchamber door, Lucy refolded her father's letter and pushed it into her jewelry box. It was one of the chambermaids with Lucy's breakfast tray—a simple repast of hot chocolate and honeyed crumpets—and to Lucy's surprise, the butler, bearing a silver salver upon which lay a rich cream envelope.

"Redmond, it's a bit early for the post, isn't it? It's not even nine o'clock," said Lucy as she reached for the letter.

"It is, but this missive came via a private messenger—a liveried footman in fact, Miss Bertram," said Redmond. "He's presently waiting downstairs for your reply."

"A liveried footman?" Lucy examined the familiar script on the front of the envelope and then squealed. "Oh, my goodness!" She flipped it over and the crest stamped onto the red wax seal confirmed her suspicions.

It was from Artemis Winters, the Duchess of Dartmoor!

Lucy hastily cracked the seal and read the contents eagerly.

My dearest Lucy,

I hope this letter finds you well. I've missed you and Jane terribly, and I'm so excited to be back in London!

Dominic and I arrived home late yesterday—what a time we've had—and I can't wait to tell you all about our adventures on the Continent. And of course I just have to see how you are faring too, my sweet friend. In light of that, I propose that you and Jane come to Dartmoor House at one o'clock today for luncheon and a Byronic Book Club Meeting. We can talk all afternoon about whatever we like. I know it's short notice, but I do hope you'll say yes.

    Love,

                                     A xx

Lucy was glad she was sitting down because it seemed like her knees had turned into jelly with the feeling of sheer relief flooding through her. She had to blink away tears before she could address the butler. "Please tell Her Grace's footman that I will be at Dartmoor House at the prescribed time."

Even though her appetite had all but fled because of the excitement dancing in her belly, Lucy made herself take a few bites of crumpet and a few sips of hot chocolate before she raced downstairs to see Will. He was currently ensconced in Mr. Gilchrist's office, conducting a search. According to Mrs. Gilchrist, her husband had ventured into Town to conduct some business at the Metropolitan Cattle Market and she didn't expect him back until late in the afternoon. Which meant Will could search without fear of interruption.

Nevertheless, Lucy had given him the key to the steward's office just in case one of the maids decided to beat the rugs or dust the furniture. At her quiet knock, and her murmured, "It's only me...Lucy," Will opened the door almost at once.

"*Only* you?" he repeated as he whisked her into the room then shut the door behind her and locked it.

"Yes. Just me."

"There's nothing 'only' or 'just' about you, lass. You're so much more. In fact, after last night, I canna stop thinking about you."

And then with a groan, he crowded her against the door, his strong, muscled arms bracketing her in, and he kissed her. His hips pressed forward, crushing the silk skirts of her blossom-pink gown as his mouth hungrily claimed hers. And Lucy melted into him because how could she not? Will made her feel so very special and alive and wanted. And yes, "more." Like he actually needed her. And she'd never felt like this before. It was a heady feeling indeed. The *best* feeling. If only...

If only what, Lucy?

Before she could contemplate the full ramifications of her wayward thoughts, Will drew back and he was smiling down at her. His irises reminded Lucy of a deep blue ocean on a summer's day. Or perhaps a cloudless blue sky. She wasn't sure if she was drowning in the depths of those magnificent eyes or if she'd ascended to heaven. Either way, she was momentarily lost.

"You taste good, like honey and chocolate and sweet essence of 'Lucy,'" he murmured huskily. "I could just eat you all up." His lips caressed the edge of her ear. "*All* of you..."

Oh, figgy jam. Lucy's fingers curled into Will's shirt, and she tilted her head to the side so he could easily sip at her neck and throat. They'd both agreed that this wouldn't be a genuine courtship, but why did it suddenly feel real? That maybe thoughts like "if only" weren't futile at all, or merely a hazy, insubstantial dream? That a dream of more *was* possible.

She wanted *more* of this moment. *More* of these feelings.

More of Will.

Although it could very well just be lust that is making your mind race off down irrational, even hazardous paths, Lucy told herself as Will's hand that had been spanning her rib cage rose higher to cup her breast, setting off sparks and lighting embers of desire…

We're just having fun. Letting our natural instincts run wild…

It's just biology. It's better if it doesn't mean anything. The real danger here is to your heart…

At last marshaling her unruly thoughts, Lucy gently tugged on Will's hair and said with mock sternness, "I came here for a reason, Will. You cannot distract me, no matter how much you try."

"Is that a challenge?" Will began to nuzzle her ear again. "Because I'd be verra happy to take you up on it." His lips grazed her cheek. "I willna lie. I'm as distracted as hell."

"Perhaps if I tell you I have good news, would that gain your attention?" she asked, and at last, Will took pity on her and lifted his head.

"What is it?"

Lucy smiled. "My dear friend, Artemis, has arrived back in London. She just sent a message, inviting me to her house in Belgravia this afternoon and when I see her, I shall ask her if I can stay there. So it seems I won't have to impose on Jane and her family or take off to the Continent."

Will frowned. "Artemis is your elevated friend?"

Lucy couldn't help it if her smile turned a little smug. "Yes. Artemis Winters, the newly wedded Duchess of Dartmoor."

Will's eyebrows shot up. "You're friends with the Duke of Dartmoor's wife?"

"I am. Actually, Artemis was at Lord and Lady Castledown's ball too. Do you know His Grace?"

"Not well, but yes, we know each other through Castledown. Dartmoor also has ties to the Home Office."

"And does he know you're a spy?"

"Aye, he's one of the few peers that does."

Lucy nodded. "Well, perhaps mentioning that both the duke and Lord Castledown know you will help to convince my father to accept that you are indeed Lord Kyle when you see him."

"Aye, I hope so."

"And how is your search going, by the way?"

Will stepped back from the door and gestured at the room. "I've found nothing of note. Just estate ledgers, accounts, bills. It's clear the estate has financial troubles, but I havena discovered anything else that ties your father to Litchfield or Thorne so far. No letters, no journal entries. Nothing. Is there any place your father might keep a more personal sort of diary?"

Lucy shook her head. "I don't believe so. To begin with, I don't think he has a diary or journal of that nature. Only one for business appointments, and even then his use of it is haphazard at best. If a journal like that isn't in my father's study or in the desk in his sitting room upstairs, I have no idea where he might keep it." Lucy arched a brow. "I take it you've searched there already during one of your middle-of-the-night excursions?"

Will rubbed his chin. "Aye, I have. And it certainly seems as though the evidence I'm looking for isna at Fleetwood Hall. My investigation here is at an end. But"—he caught Lucy's gaze—"I have other leads now. As soon as you are ready to leave, I say we head into Town."

"It won't take me long…although I'm not due at Dartmoor House until one."

"Excellent," said Will. "Because I can think of something else for you to do that could help the investigation a great deal. If you wouldna mind lending me your scientific eye and opinion."

"Of course," said Lucy. "I'll do anything I can to help things along." She sighed. "You've only been here at Fleetwood such a short time. It's such a shame that you're leaving so soon but I understand that you have to. I think Mrs. Gilchrist and Freddy will miss you."

Will grimaced. "I do feel a wee bit guilty about leaving Freddy to deal with the stables all by himself again. If your father is amenable, I might even offer the services of one of my own grooms to help out here. I know pride might prevent him from accepting the offer, but it canna hurt to ask."

Lucy smiled. "That is very generous of you. And yes, I have no idea what he will say, but the gesture means a lot. To me, at least." She stood on tiptoe and kissed his cheek. "Shall I see you in half an hour? I'll be waiting in the hall."

He smiled wolfishly. "Aye. You'd best go, lass, before the wild, savage Scotsman in me decides to make use of your steward's desk for all kinds of wicked purposes."

Lucy's eyebrows shot up. "You can make love on a desk?"

"You can make love anywhere. Considering we'll most likely be a courting couple verra soon, I'd be happy to demonstrate what I know anytime."

Lucy felt herself blushing. "Goodness, and here I was thinking I was so worldly because I have some theoretical knowledge about what goes where."

"Ah, but it's really the 'how' of the business rather than what goes where that's most important." Will winked. "I dinna imagine that you'd be reading about that sort of thing in a scientific text." He leaned close and whispered in her ear, "I'd suggest you go, lass, unless you want a practical biology lesson right here and now."

"I think you underestimate my scientific curiosity, my lord," whispered Lucy. "But you're right, I should go. I'll hold you to your offer though. Sometime, in the not-too-distant future, you will show me the 'how' of making love on a desk. Or any place at all."

She was about to turn the key in the lock when she heard

Will mumble something that sounded like "cheeky wench," and she smiled.

Light and fun and playful was good. It was always safer when one didn't hope for "more."

But what if you could have more, Lucy? What if you could have everything?

A knock on the door immediately made Lucy jump, and Will swore softly beneath his breath.

"Miss Bertram? Miss Bertram? Are you in there?"

It was Redmond. Will stepped to the side, then nodded at Lucy to respond.

"Yes?" she called, hoping she didn't sound as breathless as she felt. She smoothed her hair, then her skirts. "I'll be out in a minute."

"Oh, it's just that a message arrived for Mr. Armstrong via courier, and he can't be found. Apparently it's an urgent matter."

Urgent? Lucy's gaze darted to Will, and he nodded again. When she opened the door, he was safely concealed in the shadows behind it.

"I'll see that Mr. Armstrong gets this," she said, taking the envelope from the butler before shutting the door again. If Redmond was taken aback by her abruptness, she didn't have time to dwell on it.

As Will scanned the contents of the missive, he paled. "There's been another murder."

Ice-cold fear gripped Lucy's chest. "Who?" she whispered.

"Another member of the Linnean Society Council who's been in the murderer's sights. Professor George Fitzroy. He apparently died while drinking his morning coffee. Poisoned. Strychnine is suspected based on the manner of death." Will's grim gaze met Lucy's. "A visit to Scotland Yard is definitely in the cards."

Chapter Nineteen

ALTHOUGH THE HEADQUARTERS OF THE METROPOLITAN Police, or "Scotland Yard," were officially situated in Whitehall Place, Will directed Nutmeg and the Bertrams' gig to the rear entrance of the building at Great Scotland Yard where the constabulary's stables were also located. After Will handed the reins to Freddy, who'd willingly accompanied them on the journey to act as a tiger, he helped Lucy alight into the busy street.

"I'll need to have a wee chat with Detective Lawrence before I bring you into his office," said Will. "This change in tack will be a huge surprise for him as well, but I'm sure I'll be able to convince him this is the best way to proceed with the investigation from this point onwards."

Lucy nodded as she lifted her silk skirts to negotiate the short flight of steps leading up to the Scotland Yard offices. "I hope I'm not going to cause a huge kerfuffle by joining the investigation," she said.

"Only a minor one, I'm certain." The vestibule inside was bustling with activity, so Will drew her to a slightly quieter corner near a marble pillar. "Just a word of warning, lass..." He drew a deep breath. "I'll no longer sound like a Scotsman when I'm talking to Detective Lawrence or, indeed, anyone from the peerage."

Lucy frowned. "What do you mean?"

"I mean I'll sound just like you. English..." Will winced. "I had to cease using the Scot's brogue of my youth—the brogue I've been using as Will Armstrong—as soon as my grandfather sent me away to Eton because... Well, suffice it to say, it made life easier for me at school if I blended in. And I've spoken like an upper-class Englishman for years, except for when I'm in disguise. So it might come as a shock to you, and of course I would hate to think that you don't believe I've been genuine with you this whole time." He caught her gaze. Held it. "With you, Lucy, I can be myself and I wanted to reassure you that I'm still the same man, no matter the accent I use."

"Oh... Oh, I..." Lucy searched his eyes. "Thank you for letting me know..." She gave him a shy smile then. "So how many different accents have you mastered over the years?"

Will was so relieved that she trusted him that he couldn't help but cast her a rakish smile. "Just about any British accent, whether that be Scottish, Welsh, or Irish, or any of the regional county accents. I can also speak fluent Russian, French, and Italian. So you might say I'm a master linguist."

Lucy's eyes shone. "I'm impressed, Lord Kyle. You have many hidden talents."

Will leaned close to her ear. "As I mentioned earlier today, I'll be happy to demonstrate all of them. Verra soon, I hope." Pushing down the almost irresistible urge to spirit Lucy away to Kyleburn House so he could show her right now, he offered her his arm instead. "I'll escort you to an anteroom off Lawrence's office. It will be less busy there. Hopefully I won't be too long."

Will found not only Detective Inspector John Lawrence but also Lord Castledown ensconced in the detective's office on the first floor. Both the gray-haired earl and Lawrence greeted Will with grim expressions.

"Thank you for coming so quickly," said Lawrence, who

then promptly brought Will up to date on the morning's gruesome developments.

"Apparently Professor Fitzroy's housekeeper found a jar labeled 'Ceylonese Ground Coffee' in amongst the early-morning deliveries to the kitchen," explained the detective. "Thinking nothing of it, the footman prepared the professor's pot of coffee as was his usual custom. But not long after Fitzroy had taken a few sips, the poor man began to have severe convulsions and died within minutes. He was a widower with no children, so thank God no one else drank that coffee."

"Agreed," said Castledown grimly. "I also think it's a very good idea to be looking closely at this fellow Zachariah Thorne. Lawrence has filled me in on your suspicions, Kyle, and your reasoning is sound."

Will bowed his head in acknowledgment. "My suspicions are even stronger considering Thorne owns coffee plantations in Ceylon." He turned to Lawrence. "Has the postmortem been conducted yet? Are we sure there *was* strychnine in the coffee and Fitzroy didn't die from a stroke or some disease of the heart?"

"Mr. Dalrymple, the divisional surgeon, is still examining the body, but I expect to hear from him soon," said Lawrence. "To answer your second question, the staff present in the professor's morning room have all reported their master died quickly and in a manner consistent with strychnine poisoning. Their reports also match those of the witnesses who observed Lord Litchfield's death at the Raleigh Club. We've also identified a fine white powder in amongst the coffee grounds that could be strychnine, but it's yet to be identified. That might take some time as we'll need to send a sample off to a division-appointed pharmaceutical chemist or toxicologist along with the powder posted to Darwin. We have a contact at the Royal Pharmaceutical Society in Great Russell Street."

"I see." Will crossed his arms. "Gentlemen, it certainly seems like our murderer has struck again, and now more than ever we need to catch him… Unfortunately, even though we are at a critical juncture of the investigation, necessity compels me to change tack. I can no longer remain a covert agent." And then Will proceeded to explain his present circumstances in relation to his grandfather's poor health and that this current case would be his last. That he needed to reenter society as the Earl of Kyle.

"It will be a shame to lose your services, Kyle, especially given the recent developments," said Castledown, "but I do understand when familial duty calls."

"As do I," said Lawrence. "And I appreciate that you are willing to continue to see this case through to the end. Actually, I'm beginning to think it might work in our favor if you enter the scene, so to speak, as Lord Kyle."

"Yes," agreed Castledown. "It will certainly rattle both Sir Oswald and Thorne."

"I intend to do just that," said Will and then he briefly outlined his plan to catch Zachariah Thorne, including his idea of playing the role of rival suitor. "For various reasons, I had to share my real identity with Miss Bertram, and she is willing to go along with the scheme."

Lawrence and Castledown exchanged speaking looks. "I must say, this is highly irregular," said the earl. "Involving the daughter of a key suspect could compromise the investigation. You're sure she can be trusted?"

"Yes, I am. In fact, I'd trust her with my life," said Will. "And you both know I am not one to trust easily. Aside from that, Miss Bertram is determined to avoid marrying Thorne. And while she loves her father, she won't be pushed into anything. She wants to find out why her father is insisting on this match, just as much as we do. There must be something there that we don't know about yet. I can feel it."

"From what you've already told me, I strongly suspect that something odd is going on too." Lawrence's gaze narrowed. "Although are you sure that you can get Sir Oswald to accept your story about how you came to be in his employ?"

Will raised an eyebrow. "The best lies are based on half-truths. He might have suspicions about my integrity, or even my state of mind, but I doubt he'd fathom that I've been spying on him. My hope is that Sir Oswald might finally disclose why he's willing to marry his daughter off to a disagreeable character like Thorne. It's clearly to do with money, but as you pointed out last time we met, Lawrence, what does Thorne gain besides a wife? Is it access to Sir Oswald's expertise and a stash of rare poisons?"

"All valid questions we'd like answers to," said Lawrence. "As for the best way to tackle Thorne... As much as I'd like to have him brought in for questioning, I don't think we should alert him to the fact he's also under investigation for murder just yet. If his suspicions are aroused, he might go to ground."

Castledown concurred. "Yes, better to rile Thorne in the hopes he might make some sort of verbal blunder. I must say, Kyle, I do like your idea of joining the Raleigh Club to put the wind up the man. He'll be so ruffled by your presence, he might very well say something he shouldn't. I'll sponsor you myself."

"I think it's a sound plan all round," said Lawrence. He sent Will a knowing look across his cluttered desk. "I'm especially impressed how quickly you've managed to enlist Miss Bertram's support."

Castledown winked. "No doubt it helps that our Lord Kyle is a handsome-as-sin Scotsman who knows how to charm the opposite sex when the occasion calls for it, hey what?"

Will shrugged. "Must needs when the devil drives." Of

course, he didn't mean that at all, but as usual he felt protective
of Lucy's reputation. He didn't want Lawrence or Castledown
to think she was gullible or easily manipulated. Or seduced.
"Now, might I suggest that this might be a good time to bring
Miss Bertram in? She's actually waiting just outside this office."

Castledown's silvered brows shot up. "She is?"

"Yes, at my request. Because Miss Bertram possesses expert
knowledge about all types of botanical poisons, including
strychnine, I have no doubt that she will be able to quickly
identify the toxin in Fitzroy's coffee as well as the mysterious
powder sent to Darwin. I know you plan to involve the Royal
Pharmaceutical Society in the investigation, but speed is of the
essence, after all." Will turned his attention to Lawrence. "I trust
you have samples of both substances at hand?"

Lawrence nodded. "I do. If you don't mind, I'll also summon
the divisional physician, Mr. Dalrymple. I'm sure he will want
to be present while Miss Bertram conducts her analyses."

After Lawrence sent for Dalrymple, Will escorted Lucy into
the detective's office and made the introductions. Upon meeting Lord Castledown again, she promptly blushed and stam-
mered something about how much she'd enjoyed herself at his
spring ball at the start of the Season.

Lawrence was scrupulously polite, and after thanking Lucy
for lending her expertise to the investigation, he asked if she
required anything.

"Only a microscope and some microscopic glass slides,"
Lucy said matter-of-factly.

Lawrence's eyebrows shot up. "You want to examine both
powders under a microscope?"

"Of course," rejoined Lucy. Her shyness had been replaced
by a quiet confidence as she continued. "How is one to identify
a substance if one cannot see all of its minutiae in detail?" Her

brows dipped into a frown. "Detective, you don't mean to tell me that Scotland Yard doesn't routinely examine all pieces of evidence in this manner. Mr. Armstrong—pardon me, I should say Lord Kyle—informed me that you're already working on the theory that the strychnine found in Lord Litchfield's absinthe was a particularly potent form of *Strychnos nux-vomica*. Surely you didn't just rely on witness accounts of Litchfield's death to arrive at that conclusion. There must have been some sort of postmortem examination of Litchfield's stomach contents at the very least, as well as a forensic toxicology investigation, no? Given the notable contributions of the late Mathieu Orfila to the emerging science of forensic medicine, I believed such practices would be commonplace in England by now."

Lawrence puffed out his chest. "Of course there was a postmortem, and yes, a toxicology investigation, but it took us some time to find someone suitably qualified. A pharmaceutical chemist with additional medical training, actually. And while I am familiar with Orfila's work, I'm afraid I'm merely a detective, not a man of science.

"At any rate, Mr. Dalrymple, the divisional physician, will be here soon, so I'm sure he can elaborate on what has or has not been done to date." Lawrence picked up a small stoppered vial that contained a tiny amount of a pale, beige-hued substance that looked like sand. "Here's a sample of the powder that was contained in the envelope sent to Darwin if you'd like to take a look, Miss Bertram."

Lucy inclined her head. "Thank you," she said as she took the sample with gloved fingers and then crossed the room to the one small grimy window. She held the vial up to the light. "It looks like a mixture of two powders—pounce powder perhaps and something else. I suspect it's the 'something else' that caused the skin reaction. It looks organic to me. And I think I do know what it is, but I'd rather not say until I've examined it microscopically."

"I'll send for that microscope right away," said Lawrence. "And perhaps we can all take tea while we wait."

Lucy smiled. "That would be lovely."

Within the space of half an hour, Mr. Dalrymple—a portly, middle-aged man wearing spectacles—the jar of poisoned coffee, the microscope, and a small box of glass slides had all arrived. The physician looked Lucy over with a gimlet eye as Detective Lawrence introduced her.

"And what did you say your qualifications were again, Miss Bertram?" asked the doctor, his manner gruff and rudely dismissive.

Will bristled at the man's attitude, but despite the fact Lucy's cheeks had pinkened to the same color as her gown, she held her ground. "I didn't, Mr. Dalrymple. But while I do not possess a university degree, I have acted as a research assistant for my father, Sir Oswald Bertram, for many years. He's a botanical poisons expert."

Dalrymple made a scoffing noise in his throat. "I know of him. Odd that the daughter of a potential murderer is here to give her 'expert' advice though."

Will couldn't hold his tongue this time. "It's not your place to comment on how an investigation is conducted, Doctor, nor to cast aspersions on Miss Bertram's level of expertise or impartiality. Detective Lawrence sent for you out of common courtesy. Indeed, perhaps you might learn something today."

The physician's mouth twisted with annoyance, but nevertheless he didn't say anything else as they all watched Lucy take a seat behind Lawrence's desk where the microscope had been set up. After removing her bonnet, she took a silk kerchief from her reticule and fashioned it into a makeshift mask to cover her nose and mouth. She also donned a pair of cinder goggles.

Dalrymple snorted. "Egads, is that really necessary, Miss Bertram?"

"Considering Professor Fitzroy is now dead, and everyone suspects the weapon of choice is strychnine—a poison which *can* be absorbed through the skin—I would contend that yes, it is necessary," she replied coolly. "Aside from that, no one knows what's in this particular powder that made Charles Darwin ill. If it's all right with you, I'd rather not inadvertently breath in any particles or get them in my eyes." And then with gloved hands, she uncorked the vial and very carefully tipped a small amount of the powder onto a glass slide, covered it with another, then slid it beneath the microscope's lens to examine it.

Bending her head, she peered into the eyepiece and then adjusted the focus. After only a few moments, she said, "It's just as I thought... Cuttlefish pounce, and the light-brown 'something else' that caused Darwin's rash is organic in nature. In fact, it's a very common substance known to cause skin irritation." She raised her head and caught Will's gaze. "It's simply rosehip powder. It's an ingredient in itching powder and altogether harmless. Well, aside from the fact it causes a mechanical prickle, a bit like the irritation caused by roughly spun wool fibers or coarse sackcloth. While one can even ingest rosehip for medicinal purposes—rosehip tea is quite popular—it can cause gastric upset in some if taken in large amounts. I can't imagine Darwin deliberately ingested this though. His nausea must have some other cause."

"Rosehip powder?" said Dalrymple. "Surely you jest, Miss Bertram."

Lucy raised an eyebrow. "Now why would I do that, Doctor? If you would like to take a look at the sample under the microscope, it's as plain as day it's ground rosehip. You can see the fibers have a small basal attachment, a large lumen, and they end in a characteristic sharp point. There's no doubt at all."

Dalrymple rounded the desk and Lucy vacated the chair so the doctor could have a look. "Humph," he said after a brief pause. "So that's rosehip powder, is it? Bully for you, Miss Bertram. Although it's hardly a groundbreaking discovery that will change the course of the case."

"Yet it was an easy enough discovery to make if one made the effort to examine the evidence properly," said Will dryly, earning him a glare from Dalrymple. "It's quite amazing, really."

Lawrence frowned. "It may not be a significant development, but we've learned our perpetrator merely wanted to scare Darwin on this occasion rather than cause real harm."

"Or it's a warning to take the threat to his life seriously," added Will. "It's almost as though the murderer was mocking him and us. An 'I-can-reach-Darwin-or-anyone-else-on-my-list-anytime-I-like' sort of warning. And now Professor Fitzroy, another supporter of Darwin's, is dead." He addressed Lucy directly. "If you wouldn't mind examining the coffee, Miss Bertram…"

"Of course," she said. She efficiently prepared a new set of slides and then, after examining the sample briefly beneath the microscope, looked up. "There's definitely powdered Ceylonese *Strychnos nux-vomica* seeds present in these ground coffee beans," she said. Behind her cinder goggles her eyes were clouded with worry. "At the risk of incriminating my father, I can attest he also possesses the same sorts of seeds in his poisons collection. But so do many apothecaries and physicians throughout Britain. *Strychnos nux-vomica* is endemic throughout Ceylon and the subcontinent in general. What I'm trying to say is it's not *un*common. As to whether *this* strychnine"—she gestured at the microscopic slide—"is more soluble and therefore potentially more potent when mixed with liquid, I couldn't say. I'd have to conduct further experiments."

"Thank you, Miss Bertram," said Detective Lawrence. "Your observations thus far have been more than helpful."

Dalrymple grunted as he pushed himself to his feet. "Right, I have living patients to see so I'm off then," he said. "And in case you're wondering, Lawrence, I've already sent a sample of Fitzroy's stomach contents off to the chemist you used in the Litchfield case." He nodded at the detective and bowed to Lord Castledown. "If you need my services again, you know where to find me." And then he quit the room without farewelling Lucy or Will.

The detective sighed heavily as the door shut. "My apologies for Mr. Dalrymple's behavior, Miss Bertram," he said. "I'm afraid he gets rather terse on occasion."

Especially when a woman shows him up, thought Will. *What an arrogant ass.*

Lucy shrugged. "It's not your fault, Detective," she said as she carefully removed her gloves, then her goggles and makeshift mask. "It's not as though I'm not used to my opinions being dismissed by most men. But I do appreciate the fact that both you and Lord Castledown as well as Lord Kyle sought my advice."

Lawrence inclined his head. "And I shall keep in mind that perhaps we need to utilize microscopes here at Scotland Yard when the occasion warrants it."

The carriage clock on the mantel struck half-past twelve and Will caught Lucy's eye. "Right, we need to get you to Dartmoor House."

"Dartmoor House?" Lawrence cocked a brow. "Are

you acquainted with the Duke and Duchess of Dartmoor, Miss Bertram?"

Lucy smiled as she tied her bonnet in place. "I am indeed, Detective Lawrence. The duke and duchess have just returned from their honeymoon."

"Please pass on my regards to them both." When Lucy gave the detective a quizzical look, he added, "I worked on a case involving the duke earlier this year."

"Ah," said Lucy. "I thought your name was familiar. And yes, I will quite happily pass on your regards."

"Mine too," said Lord Castledown. "The duke and I are old friends."

"Of course," said Lucy.

As soon as they stepped outside of Lawrence's office into the busy corridor, Will said to Lucy in a low voice meant only for her, "You, my dear Miss Bertram, are impressive."

Even though her bonnet hid most of her face, Will could see a pretty pink blush had suffused her cheeks. "Thank you," she murmured. "And thank you for your support. It means a lot to me. More than I can say, actually."

"It's my pleasure, lass," he said, slipping back into his Scots brogue. And that drew Lucy to an abrupt halt.

Turning to face him, she searched his gaze. "Your English accent is impeccable, Will. But what feels natural to you? How do *you* want to speak? How do *you* want others to see you? It seems to me, now that you've decided to be the real 'you' again, you can do whatever you like." Her expression softened and she touched his arm. "You're no longer that young boy who got sent away to Eton. You're a powerful man. A member of the peerage. You don't have to just 'fit in' or be someone you're not just because it's supposedly required. It should be your choice."

"I..." Will studied her lovely face. Her gaze was filled with such tenderness and understanding, it made his breath catch in his chest. It was as though she knew him. *Really* knew him. She saw straight through all his masks, right down to his very soul. The noise and people brushing past them—the constables and clerks and the apprehended—seemed to fade and disappear and all that mattered was Lucy and this moment. "I...I don't know," he managed at last. His heart beat loudly in his ears. He felt as though he was standing on the edge of something important and he needed to get the answer right. Both for himself and for this incredible woman. But he was floundering. Lost. Unsure of himself, which was not like him at all.

And then she smiled and everything that felt wrong and out of kilter in his world suddenly felt so right, especially when she said, "Just so you know, I like whatever version of 'Will' you want to be. You are a good man." Taking his arm again, they proceeded toward the staircase that would lead them downstairs to the Great Scotland Yard entrance and into the bright summer's day where suddenly anything and everything seemed possible.

Chapter Twenty

As soon as Lucy stepped into the grand vestibule of Dartmoor House in Belgrave Square, Artemis Winters, the Duchess of Dartmoor, enveloped her in an enormous hug. "Lucy, my darling friend. I've missed you so much."

As Lucy hugged her back, she discovered her throat was tight with unexpected tears of happiness. And also relief. "I've missed you too," she managed. Drawing back, she added, "It's so good to see you. I can't wait to hear about all of your travels. You must have some wonderful tales to tell."

"I do." Artemis's dark brown eyes glowed with warmth. "And I will fill you in on everything as soon as Jane arrives. I doubt there will be much book chat this afternoon."

"Today, I wouldn't have it any other way," said Lucy.

At that moment there was a smart rap at the door and the butler admitted Jane. There were more hugs and happy tears, and within minutes, they were all scaling the grand staircase, arm-in-arm to the first floor where the elegant drawing room lay. A light luncheon of sandwiches, delicate pastries, and petit fours had already been laid out on platters between the gleaming silver urn, the tea caddy, Spode china teapot, and other tea paraphernalia.

Once they were all settled on plush, plumply cushioned sofas, and Artemis had dispensed the tea, Lucy and Jane plied her with questions about her travels about the Continent with her besotted husband, Dominic.

"I must say, married life seems to suit you very well," said

Jane after Artemis had finished regaling them with an amusing anecdote about a *strega* in a northern Italian village who'd been particularly taken with the darkly handsome duke and had tried to cast a love spell over him. "Next you'll be recommending it to both Lucy and me."

"While it's true I've never been happier, I would never do that," said Artemis. "Unless either of you did meet the 'right' man, so to speak. But I fear men like Dominic are few and far between. It did take me twenty-nine years to meet someone as wonderful as him, and even then I wasn't looking for a husband. And as you both know, it took a lot to convince me to change my mind about marriage."

"But it seems love-matches *do* exist. And not just in the books we read," said Lucy with a deep sigh. Such a notion should bring her joy. But it didn't. With love also came pain. Her parents had once loved each other, very deeply. But after her mother had passed away, her father had gone into a decline for over a year until the study of botany became his *raison d'être*. It was a strange sort of madness that had consumed him at the cost of everything and everyone else. And that was why she was now in her current pickle—her father needed to barter her off so he could continue with his obsession. And it wasn't fair.

Lucy's mind strayed to Will and how he made her feel when she was with him. Was this warm flood of emotions—excitement and hope and, yes, a good deal of desire—that welled inside her heart whenever she thought of him the beginnings of love? Was he beginning to feel that way about her too? She could hardly tell.

But if either one of them did fall in love, what would that mean for them both? Would she ever consider marriage to an earl who one day would become a duke? Could she risk the pain of finding out her love was unrequited? Could she risk giving up all of the things she held dear—her own dreams of traveling abroad and professional aspirations of writing a book on the medicinal uses of plants—to become the wife of a nobleman?

But your friend has both of those things, Lucy. The love of a wonderful man and *according to Artemis, her new academic ladies' college is due to open in a month's time… What if you could have love and a career?*

Will was nothing but proud of you today. He said you were "impressive," *and you know that he meant it…*

She replenished her tea, and when she looked up, Artemis was studying her with her far too perceptive gaze. "Is everything all right with you, Lucy? You've gone awfully quiet. I've been talking so much about my adventures abroad, I haven't yet asked you about your situation. I hope your father hasn't still been pressuring you to wed." She winced. "Although I fear he might be…"

Lucy tried to summon a carefree smile but suspected she failed miserably when Artemis's look of concern deepened. "Now that you mention it, I'm afraid he has." And then she poured out her heart about her concerns in regard to the odious Zachariah Thorne. That he might take some sort of action that might force her into marriage. She didn't mention anything about the Yorkshireman's possible role in the murders of Lord Litchfield and Professor Fitzroy because she'd promised Will that she wouldn't. "I know it's a terrible imposition," she concluded, "considering you and Dominic have only just arrived back in London, but I *had* rather hoped that I might be able to stay with you for a little while. Just until I can convince my father that I have another, far more suitable suitor in mind. Which I do…"

Both Artemis's and Jane's eyes widened to the size of saucers.

"Heavens," said Artemis after she seemed to recollect herself and her eyebrows returned to their usual position. "Where to begin with all of that. First of all, of course you can stay here at Dartmoor House. For as long as you like. That should go without saying." Leaning forward in a conspiratorial fashion, her eyes gleaming with interest, she added, "But what do you mean you have 'another, far more suitable suitor in mind'?"

"Yes," said Jane. "I'm as curious as can be, considering you haven't said a word to me about it. I knew about Mr. Thorne— indeed I don't think I will ever forget our recent encounter at Fortnum & Mason's—but pray tell, who is this other mysterious contender? And when and where did you meet him?"

Lucy felt her cheeks grow hot. "We've only met recently... Actually, it's a little more complicated than that." *Oh, Barnaby Rudge.* How could she explain how she'd met Will without giving away his secrets? "Lately, he's been staying in the environs of Heathwick Green. But we first met months ago— albeit briefly—in April. His name is William Lockhart...the Earl of Kyle."

Two pairs of eyebrows shot up again. "Lord Kyle?" repeated Artemis and Jane in unison.

"Yes, Lord Kyle," said Lucy. Oh, she was such a bad liar, and she was liable to blurt out something she shouldn't if she wasn't careful. It was best to stick to facts she could safely share. And that didn't include recounting her amorous shenanigans with Will on numerous occasions. Even though her cheeks were burning, Lucy took a deep breath and added, "He's a Scotsman. Of course, that particular detail is really neither here nor there, is it? It's probably more pertinent to say he's quite the gentleman." *Well, in all the ways that really matter he is,* thought Lucy. "In any event, I rather like him, and I think he likes me. In fact, he's speaking with my father this afternoon to ask his permission to formally pay court to me."

Artemis grinned. "Well, I never," she said. "Who'd have

suspected that our sweet, shy Lucy would have developed a tendre for a Scottish earl."

Jane's gaze narrowed. "Why do I feel like there's more to this story than you are letting on? And I hope you'll forgive me for being a tad apprehensive, but how do you know he *is* a trust-worthy gentleman? Or that he's even an earl?"

"Aside from the fact I've seen Lord Kyle's signet ring that bears his seal, the earl and I met at the Castledown ball. Apparently, Lord Castledown knows him well."

"I honestly had no idea." Artemis's gaze turned curious. "You never mentioned him at the time."

"As I said, our encounter was brief, and honestly I never thought I *would* see Lord Kyle again," said Lucy. She felt bad about not being able to share the entire truth with her friends, but at least she wasn't lying outright. "Artemis, he's even acquainted with your husband," she added for good measure. "Via Lord Castledown, of course."

"Well then," said Artemis. "He sounds like an entirely suit-able match. If you *did* wish to marry…" Her expression grew a little sly. "I hope you'll forgive my bluntness, but knowing you as I do, that's the real question, isn't it, my dear friend? Do you want to wed? For years and years, all of us declared that we were confirmed spinsters, and now look at me." She laughed. "I now highly recommend the institution. As long as one finds the right man, of course. Marrying the wrong man would be quite a disaster."

"I…I'm not sure about anything yet," said Lucy. And that *was* the truth. "For so long, I've avoided even thinking about getting married at all. But Lord Kyle is…different." She shrugged. "For the moment, I'm treating it as a courtship-of-convenience."

"And what of Lord Kyle? Does he feel the same way?" asked Jane. "Is it purely a matter of convenience for him too?"

"He knows I have reservations about marrying," said Lucy. "And that I have professional aspirations. Which he approves of. He's not in any rush to wed either."

Jane's frown deepened. "Then why is he courting you?"

"He, ah…he knows Zachariah Thorne and he's happy to play suitor to put the man off."

"How very noble of him," remarked Artemis with a knowing smile.

"Very admirable," agreed Jane. "He sounds like a veritable knight in shining armor. I for one can't wait to meet him."

"Neither can I," said Artemis. "In fact, I'll make sure he's issued an invitation to the ball that Lord Castledown has generously offered to throw for Dominic and me next week. A 'Welcome Back to Society' ball of sorts."

"That would be lovely. Unfortunately, my father still has to agree to Lord Kyle's proposition," said Lucy with a sigh. "He could very well say no."

If he did, she had no idea what she would do. She couldn't stay in hiding forever, and besides, she'd already left a note for her father at Fleetwood Hall informing him where she was staying and that she wouldn't change her mind about getting married to Thorne no matter what he said.

Of course, she wouldn't mind being courted by Will. *Just for show,* she reassured herself. *Just to discourage Zachariah Thorne.* Although now that her father knew she was at Dartmoor House, maybe he would tell Thorne.

Hopefully, the horrid man wouldn't come calling.

———

"Sir Oswald Bertram is here to see you, my lord," announced Kyleburn House's butler, Hillier.

Ah, so the baronet had taken Will's bait. Excellent.

After Will had made sure Lucy was safely installed at Dartmoor House, he'd returned to his own Belgravia residence and had done two things. First of all, he'd secured the services of a canny inquiry agent—a former police constable at Scotland Yard—to track down Monty Bertram. And second, he'd dispatched several footmen to various locations where Sir Oswald might be found—Thorne's town house, the Linnean Society headquarters, and Fleetwood Hall—to deliver a short message: that the baronet's presence was requested at Kyleburn House at three o'clock sharp to discuss "a matter of grave importance with the Earl of Kyle."

Even though Sir Oswald had never met "Lord Kyle," he was clearly a curious man.

Whether he was an accommodating man remained to be seen.

Will addressed his butler: "Thank you, Hillier. Show the baronet to the library. Tell him I'll be with him presently."

Hillier bowed. "Of course, my lord."

The door to his private sitting room shut and Will examined his appearance in the mirror above the fireplace. Thanks to his trusty valet, Symington, he was clean-shaven, and his hair was relatively neat for once—well, as neat as could be expected considering he needed a good haircut. His charcoal-gray suit fit him well and the black neckcloth at his throat sported a silver and sapphire pin. Oh, and of course, he was wearing his signet ring.

He looked the part of the Earl of Kyle, heir to a dukedom, even if Sir Oswald was disinclined to believe his claim.

He also wasn't in a hurry to meet with Sir Oswald. He wanted Lucy's father to be a bit rattled when they met. Flustered men tended to misspeak, and that might work in Will's favor. Perhaps the baronet might inadvertently drop a bread crumb of a clue or two in relation to Thorne. It was a strategy he was going to use with Thorne tomorrow at the Raleigh Club after Castledown made him a member. There had to be something between Thorne and Sir Oswald that was the key to solving this murder and extortion case.

And hopefully, it wouldn't be long before he was openly courting Lucy. While their clandestine liaisons had added an extra layer of excitement to their fledgling relationship, he was actually looking forward to being able to squire her about Town and to functions as the real William, not some manufactured version of himself. The fact that he felt that way was telling indeed.

When he was with Lucy, she made him feel content. At home. *Cared for.* Like he could be himself and that was all that mattered.

Except... This idea of belonging and being accepted for who he was also felt unfamiliar. It was as though he'd entered a strange land or realm and had no clue as to what the rules were anymore. Which way was up, or which was down, or how he was supposed to act. He was not used to any of this.

One thing was certain though: he didn't want to leave. Didn't want to say goodbye to Lucy if he didn't have to.

While he understood Lucy's need to maintain her independence so she could continue with her botany career, he also wondered if she'd ever given thought to the idea that maybe she could have both—a career and marriage. If she were to wed the right sort of man who wasn't in a hurry to settle down and start a family straightaway...

He was also sure that these feelings of warmth and tenderness that had taken root in his chest weren't one-sided. He knew Lucy desired him, but he was also sure she was developing genuine feelings for him too. Why else would she have told him that he should be himself? That he was a good man?

That *had* to mean something.

But he was getting ahead of himself. First, he had a father to convince he was a worthy suitor. That he was a better choice than Zachariah Thorne. And that would be no mean feat considering Will had misrepresented who he was from the outset of their acquaintanceship.

Will tugged at his cuffs and squared his shoulders. He was dithering now. He just needed to get on with this interview. Rip off the bandage and expose his subterfuge—well, at least some of it.

He found Sir Oswald installed in the library, pacing the Turkish carpet. As soon as the baronet laid eyes on Will, his grizzled brows shot heavenward.

"Will Armstrong! What the devil are you doing here?" he demanded. His gaze traveled over Will's attire and then his brows descended into a deep frown. "And why the hell are you dressed like..." He waved a hand in Will's direction. "Like that? In gentlemen's attire? Here"—his gaze narrowed with suspicion—"what are you up to? Something's not right." He straightened his shoulders and glared. "Where is the Earl of Kyle?"

Will had to suppress a smirk. "So many pertinent questions, Sir Oswald," he said in his Scots brogue. The baronet was already sufficiently shaken. There was no need to use a cultivated accent. And he rather liked the idea of being himself for once. "But to answer your last one, Lord Kyle *is* here."

"Stop playing games. What do you mean? There's no one here but you and..." The baronet's voice trailed off as the truth hit him. "You mean to say *you* are Lord Kyle?"

Will inclined his head. "I am. William Douglas Lockhart, the Earl of Kyle, at your service."

The baronet's face had turned an alarming shade of mottled puce. "But this is outrageous! You're talking utter nonsense. You must be mad."

"Not at all." Will gestured at the arrangement of leather chairs before the fireplace. "I know this is a wee bit of a shock, and I will endeavor to explain it all to you. But first, would you care to take a seat? Can I offer you a drink, perhaps? I have some verra fine Scots whisky…" He nodded at the drinks tray on the mahogany sideboard near his desk.

"No. I do not want a goddamned whisky or any other sort of drink for that matter." Sir Oswald's lip curled with a derisive sneer. "I want answers, *Lord* Kyle."

"Verra well. You shall have them." *Or at least the version I'm prepared to give you.*

The baronet claimed a wingback chair and Will settled into the opposite one.

"Now, the truth of the matter is, I've been using the name William Armstrong for at least a year now," he began. "Armstrong was my mother's maiden name." That was true. "Indeed, Lady Anne Armstrong was the daughter of the Earl of Eskdale. But I digress…"

"Yes, you bloody well do. Get to the point, *Kyle*. Why have you been pretending to be a groom in my household?"

Will affected a sigh. "I wish there was an easy answer. But the truth is I've fallen out with my grandfather, the Duke of Ayr. It's been well known in many circles that even though I am his heir, we have been estranged for some time… Actually, the reason I joined the British military a decade ago was to thwart him."

Sir Oswald made a scoffing noise. "*You*—a man who is undoubtedly a liar and a scoundrel—served in the Queen's army? Pray, what regiment and rank?"

"Aye, I did serve, and I rose to the rank of major before I resigned my commission. When I fought in the Crimean War, I served with the cavalry regiment, the Scots Greys. I have men you know who can vouch for all I say, by the way. Lord Castledown for one. And the Duke of Dartmoor."

Sir Oswald grunted. "You can be sure that I will be checking your credentials and story, *sir*."

"And I wouldna have it any other way," said Will. "Now, to continue with my explanation as to what brought me to your door." He affected a deep sigh and fiddled with his cuffs. "I'm afraid I was injured during the Crimean conflict." He lifted the hair covering his brow to reveal the jagged scar over his left eye. "Needless to say, I was removed from active duty at that point, and as the war was drawing to a close, I resigned my commission. I'd had enough and I had begun to question what I'd been doing all those years. Facing battle year in and year out, and then almost dying, had affected me in ways that I didna quite understand, and I felt all at sea. Disillusioned. I needed some time to find myself again. I craved simplicity. So I decided to step away from my duties as an earl for a year and turn my attention to doing what I loved most—spending time with horses as a groom."

The baronet snorted. "Poppycock. You expect me to believe all that?"

"War changes a man, Sir Oswald. In profound ways. Unless you've faced death on a regular basis, I wouldna expect you to understand. But that is the truth of the matter. And as I said, men like Lord Castledown can vouch for me."

A grunt from the baronet. "I will certainly be following up with the earl." Sir Oswald's eyes narrowed with suspicion. "But what I want to know is why are you telling me all this now?" Another sneer. "Have you grown tired of being a groom after all? Too much work for you, eh?"

"No. No' exactly." Will sighed again for show. "To be perfectly frank with you, it's several things that have recently changed me. That have made me question the direction I've taken in life yet again. You see, yesterday I received word that my grandfather had suffered a stroke. I can show you the missive if you'd like. It's just on my desk."

But Sir Oswald waved his offer away and grumbled, "Just get on with it, why don't you?"

Will tilted his head. "Verra well. The physician has advised that my grandfather is out of danger for now, but I've realized that if he *should* pass away, I do need to overcome my past personal grudges and face up to my responsibilities. I can't hide forever from the dukedom—or my current duties that come with being an earl.

"And then"—he caught Sir Oswald's eye—"neither can I deny the positive effect working at Fleetwood Hall has had on me. Since I took up the position as your head groom, my spirit has lightened. And again I'm going to shock you… It's all because of your daughter."

"Eh? What's Lucy got to do with this?" The baronet's face turned red again and his voice shook with anger as he bit out, "Don't tell me you've been skulking around with her behind my back. Trying to seduce her. If you've laid one filthy finger on her, I'll have your guts for garters, young man. I can see you're a ruggedly handsome devil and likely to catch a lady's eye. And even though my Lucy is eight-and-twenty, she's still an impressionable, naive young woman."

Will held up a hand. "I assure you that nothing like that has gone on, Sir Oswald," he said. Good God, if the baronet had any inkling of what they *had* been up to, Will suspected Lucy's father might even call him out. "I both like and respect Miss Bertram, and our interactions have been nothing but appropriate. I give you my word as a former officer of Her Majesty's army and as a gentleman and nobleman." He only flinched a little on the inside at his bald-faced lies. Protecting Lucy's reputation was paramount. "However, because I have developed a fond regard for your daughter, combined with the fact I am taking my place as the Earl of Kyle in society again, I would like to court her with a view to asking for her hand in marriage sometime in the future. With your permission, of course."

"What?" Sir Oswald's face was like thunder. "A scoundrel like you wants to court my sweet Lucy?"

"My dear Sir Oswald, I think you do protest too much. Let's not pretend that you haven't been actively trying to pair your daughter with Zachariah Thorne, ostensibly for financial reasons. Don't think I haven't noticed firsthand your issues with money—the penny-pinching going on at Fleetwood Hall, or the talk about Town that you wish Thorne to fund your next expedition to the Malay Peninsula. I too am as wealthy as Croesus and could not only help you out of the deep financial sinkhole you are in but also offer Lucy a good life. A wonderful life. In fact, one day your daughter would be the Duchess of Ayr, not a mere industrialist's wife. Just think of that."

Will waited while the baronet did indeed contemplate his offer. It was a good offer. A sound offer. An offer no sane man would refuse.

But Sir Oswald was being obstinate, clearly for reasons known only to him. "And what does Lucy say?" he said mulishly. "Does she even know your real name, *my lord*?"

"She does," returned Will. "I shared the truth with her earlier today." *In my bed.* But Lucy's father didn't need to know that. "And I believe your daughter holds a degree of regard for me too," he continued. "She has informed me that she would welcome my suit, over and above that of Thorne's. And we both know that she canna abide the man. At all. Indeed, if they did wed, I believe Miss Bertram would be miserable. You canna want that for her."

The baronet's jaw twitched. "First of all, Lord Kyle, why should I trust you? You've misrepresented who you are from the outset. You could be a scoundrel of the highest order. Aside from that, I no longer have a head groom."

Will held the baronet's gaze. "And you have my sincerest apologies for misleading you. I hope I've already begun to make amends by sending one of my own grooms from my stables here back to Fleetwood Hall to help Freddy."

Sir Oswald grunted at that, but as he didn't make any further protest, Will took it as a sign to continue. "And as I said, I am verra happy to show you the letter from my grandfather's physician. The paper bears the Duke of Ayr's seal." He lifted his left hand. "I'm also wearing a signet ring which bears the Earl of Kyle's official seal. Ask any of my staff here at Kyleburn House who I am. And lastly, I encourage you to speak to Lord Castledown and to the Duke of Dartmoor who has just returned to Town. Lord Castledown, who knows me verra well, will attest to all I have told you today."

Sir Oswald's chin hiked up a notch. "You can be certain that I will, young man," he said. "But even if Castledown and Dartmoor do back up your claims, I still may not give my consent to your proposal."

Will frowned as he studied the baronet's face. "Now I'm beginning to wonder why you would no' accept my offer to court your daughter. I'm a wealthy earl who is the heir to a vast dukedom in Scotland. Miss Bertram and I both like each other..." He shrugged and let the silence extend.

A shadow of emotion flickered across Sir Oswald's face, and his focus darted off to a far corner of the room. "It's complicated," he said stiffly, "and it's not something I wish to discuss." His frost-filled gaze settled on Will again. "Especially with someone I have no reason to trust."

"I understand," said Will. He paused again, watching the baronet carefully. "Sir Oswald, I canna help but feel that something untoward might be going on between you and Thorne. Otherwise, I canna fathom why you would favor his suit above mine when your daughter clearly objects to the match. If you are in any sort of trouble, perhaps I can help…"

As Will expected, the baronet immediately bristled. Leaping to his feet, the man fired a fulminating glare at Will. "And I resent your suggestion that I would sacrifice my daughter to get myself out of some sort of bind! How dare you! If I were a younger man and a sure shot, I would call you out for the insult."

With that, Sir Oswald stormed out of the library, slamming the door behind him with such force that the doors of a nearby glass-fronted bookcase shook.

Well, that could have gone better. Will sighed and went to the mahogany sideboard to pour himself a whisky. Sir Oswald might have gone off in a self-righteous blaze of anger, but it wasn't as though Will hadn't made some progress with the investigation. Because without a doubt he'd pressed on a nerve. A source of deep irritation for Sir Oswald.

He was getting closer to finding out the truth, even if Sir Oswald didn't want him to get closer to Lucy.

Well, he had bad news for the baronet. He was going to do that anyway.

And he was also going to provoke Thorne.

It was definitely time to stir up the hornet's nest.

Chapter Twenty-One

"MISS BERTRAM…" DARTMOOR HOUSE'S BUTLER ENTERED the drawing room and approached the sofa where Lucy was settled with a new Gothic romance that Jane had lent her from Delaney's bookstore. In his gloved hand, he held a silver salver upon which sat an ivory-hued card. "You have a caller."

Artemis set aside her leather-bound notebook where she'd been plotting her next novel. "A caller?" Her gaze flitted to the longcase clock in one corner of the room before returning to the butler. "Six o'clock is rather late, isn't it? We'll be getting ready for dinner soon."

Lucy's stomach fluttered with nerves. Lord above, she prayed her father hadn't sent Zachariah Thorne to Dartmoor House. She took the card, and then her heart did a happy jig. "It's Lord Kyle," she said softly. Her cheeks grew warm as she looked up at Artemis. "I think I can forgive him the transgression. He's probably here to tell me how his interview with my father went."

"Hopefully well," said Artemis with a smile. "In any event, tell him he must stay for dinner if he's free. We'll make quite a merry party."

"Are you sure?" asked Lucy. "I don't want to impose any more than I have already."

"Oh, fie. As if you could ever do that, darling Lucy," returned her friend as she rose to her feet, notebook in hand. "Besides, I'm sure Dominic will be happy to have some masculine company at dinner for once." Her smile turned sly. "Actually, if Jane hadn't been obliged to attend another function with her mother, I would extend an invitation to her too so she could meet your Scottish earl. But alas, that shan't be the case tonight." She addressed the butler. "Please show Lord Kyle into the drawing room." To Lucy she said in a low voice, "I'll go and see Cook about the menu, shall I? I'm sure you won't mind if I leave you unchaperoned." And then Artemis also quit the room.

Lucy didn't mind at all. She hastened over to an oval gilt-framed mirror to check her appearance. Her ringlets were neat enough and her cheeks were so flushed with excited antici-pation that she didn't need to pinch them. Indeed, they were the same hue as her pink gown. Who'd have thought that Miss Lucy Bertram would ever feel as giddy as a schoolgirl over seeing some man?

But it wasn't just any man. It was Will. They had much to talk about but suddenly all Lucy could think about was how much she wanted to be with him. To be the object of William Lockhart's attention and affection. To be the woman that he yearned to have in his arms. The woman he wanted to intro-duce to the art of lovemaking...

A deep thrill began to hum through her veins.

A footman announced, "The Earl of Kyle," and Lucy couldn't suppress a small gasp at the sight of him, framed in the doorway like a work of art. The epitome of the darkly handsome hero in her favorite amorous daydreams. Attired in fine gentlemen's garb, he was clean-shaven for once and so obviously a noble-man that Lucy wondered how on earth she couldn't have seen it before. When his deep-blue gaze connected with hers, Lucy's heart all but stopped.

As soon as the door shut and they were alone, Will strode across the room, gathered her into his arms, and kissed her with a heated ardor that bordered on desperation. As though she was his and he'd missed every minute he'd been away from her. As though he couldn't get enough of her.

And the feeling was mutual. Lucy's fingers tangled in Will's hair, and when she tasted him with her tongue, pulling a deep groan from his throat, her pulse capered with joy and desire and triumph.

This. This was what she wanted. All of this and more...

But all too soon, Will was drawing back. "We must slow down, lass," he murmured huskily. "I might be labeled an uncivilized Scot by some, but I willna seduce you in the Duke and Duchess of Dartmoor's drawing room."

"I like it when you are uncivilized," she whispered, stroking his hair back from his forehead. "But you are right. We should behave. And of course I'm eager to hear how your discussion went with my father."

She led Will to the sofa she'd only just vacated, and after they were seated, she searched his face. "You must tell me everything."

Before discussing his meeting with her father, Will informed her that he'd employed an inquiry agent who used to be a former police constable and possessed in-depth knowledge of St Giles and Covent Garden. He was now scouring the streets for her brother and would send regular reports to Kyleburn House. As soon as Will heard anything of import, he would let Lucy know. However, by the time Will had recounted how the interview with her father had gone, Lucy's buoyant mood had dissipated, and she was left feeling both disgruntled and anxious. "I cannot believe he said no, Will. That he'd rather Mr. Thorne pursue me than you."

Will's expression was grave. "Neither can I, lass. But fear not. I willna let Thorne come anywhere near you. Somehow, some way, I will unravel this mystery and expose the man's crimes."

"I believe you," she murmured.

He gave a crooked, rakish smile, but his eyes held a serious, perhaps even expectant light as he said, "Might I suggest another, entirely practical solution to keeping Thorne at bay? I know how much you relish your independence, but if all else fails, we could always elope and get married at a registry office. Or I could obtain a special license. We dinna need anyone's permission. I'm a pragmatist at heart and if you were my wife, Thorne couldna touch you…"

"Marry you?" Lucy exclaimed. "Oh, flapping flapdragons." And then she clapped a hand over her mouth when she realized what she'd just said. "Oh, Will. I'm so sorry about how that sounded. I don't mean to insult you. I'm certain most women *would* want to marry you. How could they not? I mean, you're handsome, and intelligent, and considerate, and all kinds of wonderful. And of course I'm…I'm deeply flattered you would even suggest such a thing to save me. But…part of me also thinks it wouldn't be fair to you if I married you as a last resort." She winced. "I can't be the sort of wife you are looking for. Not really."

But Will didn't look affronted. Indeed, he seemed to be biting the inside of his cheek to stop himself from laughing. "I'm not offended," he said. "However, I do feel compelled to ask: Why on earth do you say things like 'flapping flapdragons'? Actually, I think I might have heard you say something like 'Barnaby Rudge' when I first came upon you in Fleetwood Lane."

Lucy's eyebrows shot up. "You did?"

"Aye," he said. "It was one of the most amusing and delightful things I'd ever heard."

"Well, I am grateful you didn't think I was altogether mad," she said. "But to answer your question… I promised my dearly departed mama a long time ago that I would always behave in a ladylike manner and never use vulgar words. So over the years I invented my own form of harmless cursing to honor my promise. 'Flapping flapdragons' is but one of my own manufactured maledictions."

Will's mouth twitched. "I'd love to hear the others if you'd care to share them."

Lucy donned a mock frown. "You *are* laughing at me."

"Only a wee bit. But seriously, you *should* tell me the rest of your 'manufactured maledictions' so I can check if they might have an alternative meaning you're unaware of."

"Very well." Lucy drew a deep breath and listed them off. "It's an ever-evolving lexicon," she concluded.

"I love them all," said Will. "And I especially adore the fact that you love and respect your mother so much." His chest rose and fell with a heavy sigh. "I loved my own mother deeply too. Her name was Anne. Lady Anne Armstrong before she married my father. I think she would have liked you." His expression grew grave. "I miss her verra much. She had blue eyes. The same blue-gray of mist-wreathed heather on the moors around my home, Kyleburn Castle."

Oh... Lucy's heart clenched with sadness for the boy who'd lost his mother and the man who missed her still. He never talked about his father though. She wanted to ask him more about his family, but she sensed that it was a difficult subject to talk about. Not wishing to pry, she said the first thing that sprang to mind. "You live in a castle?" And then her cheeks burned. "Oh, goodness. What a silly thing to say. I must seem very gauche to someone like you."

"No, no' at all," he replied softly. "Aside from being beautiful, you're open-minded and sweet and kind and loyal and so damn smart, I feel as intellectual as a lump of wood next to you. Do no' underestimate your abundant charms, Lucy Bertram." He raised her hand and kissed it. "And dinna worry about hurting my feelings by saying no to my suggestion to wed. It was merely a spur-of-the-moment offer when I saw how upset you were about your father's rejection of my suit. My natural instinct is to protect those I care about, and if you were my wife and countess, no harm would ever come to you." His expression grew fierce. "No one with any sense of self-preservation would dare hurt you."

Lucy's heart performed an odd little tumble. "You...you care about me?" she murmured. She could hardly fathom such a remarkable thing.

"Of course." He smiled and his fingers lightly caressed her cheek. "How could I not? And rest assured, I do understand how important your career as a botanist is to you and why you have reservations about marriage. And I dinna think that is odd or strange or unnatural. To me, you are quite extraordinary." And then he kissed her with such lingering tenderness, Lucy's toes curled in her embroidered silk pumps.

"I dinna care what your father says, we *are* courting, Lucy," he said, his voice resonating with deep assurance. "I mean to have you. Do you understand?"

"Yes," she whispered. "I do. And I want that too. I mean, I want you. More than I can say."

Will smiled his wicked devil's smile. "I suppose I should bid you adieu before I do make you mine right here in the duke and duchess's drawing room."

"Oh...oh, you don't have to go," said Lucy. "I forgot to tell you that you can stay for dinner if you'd like. Artemis has extended an invitation. It will just be a small party. The Dartmoors and us. What do you say?"

Will's grin grew deliciously wolfish. "I would say it's an offer I canna refuse, my sweet. Especially if there will be an opportunity to be alone with you again later on tonight. I still haven't demonstrated all of my linguistic skills. Or the many different places, and ways, one can engage in intercourse."

Lucy's belly fluttered with excitement. "Of the nonlinguistic variety, I take it?"

Will's smile turned enigmatic. "Perhaps," he said, his voice low and cloaked in dark velvet promise. "You'll simply have to wait and see."

———————

The Duke and Duchess of Dartmoor were charming, entertaining hosts and Will enjoyed every minute of his time at their dinner table. It was especially lovely to see Lucy so at ease as she freely laughed and chatted with her lively friend Artemis.

It had been a while since he'd last talk with Dominic—and that had been only briefly during a meeting at the Home Office two years ago—but it was clear that married life suited him well. Gone was the darkly brooding duke who, back then, more often wore a scowl than a smile. Indeed, Dominic said as much himself after the ladies had retired to the drawing room for tea while they sipped port in the dining room.

It made Will question his own jaded views about the institution of matrimony. This arrangement he had with Lucy was only supposed to be a courtship of convenience. They'd both agreed it wouldn't end in a proposal. So his off-the-cuff suggestion about marrying her for the sake of expediency had not only startled Lucy but had shocked him as well.

One thing Will *was* entirely sure about was how much he wanted this woman. It was in a way he'd never wanted anyone else before. So he would continue to woo Miss Lucy Bertram *and* if they both began to explore the possibility of a future together along the way, so be it.

He certainly wouldn't run from his feelings. He hadn't lied when he'd admitted to Lucy that he was starting to care for her.

Dominic was just about to pour them a third port when Artemis returned to the dining room with Lucy.

As Will and the duke rose from their seats, Artemis declared, "My dearest husband, I hope you can forgive me for interrupting your tête-à-tête with Lord Kyle, but as it's almost midnight, I thought it was about time that you and I retired for the evening." She turned her enigmatic smile on Will. "As you know, we've only just returned from our honeymoon on the Continent, and Dominic is liable to turn into a disagreeable, misanthropic beast if he doesn't get enough sleep."

The duke's mouth twitched with amusement. "It would be a foolish man indeed who disagreed with his wife this early on in the piece," he said. He caught Will's gaze. "I hope you understand, my friend."

Will emitted a quiet chuckle. "Perfectly," he returned.

His gaze drifted to Lucy, drinking in the sight of her in an exquisite evening gown—her smooth-as-satin shoulders lit by gaslight, the luster of her pale golden curls, the mounds of her perfect breasts, and her slender waist encased in rich blue silk.

Perhaps she discerned what he was thinking because color bloomed in her cheeks as she said, "I would be happy to see you out, my lord."

"Wonderful. Then it's all settled," said Artemis with a bright, bewitching smile. Will could see why the duke found it almost impossible to resist the woman.

He, on the other hand, was going to find it absolutely impossible to resist Lucy. After they'd bid the Dartmoors good night, he tucked Lucy's hand into the crook of his arm and escorted her down the main stairs to the grand entry hall, which was presently deserted.

All was silent save for the soft patter of rain outside and the thud of Will's heart.

"You know, if this evening's weather wasn't so inclement, I'd offer to take you for a tour around Dartmoor House's back garden before you left. It's quite lovely. But as it is rather horrid outside"—she paused and smiled softly—"I wondered if you'd be happy if we took a turn about the conservatory instead. I believe there are some rare plant specimens I could show you."

"Ah, you know I'm always in the mood for a biology lesson," murmured Will. "But the question is who will be tutoring whom?"

Lucy laughed. "Oh, but I rather hoped that there would be time for a language lesson. Because you did promise to demonstrate how lingually adept you are."

A powerful pulse of lust shot through Will's veins and straight to his cock at the thought of showing Lucy what he'd been dreaming of doing with her for so very long. "There's no reason in the world why we canna do all of those things," he said in a voice roughened with acute hunger. "Now, where is this conservatory, lass?"

In all of his thirty-two years, Will had never been so keen to visit a hothouse.

Chapter Twenty-Two

THE CONSERVATORY WAS SITUATED AT THE BACK OF Dartmoor House and at this late hour of the night was swathed in soft, velvet darkness. After locating and lighting a pair of gas lamps, Will threaded his fingers through Lucy's as she led him into the elegant glass-enclosed structure. The dome arching over their heads was lost in shadows, but the lamps cast enough light to illuminate the feathery fronds of palms and ferns and the fruit-laden branches of orange and lemon trees as they picked their way to a secluded, cushioned bench seat at the very back of the greenhouse. Surrounded by exotic flowering plants like fuchsias and orchids and lilies and cyclamens, it was a delightfully romantic grove. The air around them was pleasantly humid and fragrant with heavy perfume and earthy scents. Lucy fancied they'd found their own miniature version of Eden.

And she was certainly tempted to taste as much carnal pleasure as she possibly could with Will.

He set their lamps on the flagged floor by a small tinkling fountain, and then they both sat on the bench. The rainfall had grown heavier—but the rhythmic tattoo upon the glass roof and walls enhanced the illusion that she and Will were all alone. That the rest of the world had disappeared, and they were free to do whatever they liked with no one to naysay them.

The soft glow of the lamps highlighted the strong, savagely handsome planes of Will's face. His eyes were a deep midnight blue, his expression rapt as he gently cupped Lucy's face between his hands. As though she were the most delicate bloom in the world.

"My fair Lucy, do you know how beautiful you are? How precious?" he breathed. His thumbs caressed her fevered cheeks. His heated gaze grazed her lips. "Sweet Jesus. Do you know how much I want you? How I ache for you? How I burn to taste you?"

"If your hunger matches mine, then yes, I do," she whispered. Her lower belly throbbed with sweet anticipation. Her nipples ached. Her blood hummed. "I'm yours, Will. To kiss. To taste. You can have everything."

"Are you certain?" His dark eyes searched hers.

"Yes."

In the next instant, Will's mouth was on hers. His kiss was hot and demanding. Desperate and devouring. He tilted her head backward and she opened wider, reveling in the feel of his slick tongue stroking deeply. She was so desperate for him, she couldn't work out where her hands should go. They were in his hair, then clutching at his shoulders. Gripping his upper arms where his bulging biceps flexed and twitched. Sliding to his chest and kneading his marble-hard pectoral muscles through the cool satin of his waistcoat. And then she was pulling his shirt from his trousers and exploring the bare flesh of his lean, ridged torso.

She wanted to touch him everywhere. And it seemed Will wanted to caress all of her body too. Somehow, he managed to wrench down her bodice and the top of her corset so that one of her breasts was exposed. His mouth claimed her sensitized nipple, and she whimpered with delight as he feasted on her with long, hard, pulling sucks.

When he raised his head, he was all but panting and his eyes were heavily hooded with arousal. "Take off your crinoline and drawers," he rasped. "I want to put my mouth on your cunny. I want to slide my fingers inside you and feel how tight and wet you are. I need the taste of you on my tongue. But most of all, I want to hear you scream when I make you come."

Lucy's heart beat double time. "Yes, to all of that," she whispered raggedly. Will moved back so she could stand, and then after she lifted her heavy skirts, he helped to loosen the tapes securing her petticoats and the ribbon securing her drawers. As soon as she stepped out of the confining acres of wire and fabric, he was on his knees in front of her.

"Lift your skirts and place a foot on the bench," he ordered. "Grip my head or my shoulder if you need to. I want you open and exposed. Bared to me."

Oh, sweet figgy jam. Lucy was so awash with arousal and anticipation that she could barely make her limbs function. Her knees were shaking as she bunched up her silk skirts with one hand and then lifted her leg to place her pump-clad foot on the cushioned seat. With her other hand, she clutched at Will's broad shoulder so she wouldn't lose her balance.

"Gorgeous…" Will's breath was warm as it ruffled the curls of her sex and teased her hot, quivering intimate flesh, making her shiver. "So wet. So slick." She felt the tip of one of his fingers gently sliding through the moisture at her entrance before tracing a path along her cleft, up to her throbbing clitoris. When he parted her folds and blew on her sex, she gasped at the exquisite yet shocking sensation. Part of her—the sensible, buttoned-up, ladylike part—knew she should probably be embarrassed or ashamed about what Will was doing to her, and that she was a willing participant. But the wicked, wanton woman in her was reveling in it.

And then all rational thought disintegrated when the tip of Will's tongue touched her clitoris. A bolt of pleasure sizzled through her, setting every nerve ending alight.

One of his hands slid to her bare buttocks, holding her completely captive. His splayed fingers squeezed her flesh as his dexterous tongue flicked and swirled and lapped and taunted her tiny nub, eliciting the most decadent, excruciatingly divine sensations. Driving her wild. She was so drenched, there was no resistance at all when Will slid one long finger and then another inside her and began to gently thrust in and out. The friction, the way he rubbed and teased some special part inside her was sublime, and she mindlessly undulated her hips, matching his rhythm.

Between the wicked ministrations of his tongue and the sweet torment of his fingers, it wasn't long until Lucy sensed that her orgasm was drawing closer. That it was hovering just out of reach. Building, building, building like an oncoming tempest that she couldn't wait to be caught up in.

The pressure was too much. She couldn't take any more. Her fingers tangled in Will's hair and her insides quivered. Her knees shook and tiny moans and whimpers tumbled from her throat.

She had to come. She had to let go. Let herself get swept away.

Perhaps sensing her acute need for release, Will's lips surrounded her clitoris and when he suckled with relentless intention, she at last fell over the edge into blinding, swirling, pulsing ecstasy. She couldn't suppress her cry of elation. All she could do was hold on to Will as wave after wave of pleasure engulfed her. But he was there for her, anchoring and supporting her body until the tremors eventually subsided, leaving her panting and gasping and trembling and so replete, she was certain she'd touched heaven.

"Oh… Oh, Will," she whispered hoarsely as she subsided onto the cushioned bench. "You've utterly devastated me. Ruined me in the best way possible. I've never felt so wonderful."

He joined her on the seat and pulled her against him so that her head rested on his shoulder. "I'm verra pleased to hear it," he murmured. "And I'm deeply honored to be the man to bring you so much pleasure."

Lucy sighed with contentment, but when her gaze drifted downward, she immediately noticed that Will's trousers were tented in the most alarming fashion.

"Good heavens, Will." She straightened and caught his gaze. "Here I am lounging about like I'm the Queen of Sheba, and here you are with an enormous erection. You must be in agony."

He gave her a crooked smile. "Dinna worry about me, lass. My cockstand will subside eventually."

Perhaps emboldened by the pleasure still humming through her veins, Lucy arched a brow. "Or I could give you a helping hand like I did last night…or I could use my mouth on you…"

Will's gaze narrowed but his eyes gleamed. "Och, I couldna ask you to do that for me, lass."

"But you're not asking," she said softly. "I'm offering." A dark thrill running through her, Lucy dared to curl her fingers around Will's shaft. "I want to return the favor and bring you pleasure too." Through the fabric of his woolen trousers, she gave him a gentle squeeze. "Tell me you don't want this."

"God help me," he groaned. "I canna say no. I do want it. You've ensorcelled me, Lucy."

"Good," she said with a smile. "Then we are in agreement."

───────────

What the hell had he just agreed to?

Will felt helpless, completely bewitched, as Lucy, the woman who effortlessly aroused him like no other, slid off the bench and wedged herself between his thighs.

He *should* say no. He shouldn't let someone who was such a novice—a *virgin*—perform such a carnally decadent act. "Lucy," he managed as she began to unbutton the fall of his trousers with deft, determined fingers, "Do you ken what will happen when I come?"

She looked up through her lashes at him, and her lips curved in a knowing feline smile that did nothing to lessen his thundering need. "Of course I do," she murmured. "I might not have done this before, but I have an idea of the mechanics involved. I haven't forgotten what happened when you came last night." She arched a brow. "I'm game if you are, my lord."

Christ. When had shy Miss Lucy Bertram turned into the siren of his own wicked, erotic fantasies?

Will hardly knew. But then thinking almost became impossible when his throbbing member sprang free, and Lucy wrapped her small hand around his engorged shaft and then licked her lips. At the sight of her small pink tongue darting out to moisten that plump sweet flesh, Will almost came then and there. Indeed, a droplet of his seed was already welling from the tip of his cock's swollen head. And Lucy had noticed it too. "Can I taste you?" she whispered. The muscles in Will's belly and thighs tightened and his hands clenched into fists upon the seat.

"Yes," he gritted out. Sweet Jesus, he prayed he wouldn't erupt like a volcano as soon as her tongue and lips touched him.

She bent her head, and when that pretty tongue of hers darted out again to give him a tentative lap, he growled, and his hips bucked. He was so aroused, so primed to explode, he knew he wouldn't take long to lose all control.

"What should I do?" she whispered. "What do you like?"

"You can do whatever *you* like, lass… But I like sucking and licking and squeezing. And you can always fondle my balls, and oh…God…"

Will's head fell back as Lucy began to do all of those things. And with gusto. What she lacked in finesse, she certainly made up for with unbridled enthusiasm. And as he'd predicted, in no time at all Will was shaking and cursing and hurtling toward an orgasm that was sure to blow the top of his head off. The exquisite suction, the squeeze and slide of her fist, the heat of her mouth and the swirling of her tongue...

It. Was. Agony.

It was pure bliss.

And then he was there. Catapulted skyward and his body exploding like fireworks. Indeed, he might have actually seen stars behind his closed eyelids as he groaned and jerked and shuddered and expelled his seed in a series of hot, violent spurts. And somehow Lucy held on and took everything that he gave her until he was empty and spent and so satisfied he didn't think he'd be able to move for hours, if not days.

Dear God. What a revelation she was. Too perfect for words.

Dragging himself from sweet oblivion, he opened his eyes and then pulled Lucy up and onto his lap. She was smiling as he pressed his forehead against hers, then kissed her flushed cheek. Her swollen lips.

"You are amazing," he murmured huskily.

One thing was clear to him: He might not be able to predict what tomorrow would bring, but right now he knew that without a doubt—right down to his very bones— he could never let this remarkable woman go.

Ever.

Somehow, some way, he would make her see that they were meant for each other.

Chapter Twenty-Three

THE RALEIGH CLUB WAS LOCATED IN ST. JAMES'S, NOT FAR
from Piccadilly and the gentlemen's clubs White's, Boodle's, and
Brooks's. As they'd planned during their meeting at Scotland
Yard, Lord Castledown had "sponsored" Will to become a
club member.

When the Earl of Kyle walked into the main club area furnished with overstuffed leather chairs, heavy teak tables and
cabinets, Persian rugs, and an abundance of potted palms—
perhaps to evoke an atmosphere of warmer, more exotic
climes—he immediately scanned the area, looking for Thorne.
According to a plainclothes Scotland Yard officer who'd been
tracking Thorne's movements, the Yorkshireman quit his
Lowndes Square residence at about three o'clock in the afternoon and caught a hansom cab to the Raleigh Club.

No doubt Thorne had already heard from Sir Oswald that
Will Armstrong, his erstwhile groom, was really a Scottish peer.
And that he intended to court Lucy.

This was going to be an interesting encounter indeed.

Will soon found Thorne in a relatively secluded reading room, installed in a wingback chair by a bookcase packed
with leather-bound volumes. A nearby table contained neatly
arranged piles of the latest broadsheets, journals, and gazettes.
With a pot of coffee and a plate of neatly cut sandwiches at his
elbow, the Yorkshireman was perusing the *Times*.

Will snagged a copy of one of the papers and then claimed

the wingback chair closest to Thorne. As he made a great fuss of opening up the newspaper, crinkling its pages, and then riffling through them, Thorne soon looked up. The second he recognized Will, his expression changed from "mildly annoyed" to "positively ferocious." If scowls could kill, Will would be a dead man.

"What in the devil's name are you doing in here, you filthy bastard?" hissed Thorne over the top of the *Times*.

Will put down his own paper and smirked. The more he could rile Thorne, the better. "First of all, while I might use a filthy word or two on occasion, I assure you I'm not unwashed, nor am I baseborn. And the reason I'm here? I'm a member of the club, just like you. It's verra easy to join when one has the right connections. And considering I'm the Earl of Kyle, I'm no' short of those..." He leaned closer to Thorne in a conspiratorial fashion. "I for one am especially interested in your connection to Sir Oswald. For the life of me, I canna work out why you two are such bosom friends."

A muscle pulsed in Thorne's jaw. "The way you misrepresented yourself to Sir Oswald and Miss Bertram—yes, Sir Oswald told me everything after your meeting with him yesterday—you're nothing but a lying, deceitful scoundrel. What are *you* up to? That's the more pertinent question."

Will cocked a brow. "But I could say the same about you, no? Because surely you are up to something. Why throw your money away by funding one of Sir Oswald's expeditions in some far-flung place on the other side of the world? Why pursue his all-but-penniless daughter when you have nothing in common and no regard for one another? That is the greater mystery."

"You know nothing of my relationship with Miss Bertram."

"Oh, I dinna think that is the case at all. I was there in the dining room at Fleetwood Hall when you insulted her reading choices and her scientific beliefs. I have also heard from Miss Bertram herself that you recently insulted her character most grievously when you suggested she was sinful. I'd hardly call that a sound relationship on which to build a union. No, something untoward is going on between you and the baronet. And I mean to find out what it is."

Thorne emitted a derisive snort. "That's pure speculation on your part."

"Perhaps… But my gut tells me that you are not to be trusted. That all your talk about fire and brimstone and sinning conceals a dark, dark nature. I wouldn't trust you to take care of my horses or dogs, let alone take someone like Miss Bertram to wife."

"How dare you talk to me about sinning, you vile, untrustworthy blackguard!"

Will threw down his paper on the low table between them. "How dare I indeed, *Mister* Thorne?"

Thorne glared at him, daggers in his dark eyes. Will wondered if the man was contemplating calling him out and what his odds of surviving such a deadly encounter with a former soldier would be. He imagined that Sir Oswald shared the fact that he'd served in the military for some years.

Will lounged back in his chair and steepled his fingers beneath his chin. "What, you've nothing more to add to the conversation?" He couldn't resist irritating the man a wee bit more.

Thorne slapped down his own newspaper, stood, and then stepped close, attempting to tower over Will. "Do not push me, Lord Kyle. Or whatever your misbegotten name is. Rest assured I will be speaking to the club management about your recent addition to our membership's ranks. Your shadow shall not darken the Raleigh Club's doorstep, or indeed any of its rooms, for much longer, you mark my words."

"Och, well, it might be worth my while to have a word with

them about your reputation, *sir*, and your unsavory dealings. Or perhaps *sinful* goings-on would be a better way to characterize your recent activities."

Thorne paled. "What do you mean?"

Will shrugged a shoulder. "One hears whispers in certain circles. About grudges and disagreements and secret liaisons." He locked eyes with Thorne. "About threats. You ken, that sort of thing." Of course, Will was lying and making all sorts of unfounded assertions, but his aim was to rattle Thorne. To strike a vulnerable sore spot. To needle him into asserting his dominance. The Yorkshireman wasn't the sort of man who would cower in fear. He'd strike out. He would want to smite whoever opposed him. It was a matter of pride as much as vengeance.

The man's lips thinned to a flat, bloodless line. His dark eyes glittered dangerously. "Are you threatening me, Lord Kyle? Because I do not take kindly to threats."

"You can take it as a warning that I do not like you or what you stand for." When Will rose to his feet, he was almost nose to nose with the Yorkshireman. His voice was a low threatening growl as he added, "And if I hear that you've gone anywhere near Miss Bertram again, I willna threaten you, I will end you. Do you understand?"

Thorne's nostrils flared. "Perfectly."

"Good." Will moved away, then paused on the threshold of the room. "You have a verra good day now, won't you, Thorne." And with that, he quit the Raleigh Club before he did pummel Thorne to dust.

———

Jane's grandfather, Mr. Delaney, smiled as he handed the brown-paper-wrapped book over to Lucy. "I'm sure you will enjoy this one, Miss Bertram. Jane said it would be your cup of tea."

"I'm certain it will be too," said Lucy. Jane was still staying with her mother, but during their Byronic Book Club meeting the day before at Dartmoor House, she'd mentioned she'd set aside a thrilling Gothic-themed title for Lucy at her grandfather's bookstore—Catherine Crowe's *The Night–Side of Nature*. The book was apparently filled with "real" ghost stories and hauntings and tales of those who'd had dreams that foretold the future. Lucy couldn't wait to dive in.

It might be the diversion she needed to stop obsessively thinking about Will and their erotically romantic tryst last night in Dartmoor House's conservatory.

It had been one of the most wonderful nights of her life. And it made her realize that she could hardly bear to think about facing a life without Will. Proclaiming oneself a hardened spinster was all well and good when one hadn't tasted real passion. But after one had… When one had glimpsed heaven in the arms of a man? When that man wasn't just a masterful, caring lover but supportive in every conceivable way? A man who understood her? Who believed she was impressive and remarkable *and* pretty?

How could she give that up?

So yes, until she mustered the courage to talk to Will about her feelings in regard to their budding relationship, she needed something else that was thought-provoking—like real-life, thrilling tales of the supernatural—in order to engage her mind and to keep herself from fretting about every little thing. Including the fact that she might have fractured her relationship with her father forevermore.

Since she'd quit Fleetwood Hall and had only left him a note informing him of her decision to stay with Artemis for the foreseeable future, since Will had informed him of his intentions to court her, she'd heard nothing from her father. There'd been no word from the inquiry agent on Monty's whereabouts yet either. Even though it had only been a day since the search for her brother had begun in earnest, Lucy couldn't shake the feeling that it would all be for naught. To her anxious heart, it seemed as though the Bertram family was on the brink of disintegrating into nothing.

If Lucy didn't have Artemis and Jane and now Will in her life, she'd feel so terribly alone.

After paying Mr. Delaney for the book—he'd initially insisted it was a gift from Jane, but Lucy wouldn't hear of it—she tucked the small package beneath her arm and then pushed through the door onto Sackville Street. It was raining softly, and Lucy paused beneath the shop's narrow portico to put up her umbrella. Artemis had a series of engagements that afternoon—one with her publisher and then another to commence setting up the premises of Dartmoor Ladies' College in Tyburnia, not far from Paddington Station—so Lucy had ventured out on her own. Piccadilly and Delaney's were but a mile from Belgrave Square, and while she could have taken a hansom cab, she felt like she needed a good stroll to clear her mind.

Of course, Artemis had insisted that one of the duke's footmen accompany her, and because Lucy was still hesitant about Mr. Thorne accosting her—and because she also didn't want Will to worry about her safety—she'd readily agreed. She wasn't foolish. Ever since that frightening incident in the Rookery of St Giles, she knew she had to be careful.

The footman matched her pace while maintaining a respectful distance as she struck out along Piccadilly. He'd brought his own umbrella, so she didn't have to worry about his immaculate livery getting all wet or that he might catch cold on her account.

As Lucy approached the grand arched entrance of Burlington House, she wondered how Will's—or perhaps she should say Detective Lawrence's—murder investigation was progressing.

How disconcerting to think that perhaps poor Lord Litchfield and Professor Fitzroy had been poisoned by someone from within the Linnean Society's ranks. Lucy wondered yet again why her father hadn't spoken to her about the fact he'd been a suspect in the viscount's murder, or that other members of the society, including Charles Darwin, had been threatened with death all because of a scientific paper.

And then her thoughts wandered to Mr. Thorne and his staunch, narrow views of the world. Would he really murder Darwin and several of his supporters just because their beliefs didn't align with his own? It seemed quite bizarre to her. No, it was more than bizarre.

It was mad.

The words that Thorne had spoken during their first dinner together returned to her: *It is heretical, in my opinion, to believe that humans aren't unique. We are not related to other animals. One species does not simply transform into another. That goes against the laws of both God and nature and everything I believe in. Species are an unchanging part of an intelligently designed hierarchy. A divine hierarchy.*

Did Thorne truly believe Darwin was a "heretic," and thus should be removed from this earth?

If Thorne *had* murdered Litchfield because he was a supporter of the naturalist, and if her father had known all this time... Lucy shivered, and her stomach pitched and roiled. All of it was far too disturbing to even contemplate.

Lost in her own thoughts, it took a moment for her to register that a tall gentleman in a dark coat and top hat was also keeping pace with her. The collar of his coat was pulled up, obscuring his jawline, and an enormous black umbrella hid almost all of his face.

There was something about him—his closeness to her—that was off-putting, so she slowed down. And then so did he. A frisson of unease tripped down Lucy's spine, and just when she was about to stop and call out to the footman, the man's gloved hand shot out and gripped her elbow. And she shrieked. It was Mr. Thorne.

He loomed close, his black, soulless eyes boring into hers. "I know that morally repugnant cur Lord Kyle means to have you," he rasped, "but he won't. You're mine, Miss Bertram. *Mine.* You've been promised to me, and I staked my claim first. Don't ever forget that."

And then before she could find the air to protest or scream or do anything at all other than gasp in open-mouthed shock, he released her and strode away into the rain and the traffic rattling along Piccadilly.

"Miss Bertram! Miss Bertram! Are you all right?" The Dartmoor footman rushed to her side. His face was as pale as the pristine white collar of his cambric shirt as he peered down at her from beneath the shade of his umbrella. "I'm so sorry I wasn't closer to stop that man from approaching you."

Lucy nodded. "I... Yes, I am all right." Of course, she was shaken to her very bones, but it wasn't the footman's fault a madman like Thorne had waylaid her in the street. "I mean, I'll be fine. Although perhaps I might feel better if we hailed a cab."

"Lucy?"

At the sound of her name being called, Lucy turned and peered into the arched entranceway of Burlington Arcade. And as soon as she saw the man sheltering in the shadows, she gasped in shock for the second time that afternoon. "Monty? Oh my God! Is it...is it really you?"

Even though Monty's face was thin and haggard, his blond hair unkept and far too long, and the coat he was wearing frayed at the cuffs and rumpled, his mouth lifted into a small, familiar smile. "It is, darling sis. It's me."

"Oh, Monty!" Tears blurring her vision, Lucy dropped her umbrella and her new book and rushed over to her brother and threw her arms about him. She hugged him with such vigor, she thought she might have cracked his ribs. But he was embracing her just as tightly. So tightly that Lucy was breathless when they at last released each other. There were tears welling in Monty's eyes too.

"How did you find me here in Piccadilly?" she demanded in a voice choked with emotion.

Monty swiped at his eyes with his wrist. "It was simple, really. A few hours ago, I confronted a man who'd been following me around Covent Garden all morning. He confessed he was an inquiry agent. That you and some peer—the Earl of Kyle—had hired him to find me because you were in some sort of trouble and needed me. I wasn't sure whether to believe this chap at first, but when he told me that you were currently staying with your friend Artemis at Dartmoor House in Belgrave Square, I decided to track you down myself. To see if what he'd said was true. When I caught sight of you leaving Belgrave Square, I followed you here." He reached out and touched her arm, his expression now grave. "What's going on, Lucy?"

"What's going on?" Lucy repeated, unable to hide the incredulity in her voice. "I could ask you the same question, along with 'Are you all right?' and a half-dozen others. I've been so worried about you, and of course you know how stubborn Father is and he just won't talk about what happened between you two. And I got your letter, but, you oaf"—she gave his arm a playful thump—"there was no address on it. Jane Delaney and I worked out you'd posted it from the High Street in St Giles. But looking for you there was like searching for a needle in a—"

"That *was* you? In the High Street a few days ago?" Monty

swore beneath his breath. "I nearly died from shock when I thought I saw you in the crowd. But then I told myself surely not. My sister wouldn't be so foolish." A frown marred her brother's brow, and his voice shook as he said, "Good God, Lucy. What were you thinking? That place is horrendously dangerous."

"Yes, it is. So why were *you* there, Monty?" Lucy demanded. "Have you been living there all this time? Since April? For these last five months? What were *you* thinking?"

He winced. "The situation I'm in is…complicated."

"Complicated? Well, that's not good enough, dear brother. Not when I've been worried sick. And not just about you. About my own situation. I was looking for you because I needed you to help me, most urgently."

Monty ran a hand down his face. A shadow of guilt clouded his eyes as he murmured roughly, "Sweet Lord above, what's Father done now?"

"Oh, nothing much"—Lucy lowered her voice—"other than he's determined to marry me off to a horrid, staunch religious zealot by the name of Zachariah Thorne who believes I'm wicked but that somehow I'm his property already. A madman who might very well have committed unspeakable crimes. But apparently, that's all right with Father because he's an obscenely rich industrialist. So, yes"—she emitted a bitter laugh— "nothing much at all, really."

"Christ, Lucy. I'm so, so sorry." Her brother shook his head, his expression guilt-stricken. "That's…that's unconscionable. If I had any idea at all that he would put you in such an impossible position…" He reached out and lightly grasped her shoulder. "That's why you've been staying with Artemis, isn't it?"

"Yes…I was getting rather desperate. And because I hadn't had much luck searching for you myself…" She shrugged.

Monty's mouth flattened into a grim line. "You really

shouldn't have ventured into St Giles though. I feel sick whenever I think about it. If anything had happened to you, I'd never be able to forgive myself."

"I–I had an escort," said Lucy. "I wasn't silly enough to go by myself."

"An escort?" Monty's gaze narrowed. "Who? This Lord Kyle?"

"Yes," she said. "He's my new suitor. And he was the gentleman who accompanied me into St Giles on each occasion. I was quite safe."

"Safe my arse, Lucy. What the hell was this Lord Kyle thinking?" Monty's scowl was fearsome. "Aside from that, you searched the streets of the Rookery more than once?"

"It was only twice. And Lord Kyle is a good, noble man. A very capable man. He once served in Her Majesty's army, so he knows how to handle himself in a difficult situation."

Monty snorted. "It sounds as though you like this fellow. So why is Father trying to marry you off to Thorne instead of Lord Kyle? What's wrong with him? Is he an earl who's as poor as a church mouse?"

"No, he's not poor. Far from it. He actually hired the inquiry agent to find you because he knew that *I* couldn't afford to. Well, not unless I sold some of Mama's jewelry. It's… In your words, the situation is complicated," said Lucy. "I'm happy to tell you more. Everything, in fact. Just not here." Discussing her relationship with Will and everything they'd been through wasn't the sort of topic one should go into in the middle of Piccadilly, especially when the rain was growing heavier by the moment. Thank goodness the footman had thought to rescue her discarded umbrella and book. He was presently standing a few feet away, steadfastly studying the pedestrians and the passing traffic. No doubt he was also keeping a look out for Thorne.

Her attention returned to Monty, who'd turned very pale. "If you mean to suggest that we return to Fleetwood Hall, Lucy, I just can't," he said. "Not today, at least. I can't face the idea of having another row with Father, not after we've been reunited."

"No, I wasn't going to suggest that at all." She drew a deep breath. "I have the perfect place in mind. The Earl of Kyle's house, in fact. Even though you don't know him at all, I promise you that he can be trusted." She put out her hand and touched his arm. "Does that sound all right, Monty?"

He sighed and nodded. "My dear Luce. After the hell I've been through these past months, I won't say no. I trust your judgment."

She smiled. "Good. We'll hail a hansom cab and be there before you know it."

Chapter Twenty-Four

By the time Will returned to Kyleburn House, it was early evening. While he was exhausted and damp from striding about in the rain for far too long, he was also itching for a dram or two of whisky and dinner before he retired for the night. Hopefully, the spirits and a good meal and hot bath would take his mind off the fact he couldn't very well show up on Dartmoor House's doorstep again asking to see Lucy. That wasn't the done thing.

After he'd quit the Raleigh Club, he'd stopped by Scotland Yard to provide Lawrence with the details of his encounter with Thorne and to plan their next move: whether to bring the man in for an interview or to search his Belgravia residence and business premises for evidence implicating him in the murders of Litchfield and Fitzroy.

Lawrence had pointed out that Thorne would most likely claim he'd barely known Lord Litchfield, and that while he'd been at the Raleigh Club on the night the viscount was murdered, he hadn't a clue why anyone would kill the man. He imagined Thorne would say the same about Professor Fitzroy—that he didn't know the man. Even if they uncovered Ceylonese coffee and some form of strychnine at Thorne's home or office, both substances were easy enough to come by and any decent solicitor would be able to argue that point.

Of course, they would have the strychnine analyzed by a pharmaceutical chemist or toxicologist, and if it turned out to be a more potent form of *Strychnos nux-vomica*—the type of strychnine that had been used in both murders—that still might not be enough evidence to gain a conviction. Sir Oswald possessed the same sort of strychnine in his poisons collection, so the defense counsel would argue it still could have been the baronet who murdered both men. And Thorne wasn't the only man in Britain who was opposed to Charles Darwin's recent paper on natural selection and evolutionary principles.

There were too many "ifs" and they'd be relying on circumstantial evidence and hearsay at best. Time was running out—the general consensus was the murderer would strike again very soon—and it would be difficult to infiltrate Thorne's household with another spy. What Scotland Yard needed was irrefutable evidence. A "smoking pistol," so to speak.

Of course, Lawrence and Will had known Thorne wasn't likely to incriminate himself this afternoon at the Raleigh Club, but given the man's proud, altogether arrogant nature and his tendency to anger at the drop of a hatpin, they'd rather hoped that he would be goaded into action. It was a risky ploy, but at this point it was the only plan they had that might bring them *some* sort of result. According to Lord Castledown, certain Linnean Society Council members who'd also been threatened were getting twitchy and making noises about "taking the matter higher"—and no wonder. The investigation was as stagnant as the Thames at the height of summer. Lawrence agreed with Will that they really had nothing left to lose.

Thorne had to be tempted into a trap, and Will would be the bait. What the precise nature of the trap would be was yet to be decided.

As Will handed his hat, gloves, and coat to one of his footmen, Hillier appeared.

"My lord… You have a message from the inquiry agent you

recently engaged. It's on your desk in the study. And you also have unexpected visitors. A Mr. Egmont Bertram and a Miss Lucinda Bertram. Although they did not say so, I believe they are siblings. I've installed them in the drawing room with a tea tray."

What? Will's eyebrows shot up. Lucy's brother had at last been found?

Thank God and hallelujah!

Glancing at the longcase clock in the entry hall, Will could see it was almost seven. "Tell Cook there will be three for dinner at eight," he said. And then he passed a hand through his rain-damp hair. Lucy had seen him in an unkempt state and no doubt she wouldn't care if he was slightly disheveled. If her brother had been living in St Giles, he probably wouldn't care either.

Hillier bowed. "Of course, my lord."

When Will entered the drawing room, he had a difficult time controlling the overwhelming urge to sweep Lucy into his arms and kiss her senseless. Instead he forced himself to focus his attention on her brother. Egmont, or "Monty," Bertram was a tall, fair-haired young man who'd clearly been having a rough time of it of late. His face was drawn and there were deep bruise-like shadows beneath his blue eyes. His hair wasn't "artfully tousled," but simply messy. His jaw was covered in stubble, his clothes were rumpled, and his shoes were scuffed.

However, the man's manners were impeccable after Lucy made the introductions. "Lord Kyle, I know I am imposing on your time and have ostensibly invaded your home," he said in the cultured accent that marked someone as upper class. "But Lucy insisted that it would be quite all right to come here..."

"It is. Of course it is," said Will. "Please, let us take seats." He gestured to the arrangement of chairs around the fireside where a low fire burned. He poured himself a whisky and offered Monty one, which he readily accepted. Lucy declined a sherry in favor of her tea. Once they were settled, Will ventured, "I'm thrilled to see that you are indeed hale and hearty, Mr. Bertram. I'm sure you already know that your sister has been verra worried about you. Indeed, it was her brilliant idea to hire an inquiry agent to find you. Considering I have a message from the man, and you are now here in my drawing room, I'd say it worked."

"Yes, it did. And I'm glad. Although I do deeply regret that Lucy has had to endure so much since I left." Monty's remorseful gaze skipped to his sister. "If there had been another course of action I could have taken to deal with the situation I found myself in, believe me, I would have chosen it."

Will gave him a measured look. "And what situation was that, exactly? Perhaps if you disclose what the issue is, others might be in a position to help you. It's clear that something is amiss."

"That's what I've told Monty too," said Lucy gravely. "But he's as stubborn as an ox. He will not budge. He will not say a word."

"Oh, Lucy, as I've told you at least a dozen times already," said Monty, "my situation is complicated."

Will's gaze narrowed with suspicion. "Have you committed a crime, Mr. Bertram?" When Lucy's brother immediately paled, Will knew he must have hit close to the mark.

Monty's next remark was telling. "I suppose it depends on your point of view," he said, his eyes shadowed with wariness. "In my opinion, no, I haven't. Others might condemn me though." A mirthless bark of laughter escaped him. "My father certainly does. I'm sure someone like Zachariah Thorne would too, given what I've heard about his staunch religious beliefs from my sister."

"Oh, Monty, what did you do?" entreated Lucy. Her hands were clasped so tightly together in her lap that her knuckles had turned bone-white. "I can't imagine it was anything *that* terrible.

You're not a bad person. In fact, you're charming and generous and have a good heart. And besides"—her gaze softened—"you're with people who care about you. You can trust us not to betray you."

Monty's gaze shot to Will. "I hear you are courting my sister, Lord Kyle. Not only that, I understand you've been protecting Lucy from the blackguard our father wants her to wed. You might have developed a fond regard for her, but I'm not sure if I can trust a man I barely know with a volatile secret that could destroy me. For me to share it, I would have to be convinced that you…" He swallowed. "That you aren't the sort of man who would judge a fellow simply on the basis of who he loves."

What an interesting choice of words. And how brave it was of Monty to share something so very personal with a man he barely knew. While Will's interest was piqued, he was also aware of the trust that had been placed in him. He definitely had an inkling about the nature of Monty Bertram's "volatile secret," but he needed to make sure his assumption was correct. After serving as a spy, he'd seen and heard just about everything. "Are you reluctant to share your secret with Lucy because you think it will shock her?" he asked carefully. "Because she's a woman and might not have come across such a thing before? And do you believe I might use that information against you? Because I might be a narrow-minded man?"

When Monty didn't do anything but sip his whisky, Will persisted as gently as he could. "Is it something to do with the company you keep? Because if it is, I assure you I am not easily shocked. And neither would I condemn you. Lucy is right. I would not betray you. I *can* be trusted with your sort of secret. In my eyes, it's not a crime at all."

Monty's gaze darted away to a shadowed corner of the room.

He sounded both bitter and resigned as he eventually muttered, "The answer is 'yes.' To all of your questions."

Lucy was frowning. "Whatever are you two talking about? I don't understand. But I agree with Will—" She broke off. "I mean, Lord Kyle. Oh, bother!" She caught the eye of her brother. "Monty, I can see you are about to protest, but don't you dare say anything about the fact that Will and I are on familiar terms. We *are* courting, and besides that, I'm a twenty-eight-year-old woman who already knows a lot about the world. And as I started to say a moment ago, I agree with Will. I'm not easily shocked. I want to know what it is you've done. What has driven a wedge between you and Father?"

Monty put down his tumbler. "I..." His brow furrowed. "Lucy, I know you've been annoyed with me for some time. For not doing my bit to help Father out of the financial hole he's dumped us in. But you see..." His Adam's apple bobbed above the graying, limp collar of his shirt. "I would have married an heiress some time ago if I hadn't been so confused about whether I wanted to wed or not. Not because I'm determined to remain a bachelor forevermore just for the sake of it. But because..." He inhaled a fortifying breath. "I *do* like the company of women. But..." His gaze flitted to Will again as if seeking reassurance before darting back to his sister. "But I also like the company of men. In a romantic sense. If you take my drift."

Lucy blinked. "Oh... Like Herr von Schmidt, the maître d'hôtel at Fortnum & Mason's tearooms? He prefers the company of men. I'm certain of it. He's never said so—and of course I know he cannot risk being arrested—but I've noticed the way he smiles at handsome gentlemen sometimes. And even at you, Monty. He's quite the flirt with both sexes."

Monty's mouth tilted into a relieved smile. "Yes, I'm exactly like Herr von Schmidt. It's been so long since I've been to

Fortnum & Mason's that I had no idea he was still working there. I'm sure he's as charming as ever."

"Oh yes, he is." Lucy's brow wrinkled. "Father forced me to take tea with Mr. Thorne there recently. Of course, you're right about Thorne. He was smirking and sneering about Herr von Schmidt's manner of dress and speaking and making all kinds of disparaging remarks that made me want to toss my cup of tea in his horrid face, so there's no doubt in my mind that he would not view 'your situation' with one iota of understanding. He's the sort of judgmental prig who'd go running straight to the police…"

Lucy blushed bright red. "Oh… I…um…I didn't mean anything by that, Will. I know you wouldn't do anything."

Monty's brow plunged into a frown. "What do you mean, Lord Kyle wouldn't do anything? What on earth is going on?"

Will caught Monty's eye. "I am going to take you into my confidence now. But before I make my disclosure, I want to reassure you again that your secret *is* safe with me. All right?"

Monty's eyes still glinted with suspicion, but nevertheless he inclined his head. "Very well."

"For the past three years, I've been working for the Home Office and occasionally the Foreign Office on hard-to-solve cases. I'm not a detective, but a spy of sorts."

"A spy?" Monty's shocked gaze shot to Lucy. "Do you know this, Luce?"

Lucy nodded. "Yes, I do. I only found out recently too. But do not worry. Will is on our side, Monty. Unlike Father." She frowned. "You still haven't told us what happened that night in April when you left. Did…did Father find out that you like men too? Is that why you fought?"

Monty sighed heavily as though the weight of the world was pressing down on his shoulders. "Yes. That's exactly what happened," he said. "I...I wasn't careful enough. I got cocky. My...my paramour, the man I'd fallen in love with, escorted me home and I asked him inside for a drink. To share a brandy in the drawing room. The townhouse was so quiet, I thought you and Father had retired for the night... But unfortunately, Father hadn't. He walked in and caught my lover and me kissing. To say he wasn't happy about it would be a gross understatement." Monty shrugged and sighed again. "There was no reasoning with him. He told me that he was disgusted. That I was no son of his and the mere sight of me made him feel ill. And so I left. I had no other choice."

"Oh, no, Monty. I'm so, so sorry," murmured Lucy. There were tears in her eyes. "He was wrong to say all of those things. No doubt he was shocked, but to treat you that way." She shook her head. "It isn't right. He shouldn't have disowned you like that."

"I'm verra sorry too," said Will. "I've been estranged from my grandfather for many years. And before that, my own father."

Lucy cast him a sympathetic glance, but then she turned her attention back to her brother. "So where have you been living all of this time, Monty? Have you been staying in St. Giles?"

He reached for his whisky and took a large sip as though fortifying himself to continue with his story. "For the last month, I've been renting a room above a tobacconist's shop in Covent Garden, so not St. Giles exactly. I've been trying to take on odd jobs as a stagehand at the theaters—managing props, acting as a prompt. Anything, really. But it's been quite a hand-to-mouth existence and there's not much money left in the old pocketbook." He sighed. "Before that, I was living in bachelor digs in Chelsea that..." He raised his chin as though daring anyone to challenge him. "That my lover paid for. And we were happy. Blissfully happy, in fact. But then..." A dark shadow, perhaps even a haunted look, crossed the young man's face and tears gleamed in his blue eyes. "The man that I loved, he was killed. Murdered... And the killer still hasn't been caught."

"Murdered?" gasped Lucy, a hand flying to her throat. "Oh my God, Monty. That's so incredibly awful and heartbreaking. Not only that, how terrifying. I can't even imagine what you've been through."

"If you can bear to talk about it, what happened?" said Will gently. "And if the investigation has stalled in some way, perhaps I can help. I have close connections at Scotland Yard."

Monty's mouth twisted with a wry smile. "From my under-standing from what I've read in the newspapers—the inves-tigation is still ongoing but there haven't been any recent developments. At least not of late. You've probably even read about the case yourself, Lucy. You see, my lover was a noble-man. A man our father knew too. Roger, Lord Litchfield."

"Roger? Lord Litchfield?" Lucy turned as white as a ghost. "You...you can't be serious."

Monty frowned. "Why would I jest about a thing like that? And why are you so shocked?"

"Because"—Will exchanged a speaking look with Lucy—"I've been investigating Lord Litchfield's murder. And Scotland Yard's prime suspect at the present time is Lucy's would-be suitor, Zachariah Thorne."

"What the blazing hell?" Monty's gaze darted between Will and his sister. "This must be some kind of sick joke. Lucy, why would Father make you marry a man who could very well be a murderer? It doesn't make any sense. Unless..." His eyes wid-ened. "Do you think Father put him up to it? To get back at me? To punish me? He knew that I loved Litchfield." Monty shook his head in disbelief. "I never thought he'd stoop so low."

Will frowned. "I… To be perfectly honest, that's not a line of inquiry we've been pursuing, simply because we had no idea that Lord Litchfield was in a relationship with anyone at all."

"For obvious reasons, we took great pains to hide it from the world," said Monty, and then his mouth curved with a rueful smile. "Until I made the mistake of bringing Lord Litchfield home, of course. I was such an arrogant fool to think we wouldn't get caught."

"Monty, I know Father was angry with you," said Lucy, "but I am struggling to believe that he would do something so heinous. And why would he ask Thorne to do his bidding? Besides, you'd been gone months and months. It doesn't make sense that he would go after Lord Litchfield after so long. At least I don't think so."

Will rubbed his jaw. "I'm no' so sure, lass. Your father was originally our main suspect, remember? When we couldna find any direct evidence implicating him in Lord Litchfield's murder, that's why we turned our attention to Thorne. But now…" He grimaced. "I'm afraid to say that this could be the motive we missed. And who's to say they're not both involved?"

Lucy's forehead dipped into a puzzled frown. "But other prominent members of the Linnean Society have been threatened with murder too. And then there's poor Professor Fitzroy, the latest victim. From what I've heard, he was once married. How does any of that fit within your new theory that Litchfield was murdered because of his relationship with my brother?"

"Perhaps Fitzroy's murder and those other threats were just a ruse to throw the police off," said Will carefully. "The murderer could have simply been attempting to muddy the waters to confuse us. And even though I'm speculating, maybe Fitzroy had a male paramour too. Someone we don't know about yet. He's been a widower for some time. It's certainly a line of inquiry we could look into."

Lucy shook her head. "No…no, I don't think so. Something doesn't feel right about this. Father isn't perfect, but he wouldn't commit murder. For any reason. I know he wouldn't."

"Lucy, you didn't see him when he walked in on Roger and me," said Monty sadly. "His gaze was filled with so much outrage and loathing. Once upon a time I would have agreed with you, but not after the fight we had."

But Lucy would not be swayed. "I still don't believe he would enlist Thorne to take part in such a wicked scheme. And while Thorne is zealous about many things, do you really think he'd commit the sin of murder just because Father asked him to?"

Monty shrugged. "From what you've told me, Thorne sounds rather unhinged, if not altogether mad. He might."

"Aye," agreed Will. "Although Thorne could just be acting on his own and not at the behest of your father. If Thorne *did* find out that Litchfield preferred the company of men, he might have viewed him as an evildoer who was violating the laws of nature and God. Someone who should be dispensed with and sent to hell's fiery pit."

Lucy sighed. "You're right. And I suspect that's the exact sort of thing he would say to Monty too. But I still can't see my father subscribing to this school of thought. This is all so confusing and demoralizing."

"We seem to be going around in circles at this point," Will said gently. "I think the only way to clarify any of this is if I go talk to your father. On the morrow."

Monty nodded. "I think that would be a good idea."

"So do I," said Lucy. "In fact, I think we all should speak with him. How do you feel about that, Monty?"

"I…" Her brother swallowed, then nodded. "Very well. I

think you're right. There's no point in hiding from Father any longer. Even though we're likely to exchange words, I want answers from him too."

"Excellent. We have a plan. Tomorrow afternoon we'll visit Fleetwood Hall together." Will glanced at the Boulle mantel clock. "It's almost eight and I dinna know about you two, but I'm starving." He caught Lucy's eye. "Would you like to stay for dinner?"

Lucy blushed ever so slightly. "I... Yes, Monty and I would love to, wouldn't we, Monty?"

Her brother inclined his head. "Yes. You are too kind, my lord."

"Please, call me Kyle or Will. Whatever you feel comfortable with. I'm not one to stand on ceremony."

"As long as you call me Monty," he replied.

"Of course. By the way, where will you be staying from now on?" Will raised a brow. "I hope you're not intending to go back to your room at Covent Garden. It doesn't sound at all adequate."

A ruddy flush marked Monty's cheekbones. "I..." He glanced at Lucy, and then she caught Will's gaze.

"I hope you don't think it's too presumptuous," she said, "but I was rather hoping Monty might be able to stay here at Kyleburn House a little while. At least until things are resolved with our father. I would have asked Artemis and her husband, but I've already foisted myself on them at short notice."

Will held up a hand. "Worry no more. Monty is welcome to stay here for as long as he likes. I'll send a footman to collect his things from Covent Garden right away. How does that sound?"

"You are too generous, Kyle," said Monty. "Lucy was right about you. You are a good man. For what it's worth, you have my resounding support to court my sister, even if our father doesn't approve."

To Will's consternation, he felt his own cheeks grow warm

and an uncharacteristic knot of guilt twisted in his belly. *Bloody hell*. If Monty knew what he'd been up to with Lucy in a dark conservatory last night, the man wouldn't think that. He'd probably call him out for debauching his sister. Even though said debauching was completely consensual.

But then, it would hardly come to pistols at dawn if Will married Lucy...

Good God, he wanted her with an intensity that took his breath away. He didn't care what Sir Oswald had or hadn't done. Who Lucy's brother loved didn't matter to him either. Love was love and it seemed this battle-hardened, world-weary, cynical Scot had been hit with Cupid's arrow. Hard.

He could no longer deny the truth beating in his chest. The longing in his veins. His heart was no longer his own. It belonged to a beautiful, intelligent, sweet yet sensual-as-hell botanist.

One way or another, he meant to make this woman his wife when the time was right. He just had to convince Lucy that if they wed, they could both have everything they'd ever wanted.

How hard could that be?

Chapter Twenty-Five

DINNER AT KYLEBURN HOUSE WAS A DECIDEDLY PLEASANT affair. Just lovely.

No, it's more than just pleasant or lovely, Lucy told herself as she picked up her almost empty crystal wineglass and took a final sip of her Chablis. She sounded like she was describing the weather or a new gown or even a new variety of rose. *No, tonight is wonderful, and diverting, and altogether memorable.*

One of the best nights of my life.

Monty was back safe and sound, and she'd just spent the last two hours eating exquisitely cooked food and drinking fine French wine while she chatted and laughed with both him and Will.

For once, it felt like everything was right with the world rather than wrong. Like the ever-present anxiety simmering in her veins had dissipated and dispersed as effortlessly as the bubbles in the champagne she'd been drinking earlier. She felt as though she could breathe again. Smile freely and be herself instead of worrying about where Monty might be, or what others thought of her, or what would happen if she didn't do this or that quite the right way and then the sky cracked and fell and crashed down about her ears and somehow it would all be her fault.

She was relieved. And content. And full of delicious anticipation.

Monty had already said good night and quit the room in the company of Will's butler, Hillier, who'd been tasked with showing him to one of Kyleburn House's guest rooms. It was as though her brother had already accepted that she was a woman who didn't need his protection and could make her own decisions about the company she kept.

Or, she thought with a wry smile to herself, perhaps he'd simply been too tired to create a fuss about the fact that once he left, she'd be lingering alone in the dining room with the very eligible, very handsome, far-too-charming-when-he-chose-to-be Earl of Kyle.

Her suitor.

Her lover.

The man she was falling deeply in love with.

Lucy couldn't hide from her feelings anymore. They were swirling around inside her, a gentle eddying current of warm emotion at present. But when Will looked at her with that deep, hungry, focused look in his eyes, she knew those same feelings would soon whirl faster, hotter, sweeping her into a firestorm of passion that she couldn't hope to escape from. Or more to the point, she didn't want to escape from. Ever.

Yet…even though she belonged to this man, heart, body, and soul, she still faced a conundrum: How could she be with him forever if she didn't become his wife?

After Will had made his off-the-cuff suggestion to wed her as a last resort to save her from the clutches of Mr. Thorne, a tiny seed of what-if had been planted in her brain. If she surrendered all of herself to Will tonight, would that be enough? Would she want more nights by his side? A lifetime?

Of course, Will might never actually offer her a proper proposal. He'd already said once before that he wasn't looking for a wife yet.

But *if* he did, and she accepted, would she risk losing herself altogether? Could a countess—who would become a duchess one day—still manage to maintain a career as a botanist? Aside from the fact that noblewomen didn't "work" per se, she'd have other duties she'd have to prioritize ahead of her personal ambitions. No doubt bearing the Earl of Kyle's children would be at the top of the list. Will would need an heir and a spare one day.

But that day wasn't today, she reminded herself.

Yes, she and Will were simply "courting," which gave them the freedom to do whatever they liked. To explore if they were indeed compatible in every way. At least Lucy thought so. Tonight, she would set aside all of her worries and cares and just live in the moment. Enjoy herself and damn the consequences.

She pushed her empty wineglass away and placed her napkin carefully on the table. And then her gaze locked with Will's over the sea of white linen and crystal and clusters of candles.

To her delight, Will's dark-blue eyes were fairly smoldering with heat. He raised his hand and waved away the two remaining footmen in the room with a curt "Leave us."

Oh, sweet, sweet heaven. Could the man detect that the pursuit of pleasure was on her mind too?

As soon as the dining room doors shut behind the servants, Will tossed his own napkin onto the table and rose from his chair. Rounded the table and prowled toward her with calculation and hunger in his gaze.

As he approached, Lucy got to her feet too. Her heart was pounding, and her breathing had quickened. Lust fluttered and gathered between her thighs.

"I didn't have a chance to mention it earlier because Monty was with us, but Artemis is not expecting me to return to Dartmoor House tonight," she said in a low voice. "Before I came here, I left word with her that I might be staying here. She won't judge me for doing such a thing."

"And what will your brother say in the morning if he discovers you spent the whole night with me?" Will slid a hand about her waist and drew her closer. "Will he be angry?"

"I'm not sure, to be honest. But I'm a grown woman. An adult who's free to make my own decisions. If he voices any complaint, I shall counter that I respect his choices so he should afford me the same courtesy."

Will nodded, seemingly satisfied with her response. "So he should." He leaned down and his lips brushed her ear. "I must warn you, lass," he murmured huskily, "I mean to make you mine tonight." Drawing back, he cupped her jaw with gentle fingers. Trapped her gaze with his. "But before I do, I need to know that you want this too."

Oh... A dark thrill shot through Lucy. "I do," she managed, her throat tight with longing. "Of course I do. There's no one I'd rather be with for my first time. After today, one thing is clear to me: Life is too short to wait forever for the things one really wants. I want to experience the unbridled joy of lovemaking. I don't wish to remain a virgin forever, and why should I wait until I'm wed if I've found a man I truly desire? You are all I want in a lover, Will."

His mouth curved in a slow rake's smile. "Tonight, I will make it my mission to please you until you are boneless and speechless and canna stand the pleasure anymore."

Lucy slid her hands about Will's neck and her fingers flirted with the overly long locks grazing his collar. "Lord Kyle, I'm beginning to think you mean to ruin me for any other man."

"Ah, you've worked out my evil master plan at last," he said. His fingers tightened about her waist. "I willna just ruin you. I will devastate you."

"I can hardly wait," she whispered.

Will took Lucy by the hand and led her to his suite of rooms. He was so impatient for her, his hunger so acute, that he had to force himself to slow down and not rush up the stairs and along the hallway. He had to remind himself that they had hours and hours alone together. All night.

But upon entering his sitting room, it was to discover that his valet, Symington, was still lurking in the dressing room, fussing about with God knew what.

Curse him. Will hoped to Hades the man didn't notice his master had a raging erection. He put a finger to his lips and bade Lucy wait in the shadows by the sitting room door before he adjusted the front of his trousers and coat, then strode through to the bedchamber to dismiss the man for the evening.

His valet frowned but other than informing Will that he'd left a pitcher of hot water by the fire for bathing, he didn't argue when he was dismissed for the night and instructed not to enter his master's suite again unless summoned.

Once the coast was clear and the doors to his suite were all locked, Will returned to Lucy who was now waiting by the sitting room fireplace. The leaping flames and the low-burning gas lamps gilded her hair and lovely countenance. Highlighted her flushed cheeks and the light of desire in her wide, blue-gray eyes. When she smiled, Will's blood pounded hot and hard through his veins, thickening his cock. His mouth watered as inspiration struck. After shrugging off his coat and tossing it onto a nearby wingback chair, he pulled her into his arms.

"I've a mind to start here in this room before we retire to my bed." Dipping his head, he traced the seam of her sweet lips with the tip of his tongue, making her shiver. "Remember, I'm a wild, savage Scotsman who can make use of any type of furniture for any wicked purpose."

"I do remember," she said. "And that it's the 'how' of the business rather than what goes where that's most important."

Will turned her about to face the other side of the room. "Well, I've decided I'm going to demonstrate the best way to use that oak desk." His lips brushed her ear. "But first, I'm going to undress you. I want to see you naked. I've been dreaming of that for days, lass. Picturing all of your glorious curves in my head, but now I need to see it all. Do you understand?"

"Yes…" she whispered.

Even though his fingers were practically shaking with need, Will somehow helped Lucy to remove her gown, crinoline cage, petticoats, corset, fine lawn chemise, and drawers. With each garment that fell to the floor, he lavished Lucy's smooth-as-satin flesh with kisses and caresses: the column of her throat where her pulse beat wildly, the sweet hollow between her collarbones, her rosy-pink nipples, the elegant length of her neck, the two tiny dimples at the base of her spine just above her lush, peach-shaped derriere. Her gasps and shivers and sighs were music to his ears.

When Lucy was at last wearing nothing but her stockings and silk heels, Will caught her about her slender waist and pulled her against him, her back to his front. "My bonny Lucy," he groaned, pushing his hips into her bare behind. "You're so beautiful. So desirable. Can you feel how hard I am for you? How aroused?"

She gave a soft, throaty laugh. "As stiff as an iron poker, I'd say."

Will slid a hand to her throat, grasping gently, and then dropped a kiss on one pale shoulder. "That's because I've been thinking about what I'm going to do to you. I want to taste you before I have you." He scraped his teeth along a delicate tendon of her neck, then whispered, "You're now going to walk over to my desk, place your forearms on the blotter, and then bend over. Will you do that for me?"

Her reply was a breathless "yes," and then Will released her and watched in a fever of lust and sharp anticipation as she sauntered across the plush Persian rug and did exactly as he'd asked. When she looked back over her shoulder at him, her eyes heavy-lidded with desire, Will almost came in his trousers.

Within a handful of strides, he was behind her and dropping to his knees. "Spread your lovely thighs, my lass," he commanded, his voice low and rough. "Let me see your pretty wet cunny."

Lucy complied immediately and Will couldn't contain an outpouring of crude praise. Never in his life had he seen a more erotic sight. Never had been so aroused by the musky scent of a woman. His head was spinning, and his cock was throbbing.

But the most thrilling part of all was that Lucy gave him everything, surrendering all of herself to live in the moment. Allowing him free rein to pleasure her. He gently parted her slick folds, then slid two fingers into her tight, lust-drenched sex. She gasped and pushed back, and he thrust in and out several times, before spreading her sweet nectar up to the apex of her folds.

"Oh…God," she moaned. "Oh, Will. Please… Use your mouth on me."

And he did. He feasted and gorged, tormenting the hard pearl of her clitoris with his tongue and lips, alternately flicking and swirling and suckling like a starving man who'd found ambrosia and couldn't get enough. He licked every part of her sex and plunged his tongue inside her. It was only when Lucy had reached her peak and her thighs were trembling and she was begging for mercy that Will relented and ended the exquisite plunder of her most intimate flesh with one long, slow, decadent lap.

Rising to his feet, he leaned over her, covering her back with his front. His hands cupped her plump breasts and he pinched her tightly furled nipples, eliciting another moan from her. "Are you ready for me to take you?" he whispered huskily against her ear. "Do you want me to lay you upon my bed and fill you with my throbbing cock and hammer in and out of you until I make you come again? Is that what you want?"

Lucy whimpered and arched against him. "Yes. Please, yes," she moaned.

Will eased himself up, then swept Lucy into his arms. As he carried her through to his bedchamber, he caught her gaze. "You have nothing to fear. I willna come inside you."

"I trust you," she whispered, her eyes shining.

"Good." He lay her very gently upon the crimson silk counterpane of his tester bed. Then bending low, he claimed her delectable mouth, kissing her with lingering tenderness. The importance of this night, these next minutes, was not lost on him. "I'll be as gentle as I can when I enter you," he said. "It can hurt the first time."

"I know and I'm not afraid." Her mouth curved in a smile. "I'm a keen horsewoman, remember? I've heard that can help."

Will grinned. "Aye, it can."

Reaching up, Lucy tugged at the waistband of his trousers. "Now, hurry up and get undressed," she demanded with a mock frown. "Turnabout is fair play, after all. I want to see you naked too."

Will laughed. "I canna argue with that." But then he sobered as he stripped. Lucy had jested earlier that he was planning to ruin her for all other men, but deep down he'd been serious. He had to show her that they were made for each other. That they belonged together.

This night, he realized as he tugged off his shirt and Lucy's adoring gaze traveled over him, was also deeply significant for him. He had to get this right.

For the first time in his life, he wouldn't just be slaking his lust. This would be making love.

Lucy watched Will avidly as he divested the rest of his clothes. Her gaze drank in the breath-stealing sight of him. All of his sleek, rippling muscles and masculine perfection. His impossibly wide shoulders, and the well-developed mounds of his pectoral muscles with their scattering of dark hair and ha'penny-sized nipples. His ridged torso, the taut plane of his belly. The sharp crests of his lean hip bones and his heavily muscled thighs. And then there was that huge hard cock that sprang forward from its nest of fearsome dark curls.

She could hardly fathom that last night she'd taken that impressive part of Will in her mouth. That she'd cradled and fondled his heavy ballocks and readily swallowed his seed. When had she become so wicked and brazen and carefree? Shy, anxious Lucy disappeared whenever she was with William Lockhart. And indeed, perhaps it had been that way from the very beginning, when they'd braved that fierce summer storm together on the way back to Fleetwood Hall.

Her gaze fell to his enormous member again. Will had taken it in his hand and was stroking himself as he climbed onto the bed. Very soon, that cock would be inside her, sweeping her away into another storm, bringing her untold pleasure. Her sex throbbed in anticipation.

Instead of lying down, Will sat back on his haunches and studied her through heavy, half-mast lids. "Och, lass. You are the most exquisite thing I've ever seen," he whispered, his voice hoarse. He reached out with his free hand and his fingers lightly traced over her collarbones, then slid between the valley of her breasts until they reached her mound and ruffled the curls in a whisper-soft caress.

Lucy kicked off her shoes and then stretched her arms up above her head, arching her back, reveling in the unabashed adoration in her lover's gaze. She felt no shame at all, only desire. "You make me feel so very beautiful," she whispered in wonder. "And truly wanted."

"Aye to both of those things. Never doubt that." And then at last Will slid on top of her, covering her with his large body. He was so wonderfully hot and hard all over, and his engorged manhood jutted into her soft belly with an insistence that could not be denied.

When he swooped down for a searing kiss, Lucy instinctively parted her thighs, silently urging him to possess her. Will immediately accepted her invitation. Taking his weight on one arm, he took his cock in hand and swept the velvet-smooth head through the slick moisture welling between her folds. Then he positioned himself at her entrance.

"Are you ready, lass?" he murmured.

She clasped his shoulders and smiled. "Aye, make me yours, Lord Kyle," she whispered.

He pressed forward in a series of small but insistent nudges and Lucy closed her eyes and bit her lip to stifle a whimper. There was a brief, flaring sensation of burning, of excruciating tension, and then the discomfort of his incursion eased. Indeed, her sex seemed to clutch at him, greedily sucking him in farther. She was crammed full of rock-hard cock, and it was wonderful.

Will held perfectly still on his braced arms, and when Lucy opened her eyes, all she could see was concern in her lover's gaze.

"You're inside me," she murmured.

"Aye. To the hilt." He kissed her forehead. "How does it feel?"

She smiled and caressed his beloved face. "It feels right."

"Och, lass." Will's answering smile was warmer than a midsummer's day. "You make my heart ache in the sweetest way."

As he claimed her mouth in a hot, urgent kiss, he began

to rock his hips, sliding in and out of her. The friction of his gliding cock was exquisite, and very soon Lucy had the urge to move her own hips, to meet each of his thrusts, matching his rhythm. As Will increased his pace, she wrapped her legs about him and grasped his shoulders. She began to pant, and then moans and gasps she couldn't hope to contain tumbled from her throat. She was being taken on a wild, wild ride and heaven was fast approaching.

Indeed, she could feel the familiar coiling tension inside her, twisting tighter and tighter as Will's pumping grew harder and faster. His cock seemed made for her. It stroked some secret place deep inside her, setting off sparks and tremors, and all at once her sex began to clench tightly in anticipation of the enormous wave of pleasure that was about to break over her.

When it did, Lucy cried out, calling Will's name. Her whole body arched and her sex spasmed as she was engulfed in ecstasy. A moment later, Will pulled out of her body and succumbed to bliss too. On a roar, he came, and his seed coated her lower belly before he collapsed on top of her, his chest heaving, his body slick with sweat. When he rolled to the side, gathering her into his arms, he whispered her name like it was a plea or perhaps a prayer. Or even a declaration of love...

Love... If this was love, Lucy wanted more of it.

After they'd both bathed and were nestled back in bed beneath the sheets, Lucy nuzzled her face against Will's chest. Inhaled his delicious spicy scent as she listened to the steady thud of his heart. Satisfaction like she'd never known hummed through her veins and drowsiness tugged at her, beckoning her toward sleep. And then her heart clenched as the realization hit her. Will had indeed devastated her with pleasure. In a way, he *had* ruined her because she didn't want anyone else.

Only this man would do, now and forever.

It was wonderful and terrible all at the same time. She didn't know if the tears welling in her eyes were tears of joy or sadness.

Will had suggested they could marry as a last resort to save her from a life of misery with Thorne, and she'd balked at the offer. But now…she was confused.

She didn't know what she wanted anymore, what was most important to her.

Did she want a life with Will—a wonderful man who might very well be in love with her and she with him—or the promise of a career? A career that she loved, but given her lack of financial resources she couldn't afford to pursue in the way that she wanted to? A career that was almost impossible to become established in, never mind recognized as a serious contributor, if one was a woman without a formal university qualification? A career that was incompatible with having children if one's aim was to travel abroad in the hope of making groundbreaking discoveries?

But maybe you can have both, a small voice whispered inside her. *What if Will agreed to help you, which he might do if he sincerely cares for you? What if you could travel abroad and have a family? What if you could use your elevated position to convince universities like Cambridge and Oxford to accept women into their ranks?*

Perhaps it was just a matter of logistics and a bit of give-and-take…

One thing was clear: In the coming days, she needed to have a serious conversation with Will, the man who'd stolen her heart and made her question everything about her life. A man who'd made her yearn for something she used to be part of long ago and—if she were honest with herself—she missed desperately. A happy family.

Then, and only then, could she make an informed decision.

Chapter Twenty-Six

LUCY AWOKE FROM A DEEP SLEEP WITH A START, AND FOR A moment she forgot where she was. As her eyes adjusted to the dim light, she realized she was lying naked beside Will in his enormously sumptuous tester bed.

For some reason she couldn't fathom, her heart was pounding.

And then she heard it. A strange noise. A strangled choking sound followed by a whimper. That's what had woken her, she was certain of it.

It was Will.

He must be having a nightmare.

Lucy's heart cramping with concern, she turned her head on the pillow, but she could barely see his profile. Because the fire in the grate had burned low and the gas lamps had been extinguished, he was little more than a dark silhouette. But she sensed his whole body was rigid and the sheets seemed to be twisted about his hips.

She pushed herself up against the carved bedhead and reached for his shoulder. Touched him gently. "Will?" she whispered uncertainly.

All at once, his whole body jumped and then he bolted upright, muttering something that sounded a lot like "Christ on a cross." His shoulders were rising and falling as though he couldn't catch his breath, and when Lucy dared to reach out and touch him again, she felt that his skin was slick with sweat.

"Will... Are you all right?"

He turned toward her and reached for her hand. Gave it a reassuring squeeze. "Aye. I... It's just a bad dream. One I havena had in a while."

"You've had it before? I'm so sorry. How awful."

"Aye. But dinna worry, lass." He wiped a hand down his face, and then she imagined he was attempting to smile at her even though it was dark. "I will be all right. I apologize if I frightened you."

He climbed from the bed and padded across the room to his dressing room. She heard sounds of rummaging, and in a minute he returned with a lit gas lamp. He'd donned a silk banyan, and in his other hand he carried a second garment which he offered to her—another quilted silk robe. His mouth curved in a lopsided smile. "Since the fire's gone out, it's a wee bit cold in here," he said. "You might like to put this on."

"Thank you." She took the robe, then shrugged it on. It was far too big, but the smooth silk smelled like Will and his cologne as she wrapped it about herself. She wanted to ask him what his recurring nightmare was about but he was busy restoking the fire, and when there were bright flames leaping up the chimney, he poured himself a drink from one of the crystal decanters kept on a side table by the fireplace.

"Would you like something?" he asked over his shoulder as he replaced the stopper in the decanter. "I'm having whisky, but I also have sherry. Or I could ring for tea, perhaps? I dinna know if we have chamomile tea though."

Lucy slid from the bed and approached the fireside. The ormolu clock on the mantel proclaimed the hour to be almost midnight. She always felt guilty waking the servants to do her bidding in the middle of the night, but it wasn't *that* late. "If I ordered tea, perhaps we could also order some warm milk for you. I know how much you like it, and it might help you sleep."

Will looked at her over the rim of his crystal tumbler as he took a pull of his whisky. When he lowered the glass, Lucy was surprised to see that he looked guilty. "I have a confession to make," he said, holding her gaze. "I dinna want to upset you, but I actually loathe warm milk."

Oh… Lucy blinked. "Then…then why didn't you say something at the time? Why did you drink it? On both occasions?"

He gave an apologetic grimace. "That first time you caught me trying to skulk about Fleetwood Hall searching for evidence, I had to think of some excuse for my late-night visit. And needing a drink of warm milk to help me sleep was the first excuse that sprang to mind."

"You scoundrel! You lied to me," cried Lucy. "And watched me painstakingly prepare it for you—stirring and stirring it for ages so it wouldn't catch on the bottom of the pan. And oh…I should pummel you with a pillow."

"In my defense, I did drink it though," he said. "All of it. I didna want to hurt your feelings. And if it helps, I just want you to know that it was at that precise moment that I realized how sweet and lovely you are. Aside from my dearly departed mother, I couldna think of anyone else who's ever taken such pains to do something like that for me. It meant a lot. It still does."

Oh… The spark of indignation firing Lucy's chagrin was immediately snuffed out. "Oh, Will. That's such a lovely thing to say. You're forgiven. And…and I'll have a sherry."

His answering smile was so warm, Lucy's heart melted into a puddle of something altogether soft and syrupy like honey or treacle or sweetened hot chocolate.

Once Lucy had her drink, they returned to the bed. Will

leaned back against the pillows, and when Lucy settled against his chest he draped an arm about her shoulder, drawing her closer. As though she belonged there. Indeed, she fit so well, perhaps she did.

Before her own thoughts could turn to the ever-present conundrum of whether her future would include Will or be Will-less, he kissed her temple, then broke the silence with a thought of his own. "No doubt you're wondering what my bad dream was about."

"I won't lie. I am curious," she said. "But please don't feel like you need to tell me if it's too painful to speak of."

"It is painful, but you and I... I feel like we've become verra close. In a verra short space of time. Yet you dinna know everything about me, including my family's skeleton in the closet, so to speak."

Goodness. What on earth had happened in this man's past that had scarred him so badly that it still gave him nightmares? "You don't have to tell me anything at all if it's difficult," she said softly. "All of us have secrets of one kind or another."

He kissed her forehead again. "I dinna want to keep anything from you."

His voice was so deep and low and weighted with sadness that Lucy turned in his arms to face him. "I'm here to listen, then. I do have to wonder though. Is this about your estrangement from your grandfather and your father?"

"Aye..." Will released a heavy sigh and then his mouth flattened. "Some things in life are unforgivable. What my father did and then what my grandfather failed to do when I was only a twelve-year-old lad definitely fit into that category."

"You've mentioned before that your mother died when you were twelve. And then you were sent away to Eton." She was almost afraid for Will to continue with his story, but for him she would be brave and listen to whatever he had to say.

"That is indeed what happened," he said. "She did die. But…" Will paused to throw back the rest of his whisky, then put the glass down on the bedside table with such care that Lucy wondered if he was trying to stop himself from hurling it across the room. He seemed tense and angry and sad all at the same time.

He started again. "But the word 'dying' doesna accurately portray the circumstances." He looked into Lucy's eyes. His own gaze was a stormy dark-blue as he added gravely, "I havena told another living soul any of this before. But my mother didna just die… The coroner ruled it was an accidental death. That she tripped and fell down the stairs of Kyleburn Castle late one night when she was addled with laudanum and wine. But that's not what happened at all. She was killed. Murdered. At the hands of my rotten-to-the-core father. And…" His eyes filled with tears. "I witnessed it. I saw it. And I couldna do anything to stop it."

Lucy couldn't suppress a gasp of horror. "Oh, my God, Will. How…awful and terrifying and I have no words that can adequately express my dismay. My heart weeps for you. But surely you couldn't have changed what happened. You mustn't blame yourself for what your father did."

He nodded and roughly dashed away a tear that had slipped onto his cheek. "What you say is true, but part of me canna help but wish things had turned out differently," he said, his voice clogged with so much raw emotion that Lucy's own throat began to ache with the effort not to cry too. "I will never, ever forget that night."

He pressed his lips together as though willing himself not to cry anymore, but after a brief pause, he swallowed and continued. "My mother had been unwell for a number of years," he said. "The doctors declared that she had rheumatism, but more often than not she was plagued with headaches and fatigue and various maladies that confined her to her bed for days, sometimes weeks. And she did take laudanum on occasion to relieve her pain, but I didna think it was to excess. Nevertheless, she always had time for me. We used to read to each other in her rooms when she was well enough." His expression softened as he looked at Lucy. "One of the last books we read together was Mary Shelley's *Frankenstein*. She was fond of Gothic novels too."

Then Will's mouth flattened into a hard line again. "The real monster though was my father. He was a rough, hard-hearted man with a fierce temper and no patience, but a fondness for whisky and cards and wenching. If I ever did anything to displease him, he was quick to whip out a leather strap to discipline me. And if my mother spoke out in protest, he would slap her too."

"Oh God. I'm so, so sorry." This time, Lucy couldn't swallow back her tears. "He was a monster. A bully. No wonder you have nightmares."

Will gave her a tender smile. "Och, dinna cry for me, lass. It was a long time ago and I survived. It didna take me long to learn to stay out of his way, and fortunately, he was hardly ever at home. He preferred to spend most of his time in Edinburgh and London, which suited my mother and me well. Kyleburn was a far more pleasant place without him there."

"And your grandfather? Did he not have anything to say about your father's shameful conduct, given he would be the next Duke of Ayr one day?" asked Lucy.

Will's mouth twisted with a sardonic smile. "My grandfather didna think his son could do any wrong. That he was simply a braw Scot, just like he was, with a strong appetite for 'wine, women, and song.' He also tended to avoid his own seat at Braeburn Castle in favor of spending time carousing in Edinburgh and London. How both of them didna manage to run the estate into the ground, I'll never know. My grandfather hardly ever visited us at Kyleburn, but he *was* there the night my mother was killed."

"What happened?" whispered Lucy.

"My father and grandfather were holed up in the dining room with several other clansmen along with their wine and whisky. But when one of the servants informed my mother that several women from the local tavern had been ferried into the castle for the men's entertainment—I was with my mother in her suite, reading, so I heard the exchange—she stormed into the dining room to break up the so-called party. I think it was the last straw for her. She and my father traded a few angry words in front of my grandfather and the other guests, but then she returned to her bedroom and wouldn't speak of it to me."

"How awful to hear about such debauchery at a young age. And your poor mama…" Lucy shook her head. "I don't know how you bear it."

Will's mouth curved into a sad yet wry smile.

Lucy caressed his cheek. "I've interrupted you. But only continue if you feel that you can."

"I canna stop now. I want you to know everything." He sighed, his expression grim. "Later that night, after the women from the tavern and the clansmen had gone, my father returned to my mother's apartments even though she'd retired for the night. Their argument was so loud it woke me, and I crept from my bedchamber on the floor above and hid behind the stone newel-post at the top of the staircase. I didna know what I could do to help. I was quite a scrawny twelve-year-old and my father was a large, brutish man. Nevertheless, I felt compelled to do something. Anything."

A haunted look filled Will's eyes. "I'll never forget what happened next. My father burst out of the bedroom, my mother at his heels. She was crying. Sobbing. At the head of the stairs near her suite, she grabbed his arm, but then he swung back around and gripped her by the arms. Shook her. Yelled a foul string of obscenities that I canna repeat. He raised a hand to slap her face and she jerked away…and then somehow she lost her balance and stumbled backward, then fell down the stone staircase. All the way to the bottom… And all my drunken father did was shrug and return to his own suite of rooms."

"Oh my God. Oh, Will." Tears were streaming down Lucy's face. Horror compressed her lungs. "What did you do?"

"I was frozen to the spot. I couldna believe what I'd just seen. Then my grandfather was there, turning me around, leading me back to my own bedchamber. I tried to tell him about what I'd seen, but he wouldna listen. He just locked me in. And then after that…" Will wiped a hand down his face. "It was as though my father hadna done anything wrong at all. It was all covered up. Glossed over."

"But…how?" asked Lucy. "Surely that couldn't happen."

"When your grandfather is a wealthy duke, anything can happen," said Will bitterly. "A physician and the local coroner came in the morning and decreed the Countess of Kyle had died from an accidental fall. My father left Kyleburn for Edinburgh or London. I'm no' exactly sure which because no one ever told me. And my grandfather sent me away. When I received word from him at Eton that my father had died—apparently he was so drunk one night when leaving a tavern on the Royal Mile in Edinburgh that he slipped on the cobblestones and was hit by a carriage—I wasna sorry at all. I didna a shed a single tear.

"Over a decade later, when I finally confronted my grandfather about what had happened that night at Kyleburn—how he'd let my father get away with murder—he told me he'd done what he'd done to protect the family name from scandal. He hadna seen the moment my father had let his wife fall to her death. He only had my word about what happened and he wasna inclined to believe a 'puling twelve-year-old lad' over the word of his son. It was then that I told my grandfather that I never wanted to see him again. That I would never marry, and the dukedom could die with me because I'm the last Lockhart male in line for the title. My grandfather only agreed to purchase a military commission for me in order to buy my silence. And that was the last time I saw him."

Will blew out a sigh. "So there you have it, lass. My family history is no' something I'm proud of. I would understand if you didna want to continue pursuing any sort of relationship with—"

Lucy caught Will by the chin and turned his head to face her. "I will not hear you say such things, William Lockhart. You are the most noble, kindhearted, brave, and caring man I've ever met. Any woman would be mad not to want to share a life with you."

Some sort of powerful emotion—perhaps it was stark longing and sharp want—flared in his deep-blue eyes. "Do you mean that, Lucy?" he whispered hoarsely. "Truly?"

Lucy swallowed. "Yes, I do."

And then Will kissed her. Passionately. With an intensity that soon had Lucy moaning in his arms.

This time when Will made love to her, Lucy did know, deep in her heart, what she was going to do if Will ever *did* propose.

There was no other option.

Chapter Twenty-Seven

WHEN WILL AWOKE THE NEXT MORNING JUST AFTER SEVEN o'clock, it was to discover that Lucy had already risen, dressed, and quit Kyleburn House. She'd left a note on the pillow beside him where her head had rested.

My dearest Will,

Last night was absolutely wonderful—the best night of my life—but when I woke this morning, I thought it best to discreetly return to Dartmoor House after all. I hope you understand, but there's been enough discord in my family to last a lifetime, and despite my words of bravado last night, I really couldn't face the prospect of dealing with an upset Monty. Neither of us needs that right now, so I thought it would be best to err on the side of caution.

I shall return to Kyleburn House later in the morning, at eleven.

I trust you slept well.

Yours,

Lucy

Trying to ignore the sinking feeling in his heart that Lucy wasn't in his bed, in his arms with her head upon his chest,

Will rose to face the day. He rang for Symington and subjected himself to the man's attentive ministrations. Once he'd bathed, shaved, and was attired in gentlemen's clothes befitting his station, he descended to the morning room to take breakfast. He was uncommonly hungry for once and piled his plate with bacon and kidneys, poached eggs and toast, and tucked in with gusto. He suspected that his amorous exploits with Lucy last night had worked up his appetite.

Lying in the dark with her in his arms after their second round of lovemaking, Will had wanted to say "I love you," but he hadn't been able to. The air seemed to freeze in his lungs and the words lodged in his throat because if he uttered them, he was worried that Lucy would balk and retreat from him like a startled hind.

As a grown man, he'd never been a coward, but he'd never had something so precious to lose. Somehow, he had to find the courage to say what needed to be said. When the time was right. But that wasn't today.

Today he had to arrange a meeting with Sir Oswald. He wouldn't interview him at Scotland Yard. Such a formal setting was likely to intimidate rather than encourage the baronet to open up. And he doubted that Monty would want to visit Scotland Yard either. The fact that he'd trusted Will with his secret—one that could land him in very hot water with the law too—was not lost on him. And Will would do his utmost not to break that trust. He wouldn't divulge Monty's secret unless he had his permission.

Of course, Will would let Detective Lawrence know what he was up to in a general sense—that he'd unearthed a potentially significant lead but things were at a "delicate stage" so he couldn't say any more *just* yet.

He'd begun to pour himself another cup of coffee and was

thinking of helping himself to another slice of toast when Hillier announced that Detective Lawrence was asking for him and that he'd installed him in the library. At that moment, Will knew something was afoot. Whatever it was, it couldn't be good.

Indeed, as soon as Will spied Lawrence's grim countenance, he knew his suspicions had been correct.

"What is it?" he asked without preamble.

The detective handed him a piece of paper. "More threats," he said. "Every single Linnean Society Council member who's been previously threatened received one of these during the night. It was pushed under the front door of each of their homes. I think your stirring up the hornet's nest yesterday worked after all."

Will glanced over the note and its messily scrawled contents, and his blood ran colder than a Highland burn in midwinter.

> *Time is running out. Tick tock, tick tock.*
>
> *Expel Darwin, the heretic, the perverter of God's Divine Law, or meet the same fate as Litchfield and Fitzroy. I'm watching and waiting, and my pockets are full of poison...*

"Thorne's goading us," said Will, passing the note back to Lawrence. Last night he'd told Lucy and Monty that their father could still very well be a suspect, but this note sounded exactly like something the arrogant Yorkshireman would have penned. "Did anyone at all—a night footman, a maid, a deliveryman, a lamplighter, a knocker-up, any passerby on the street—witness who delivered these notes? Even though it's only a handful of Linnean Society members, surely someone saw something useful."

"I have uniformed officers out asking those questions as

we speak. But so far, it seems no one has witnessed anything remotely helpful." Lawrence sighed. "Of course, I'll be visiting Thorne shortly to find out what his movements were last night and if anyone can provide him with a decent alibi. The problem is he's so wealthy that he could have paid half a dozen lackeys to deliver these notes—or even street urchins desperate for a few coins."

Will agreed. "I really do think we're going to have to set a trap for Thorne. It's the only way to stop him quickly."

The detective cocked a brow. "You have something particular in mind?"

"Aye," said Will. "I do. But I willna be at liberty to discuss it with you and Lord Castledown until later this afternoon or this evening."

"I'll set something up with Castledown, if you like. Six o'clock at my office?"

"Done," said Will.

———————

As Will's carriage crunched over Fleetwood Hall's gravel drive, Will grasped Lucy's hand and gave it a squeeze. "Everything will be all right, lass," he said gently. "Dinna fash yourself."

Lucy offered him a smile, but she couldn't quite quell the race of her pulse. Inside her gloves, her palms felt damp, and her corset felt far too tight. Monty, who sat on the opposite bench seat, appeared to be tenser than a pianoforte wire too. She could tell by the set of his jaw and the lines of strain about his mouth and eyes. There was no way to tell how this reunion between father and son would go. Or if their father would at last shed any light on why Thorne seemed to be controlling him like a puppet on a string.

If her father didn't share what was going on, Lucy feared he might be arrested for obstructing the course of an investigation, or even for the murders of Lord Litchfield and Professor Fitzroy. At some point, Will and Scotland Yard were going to lose patience with him.

Clarke, the footman, gaped like a floundering codfish as soon as he saw who was walking through Fleetwood Hall's front door. Not only had Monty returned, but Will was now dressed like a gentleman, not a mere groom.

"Lord Kyle," he repeated like a mindless automaton after Lucy had introduced him to the footman by his title.

"Yes. Lord Kyle," said Lucy. "Won't you take his hat?"

"Of course. My apologies, Miss Bertram. Lord Kyle..." He bowed to Will, then to Monty. "Mr. Bertram, welcome back."

"Thank you. I take it my father is in?" said Monty.

Clarke took everyone's hats. "Yes, he is, sir. In his study, I believe."

"Excellent," remarked Will. "And he's by himself?"

The footman nodded. "Yes, my lord." His gaze darted about the entry hall before it returned to Lucy and Monty. "Miss Bertram, Mr. Bertram...I know it's not really my place to say anything, but I'm so relieved that you are both back. We're all quite worried about the master. He's not been himself these past few days. Mrs. Gilchrist says he's not eating, and Mr. Redmond says he's not been sleeping. That he paces his rooms all night."

Lucy frowned and traded glances with Will and her brother. "Thank you, Clarke," she said. "We appreciate your candor. Hopefully things will be back to normal very soon."

Clarke offered her a shy smile. "I knew you'd understand, miss. Thank you."

Lucy faced Will and Monty. "Are we ready?" she asked.

Monty nodded, his expression grim. "No, but I'm grateful that you are here, Luce. And Will."

Lucy grasped his arm and gave it a squeeze. "We'll both be here for you, no matter what."

"Aye," said Will. "You can count on our support. And one way or another, we should have some of the answers we need."

Lucy led the way to Fleetwood's study, Will and Monty trailing behind her. When she entered, it was to discover that her father was standing at one of the room's wide windows, staring out at the poisons garden. He didn't even seem to register that the door had opened and he had visitors.

"Papa?" she called softly.

Her father started, then swung around to face her. "Lucy. My God, gel. I all but jumped out of my skin. What on earth are you playing at…?" He trailed off as his gaze swung to the doorway where Will stood. "You," he exclaimed, his face turning as red as a beet. He threw his hands up in the air. "What are you doing here?"

"I'm here to help you and your family, Sir Oswald," replied Will calmly, advancing farther into the room. "Each and every one of you."

Before her father could respond, Lucy jumped in. "He is, Papa. Actually, I've brought someone else to see you. He wants to help as well…"

When Monty appeared on the threshold, her father's eyes widened to the size of saucers behind his spectacles. "Oh my God," he breathed. "Monty… Is it really you?"

"Yes, Papa. It's me." Monty took a few steps farther into the room.

Her father swallowed. "You're all right," he added in a choked whisper, and then in the next instant, both men had crossed the Turkish rug and were embracing and crying and Lucy could hardly believe it.

When Will offered her a linen kerchief, she used it to brush away her own tears that had escaped onto her cheeks.

"Oh, my son. I've been so, so terrified for weeks and weeks... About whether you were safe or whether something terrible had happened to you." Her father's voice was thick with emotion as his words tumbled out. "I'm so sorry. For everything I said that night. For turning my back on you. For all of it. Can you ever forgive me?"

When Monty drew back, he was frowning. "Of course I can... But I hope you'll be able to forgive me when I say I'm so very confused by your change of heart right now. That night you came upon me and Lord Litchfield, you were adamant that I was no son of yours. What happened to change your opinion?"

Sir Oswald sighed heavily. "That's perfectly understandable that you would doubt me. And I'm ashamed of how I reacted then. If I'd been a better man—a more understanding man—I would've acted differently. But something did happen to change my perspective. It made me realize the error of my ways, and that what I thought was wrong isn't at all. That there are far, far worse things..." His voice faded away as he shook his head.

Will cleared his voice. "Sir Oswald, forgive me for interrupting, but you mentioned before that you've been terrified for Monty for weeks. What did you mean by that? I canna help but think that Zachariah Thorne is involved."

"Yes, Father," said Lucy gently. "You must tell us what's going on. *All* of us are here to help you. We've had enough of secrets and lies. It's time to bring everything into the light."

All color drained from her father's face, leaving it ashen. "I can't say," he whispered hoarsely. He took a few steps away from Monty, then walked stiffly over to the window again. "I wish I could."

Lucy approached him slowly. "You can trust us, Papa." She reached out and touched his rigid shoulder, attempting to offer comfort even though a frisson of fear was trickling down her own spine. "Lord Kyle—Will—is a powerful nobleman with connections in high places. All of us know something is terribly, terribly wrong and that Mr. Thorne is involved. We're worried he's made you do things you don't want to and—"

Her father tore away from her. His hands were shaking as he pushed his spectacles farther up his nose. "You have no idea, Lucy, my dear gel. None at all. *That* man. He—" Her father broke off and pinched the bridge of his nose. Bowed his head. "He'll be the death of me, that man," he bit out from between clenched teeth. "How I hate him. I rue the day I met him. He talks of the sin of others and that we're all damned, when he's the one who has evil running through his veins." He raised his gaze to Will's, his blue eyes blazing with indignation. "And Scotland Yard hauled *me* in for questioning. They thought I'd killed Litchfield because of my knowledge of poisons and the fact he'd withdrawn his support for my expedition to the Malay Peninsula at the beginning of the year. But I didn't murder him. I didn't want him dead. Not even when I found out about his relationship with my son."

Will stepped forward. "Sir Oswald, I can see how distressed and angry you are and I dinna doubt for a moment that what you say is true about Thorne. Would it help you to know that I have associates at Scotland Yard and at the Home Office who now suspect Thorne is responsible for Lord Litchfield's murder and a nefarious plot to oust Charles Darwin from the Linnean Society? And that he might also have claimed the life of another man?"

Her father paled. "Professor Fitzroy? I saw his death mentioned in the papers and there's been whispers of foul play between members of the Linnean Society. I did wonder."

Will nodded. "Aye. We're treating the professor's death as suspicious."

"Well, you can add blackmail to the list of Thorne's crimes," her father said bitterly. He collapsed onto the window seat as though the fight had suddenly gone out of him. "What do you want to know, Lord Kyle? I'll tell you everything."

―――――――――

Thank God and hallelujah!

Will blew out a relieved sigh before he exchanged a speaking look with Lucy and her brother. So he wouldn't tower over the baronet, he pulled up a nearby chair and then sat down, forearms resting on his thighs, hands clasped in a nonthreatening pose. Lucy selected an armchair and Monty took the chair behind his father's desk.

"Sir Oswald, if I tell you everything that Scotland Yard already knows, will that help? Then you can fill me in on the missing pieces of the puzzle. I assure you that anything you share with me now will not be used against you or Monty. Consider this discussion to be confidential."

The baronet nodded. "Yes. I'll agree to that."

Will inclined his head. "Good." When he'd finished bringing Sir Oswald up to date with the details of the case—as far as Scotland Yard knew, at any rate—the man looked far less troubled. Perhaps he even seemed a little relieved.

"You have a good deal of the details correct," he said. "Thorne did kill Litchfield with *Strychnos nux-vomica* at the Raleigh Club. He did slip it into the viscount's absinthe. As I said, I wasn't sure about Professor Fitzroy's death, but I do know that Thorne does indeed have plans to kill several other Linnean Society Council members unless Darwin is expelled and discredited in a few weeks' time. I do believe Thorne does ultimately mean to kill Darwin because of his scientific beliefs no matter what happens. The man is irrational, if not entirely deranged."

"And do you have any proof that Scotland Yard could present in a court of law that would incriminate Thorne, beyond your testimony which he's likely to refute?" asked Will.

"There's the rub," said Sir Oswald with a heavy sigh. "You *would* have nothing but my word. The worst part is anything I say may incriminate me and my son. Thorne is diabolically clever, I'll give him that."

Damn. "Why don't you provide me with some basic details, and we'll work from there," said Will. Perhaps he could draw out something useful from the baronet. A seemingly inconsequential detail that was actually significant. "When did you first meet Thorne?"

"It was a little over a year ago. He'd just returned from Ceylon where he has coffee plantations. That's when he joined the Raleigh Club and the Linnean Society. He wanted to meet with like-minded people who also had an interest in improving crop yields, especially in the colonies of the Indian subcontinent. Aside from 'rooting out evil,' Thorne is obsessed with making money, both here and abroad. He has fingers in so many colonial, industrial, and entrepreneurial pies that it's mind-boggling."

Will nodded. "You obviously got to know each other well. You must have liked him initially."

Sir Oswald's mouth twisted. "At first… After everyone at the Linnean Society heard that Lord Litchfield had reneged on his agreement to fund my expedition, Thorne approached me at the Raleigh Club one night with another proposition. This was in early May, after Monty and I had…" He threw an apologetic look his son's way. "Well, after I'd disowned you, my son. There's no sense in trying to sugarcoat the fact that I behaved abominably that night. I realize now, of course, that it felt like a betrayal to see you with the man who'd crushed my dream. But that's no excuse. And in case you're wondering, Lord Kyle"—his attention returned to Will—"no, I wasn't so disappointed that I decided to kill Litchfield for revenge. I'm not that sort of man."

"I know you're not, Papa," said Lucy softly.

Sir Oswald's eyes filled with tears. "Oh, my dear Lucy. What I've put you through because of Thorne. I do not want you to marry him. Pandering to that man's vile whims—pretending that I was in favor of a match—has been one of the worst parts of this whole sordid affair. I'm so very sorry. I kept telling myself it wouldn't go that far. That somehow I'd find a way out of this mess for all of us. And I suppose that's what this is now—this exchange of information. A way out. At least I hope so." He sighed. "But I've gone off track, haven't I?"

"It's no matter," said Will. "Please go on. You were telling us about Thorne's proposition back in May."

"Yes. Right," said Sir Oswald, sitting up straighter. "It seemed all perfectly innocent at first. He hinted that he would consider funding my proposed expedition to Malaysia in exchange for my botanical knowledge. You see, he was thinking of starting tea plantations in Ceylon but needed someone with expertise to advise him, and because I'd once written a paper on partic-ular tea varieties that grow well in India based on geographical location…" Sir Oswald shrugged. "I was flattered of course and keen to work on a project that might have some financial ben-efit in the long run. And yes, I was excited by the prospect that my expedition might actually happen after all. But then"—he shook his head—"it all went wrong."

"How so?" prompted Will gently.

"I was particularly maudlin one night. I was plagued by guilt about our family's worsening financial situation and the fact I had no idea where Monty was. I was at the Raleigh Club and well into my cups. And then Thorne appeared, and we started drinking absinthe together. I'm ashamed to say it, but I was so inebriated I barely remember the exchange. But I think I must have let slip something about you, Monty, and our estrangement." Sir Oswald's gaze connected with his son's, "And the reason for it."

"Oh, no," breathed Lucy. "You said something about Lord Litchfield?"

"I must have," said the baronet, his expression guilt-stricken. "I was such a fool."

"What happened then?" asked Will.

"Nothing immediately," said Sir Oswald. "Not until the Linnean Society's meeting on the first of July where Darwin and Alfred Russel Wallace's joint paper on evolution and natural selection was presented. I was there and so were Lord Litchfield and Thorne. Professor Fitzroy too. Everyone knew that Wallace was abroad in Borneo and Darwin wasn't present either. The poor man had recently lost his infant son. But that didn't matter to Thorne. He was both enraged and disgusted. He thought their ideas were an affront to God. Heretical. Especially Darwin's because he'd met the man on a number of occasions. Thorne didn't make his views widely known though. Only to a select few members—me and also a fellow named Cuthbert Collingwood, and then later the Bishop of Oxford, Samuel Wilberforce."

A look of revulsion crossed the baronet's countenance. "Thorne decided that it was his duty as a devout Christian to drive Darwin and his equally sinful supporters from the Linnean Society. I think he must have decided he would make an example of Lord Litchfield first, because in his eyes he was one of the worst sinners. And all because of what I'd accidentally let slip that night at the Raleigh Club."

"You didn't think to warn anyone about Thorne's plan?"

asked Monty. His voice was harsh with bitterness. "Not even Lord Litchfield?"

"You may not believe me, Monty, but Thorne never divulged to me who he considered his 'targets' until it was too late. I also had no idea that he'd stolen a sample of soluble *Strychnos nux-vomica* powder from my study, along with several other assorted potent poisons—cyanide and hemlock and aconitum—until he told me after the fact. He wanted to boast about how clever he was. And that happened to be after poor Litchfield was murdered."

"That's so terrible, Papa. I didn't know that Thorne had visited Fleetwood Hall before the evening he came to dinner," said Lucy.

"It was a brief visit in the first week of July," said Sir Oswald. "You were in Town, seeing your friend Miss Delaney. And I regret that he came to Fleetwood with every fiber of my being. Not only did he steal those vials of poison, but he saw your portrait in the hall, Lucy. And curse him, he seemed enthralled by your likeness. That's when he indicated that he wished to meet you. And I couldn't naysay him even then. He told me that he would go to the newspapers and expose Monty's affair with Litchfield if I refused his request. The scandal would have ruined all of us. Not only that, but if the police had tracked you down, Monty, you would have been arrested. Thorne has been blackmailing me for weeks to keep me compliant, and I haven't been able to work out a means of escape."

Monty nodded. "This Thorne is an evil bastard."

"Aye, he is," said Will. "When Litchfield was poisoned that night at the Raleigh Club, you must have suspected then who'd killed him. And how he'd done it."

Sir Oswald nodded. "I did. And I was horrified. But I couldn't say anything to the Scotland Yard detective who questioned me.

My hands were tied. When I confronted Thorne about what he'd done to Litchfield, he threatened me again. He said I wasn't to breathe a word about it. He wouldn't just go to the newspapers about Monty's affair with Litchfield. He said he'd tell the police that *I* was the one who'd murdered Litchfield because I was angry with the viscount for 'corrupting' my son—his word, not mine. It would mean that both Monty and I would have been arrested, and if found guilty we'd both be hanged. And I couldn't have that. I had to keep the family safe."

"That's why you've stayed silent all this time," said Will grimly.

"Yes. It's been a nightmare. And it's still my word against Thorne's. There's no evidence implicating him in anything. Not that I'm aware of. And I can't testify against him because it means he'll tell the world about Monty. The only thing that I did that was illegal was to send Darwin an envelope containing another threat—I tried to emulate Thorne's hand-writing—along with a bit of itching powder. I wanted to scare the poor man into resigning from the Linnean Society before anyone else got killed. But I also fear that Thorne will kill Darwin anyway, regardless. And his death will be the last. The pièce de résistance. Thorne wants to send a message to the world: Thou shalt not question God's law."

"That's diabolical," said Lucy. "But I was right about one thing at least."

Sir Oswald frowned. "What do you mean?"

"Your clever daughter identified the substance sent to Darwin when she examined it under a microscope at Scotland Yard," said Will.

Sir Oswald smiled. "She is clever. And I'm also guilty of never giving her enough credit for all the work she does for me. Brilliant work."

"Thank you, Papa," said Lucy. "Your words mean more than I can say."

"Well," said Will, "given we must keep Monty's name out of the papers, and out of the investigation altogether, it seems the only way forward is to set a trap for Thorne. It's risky, but he needs to be caught red-handed trying to poison someone. Hopefully me. It will be easy enough to goad him into doing it because he sees me as a rival for Lucy's affections. And of course he's so insufferably arrogant he won't be able to resist, despite the risks. He thinks God is on his side, after all."

Lucy's heart cramped with horror. "You can't be serious, Will. It's too dangerous."

Sir Oswald's brow arrowed into a frown. "And won't Thorne say something when he's arrested? About Monty?"

"Yes. I'm not sure I like the sound of all this," agreed Monty.

"He might," said Will. "But the man *has* to be stopped. And it willna be difficult to discredit him when he starts raving on about all things fire and brimstone and the end of the world being nigh because of 'evildoers.' In the end, it's a risk we'll have to take."

Lucy released a shaky sigh. "I know that your planning will be meticulous," she said. "But please, be careful."

"Aye, I will," replied Will. "It won't be long before Thorne is in custody. And then this whole nightmare will be over."

Chapter Twenty-Eight

THE NEXT FIVE DAYS PASSED IN A FLURRY OF ACTIVITY. LUCY hardly saw Will at all, much to her disappointment.

He was caught up in meetings at Scotland Yard and the Home Office with Detective Lawrence, Lord Castledown, and even Artemis's husband, Dominic. It was all to do with the trap that was being laid for Thorne and, understandably, it was all very hush-hush. Monty had continued to reside at Kyleburn House, though he was still ostensibly "in hiding." It wouldn't do to alert Thorne that Monty had been welcomed back to the family fold in case Thorne decided to use the knowledge against Monty or their father. Or do something even worse and attempt to dispense with Monty, simply because he'd dared to love Lord Litchfield.

Lucy discreetly visited her brother once in the company of Artemis to take tea with him. He was in good spirits despite everything that was going on and the ever-present Damocles sword—in the form of Thorne's threats to reveal Monty's secret to society and the authorities—hanging over his head. Sadly, Will hadn't been in at the time. And perhaps that was for the best, Lucy had reasoned, while all of this cloak-and-dagger business with Thorne was going on. The last thing she wanted to do was complicate Will's life or distract him from his work. Although she did miss her handsome Scot's company more than she could say. It gave her a glimpse of the future—what it would be like to live without Will—and she didn't like it, not one little bit.

Artemis kept her busy, so she didn't have time to fret too much. Aside from having to make umpteen morning calls every day and deal with reams of correspondence, the new Duchess of Dartmoor was madly preparing to open her ladies' college in a few weeks' time and Lucy was helping her whenever and wherever she could. She took part in interviews of prospective science and mathematics teachers and gave advice on the college's draft curriculum in those particular areas.

Her friend had also been caught up in the hubbub of visiting a modiste—Madame Blanchard—to arrange a new gown to wear to the Welcome Back to Society ball that Lord and Lady Castledown were throwing for her and Dominic. Madame Blanchard was the modiste of Artemis's aunt, Lady Wagstaff, who would also be attending the Castledowns' ball, along with Artemis's younger sister, Phoebe Jones. Jane, of course, was invited too.

Lucy had gleaned from her father that the ball might have Thorne and a few other Linnean Society members on the guest list as well.

While Lucy didn't relish the prospect of encountering the Yorkshireman again, she would be with Will and amongst other friends. She couldn't imagine that she *wouldn't* be safe. She was certain Will wouldn't let anything untoward happen to her or anyone else she cared about. At least, that's what she kept telling herself.

Still, when Artemis insisted on gifting new ball gowns to both Lucy and Jane for the occasion—she claimed Dominic had given her such an enormous budget for her wardrobe and she had simply no idea what to do with it—Lucy took the opportunity to discreetly ask Madame Blanchard to sew a secret pocket into the side of her skirt to conceal her trusty scalpel. She couldn't shake the awful feeling of vulnerability she'd had in that laneway in St Giles when confronted by the knife-wielding pimp. She never wanted to feel so unprotected again.

When the night of the ball at Castledown House finally arrived, Lucy was beside herself with nerves. For once, her apprehension had nothing to do with the fact she'd be parading about a crowded ballroom amongst strangers and had everything to do with the prospect of facing Thorne. Despite her determination *not* to be afraid, now that the evening had arrived she couldn't seem to help herself.

Maybe I won't see Thorne at all, she told herself as Artemis and Dominic's grand town coach pulled to a stop outside Castledown House. Even though it was September and not the Season, there was still a healthy number of members of the haut monde floating about London who were evidently keen for some sort of diversion, so the event was predicted to be a crush. According to her father, the Duke of Dartmoor and his captivating new wife were immensely popular, despite the duke's past notoriety.

However, when Lucy entered the ballroom a short time later on her father's arm, the first thing she did was gasp with shock. Not because she'd just spied Will resplendent in his evening attire in the crowd—although that sight was breath-stealing in and of itself. No, her lungs had all but ceased to function and fear snaked down her spine because Will was talking to her brother.

Foxing foxgloves. "Monty, what are you doing here?" she whispered urgently when she managed to reach his side. "And Will"—she lightly poked him in the ribs with her fan—"what in heaven's name are you thinking, bringing my brother here? Thorne might very well put in an appearance, and what will happen then?"

"Now, now, Lucy," said her father, who'd somehow managed to keep pace with her as she pressed through the milling throng of guests. "Don't worry so. All is in hand. Monty's here because he wants to be."

"Yes, I am," agreed her brother. "I've decided that I want to reenter society. And tonight—if you'll pardon my crude expression—I'm going to woo the drawers off some pretty heiress. Well, not literally." He leaned closer. "It was Will's and the Duke of Dartmoor's suggestion that I attend. If Thorne begins to spread rumors about me, they're not likely to stick if I appear to be actively pursuing a member of the opposite sex. Besides"—he shrugged—"I like women too. And it's been quite some time since I flirted with anyone at all. Let me have a little fun."

Lucy gave a humph. "You could have chosen another occasion to exercise your wooing skills. I'm sure they're not *that* rusty." She turned back to Will and narrowed her gaze. "Why do I have this awful feeling that Monty's presence here is all part of your grand plan to entrap You-Know-Who?"

"I canna confirm or deny anything you've just said, lass," said Will, his eyes gleaming with amusement and something else…masculine appreciation, perhaps. His dark-blue gaze traveled over her—her new ball gown was an exquisite confection of lavender-blue silk and fine ivory lace—and she found herself blushing because she couldn't shake the thought that she would actually love it if Will wooed her drawers off by the end of the night.

"But…" He stepped closer and clasped her bare arm, just below the frothy lace of her sleeve. "If it helps to allay your fears, there are officers from Scotland Yard scattered throughout the crowd and stationed at every door of Castledown House. We have men, including Detective Lawrence, watching over your brother and your father and every other member of the Linnean Society who's here tonight and on Thorne's list. And as soon as Thorne arrives I'll be informed, so you have nothing at all to worry about."

"Oh…" Lucy's scalpel suddenly felt superfluous.

Will's mouth lifted into a lopsided smile. "So, am I forgiven, lass?"

Her lips twitched. She couldn't suppress her own smile. "Perhaps…"

"Well, will you do me the honor of dancing with me, then?"

She inclined her head. "I would love to, Lord Kyle."

He offered his arm and escorted Lucy onto the dance floor. It seemed a waltz was about to begin.

Will's gaze caught hers as he took her in his arms in preparation for the dance. "I was going to ask you to waltz in April, in this very room, when I was masquerading as Adam Whittaker, but I didna get the chance."

"Is that really true?"

"Aye. Of course it is. You were the loveliest creature I'd ever seen. I was bewitched at once." Leaning down, he whispered in her ear, "I still am and always will be, my Lucy-with-lavender-eyes."

The dance began and when she glanced back over Will's shoulder, she could see that her father, Monty, Artemis, and Jane, who appeared to have just arrived, were all beaming at her. But the waltz was fast, and in a moment Will had whisked her away.

He was an excellent dancer, and despite her lingering fears Lucy felt as light as air. As though she were waltzing on clouds.

And then she saw Thorne in the crowd, dark eyes blazing.

Lucy's heart stuttered and she misstepped. But Will was there to steady her and he deftly steered her to a quieter corner of the dance floor.

"What's wrong?" he asked in a low voice.

"He's here," Lucy whispered.

Will's jaw twitched. "Where?"

She gestured with her chin. "Over there by the door to the card room."

Will's gaze darted in the direction she'd indicated, and then the light in his eyes hardened. He'd obviously spotted Thorne too. "Dinna worry," he murmured. "You're safe and so are your family and friends. As I said, Detective Lawrence and Castledown have men stationed everywhere. Thorne canna even blink without us knowing about it."

The waltz drew to a close and Will escorted Lucy over to where her father was talking to Dominic, Artemis, Jane, and Lord and Lady Castledown.

"Where's Monty?" Lucy asked, her gaze darting about.

"Chatting with a certain Lord Chumley and his eligible daughter over by the French doors leading to the terrace," said Jane. When Lucy gave her a quizzical look, her friend said, "I've been to so many functions lately, playing the part of chaperone to my new stepsister, that I can identify most of London's debutantes."

Lucy's gaze wandered to Monty again. He was reaching out to take a flute of champagne from a silver tray proffered by a liveried footman, while Chumley and his daughter already had their flutes in hand.

And then Lucy's pulse began to race. She turned to Will, who was still at her side, and whispered urgently, "You're waiting for Thorne to poison someone here, aren't you? You really do mean to catch him in the act."

Will held her gaze steadily. "It's ruthless and risky, I'll give you that, but it's the only way. As you know, I'm hoping he'll lash out at me rather than others."

"But Monty just took a glass of champagne. What if Thorne has slipped something in it already? We need to warn him."

"All the liveried footmen are actually policemen. They're

monitoring everything that's served to the guests. There's no chance of anyone actually being poisoned."

"How can you be sure? What if someone gets distracted and Thorne adds hemlock or aconite or strychnine to someone's glass?" she rejoined. Even though she'd known this might be the plan all along, she couldn't suppress the note of panic in her voice.

Will touched her arm. "I promise you, lass, they willna let that happen."

Lucy closed her eyes and nodded. "I'm sorry. I'm just worried about Monty, and Father, and you. I want this to be over."

Will brushed his lips against her temple. "Me too, Lucy, my love," he murmured. "Me too."

My love... He'd called her *lass* and *my bonny, sweet Lucy* many times. And tonight, during their waltz he'd dubbed her *my Lucy-with-lavender-eyes*, but he'd never ever called her *my love* before. Did he really mean that?

When Lucy opened her eyes to ask Will that very question, it was to discover that he'd disappeared into the crowd... And somewhere out there was Zachariah Thorne.

Chapter Twenty-Nine

As much as Will hated walking away from Lucy, he had to.

He'd left her in the company of her father, Lord Castledown, and the Duke of Dartmoor, so she was well protected. Thank God Dominic had agreed to the plan that Castledown and Detective Lawrence had put to him five days ago during a meeting at the Home Office. This wasn't much of a Welcome Home ball, but then, Dominic had never been particularly enamored of high society or what anyone thought. And he too was firmly of the opinion that Zachariah Thorne had to be stopped at all costs.

As Will pretended to nonchalantly wend his way through the tight knots of chatting guests, he scanned the room, keeping a constant lookout for Thorne. He'd meant it when he'd told Lucy that he wanted this to be over.

He'd truly had enough of Thorne's cat-and-mouse games. The endless taunts. Tonight, he was going to draw the bastard out.

It didn't take long for Will to find Thorne. He was in the Castledowns' drawing room, which had been turned into a card room for the night.

The arrogant ass had positioned himself by the marble fireplace at the far end of the room, pretending to watch the card play at a nearby table. The light of a gas lamp glanced off his black hair, slick with Macassar oil. One of his arms rested upon the mantel, and in his other hand he held a crystal glass that contained a green liquid. Will assumed it was absinthe.

How ridiculously ironic.

Thorne's lip curled a little as Will approached. "Good God, who invited Lord Kyle?" he said in a bored tone as he swirled the contents of his glass around. "You might be wearing Savile-Row-tailored evening attire, but an ignorant clodpole of a Scot like you looks out of place in a fine setting like this. You'd best go back to mucking out the stables of sodomites or licking the boots of your so-called aristocratic friends."

Will rested his arm along the other end of the mantel, mimicking Thorne's stance. "I dinna think you truly understand the precarious position you're in," he said quietly. "Sir Oswald has taken me into his confidence and has told me everything about you. How you stole botanical poisons from his study. That you murdered Lord Litchfield and that you almost certainly poisoned Professor Fitzroy. That you've been blackmailing Sir Oswald so he won't say anything to the authorities. That you wish Charles Darwin and other members of the Linnean Society dead simply because you disagree with Darwin's scientific views. And very soon Scotland Yard will know everything too." Will leaned closer. "I intend to pay the Yard a visit first thing in the morning. I know a detective or two."

The Yorkshireman sneered. "What utter rot," he said, his voice dripping with sarcasm. "But in all seriousness, if I truly had committed such crimes, *if* you and Sir Oswald had any useful evidence to present to Scotland Yard, surely I'd already be locked up in Newgate Prison awaiting my trial."

When Will didn't say anything, Thorne snorted. "I suppose you think I'll be tempted to murder someone tonight. That I'll try to dispense with the other Linnean Society Council members who are in attendance. I can see Lord Chumley and Sir

Charles Lyell right over there." He gestured toward the ball-room. "And that idiot Sir Oswald and his vile son…"

"Why not strike now?" asked Will. "There are so many opportunities. So many possible targets… Don't you have poison secreted in your pockets? Don't you want Darwin's supporters gone? Perhaps you'd even like to get rid of this great Scottish clodpole standing right in front of you…" He cocked a brow. "After all, we both want sweet Lucy Bertram. I didna think you were a coward. But here we are…"

Thorne's obsidian eyes gleamed with pure antipathy. But he didn't say anything.

Will gestured to a card table that had just become vacant. "Join me in a game?"

"I thought we were already playing one," rejoined Thorne, and then he shrugged. "In any event, I don't gamble. It's a vice I despise."

Will nodded at his tumbler. "Yet you're not averse to having a dram of the 'demon drink' on occasion.'"

Thorne arched a brow. "No one is perfect, *my lord*. Shall I get you one?"

Before Will could respond, Thorne turned away before beckoning over a nearby footman. "Another glass of absinthe is required for Lord Kyle here," he said.

The footman furnished Will with a crystal tumbler containing a sizable nip of the bitter, wormwood-flavored spirit in a matter of moments. Once the man had stepped back into his shadowy corner, Will addressed Thorne. "I prefer whisky, but thank you all the same."

Out of the corner of his eye, Will saw the footman mouth, "Watch out," before he nodded pointedly toward Thorne's drink. Will's gaze flicked downward. Was that powder in the bottom of the Yorkshireman's own glass? Had Thorne put poison in his own absinthe when he'd turned his back to call over the footman?

Anticipation tightened Will's gut. *Ha!* So Thorne wanted to play a game of wits, did he? Keeping his expression neutral, Will needlessly swirled his own drink as he said, "What shall we drink to?"

Thorne's eyes glittered and he lifted his glass halfway to his lips as though he fully intended to take a sip. "To the glory of God."

"Wait." Will held up a hand. "It's no' that I dinna trust you…" He gave a short bark of laughter. "What am I saying? Of course, I dinna trust you. Let's swap glasses before we make a toast."

Thorne smirked. "Very well."

They traded drinks and then Will raised his glass in the air. There was definitely powder in the bottom. "To the glory of God," he said, and Thorne followed suit.

As the Yorkshireman took a sizable sip, Will put his glass down on the mantel untasted and then nodded to the strapping footman. The man stepped forward and seized Thorne's arm. "Zachariah Thorne," he declared in a voice so sonorous that everyone in the card room stopped what they were doing and turned to stare, "I am a police officer and I'm arresting you for the attempted murder of Lord Kyle."

"What the blazing hell?" cried Thorne. He struggled against the footman's hold. "Unhand me, you lackey. You have no right."

"I'm afraid he does," said Will dryly. "He is indeed a Scotland Yard police officer, and he just witnessed your attempt to poison me. If I'm no' mistaken, there's strychnine powder in the bottom of my absinthe glass. The one *you* gave me." He raised a sardonic brow. "As they like to say at the Yard, 'you're well and truly nicked.'"

Thorne gave an almighty roar. Somehow, he twisted out

of the policeman's grip, and in the next instant he was bolting toward the crowded ballroom, knocking card tables and chairs over as he went.

Christ! Will took off after him, not caring who he bumped into as he followed. He *wouldn't* let Thorne escape. The man was deranged. Not to be reasoned with—

Will stumbled to a halt in the middle of the ballroom floor, and his stomach lurched and tumbled to the floor.

Oh God, no.

No, no, no!

Thorne had Lucy. One of his arms was lashed about her waist, holding her back against him. And at her throat, he held a knife, a stiletto with a wickedly thin steel blade that winked beneath the gas chandelier.

Hell's bloody bells. The cur must have been secretly armed.

The stiletto was pressed so firmly against Lucy's delicate flesh that Will could already see the bastard had nicked her. A tiny trickle of red welled along the edge of the blade.

Someone, a woman, screamed. And then the entire room fell strangely still and silent.

Everyone was holding their breath. Watching. Waiting.

Lucy's wide, terrified eyes met Will's.

"Let her go, Thorne," he ground out. Out of the corner of his eye, he could see Detective Lawrence had drawn a pistol and had it trained on Thorne. But it was too damn risky for him to take a shot.

Thorne smirked. "Not a chance. Wherever I go, Miss Bertram goes. Her father promised her to me after all. Let us leave and no one will get hurt."

Will dared to take a step forward. "She's done nothing to deserve this ill-treatment. You have no quibble with her. Please. Release her."

He'd always been afraid he'd somehow fail Lucy. That he couldn't be the hero she needed. And now his worst nightmare was unfolding in front of his eyes. And it was all his fault. He'd been too arrogant. Too laissez-faire.

Not enough.

He couldn't bear it. If anything happened to her, he'd never be able to forgive himself.

Lucy's gaze connected with Will's. She was breathing rapidly, and her face was pale save for two flags of bright color on her cheekbones. One of her hands was gripping Thorne's arm at her waist while her other hand was buried in the folds of her skirts. "Please, Mr. Thorne," she rasped. "If you have any decency left within you, please… This is not how you treat someone you value or care about."

All of a sudden, Monty stepped forward and Thorne's gaze darted straight to him.

"Thorne," the young man began, "Lucy's done nothing wrong. Done nothing to hurt you. Let her go and take me with you instead—"

"Enough," yelled Thorne. "You vile, stinking swine!" He began waving the knife in the air at Monty. "You foul sod—"

All of a sudden, Thorne broke off with a strangled scream. Lucy wriggled out of his loosened grasp as the man clutched at his upper thigh.

"You bitch! You stabbed me!" he cried as Lucy scurried back toward her brother.

And so she had. A small blade—a scalpel, perhaps—was embedded in Zachariah Thorne's leg, just below his hip. Where the devil had she pulled that from?

Before Will could think about that further, Thorne's face contorted with rage, and he lunged toward Lucy, knife raised.

"No!" Will started forward, but then someone else in the

crowd—Sir Oswald—appeared and stuck out a foot that sent Thorne stumbling, pitching toward the floor where he collapsed in a sprawling heap. His knife skittered away out of reach.

In the blink of an eye, a pair of footmen—Scotland Yard officers in disguise—were hauling Thorne to his feet and frog-marching him out the door, with a grim-faced Detective Lawrence following close behind. All the while, Thorne was screeching about his leg and how the end of days was upon them and the seas would rise and the skies would fall and hellfire would rain down and burn everyone and everything to ash.

But none of that mattered. Not one whit.

All that mattered was that Lucy, the woman he loved with his entire heart and soul, was safe. What a braw, clever lass she was.

He crossed the floor toward her, and she rushed to him. In the next instant they were in each other's arms and Will was kissing her and he didn't care that the whole room was watching. He was going to make this woman his wife.

Everyone and everything else could go hang.

Chapter Thirty

LUCY SAT IN DARTMOOR HOUSE'S CONSERVATORY, BREATH-ing in the fragrant humid air, watching the water cascade from the fountain into the sparkling pool below, taking comfort in the little things that made life worthwhile. It was late, and she was so very tired. But she was waiting up for Will, because as she'd quit Castledown House in the company of Artemis and Dominic, he'd asked her to.

After tonight, there was nothing she wouldn't do for this man.

When she'd seen the bright anger and fear and helpless desperation in his eyes while Thorne had been holding that terrible knife to her throat, she'd known in that moment that he loved her. There were no more doubts. And then when he'd kissed her with passion and deep reverence in the middle of a crowded ballroom—in front of the who's who of society—she knew within her heart of hearts that he was going to propose again.

While that certain knowledge brought her such solace and joy, filled her with toe-curling delicious anticipation, it also made her impatient for Will's return.

Her fingers lifted and touched the small bandage above the neckline of her simple blue chintz gown. The small cut near her left collarbone only stung a little. Even though Thorne was now safely in police custody, at odd moments Lucy found her mind returning to what had happened only a few hours ago. To what *might* have happened. If she hadn't taken her scalpel with her...

She shuddered.

Thorne's locked away. You're safe. Will is safe. Everyone is safe, she reminded herself sternly for the hundredth time. *Don't let that monster steal your joy. Seal your horrid memories of him up tight in a vasculum and bury them. At least for tonight.*

Yes, the rest of this night was reserved for her and Will. It would be a night of making new memories. Ones that would last a lifetime.

She could hardly wait.

As if Lucy's thoughts had conjured him up, her ruggedly handsome Scotsman—the man of all her dreams, both romantic and erotic—appeared. His wide shoulders brushed past the palm-tree fronds fringing the path as he strode toward her. With purpose. With fierce-eyed intent.

Heart capering, she rose to her feet, and then Will was kissing her. His hands clasped her face as his mouth claimed hers and his tongue delved deep.

It was a possessive kiss. A fervent kiss. A kiss that proclaimed "mine."

Lucy never wished it to end.

But of course it did, and when at last they both drew back, Will was smiling down at her. "I will never get enough of your kisses," he murmured, pushing a lock of loosened hair away from her flushed cheek. "I need them more than air."

"I feel the same way," she whispered.

"You do?"

She smiled softly. "Aye, my lord. I do."

His deep-blue eyes shone with a warm, knowing light. "I think it's time you and I had a serious talk, lass."

"I agree."

They sat upon the cushioned bench, hands clasped, thighs touching, smiling at each other almost shyly. And then just when Lucy didn't think she could stand the suspense any longer, Will inhaled a deep breath and said, "My sweet Lucy, I've been meaning to say something to you for days and days, something important, but it never seemed like quite the right moment. And"—he drew another fortifying breath—"I'm almost ashamed to admit that I've been a coward. Not because I'm scared of what I feel in here." He laid a large, scarred hand upon his chest. "No, my cowardice stems from the simple fact that I've been worried I might frighten *you* away if…if I at last confess that I love you."

"You love me," whispered Lucy in awe. Of course, she'd suspected it for some time now, but to hear Will actually say the words aloud took her breath away.

"Aye…" His mouth tilted into the lopsided smile she loved so much, and he lifted her hand to his lips. Brushed a kiss over her knuckles. "I might even venture to say that I'm madly in love with you. Like a sort of I-hardly-know-how-I-can-even-think-or-breathe-without-you type of 'I love you.'"

"Oh, Will." Lucy's eyes welled with tears. "I love you too. With my whole heart. You're everything that I didn't know that I wanted or needed. Indeed, until I met you, until you pulled me out of that mud puddle in the middle of a storm, I was only half-living, I realize now. It was as though I'd been wandering through life, half-heartedly looking for something 'more' but I didn't know what that 'more'—that elusive 'something else'— was." She smiled and caressed Will's jaw. "And then you came along and woke me up to all of life's possibilities.

"But…" She paused to draw a nervous breath. "I will also own up to being frightened, because I *do* want to share a life with you, so very badly. More than anything. But I'm not sure if I can be the woman that *you* need. You're an earl who'll one day be a duke with a vast estate and a million responsibilities. And I'm a shy, slightly eccentric botanist with ambitions to travel the world and study the medicinal properties of plants—"

Will pressed a finger to her lips. "Hush," he said. "First of all, let me say that I know what your dreams are, and I want to give you everything that your heart desires. Indeed, I'd give you the whole world and the moon and the stars and the sun above if I could. So we can travel wherever you want, whenever you want. If you'd like me to help you to secure a place at university or gain admittance to whatever scientific society that you want to be a part of, I will do that too. Where you lead—even if it's to the ends of the earth—I will follow."

Lucy could hardly believe what she was hearing. "Are you certain? Because one day you *will* need an heir. And I'm already twenty-eight. And traveling abroad is not conducive to starting a family and I wouldn't want you to resent me if we left things a little too late and then I couldn't bear you a child after all… I mean, it's not that I *don't* want to have a baby. In fact, I do think I would love to have *your* baby. Just not right now."

Will shrugged. "It's true that one day I *might* want to begin a family. But remember when I told you that I was quite happy to let the dukedom die with me? Well, I still stand by that, lass. The only good reason I can think of for having a child is that we both want that. When the time is right for both of us. Your happiness and fulfillment mean more to me than anything else." He smiled so tenderly that Lucy's breath caught. "And do you know why?"

She shook her head. "No."

Will caught her chin between gentle fingers. "When I'm with you, Lucy, I can be myself. I feel like I belong and that I'm at home. You're loyal and kind. You care. And you make me smile. Every damn day. I've never experienced such things before, with anyone, and I canna give them up. You are all I want. You are, and always will be, my everything."

Lucy's heart swelled with so much emotion, she thought

it might burst. "You don't have to give it up. I'm yours, Will Forever, if you'll have me."

"Och…" Will closed his eyes. "What a daft idiot I've been. havena even proposed to you."

All at once, he hopped off the bench and knelt down before her on bended knee. Took her trembling hands in his. "Lucy, he said gravely, his eyes shining with promise and warmth and tears. "There are no' enough words to express how much I love you. Nor enough ways to show you, even if we both live unti the end of time. But you have my heart and my soul and now offer you my hand. Will you marry me, lass?"

Lucy's vision blurred and her throat was so tight with heart felt emotion that she had to swallow to make her voice work "Yes, my darling Will. Yes," she whispered. And then words were no longer needed because the love of her life—her wild, savage tenderhearted Scot—swept her into his arms and kissed her.

Epilogue

London, December 1858

"So, my learned colleagues, ladies and gentlemen, thus concludes my paper on 'The Atypical Medicinal Uses of British Plants for the Treatment of Common Ailments and Diseases.'"

Lucy Lockhart, the Countess of Kyle, blew out a relieved breath, then raised her gaze to the packed auditorium at the Botanical Society of London's headquarters. And then she gasped when everyone—every single man and woman in the audience—rose to their feet and clapped with uncharacteristic enthusiasm for such an occasion. Her father, her brother, and of course her darling friends Jane and Artemis even shouted "Brava!" Her paper might not be groundbreaking, but almost everyone in the Botanical Society of London and those she loved best knew what a personal achievement this was for her.

Tears misted Lucy's vision as she sought out one particular face in the sea shimmering before her. The one person who'd made this day possible.

Her beloved husband.

There he was in the very front row, slightly off to the left-hand side with the Duke of Dartmoor, clapping madly and cheering and beaming so widely, Lucy couldn't help but grin back at him.

Oh, foxing foxgloves and figgy jam and fiddle-dee-dee with bells on!

She'd done it.

She'd really done it!

She'd presented a research paper to a whole room full of people, and she hadn't vomited or fainted or stuttered or blushed or blathered on like a complete and utter hen-wit. She'd been articulate and quietly confident and considered and...and had been everything she'd ever hoped she could be.

And all because of Will, her champion. Her soul mate. The man who believed in her with unflagging devotion, who had coached her about public-speaking techniques and had helped her to practice. Who had spent hours and hours patiently listening to obscure botanical research that must have bored him witless.

She could never, ever thank him enough.

But perhaps she didn't need to. When one loved, *truly* loved, taking joy in the success and happiness of one's partner was a gift in and of itself.

She'd married Will in October by special license at Fleetwood Hall, and while they'd honeymooned at an isolated country house of Will's in Cumbria, Lucy had begun the research paper she'd been planning to write for several years. Those weeks had been some of the happiest of her life. Rambling the hills and woods and lakeside paths with Will, collecting plant specimens, making love every night and quite often during the day, it had been like heaven.

With Will's help, her father had started to stabilize his financial situation, so the Bertram family's unentailed assets were no longer at risk. Monty had moved back to Fleetwood Hall and had decided he would accompany Father on his next expedition to the Malay Peninsula as soon as a new investor could be secured. He professed he wanted to "expand his horizons and see some of the world" before he made any decisions about settling down with someone.

As for Zachariah Thorne...he'd been deemed unfit to stand

trial for his crimes because of his increasingly unstable state of mind. He'd accused almost everyone he knew—even Queen Victoria herself—of being Satan's minions. And so he'd been committed to an asylum for his own protection as well as that of others. He would never be a threat to anyone again.

When the audience's applause eventually died down, Lucy drew a bracing breath, then said in a clear, steady voice, "I'll now take questions."

By the time she'd finished, and after she'd spent at least fifteen minutes chatting with the Botanical Society's president and secretary and numerous other colleagues about "what was next" for her—a journey to Scotland to spend Christmastide with her husband's grandfather, the Duke of Ayr, followed by a research trip to Mauritius in late spring— Will was waiting for her with her bonnet and gloves and leather portfolio in hand.

"You were amazing, lass," he said. "I've never been prouder."

"And I've never been happier," she murmured. "I couldn't have done this without you."

As she tied the bow beneath her bonnet, Will bent down and gave her a swift kiss on the lips. "It was nothing, my love." Then his eyes gleamed. "The real challenge will be taking on academia. I've a mind to ride roughshod over a few narrow-minded professors who willna let women in their supposedly hallowed doors of learning. And that goes for any male members of scientific societies that women wish to be a part of too."

"I look forward to joining you," said Lucy as she took his arm and they quit the auditorium.

With Will by her side, life was nothing but a glorious adventure, and she intended to relish every single minute of it.

Read ahead for a sneak peek at
the next delicious adventure in
the Byronic Book Club series

Tall, Duke, and Scandalous

Chapter One

MISS JANE DELANEY BURST THROUGH THE FRONT DOOR OF Halifax House in a flurry of green silk skirts and ruffled pet-ticoats. Breathless from rushing and bristling with ill-humor, she came to an abrupt halt at the bottom of the stone stairs, then frowned as she scoured Chester Square. Well, *attempted* to scour. The heavy shroud of fog obscured much of the barely lit expanse of cobblestones and the enclosed park beyond.

Curses. Her family's carriage was nowhere to be seen amongst the other coaches, nor were her mother or Jane's stepsister, Kitty Pevensey, for that matter. Had they really left her behind at the Halifax's masquerade ball? Her mother *had* been complaining of a megrim and she could be single-minded whenever she felt unwell and was desperate for a dose of her "nerve tonic." But Jane had only been gone ten minutes. Kitty, who tended to be absent-minded, had apparently left her brand-new fan "somewhere" in the ballroom. And because it was a loss that "simply couldn't be borne," Jane had been sent on a mission to retrieve it.

Jane had eventually located the fan in the supper room, but clearly her search had taken too long. Her glove-clad fingers curled into fists at the realization she *had* been abandoned.

Forgotten about just like Kitty's blasted fan.

She gave a disgruntled huff, then swiped at one of her

domino mask's drooping feathers as she considered her options. On the long list of "Calamities that had Befallen Miss Jane Delaney" of late, this was on the less disastrous end of the scale. But still…Jane's already stretched-tighter-than-a-bowstring patience was about to snap.

The sounds of merrymaking seeped into the square as the door of Halifax House opened to grant exit to another set of departing guests.

Jane sighed heavily as the tittering couple brushed past her, barely sparing her a glance. She certainly didn't relish the prospect of a mile walk through the dark streets to the Pevenseys' town house in Pelham Crescent. The most sensible thing to do would be to hail a hansom cab in one of the busier thoroughfares. Luckily, she always kept a few coins in her reticule.

Mind made up, Jane hugged her velvet cloak more tightly about herself in a vain attempt to ward off the chill night air as she started toward Sloane Street. If either of her dear friends and fellow Byronic Book Club members, Lucy or Artemis were home— during the Season proper, they resided in nearby Eaton Square and Belgrave Square respectively—she would have knocked on their doors, seeking refuge. But alas, Lucy was in Scotland with her deliciously gruff husband, William, the Earl of Kyle, and Artemis was still ensconced in Devonshire at Ashburn Abbey, the country estate of her broodingly handsome husband, the Duke of Dartmoor.

While Jane was thrilled her childhood friends were blissfully wed, it appeared she'd been relegated to the ranks of spinsterhood. Although, once upon a time, she'd longed for a husband and children. But courtesy of a capricious turn of Fate and a lily-livered man, both of which had left her deeply scarred in more ways than one, that ship had sailed long ago.

It seemed that some things—no matter how much one secretly yearned for them—were never meant to be.

Jane lifted her fingers to her left cheek and brushed over the disfiguring scar that arced from her left ear down to her mouth. Thanks to her mask and its strategically placed feathers, she hadn't needed to endure too many shocked stares or pitying glances at the Halifaxs' masquerade ball. Not that she wasn't used to such reactions from strangers by now. But still, it was nice to feel ordinary and go unnoticed for once.

A grand town coach pulled by two pairs of perfectly matched grays lumbered into view, and Jane paused to wait for it to pass by. Over the last decade, she'd come to value her independence and the opportunity to forge her own course in life. However, writing a few literary-review articles and other dubious, and altogether insignificant, bits and pieces for various gazettes and newspapers hardly counted as a "career."

Jane sighed as she watched the horses clop past. Until recently, she'd been like those blinkered creatures. Head down, plodding forward along a path toward some foggy destination that was always a bit uncertain and out of reach. But now...now perhaps a rudderless boat tossed about in a storm-swept sea with no safe port in sight would be a more accurate description of her current state of being.

Oh, but Jane longed for a safe port. And fulfillment. She might have given up on her dream of finding a husband and having a baby, but she couldn't help being a *little* envious of her friends' situations. Like Artemis and Lucy, she wanted to make a difference in the world. To champion the rights of women. To help others in some way. Given her own fraught history, it was a drive within that was hard to deny.

It also seemed like an impossible feat given her present situation. A situation that was becoming more precarious by the day...

Jane glanced toward the indistinct silhouettes of the town

houses in Eaton Square. Both Artemis's and Lucy's wealthy, titled husbands were not just smitten with their wives but generous.

Now, if a mysterious Byronic hero with deep pockets popped onto Jane's horizon and offered to solve all her problems with a flick of a pen over a check book, wouldn't that be wonderful?

No, it was money Jane needed, not a man. *Money*. And desperately, before she drowned in a whirlpool of anxiety and scandal and ruined dreams.

A miracle wouldn't hurt either.

Through the shifting darkness, the sounds of unbridled carousing floated toward Jane—music and laughter and chatter interspersed with wild whoops and cheers. It seemed someone else was hosting a Saint Valentine's ball this evening. Perhaps there'd be a hansom cab in the vicinity.

Jane followed the hubbub easily, and before long, the lights of the town house pierced through the fog. As soon as it appeared in full view, she frowned. She knew this house. Lucy had once pointed it out to her as they'd passed by. It was the residence of the Duke of Roxby.

If society's gossipmongers were to be believed, the present duke, Christopher Marsden—a former army officer and Crimean-war hero—was now one of the country's most notorious scoundrels. A profligate, licentious cad who'd inherited the dukedom from an ancient uncle just last year. At least according to the *London Tatler*, a newspaper that was little more than a scandal rag. Jane should know because she also penned articles for the publication.

Indeed, to her shame, she'd also recently begun to contemplate the idea of secretly feeding gossip to the *London Tatler's* "social column." She'd certainly been attending enough high-society functions with Kitty of late—Jane was frequently enlisted as a chaperone—and she often gleaned all manner of juicy tidbits while waiting on the edge of the ballroom.

Of course, it was not within Jane's nature to do something so grubby and low, but she was so frantic with worry, she might just have to. *For the money,* she reminded herself. *For your family.* Namely for her grandfather, the proprietor of Delaney's Antiquarian Bookstore. And to save her mother from destroying her reputation and jeopardizing her marriage.

Blast her mother. If it weren't for Leonora Pevensey's addiction to high-stakes card play, Delaney's would not be in danger. The fact that her mother had put her majority share of the business up as collateral when she'd lost a large sum at the whist table was unconscionable. Jane loved that bookstore almost as much as her paternal grandfather did, and she would *not* let anything happen to it.

As for her own desperate need for money to solve her own dire problem...if Jane's blackmailer revealed her scandalous secret, she'd be devastated.

Crushed.

Ruined.

Somehow Jane pushed the deeply distressing thought aside. She could only deal with one pressing issue at a time.

A hansom cab clattered by, heading toward Roxby House, and Jane hastened her steps in that direction. Only, by the time she reached her destination, it was to discover a masked gentleman leaping into the cab, and within the blink of an eye, it had taken off.

Ugh. Jane batted the drooping feather away from her face once more. She'd have to head back toward Belgrave Street again. And then she turned and looked toward the front door of Roxby House. It stood wide open, the bright light of an enormous gaslight chandelier spilling out onto the stone steps. And there was no one—not a single footman or a butler—guarding the entry hall, monitoring who could come and go.

How odd.

Perhaps the scandalous duke didn't much care who attended his parties. Rumor had it that his soirees were on the wilder side and not for the faint-hearted, or indeed anyone who wished to maintain some semblance of a reputation. It was not the sort of place Kitty Pevensey would be allowed to set foot in.

Another frisson of cold fear trickled down Jane's spine. If she couldn't help her mother secure the funds to pay off her gambling vowels in the next week or two, there was a very real chance her grandfather might lose his entire bookstore.

But what if...? Jane studied the open doorway to Roxby House. What if she swallowed her scruples and sneaked inside and observed some of the antics of the elite hoi polloi? The *London Tatler's* chief editor wouldn't pay her an enormous sum in exchange for scandalous gossip, but it would be a start. It would be better than nothing. And really, if the Duke of Roxby was in the habit of leaving his front door open for just anybody to waltz in, what did he expect?

Desperate times call for desperate measures, after all.

Before she could think further on it—before she lost her nerve—Jane lifted her crinoline skirts and rushed up the stairs into Roxby House.

"Oi. You there, miss."

Oh no. Jane froze in the middle of the grand vestibule. Off to one side by a pair of enormous marble columns stood a burly footman wearing a scowl along with fine livery. How foolish of her to think there wouldn't be anyone stationed at the door.

Unfurling Kitty's fan, Jane raised it to obscure her left cheek, then pasted on a smile as she turned around. It seemed a bit of play-acting would be required to gain admittance.

Behind her mask, she fluttered her eyelashes in the manner

of a brazen minx who had every right to be attending the Duke of Roxby's ball without an invitation. "You mean me?"

"Yes, you." The strapping footman's brows arrowed into a frown as he looked her up and down. "What's the password? You can't go in until you tell me what it is. His Grace is very particular about who attends his soirees."

Somehow Jane managed to swallow a snort of laughter. *Particular?* By the sounds of it, a Roman orgy was taking place within these walls. As her mind scrabbled to come up with a suitable password for a Saint Valentine's event that most likely bordered on the bacchanalian, several coatless "gentlemen" bolted across the space between her and the footman. It appeared they were engaged in some sort of crude game of rugby as one chap tossed an oversized ham to another fellow before they all stumbled through an arched doorway into a gaslit gallery.

"Wine, women, and song?" she asked hopefully.

The footman crossed his arms. "You don't know what it is, do you?"

"How about 'tits?'" she suggested, puffing out her less than ample chest. She would not be put off.

"No."

"Cock-a-doodle-do?"

The footman was stony-faced.

"Does it really matter if I don't know it?" she asked.

"It does. I'll give you one last try before you're out." The servant gestured at the still-open front door with his thumb.

Borrowing a curse from her dear friend Artemis, Jane muttered, "Beelzebub's ballocks."

"What was that last bit?" asked the footman.

"Ballocks?" replied Jane.

"In you go," said the footman. "The ballroom is down that hall to your right." Then he grinned. "Have fun."

Well, that almost seemed *too* easy... However, Jane wasn't about to look a gift horse in the mouth. After murmuring, "thank you," she hurried away.

The first thing that struck Jane as she entered a high-ceilinged gallery embellished with the sort of frescoes and gilt moldings that might grace the Doge's Palace of Venice was the level of noise. It could only be described as overwhelming. A deafening, discordant cacophony that was bound to give one a headache. All the doors to every vast room were thrown wide open revealing one tableau of debauchery after another. In the ballroom, a small string ensemble doggedly played a rousing mazurka, while masked men and scantily clad women with champagne glasses in hand laughed and cheered and pranced about with gay abandon.

In another crowded room, hazy with the smoke of hookah pipes, a man in a rumpled, half-open shirt sat hunched over the keyboard of a monstrously carved pianoforte as he played a darkly dramatic nocturne. However, almost everyone's attention was riveted to a naked woman who was reclining on top of the piano, while another male guest was furiously painting the licentious scene.

Jane didn't like to think of herself as a prude, but even she found herself blushing at the idea of so many people blatantly ogling the artist's muse.

But that wasn't the worst of the debauchery. In the adjacent dining room, several couples in various stages of undress were fornicating on a table between the glassware and platters and several upset bottles of wine.

Good Lord above. Jane had never seen so many bare breasts and behinds in all her life. Her face burning, she rushed past and turned down another hall. She doubted she'd be able to report on any of this activity. It was too shocking even for the *London Tatler* to print. She had no idea if the duke himself was anywhere about. He obviously didn't care what went on beneath his roof.

There was also no doubt in her mind that she'd made a mistake coming here. She was clearly wasting her time and really should go before something untoward happened.

She just needed to find her way out. But that was easier said than done. Everywhere she turned was bedlam.

To Jane's relief, she soon found herself in a far quieter, deserted gallery, and halfway along, a gleaming oak-paneled door stood ajar. It was an enormous library, which seemed to be devoid of occupants. Well, as far as she could tell. The room was cloaked in dense shadows. She really should press on and escape this madness, but instead, she crossed the threshold. Perhaps it was the vastness of the room with its impressive bookcases or the welcoming pull of the flickering flames in the enormous black-marble fireplace that she couldn't resist. The familiar scents of leather and beeswax and the pleasant mustiness of old books drifted toward her, beckoning her inside.

And then she recalled something else she knew about the Duke of Roxby. Well, not the new duke, but the old duke. Jane's grandfather had once mentioned that the man had been an eccentric character and had amassed a large collection of very rare books.

Very *expensive* books.

Curiosity sparking, Jane decided to take a quick look. She couldn't resist. Antique book collections were her personal form of opium. Over the years, she'd spent countless hours in her grandfather's shop, helping to catalogue the antiquarian titles he sold, dusting and storing them carefully, and even repairing books in the store's workshop. Books were in her blood. Surely the new duke wouldn't mind. It wasn't as though she was going to fornicate between the shelves or construct a makeshift set of wickets from a stack of books for a drunken cricket game.

Ignoring the nervous fluttering in her belly, Jane carefully closed the door behind her. Her reverent gaze wandered over the shelves as she contemplated where to start.

There. Over by the far wall near a wrought-iron staircase that led to an upper gallery she spied tomes stored in a glass-fronted cabinet that might warrant a look. Hopefully the doors weren't locked. But then, nothing else that was of value in this house appeared to be kept under lock and key.

She traversed the plush Turkish rug and, upon reaching the bookcase, reached out and tried the brass handle. *Yes.* It *was* unlocked.

When she perused the titles on the spines, her heart did a little jig of excitement. Oh, wouldn't she love to spend hours and hours in this place, cataloguing everything. Reading to her heart's content.

She dared to run a gloved fingertip along the edge of a very old copy of *The Canterbury Tales* by Chaucer. Without even examining it, her instincts told her it was a first edition. Probably late fifteenth century. Possibly by printed by William Caxton.

A man like the Duke of Roxby didn't deserve to own such a treasure.

As Jane reached for the book, her mask's troublesome feather drooped over her left eye. With an annoyed huff, she blew it out of the way, but it immediately flopped down again.

Ack. What harm would it do if she took off her mask? No one else was around. It would only be for a minute or two. Decision made, Jane put Kitty's fan and her own reticule on a nearby table then removed the domino.

Once unmasked, she carefully slid Chaucer's book out from

the shelf and opened its delicate pages with suitable reverence. Aha! Her instincts had been correct. This volume had indeed been published by Caxton. It was priceless.

It would fetch a small fortune at auction...

Jane swallowed. Her breath quickened. Temptation curled its hooks into her. Whispered wicked thoughts in her ear. Made her ignore the sharp prick of guilt inside her chest. Her gaze darted to the library doors, but they were still firmly closed.

If truth be told, Jane had always been sensible. Practical and dependable. Since her nineteenth summer when she'd thrown caution to the wind and put her faith in the wrong man, she'd been the sort of woman who'd never put a foot wrong. She didn't lie or cheat or act rashly. She certainly didn't steal.

But...if she bid a hasty retreat from Roxby House with this book in her possession, would anyone notice it was gone? Did the Duke of Roxby even know that he owned something so precious?

He probably doesn't value it at all, Jane told herself, even as her conscience quailed in horror at what she was about to do. *He's too busy hosting orgies where anything and everything goes. His guests almost certainly pilfer the silver, and Lord knows what else, all the time.*

And what she was thinking about stealing—no, *rescuing,* from this madhouse—was one little book that was practically falling apart...

This book... This was the miracle Jane desperately needed. And of course, the money she'd make from its sale was going toward a very good cause. She could pay off her mother's gambling debt and save her grandfather's bookstore and...and she might be able to extricate herself from her own precarious predicament too. It wouldn't be long before her blackmailer demanded another payment. A payment she couldn't possibly make.

A soft noise made Jane jump and she nearly dropped *The Canterbury Tales*. Whirling around, her gaze darted about the room, but she didn't see anyone lurking by the fire or between any of the bookcases or by the duke's enormous desk. The soft rustling sound must have been a log crumbling to ash in the grate. Blowing out a sigh of relief, she contemplated the best way to conceal this book on her person. Her ballgown didn't have a pocket. Her reticule was far too small. She could hide the book in the folds of her cloak, but what if the footman at the front door noticed she was clutching something against her body?

Her caged crinoline skirts were so voluminous, she could practically hide a person—or even half a library—beneath them.

Yes. What if she carefully tied the book to one of her legs with a garter and stocking? No one at all would notice one foot was stockingless. She really only had to make it out the front door. This plan was the one way to ensure success.

Jane put the book down on the table, then slipped off a pump. Hiking up her skirts and petticoats, she placed her foot on a padded chair, rolled up her drawers to her knee, untied her garter, then swiftly whipped off her silk stocking. Within less than a minute, she'd firmly strapped the book to her upper thigh.

She smiled at her handiwork. *There, that will do.*

And then a distinctly masculine voice, laced with sardonic humor drifted toward her from the deep shadows to her left. "As much as I'm enjoying the show, I must stop you there."

Oh, my God. Jane froze. Her heart almost stuttered to a complete stop before taking off at breakneck speed.

Snatching a breath, she slowly turned her head. How had she

not noticed that there was someone else—an impossibly tall, broad-shouldered man—lingering here in the library with her?

Watching her every move in silence. Observing her in the act of stealing one of the Duke of Roxby's priceless books.

She'd been caught red-handed.

And she wasn't wearing a mask.

Chapter Two

"I...I..." Jane dropped her skirts and slid her bare foot to the floor. Her knees were shaking so much, she doubted she'd be able to bolt from the room. "Well, this is rather awkward," she finished in a voice husky with mortification and a good dose of fear. And smothering guilt.

Drawing a steadying breath, she peered past the man's imposing silhouette and spied a wingback chair secreted in a curtained window embrasure. A cut crystal tumbler sat on an occasional table beside it. The man must have been sitting there the entire time.

Oh God. If the floor had opened up and swallowed her whole, Jane would have been most grateful. Anything would have been better than these excruciatingly painful moments. The entire room seemed to be hushed and listening. Waiting.

"Oh, I don't know about that," the stranger said. While one of his wide shoulders was propped casually against the wall, Jane had the feeling that if she made any sudden move, he would pounce. "The words amusing and intriguing spring to mind. You've certainly aroused my interest in more ways than one."

Jane's cheeks burned. Surely he didn't mean that. Without thinking, her gaze fell to the man's lean hips, but of course, he was still cloaked in darkness, so she couldn't see if the sight of her removing her stocking had affected him. She couldn't even discern the stranger's face. But his superior, mocking tone along with the idea that he'd been watching her and hadn't said a word, rankled. Some wicked imp inside her made her say, "Actually, sir, I meant it must be awkward for you. Do you make a habit of hiding in dark corners and spying on others?"

"Or," he drawled smugly, "perhaps I'm simply lying in wait to catch out pretty book thieves."

The retort forming on the tip of Jane's tongue died as soon as the stranger stepped into the golden pool of light cast by a nearby gas lamp. In fact, all she could do was gasp. Even the word "handsome" wouldn't have done this man justice.

He was starkly beautiful. His face, all lean planes and sharply cut angles, was framed by tousled, light brown locks that bordered on leonine. Golden stubble shaded his perfectly hewn jaw. Even though his evening attire was the epitome of sartorial elegance, Jane wasn't sure if the man reminded her of a marauding Viking or an avenging angel who'd descended to Earth. If he'd drawn a flaming broadsword from a sheath strapped to his back to smite her, she wouldn't have been the least bit surprised.

Even "light brown" was the wrong phrase to describe the stranger's hair. As he raked a hand through that lustrous tawny mane, the lamp's glow picked out strands of deep guinea gold and copper and rich caramel. And then of course, it was impossible not to be mesmerized by the man's arresting eyes. Set above carved, high cheekbones, they were the ice-cold blue of an arctic wasteland. Indeed, his gaze, as it met and trapped Jane's, was sharp and hard and penetrating. There was no warmth there, only acute interest and some other emotion she couldn't quite identify.

It was Jane who looked away first to break the disconcerting glamour that had ensnared her.

She cleared her throat. "Well…" Beneath her skirts, she surreptitiously reached out with her bare foot in search of her discarded pump. "I…er…should probably be going." There was no point in refuting the man's accusation that she was a book thief, just as there was no point in paying any attention to his false flattery about her looks. Brazening her way out of this situation was the best she could hope for.

Well, she could also pray that the handsome stranger didn't say anything about her thievery to the duke. And then she nearly expired on the spot when the man held out one hand and said, "Before you do go, I'd like my book back."

"*Your* book?" Jane whispered as a wave of foreboding engulfed her.

The man's perfectly chiseled lips twitched with a wry smile. "Yes, *my* book. *The Canterbury Tales* published by William Caxton. While I admire your taste and the fact you know a valuable work when you see one, I really don't wish to part with it. I'm sure you understand."

"You're...you're the duke." It wasn't a question. In that moment, Jane *knew* it.

The man sketched a mocking bow. "I am indeed. Christopher Marsden, the sixth Duke of Roxby. And you are?"

"Horrified."

Genuine rather than sardonic amusement flickered in the man's eyes. "Come, come, I'm not that frightening, am I? I did ask that you return my book with an appropriate degree of politeness, did I not?"

"You did," agreed Jane. "But I would politely ask you to face the other way while I remove it from..." She blushed as she gestured at her skirts. There was no hope for it. She would not be leaving here with her much-needed "miracle" after all.

The duke laughed. It was a deep throaty chuckle that Jane felt all the way to her toes. "And have you abscond while my back is turned, Miss Horrified? I don't think so."

Jane lifted her chin. "Doubtless you'd catch me before I even made it halfway across the room."

"Doubtless," he returned. "But I'm sure you can appreciate that I don't quite trust you. It will be easier this way."

"A gentleman *would* turn away," returned Jane stiffly.

The duke bared his teeth in a wolfish grin, and his blue eyes gleamed. "Ah, but everyone knows the Duke of Roxby is no gentleman. Don't mistake an occasional bout of politeness for gallantry."

"Very well," Jane huffed. Her remorse and embarrassment coalesced with bristling indignation as she placed her bare foot on the chair again and raised her skirts. *At least he hasn't threatened to have me arrested and then hauled off to Newgate Prison,* she reminded herself as she plucked at the knots in her ribbon and stocking. *It could be worse.*

Fate must have been listening and in that moment, decided to punish Jane for her hubris. Because things *did* get worse. Her trembling fingers couldn't undo the tight knots. She was all thumbs. And if she tried to slide the book from its bindings, she'd be sure to damage it.

"I…um…" Jane glanced over to the duke who was watching her ineffectual plucks with an expression that might have passed for amusement. Although it could very well have been annoyance. "You wouldn't happen to have a nice sharp letter opener at hand, would you, Your Grace?"

He made a scoffing noise then marched over to the desk. When he returned with the requested implement, he eyed Jane narrowly. "Again, I hope you'll understand when I say that I don't trust you. I'm afraid that *I'm* going to have to cut those ties."

Jane snorted, even as her blood began to thrum at the idea that the duke's large hands would soon be touching her drawer-clad thigh. "I only tried to pilfer a book. I'm not a murderess. I promise I won't stab you."

"Ah, but it's a very *expensive* book," said the duke. "People will do all kinds of things for money. And I don't know you." He drew close, and Jane caught the scent of his cologne—something spicy and rich like sandalwood with a touch of citrus. "Now, hold still," he said softly as he bent low. "This will be over in a moment."

His long fingers gripped the book and with a flick of the letter opener's wickedly sharp silver blade, the silk bindings split in two with nary a whisper. Which was a shame because as the duke's fingers brushed her leg, an involuntary shiver of longing spread across Jane's skin and an agonized whimper escaped her throat. The soft sound was loud in the silent library.

Oh, dear God. Why must her body betray her in this way? Would this humiliation never end? Jane didn't want to want the duke. He was arrogant and a cad and ungentlemanly and…{~?~IQ: Editorial: Paragraph may be missing ending punctuation.}

He was probably going to let her go.

Many men in his position wouldn't. She should count her blessings.

But then again, maybe she shouldn't count them *too* soon…{~?~IQ: Editorial: Paragraph may be missing ending punctuation.}

Even though the duke had his precious book in hand, he hadn't moved away. Jane pushed down her skirts and when she looked up, he was unabashedly staring at her face.

At her scar.

She opened her mouth to say something along the lines of, "It's rude to stare," but all of a sudden, she couldn't make her lips and tongue work. Not one syllable emerged.

She was transfixed. The duke's bold, ice-blue gaze traced its way down the unsightly slashing mark to where it ended at the corner of her mouth. There his attention lingered for the briefest of moments before dipping to her chin. Then he examined her nose, and then her furrowed brow. Her bright red cheeks. She had the oddest notion that he was studying each of her features. As though he was trying to commit her face to memory.

Leaning toward her ear, his nostrils flared ever so slightly as though he was also sampling her scent. It was nothing special or exotic. Just Pears Soap and lily-of-the-valley water.

While these moments were strangely intimate, they were also peculiar and unsettling. Jane suddenly felt like a butterfly pinned beneath a sheet of glass—a curiosity—rather than a woman being admired.

At last, the duke's torturous scrutiny ended. "Remarkable," he murmured before he stepped away and crossed to his desk.

Remarkable? Bizarre seemed more fitting, but Jane kept her thoughts to herself. She didn't need her unruly tongue to get her into any more trouble tonight. Dragging in a much-needed breath, she held onto the arm of the chair as she lowered her foot and slid on her shoe. Retrieved the rest of her things, including Kitty's fan.

When she turned around, it was to discover the duke had propped one lean hip on his desk. And he was still holding Chaucer's book.

Jane affected a laugh. "All's well that ends well," she said, trying for a light and breezy tone. Instead, her voice sounded brittle and high-pitched. It was obvious she was nervous.

"Oh, our little tête-à-tête hasn't ended," said the duke quietly.

Jane swallowed. "What do you mean? As pleasant as this has been, it's rather late"—she gestured toward the library's longcase clock that showed it was nearing one a.m.—"and don't wish to turn into a pumpkin."

"Tell me why you tried to steal my book and you may go." The duke's frosty gaze was uncompromising. "I'll know if you're lying, so I wouldn't bother."

Jane gave a mirthless laugh. "Obviously I need money, Your Grace. It's a very *expensive* book after all."

The duke's attention drifted over her attire, and Jane knew he was assessing its worth. It was unmistakably haute couture. A gift from Artemis last Season, in fact. Even though the ball-gown suited Jane well—the emerald-green silk complimented her brown hair and green eyes—it was the not the kind of gown she usually wore. Of course, the duke didn't know that. He would surmise that she didn't *look* impoverished. But people needed money for all sorts of reasons.

The duke clearly thought so too. "Money for what purpose?"

Oh, but he was blunt. Jane's gaze fell to the volume in the duke's hand. "It's a complicated matter," she said stiffly. "One that's difficult to discuss with a stranger."

"I understand 'complicated' more than you could know."

The duke's voice was so soft, so imbued with compassion, Jane's gaze shot to his face. In some ways, the change in his demeanor was the most surprising thing that had happened tonight.

Or was it a trick? Some ploy to invite her to share a confidence that he could then use against her. How he would do that, she had no idea, but her instincts told her to be wary.

"I...I don't know if I can trust you," she murmured.

He nodded. "Will you at least share your name with me?"

Jane decided she could make this one small concession. "Miss Jane Delaney."

"Ah," he said. "That makes sense."

"What do you mean?"

He raised the book. "You knew the value of this straightaway. I presume you have an association with Delaney's Antiquarian Bookshop in Sackville Street off Piccadilly?"

Jane couldn't hide her astonishment. "You know about Delaney's?"

"I inherited a vast antique book collection from my uncle. Of course, I do."

"I've never seen you in the sho—" She broke off.

Oh no. She'd just inadvertently admitted she was very well acquainted with her grandfather's business. If she'd put her grandfather's reputation in jeopardy because of her own foolish, rash actions, she'd never be able to forgive herself.

"Your Grace," she began, "what happened here tonight, I want to assure you it had nothing to do with the proprietor of Delaney's. It was me and me alone who decided to come here. I'm the one who tried to take your book to serve my own ends. I accept full responsibility—"

The duke held up his hand. "That's quite enough self-flagellation, Miss Delaney. I'm not going to send for the police."

"You're not?"

"No. But that doesn't mean there won't be any consequences for your actions."

Jane's heart began to thump against her breastbone. "Con-consequences?"

The duke placed the book down very carefully upon the desk. "You don't need to look so alarmed, Miss Delaney. I don't bite..." His wide mouth curved into a rakish grin. "Well, I do sometimes, but only when invited to."

Heat suffused Jane's cheeks. She'd never blushed so much in her whole life. "Your Grace, please speak plainly. It does grow rather late, and I don't wish to worry my family unduly. I still need to make my way home."

"Very well. You do have a point. We shall finish this conversation tomorrow." He sighed and rubbed his brow as though he was suddenly weary beyond measure or even had a megrim coming on. "I mean later on today. I expect to see you back at Roxby House at three o'clock. Sharp."

Jane dipped into a small curtsy. "I'll be here, Your Grace." She had no doubt in her mind that if she didn't turn up at the allotted time, the duke would come and find her.

"Right." The duke pushed to his feet and gestured toward the door. "Let us depart."

"Wait... You're coming with me?" Did he think she would try to steal something else on her way out?

But then he said, "Only to the front door. I know how wild things get here in the wee small hours. It would be curmudgeonly of me not to see you out safely."

Jane inclined her head. "That's very kind of you, Your Grace."

Once she'd redonned her mask, the duke offered his arm, and he escorted her through the halls. Carousing guests called greetings as he passed by, and he acknowledged all with a wave and a tilt of his head. But he didn't stop to talk with anyone, and Jane was grateful.

They gained the grand entry hall, and the footman on duty bowed as soon as he saw his master.

The duke addressed him. "Please arrange suitable transport for my guest here." He turned to Jane and raised a brow. "I take it that you don't have a carriage waiting outside?"

"No. I don't. A hansom cab will suffice." Jane lifted her chin. "I have enough for the fare."

The duke smirked at her show of pride. "Tell the cab driver to return here for his payment," he said to the footman.

And then the Duke of Roxby astonished Jane again when he bowed over her hand. "Until we meet again, Miss Delaney," he said in a low voice meant only for her. And then he turned on his well-shod heel and quit the entry hall, leaving Jane with the sense that she might have unwittingly jumped from the frying pan, straight into the fire.

Author Note

My dearest readers, in penning *Curled Up with an Earl,* I hope you'll forgive me for using a little bit of literary license in a few areas...

As I mentioned in *Up All Night with a Good Duke,* the first book in The Byronic Book Club series, Heathwick Green near Hampstead Heath is my own invention and is loosely based on the hamlet of Hatch's or Hatchett's Bottom. The train station at Hampstead Heath apparently opened in 1860 not earlier as depicted in my story.

Lucy Bertram is a member of a scientific society—the London Botanical Society—that did indeed admit women to its ranks. *Curled Up with an Earl* is set in 1858, but the London Botanical Society apparently only existed from 1836 to 1856. From what I can gather though, it eventually reformed as the Botanical Society of the British Isles and is presently known as the Botanical Society of Britain and Ireland.

The Raleigh Club mentioned in *Curled Up with an Earl* was inspired by a club of the same name that became the Geographical Society in 1854.

Fortnum & Mason's tea rooms weren't actually opened until 1926, but I needed a place for my characters to "take tea" in the vicinity of Piccadilly. My fictional tea salon and the characters who work there are a pure flight of fancy on my part. In the UK, surgeons tend to use the honorific "Mr." rather than "Dr." so this is why my fictional "Scotland Yard surgeon" is referred to as Mr. Dalrymple. This tradition apparently began before 1800.

And lastly, as far as I can tell from my research, strychnine is only a partially soluble substance. To serve the story, I've suggested that the strychnine used to commit the murders in this book is possibly more potent and more readily soluble than garden-variety strychnine. Any inaccuracies related to this plot point are entirely my own.

Acknowledgments

Thank you to everyone at Sourcebooks Casablanca, including my wonderful editor, Christa Désir, for all your hard work. It's truly, truly appreciated.

My gratitude also goes to my agent, Jessica Alverez, for believing in me.

And then of course, I must thank my amazing family. I couldn't do any of this without you.

About the Author

Amy Rose Bennett is an Australian author who has a passion for penning emotion-packed historical romances. Of course, her strong-willed heroines and rakish heroes always find their happily ever after.

A former speech pathologist, Amy is happily married to her very own romantic hero and has two lovely, very accomplished adult daughters. When she's not creating stories, Amy loves to cook up a storm in the kitchen, lose herself in a good book or a witty rom-com, and when she can afford it, travel to all the places she writes about.

Also by Amy Rose Bennett

THE BYRONIC BOOK CLUB SERIES
Up All Night with a Good Duke
Curled Up with an Earl